Praise for [...] Zo[...]

"A thrilling story of lov[...] on the brink of war... Jones' main characters are wonderful—and she surrounds them with a strong supporting cast that will have audiences eagerly anticipating the next books in the series."

—*RT Book Reviews*, 4 Stars

"Astonishing. From the first word to the last, this book held me spellbound... The chemistry is simply stunning."

—*Romance Junkies*, Five Blue Ribbons

"Plenty of action and romance to keep you glued to your seat."

—*Night Owl Reviews*

"Ms. Jones... hit my romance meter and left me aching for more."

—*Just Erotic Romance Reviews*

"The world building is without a doubt superbly done, mixing military aspects with an innate sense of the paranormal."

—*Black Lagoon Reviews*

"Sexy men, strong women, a great plot, and a fascinating new world."

—*My Book Addiction Reviews*

LETHALLY PASSIONATE, WICKEDLY DANGEROUS...

He is a soldier of soldiers, an enforcer of the code of honor—expectant of greatness and tolerant of nothing less. With ruthless precision, he calculates risks as deliberately as he does his lover's satisfaction. Assessing, pleasing, and when needed... destroying. Inexplicably in control, there is absoluteness in everything he does, everything he is—everything he will make you feel.

HE IS... DAMION.

THE
Danger
THAT IS
DAMION

LISA RENEE JONES

sourcebooks
casablanca

Published by Sourcebooks Casablanca, an imprint of Sourcebooks, Inc.
P.O. Box 4410, Naperville, Illinois 60567-4410
(630) 961-3900
FAX: (630) 961-2168
www.sourcebooks.com

Printed and bound in the United States of America
VP 10 9 8 7 6 5 4 3 2 1

To Diego—whose fight for the dream keeps me fighting. And to all the brave soldiers who fight the real fight and sacrifice so much for our country.

Glossary

AREA 51 — Another name used for Groom Lake.

BAR-1 — A brainwashing program that isolates brain neurons and allows brainwashing to occur. It will only work on females, not on males.

BLOOD EXCHANGE — A part of the Lifebond process done by choice, after the Lifebond mark appears on the female's neck. This completes the female's transformation to GTECH and links the two Lifebonds in life and death. (See Lifebond Process.)

DREAMLAND — Though Groom Lake/Area 51 is often called Dreamland, in the Renegades series, Dreamland is the fictional military facility opened eighty miles from Area 51 by General Powell to take a stand against the Zodius who overran Area 51.

GREEN HORNET — Special bullet that is so powerful it not only shreds human muscle and bone, it penetrates the thin bodysuit armor that the GTECHs — both Zodius and Renegades — wear when no other bullet can do so.

GROOM LAKE — Also known as Area 51, this is the military base where the Project Zodius experiments with alien DNA took place. It was later taken over by the Zodius rebels.

GTECH—The Super Soldiers who were created under Project Zodius and who divided into two groups—Zodius and Renegades. GTECHs are stronger, faster, and more agile than humans; they heal rapidly and have low fatality rates. They can wind-walk. Over time, many are developing special gifts unique to them, such as telepathy and the ability to communicate with animals.

GTECH Body Armor—A thin bodysuit that fits like a second skin. Extremely light and flexible. The material is made from alien technology recovered from a 1950s crash site. Until the Green Hornets were created, no standard issue ammunition could penetrate the suits.

GTECH Serum—The serum created from alien DNA that was gathered at a crash site in the 1950s and then used to create the GTECHs. The original sample was destroyed. Since the alien DNA will not allow itself to be duplicated, there can be no new serum created without new scientific discoveries. The remaining serum disappeared the day Area 51/Groom Lake was taken over by the GTECH Rebels known as Zodius Soldiers. The GTECH serum cannot be created from GTECH DNA. This has been tried and has failed.

Lifebond Mark—A double circle resembling a tattoo that appears on the back of a female's neck after her first sexual encounter with her GTECH Lifebond. After the mark appears, it will tingle whenever her Lifebond approaches. Only sexual encounters with one's Lifebond will result in a Lifebond Mark appearing.

LIFEBOND PROCESS—A Lifebond is a male and female who are bonded physically for life and death. If one dies, so does the other. This bond allows the GTECH male to reproduce, and it offers the females the same physical skills as their male Lifebond. The Lifebond mark, a double circle resembling a tattoo, appears on the back of the female's neck after the first sexual encounter. A blood exchange is required to complete the physical transformation of the female to GTECH, if the couple makes that decision. There is physical pain and illness for the female during conversion.

NEONOPOLIS—The Las Vegas satellite location for the Renegades, covertly located in the basement of the Neonopolis entertainment complex off Las Vegas Avenue.

PMI or **PRIVATE MILITARY INTELLIGENCE**—A company run by General Powell, the officer who created Project Zodius. PMI is used as a cover for top secret military projects that the government doesn't want to officially show on the books.

PROJECT ZODIUS—Code name for the government's top secret operation—two hundred Special Operations soldiers who were assigned to Groom Lake (Area 51) and injected with what they believed to be immunizations, but which was, in fact, alien DNA.

RED DART—A red crystal found at the same UFO 1950s crash site where the GTECH DNA was discovered. The crystal enables a red laser beam that enters the bloodstream and creates a permanent tracking beacon that is sensitive to sound waves. These sound waves can also be used for torture and control of the GTECHs. Thus far, U.S. military attempts to use Red Dart have been fatal.

RENEGADE SOLDIER—A GTECH who protects humanity and stands against the rebels known as "Zodius." The Renegades are led by Adam Rain's twin brother, Caleb Rain.

SHIELD—A mental barrier that a GTECH uses to block their psychic residue from being traceable by Trackers.

STARDUST—An alien substance that is undetectable in human testing and causes brain aneurisms.

SUNRISE CITY—The main Renegades facility, an advanced, underground city located in Nevada's Sunrise Mountain Range.

TRACKERS—These are GTECHs with the special ability to track the psychic residue of another GTECH or a human female who's been intimate with another GTECH. If a female possesses this residue, then only that female's Lifebond can shield her from a Tracker.

WARDENS—An all-female group of women who have joined to stop the abductions of other women by the Zodius.

WIND-WALKING—The ability to fade into the wind, like mist into the air, and invisibly travel far distances at rapid speed.

X2 GENE—A gene that appears in some, but not all, of the GTECHs by the fifteenth month after injection of the GTECH serum.

ZODIUS CITY—Still known as the top secret U.S. military facility. Located in Nevada and often called Area 51 or Groom Lake, it was taken over by the rebel GTECHs led by Adam Rain. This facility is both above and beneath ground level.

ZODIUS SOLDIER—A rebel GTECH soldier who follows Adam Rain, the leader of the rebel movement. Adam intends to take over the world.

IT LIVES BECAUSE THEY LIVE...

A silent, raging battle, born of greed and lust. Of a hunger for power and a passion for misplaced greatness. A burn for control. A seed planted under the guise of growing peace. But instead, that seed evolved into death and despair, proving, as history has shown time and time again, that man is, indeed, his own worst enemy.

This war, this seed, started as a quest for the perfect weapon, the last weapon, the ultimate weapon. The one that would end all wars. In this case, a weapon neither human nor inhuman. A man, but not quite a man. Created under a veil of secrecy inside Area 51, the program, code-named "Project Zodius," recruited soldiers who were told they were being immunized against enemy pathogens. Instead they were injected with alien DNA found at a crash site the century before.

Their lives were changed forever, and perhaps the destiny of humankind as well. Possessing super strength and speed, and able to travel with the wind, these soldiers became GTECH Super Soldiers. It was hoped they would eliminate battlefields and bloodshed simply by existing, by drawing a line in the sand that our enemies didn't dare cross.

One of these GTECH Super Soldiers rose against humanity, a power-hungry soldier who thought he was the chosen one, the one who could destroy the pathetic existence of humanity in all its weakness. His name is Adam Rain, and he believes he was created for a single purpose—evolution. He will create a better, stronger race, a Zodius race. One nation under a Zodius government—his nation.

Humanity's future lies with Adam's brother, Caleb Rain, and his Renegade followers. These Renegades represent hope and honor, sacrifice and salvation. They are the last great warriors of humankind, defending their people while being shunned, even feared, by their creators.

The war rages on...

Chapter 1

THERE WAS NOTHING UNUSUAL TO A CASUAL OBSERVER about a hot woman in a white string bikini, lounging poolside, a few feet from where undercover Renegade soldier Damion Browne leaned against the cabana-style bar, a beer in hand. In fact, from a purely male standpoint, there was absolutely everything *right* with this particular woman—a brunette with long, silky, dark hair brushing creamy white shoulders. But then, he was on duty, and he took that duty too seriously to allow primal urges to distract him. Still… something about this woman set his blood pumping, and like it or not, that translated to a distraction that was out of character for him.

He told himself it was because she'd shown up ten minutes into the outdoor excursion of a Russian nuclear scientist and his family that Damion was covertly ensuring didn't end up in Adam Rain's arsenal of weapons. The last thing the Renegades wanted was the leader of the Zodius GTECH movement getting his hands on the nuclear technology Lev was selling the United States in exchange for citizenship. That's why this woman was a potential risk, he told himself, not because she had long, shapely legs that belonged wrapped around a man's waist—his waist, Damion thought with a rush of pure male heat. They belonged around *his* waist. Damn. What was wrong with him?

Inwardly he shook himself, not sure what it was

about this woman, but she could easily drag him into the linger zone when he didn't go to the linger zone on duty. Scratch that, he thought, as he glanced at Lev and family and back to her. She already had him in the linger zone, and there was no forgiving his distraction, unless… That gnawing gut feeling was telling him that underneath all that sex appeal, she was trouble, despite Adam's dislike of female operatives. Add that to the fact that the CIA team watching Lev had allowed him outside in the first place, and Damion had a bad, bad feeling about this. Suddenly, as if she sensed his suspicions, the dark-haired beauty's head snapped in his direction, her attention settling on him, her eyes shielded by white-rimmed sunglasses. Time stood still for an intense, crackling moment. Certainty filled him. She had known the entire time that he was watching her.

The microphone tucked discreetly inside Damion's ear hummed a second before the voice of his Harley-loving, wild card, second-in-charge, Chale Bonner, spoke, "We reported Lev's barking dog to the front desk several times. Looks like security is headed his way. We'll have him inside the building where he's less exposed in a flash."

Damion didn't reply. He was still watching the woman, who, as abruptly as she'd given her attention, jerked it away. Reaching for her bag, she stood up, offering him a nice, heart-shaped backside view as she sashayed away. Her pace was slow, confident, but a bit too precise. She was hiding something, beside the intimate details of her body, details he wanted to discover beneath those tiny pieces of white material. Damion knew Adam didn't typically work with women—he believed they were inferior beings—but somehow, someway, this one was the source of the warning in his gut.

"Alert," Chale added. "Doggy Patrol has arrived. Get ready for movement." Damion eyed the back door of the hotel to find two uniformed security guards and a woman dressed in a suit headed toward Lev and his brood. "I see them," Damion said, his gaze shifting to the fast-departing, bikini-clad female. But had she seen them? Was that why she couldn't get away from this place fast enough?

Damion set the beer down and discreetly touched the mike hidden in his ear. "Cover Lev. Something about that woman is bothering me." He pushed off the bar and started walking, unable to use his GTECH ability to travel inside the wind without risk of garnering unwanted attention. This woman was dangerous. The kind of dangerous a soldier, a Renegade, didn't let escape.

———

Lara's hand slipped discreetly into her oversized bag, wrapping around the hot steel of the weapon there, even as she rounded the diving board of the pool, carefully pacing herself, despite the urgency coursing through every pore. She was driven by the certainty that the man with the hot stare—and hotter body—by the pool was one of those GTECH monsters who'd killed her family.

She'd suspected as much the minute he'd walked to the bar, looking like an all-American soldier, no matter the absence of a uniform—his swagger confident, his jeans and T-shirt molding a perfectly honed physique, and his light brown hair neatly trimmed. A lethal air crackled off him, belying the casual way he leaned back against the bar and sipped his beer with an air that said that he could not only kill you if he wanted to, but he was ready to do so at the drop of a hat.

The hard edge of his assessing stare had settled on her, hot as it flickered across her barely clad body and then returned to her face. Lara had felt the intensely probing inspection with the unnerving feeling this man—this GTECH—could see beyond her dark glasses as surely as he'd glimpsed beneath the thin strips of fabric covering her. Heat had flooded her limbs at the daring way he'd looked at her, and having been warned about the unique, unpredictable abilities the GTECHs developed over time—that she too might develop over time—she'd jerked her gaze away.

It had been a foolish, amateurish reaction, unworthy of the training she'd received when she'd joined Project Serenity. Part of her welcomed the man to follow her, welcomed a chance to unload her weapon between his eyes where even a GTECH would be vulnerable, where their incredible healing abilities wouldn't matter, nor would their high-tech, second-skin armor protect them. But she couldn't risk failing General Powell and making a misstep that would allow the GTECH to get his hands on Lev. Powell had given her her life back, given her a chance to protect innocents. She now had a reason to fight and a reason to live. Her orders were clear, as well as her intel on Lev and his security detail. She was to be the silent, second level of security for Lev Egorov, the protection against the threat the GTECHs represented, Renegade or Zodius. Neither GTECH group could be trusted with nuclear technology—or trusted at all. The GTECHs outside of those on team "Serenity" were to be disposed of, before the public ever knew they existed. Only a handful inside the government knew, and the agents protecting Lev weren't included in that circle.

Determined to quickly and efficiently complete her task, she'd reached the trail directly behind the pool that led between this hotel and an adjoining property. A young couple walked toward her, delaying her plan to slip into the foliage and trees lining the path. She gave a friendly smile to the man and woman, a gesture that belied her racing heart and the worry that the GTECH would appear at any moment. She took that moment on the path to yank a red-and-white-striped cotton dress from her bag and pull it over her head. Then she kicked off her sandals and dropped a pair of Keds white tennis shoes to the ground before shoving her feet inside them. Not the perfect fighting attire, but better than a bikini.

By the time she was done, the man and woman had disappeared down another path, and from her earlier surveillance, she knew that their path lead to a duck pond.

Another quick glance around confirmed Lara was alone. She slipped off the path, behind the thick line of trees several feet deep that gave her ample cover, a mixture of pine needles and rocks crunching beneath her feet.

Lara stopped behind the thickest patch of foliage beside a chain-link fence, the steel laced with thick ivy. She inched her gun, complete with silencer, over the edge of her bag and peered through the greenery.

Surveying the pool area, Lara's breath lodged in her throat as she found the GTECH missing. He was coming for her, and if he wind-walked, he could appear near her at any moment. *Focus*, she silently reminded herself. *Do the job, then catch some wind of your own, and be gone*.

Quickly, she took aim at Lev, who was standing up and arguing with what looked like hotel security. They seemed to want him to go inside, where he should have stayed. It was too late for that. Too late because he was already on the GTECH's radar, just like she was.

The sound of female voices on the trail behind her stilled Lara momentarily. The instant they faded, her finger lifted to the trigger only to once again pause as one of Lev's little girls rushed to his side. Lara hesitated at the unexpected tightness in her chest, urging her not to take the shot. Why couldn't she take the shot? This was a big-picture job, about saving the world. She'd trained for this. She had prepared mentally and physically to do whatever was necessary to protect the innocent. She was a soldier. It hit her then, and she knew what was bothering her. *The little girl*. She didn't want the little girl to see her father drop dead at her feet, which was insane and completely unacceptable. She was part of Team Serenity, part of a greater cause to save the world from a GTECH takeover, from GTECH enslavement. She was defending millions of little girls, not one. With that thought, a steely cold began to reshape inside her. A hardness that was part of her training, part of her destiny, had taken shape the day the GTECHs had slaughtered her family.

Her finger moved a millimeter. She was ready to fire, but again, that tightening in her chest halted her. In that split-second of hesitation, an odd, dizzy feeling set her swaying. With one hand, she steadied herself on the fence, but before she'd even righted herself, a screeching sound ripped through her eardrums.

A rush of images flew through her mind like a reel from a film on fast forward. Unfamiliar images of herself, of a life she didn't know, of a man she seemed to love like a father. Of being dragged up the stairs by her hair, by someone she couldn't see, to watch that man die. A shrill sound blasted through her skull, and just like that it ended.

Lara came back to the present in a jerk and a gasp, unsure how long she'd been lost to whatever had just happened to her. *Her head.* God, her head was still pounding as if someone had beat it like a drum. She brushed at the dampness on her cheeks, shocked to realize she'd been crying. She hadn't cried since the night Powell had saved her life, since he'd given her a chance to fight back, given her a purpose.

A sudden gust of wind touched her hot skin and jolted her with full recall—the GTECH, her mission. The GTECH was coming. The GTECH *was* the wind. In a blast of adrenaline, Lara pushed herself off the fence where her fingers had somehow curled, reaching for the gun she'd apparently abandoned in her purse during her blackout, but she was too late. She could feel the heat of the body that materialized in the wind behind her a moment before strong, powerful arms surrounded her, held her.

"I wouldn't do that if I were you, sweetheart," came the rich male voice that whispered against her ear, his warm breath brushing her neck and sending a shiver down her spine. A voice that she knew instinctively, on every level, matched the man who'd been by the pool. The GTECH had found her.

Chapter 2

THE INSTANT LARA FELT THE GTECH'S BODY MOLDED far too intimately against her, her backside pressed to his hips, she tried to wind-walk, intending to reappear behind him and draw her weapon. But no wind came to her. Instead, pain splintered through her head, gray and white dots speckled with barely perceivable images, clouding her mind and sight.

Something was horribly wrong. She couldn't wind-walk. She could barely breathe, hardly think. Somehow, though, by sheer will or just plain luck, she blinked away the shadows and forced away the pain. This had to be the GTECH controlling her mind, controlling her wind-walking ability. She'd never once tried to wind-walk and not been capable of making it happen. There was no other explanation for something that had started the minute she'd found her way onto his radar.

Recalculating her options with the loss of her wind-walking skill, she tried to turn, testing her strength against the GTECH's, careful not to give away her own GTECH strength, to keep surprise as her weapon.

"You aren't going anywhere until we talk," came the low command, as he narrowed the V of his legs around her hips.

Male GTECH strength apparently trumped female GTECH strength, because Lara was immobile, and it was frustrating beyond comprehension. For the first time since joining Serenity, she questioned Powell's claims that in a world of male GTECHs, women were the unexpected weapon that would win this war. In fact, she just plain wanted to scream at the injustice of the physical differences. That left her with outsmarting him and getting to her weapon, and she would.

"What's the ETA on Lev and family being back in their room?" her captor said in a hushed tone, clearly speaking into a mike. He wasn't alone, and she was. The odds had just gotten worse. A second passed—not enough time for her to calculate her plan—and he cursed beneath his breath, before he replied, "We've gone mission ignite. Situation is hot. Get them inside now or take them into custody."

Lara cringed at what his command implied, at the idea the GTECHs would have nuclear expertise because she'd failed her mission. "Let me go," she demanded, "before I scream." It was a threat used to seem weak, to convince him to underestimate her, to let down his guard.

"And when help comes," he said, calling her bluff, "I'll show them your gun."

Her gun was the last thing she wanted him thinking about right now. He leaned in closer to her, his breath warm near her ear, his tone a primal rasp of demand. "Now why don't you tell me who you were trying to kill, Lev or Phillips?"

He was trying to figure out who she worked for, whether she wanted to capture Lev or kill him. She wasn't telling him anything or showing him one iota of weakness. No more damsel. *Never let them see you sweat.* Someone used to say that to her, though she couldn't remember who.

"Let me go, and I'll demonstrate," she said flippantly. It was all she could do not to shove him backward, not to fight her way out of this, but she couldn't wind-walk, and that changed everything. She had to be patient, wait for her moment, her opportunity to escape.

"What's the rush, darlin'?" he asked. "If you aren't careful, you're going to hurt my feelings. And you won't get another shot at Lev. My men are too good to let that happen."

"If I were facing forward, I'd hurt a lot more than your feelings," she promised with sticky sweetness, still not letting on that she could turn around if she wanted to, still hoping he believed her nothing more than human.

"You'd like that, now wouldn't you?" he mused, laughing, a sensual sound that ran up and down her nerve endings with female awareness, belying how much she hated this man and all those like him.

"You betcha, *darlin'*," she said, repeating his mockery of an endearment. She hated GTECHs, even ones that managed to smell all sexy and male. No—*especially* ones that managed to smell all sexy and male, because it proved he could somehow work seductive magic on her. She didn't like being manipulated. But then, two could play that game. She taunted him, went after his male ego. "Unless you're afraid you can't handle me." She softened her voice to a seductive rasp, "Don't worry, honey. I promise to be gentle."

His hands slid around her waist, his palms scorching her skin beneath the thin material of her dress. "The gun in your purse doesn't say *gentle* to me."

"You might be surprised," she challenged, setting aside the unexpected, uncomfortable, drugging effect of this man's deep baritone voice. "Try me." The fingers of her one hand curled around the steel of the fence, the other held her purse where her weapon rested. Oh yes, indeed, he had some unique gift of seduction. He possessed numerous special GTECH abilities, it seemed. There was no other way to explain how he'd stolen her wind-walking ability, and she was willing to bet he'd created her blackout. Otherwise, her breasts wouldn't ache with a stranger's nearness... her thighs wouldn't beg to press together.

"First things first," he said, and just like that, he snatched her purse from her grip and off her shoulder.

She reached for it, but it was too late. He had it and her gun. "You son of a bitch!" she ground out between her teeth, barely containing a yell sure to bring unwanted attention, and silently cursing herself for letting him best her.

"Such a potty mouth on a pretty woman," he chided. "Now you can turn around and apologize." He shifted his weight and hers with him, as he rotated her to face him, giving her the opportunity she'd been waiting for. The playing field was far more level in a full frontal confrontation, her skill and training able to shine against his superior strength. The instant Lara was facing forward, before he managed a solid grip on her again, she shoved the GTECH with her supernatural strength, trying to get him off her so she could wind-walk and attack him from behind. He didn't so much as rock from the shove, but adrenaline was her friend, and she quickly followed with an attempt at a strategically placed knee. He countered the knee with his hands and trapped her leg with his.

She growled with frustration. She hadn't felt this

pathetically weak since she'd watched her family get slaughtered, and she'd sworn she wouldn't ever again feel such helplessness. She was a GTECH, trained well, his equal, and she wasn't letting his size and sex dominate her. Nor was she done fighting. She shoved him and threw a punch. He captured her hand in his bigger one with ease.

He arched a brown eyebrow, amusement in his gaze. "Feisty little *GTECH* thing, aren't you?"

She kneed him in the groin, and this time she landed the blow. He grunted loudly, and she reveled in her success. "Feisty doesn't begin to describe what I am or what I'll do to you." She lifted another knee. He caught it.

She took the opportunity this distraction gave her and reached for her bag. He was too quick though, and he pulled it back. Her chin inched upward, narrowing the gap separating them, to meet his gaze with a lethal glare. "I assume you're aware that no one will ever call you a gentleman, not that I think you care. A girl's purse is sacred."

His eyes, which he'd camouflaged from the GTECH black that came with conversion, to his natural honey-colored eyes, twinkled with mischief. "So is a man's life," he countered. "And for the record, most people say I'm quite the gentleman, but then, most people don't include those who have guns in their 'sacred' purses they'd like to use to kill me." His full, dangerous lips, that she shouldn't even be noticing, twitched, before he added, "And most people don't try to knee me in the groin. I thought you promised to be gentle?"

"After you shoved me against a fence and stole my purse," she said, "I assumed you preferred things rough.

And for the record—I didn't *try* to knee you in the groin. I succeeded. Keep pushing me, and I'll do it again. This time, you won't recover so quickly." Before she knew his intention, his hand slid behind her neck, under her hair, pulling her closer. The air instantly charged with tension. Their eyes met and held, a warning in the depths of his stare. He could break her neck, and then she'd never have a chance of stopping him. They both knew it.

"I would never be anything but gentle with a woman," he finally said, his face close to hers, so close she could see the light brown stubble of fresh growth on his chin, feel that hot breath on her cheek, on her lips. "But a Zodius soldier, a willing member of the Zodius Movement, is a killer, and that changes everything." His touch remained surprisingly light, while still sure, but his voice turned rough with demand. "Tell me... since when does Adam turn females into GTECHs?"

Her hand pressed against his chest, the only thing separating them, and she could feel the steady beat of his heart, a contrast to the racing of hers. "Since when do Renegades manhandle women? I thought you liked to 'play' like you were the good guys."

"If I decide to manhandle you," he said through clenched teeth, "you'll know it. Now answer the question."

"Who said I work for Adam?"

"Don't you play me, little one," he said, his fingers stroking the back of her neck in a slow, sensual caress that hummed with threat. "I felt your strength. I know you're GTECH. If you were made that way by a Lifebond mating connection, Adam would never risk you being killed. You'd be one of the few females who could actually mate with a GTECH male. And don't tell me Adam didn't make you this way. He's the only one who has any serum left. For you to have scored some of what little bit he has left, you must be high on his list of importance. Women, apart from his Lifebond, Ava, do not make that list. They get put in sex camps where he tries to find a Lifebond match so he can breed them. Why are you different?"

"I believe this is where I give you my name, rank, and serial number," she said, ignoring the real risk that he might kill her if she allowed him to believe she was with Adam. But Serenity was top secret, and there was no negotiating that point.

The air crackled with her reply, and he stared at her, unblinking, as seconds ticked by, that honeyed ice in his eyes marbling to black and then returning to their natural shade. "Give me a good reason not to kill you," he said. "Tell me Adam has your family, that he is bribing you. Something that justifies working for him, something that can be fixed."

For a moment she was stunned. This GTECH, this cold-blooded killer, wanted a reason not to kill her. "Who says I won't lie?"

"Because I can damn near taste your fear in the air," he said. "You're too nervous and too scared to hide the truth. Which means you haven't been at this long. Before you knew I was watching you, I saw you take aim at the Russian and hesitate to pull the trigger. Adam hasn't had time to make you cold and heartless."

He was right, she realized, admitting the truth to herself, if not to him. For all her bravado about GTECHs and justice, she was afraid, but not for the reasons he assumed—not of him, and not of fighting. She was afraid she was going to die before she ensured that her family had the vengeance they deserved. With the past twisting inside her, nerves and fear turned to a bitter laugh. "What your kind has done to me can never be fixed."

Surprise and understanding flinted across his strong features, a muscle ticking in his solid, square jaw. "Who did Adam kill that you loved?"

"Not Adam," she whispered. It had been the Renegades who'd pretended to be her military father's friend, trying to find out top secret information. And that same Renegade had butchered her entire family, while she'd helplessly watched.

The wind lifted suddenly, and he cursed in anticipation of an attack. He took a step, putting his back to the fence, but not to Lara. Lara barely registered the unexpected presence of Serenity's team leader, before Sabrina fired three shots at the GTECH's head, the only place that a GTECH wasn't protected by state-of-the-art, second-skin body armor. Amazingly, he anticipated the shots, faded into the wind, and reappeared behind her team leader. God, he was fast, faster than anyone on their team.

Lara's eyes caught on the glint of steel on the ground, where her gun had fallen out of her purse. She launched herself toward it. The GTECH shoved Sabrina aside and went for the gun at the same time Lara did, and they slammed into each other. The ground disappeared from beneath Lara's feet as she and the GTECH went tumbling.

The GTECH landed on his back and Lara landed on

top of him, tree limbs and foliage scraping her arms and face. She gasped with the impact of their fall, and her GTECH attacker cursed again, no doubt taking a pounding from the bushes and rocks, not to mention her weight.

"Cover me!" Sabrina yelled, clearly determined to complete Lara's mission at all costs. If the GTECH's men hadn't already gotten to Lev, Sabrina was going to kill him in front of his kids. Lara had no idea why, but she knew in her soul she couldn't let Sabrina fire that gun.

Lara forgot everything but stopping her—forgot her mission, forgot logic, forgot the GTECH. She faded into the wind and reappeared beside Sabrina, kicking the gun from her hand.

"You bitch!" Sabrina screeched in outrage and launched herself at Lara. "I'm going to kill you."

Lara hit the ground in a skid that ripped her back and legs, snapping her head back to crack on a rock. Pain splintered down her skull and left her gasping for air, but air lost its importance when Sabrina flattened on top of her and threw a punch. Lara blocked the jab and threw her own, fighting back with all she had, until the GTECH ripped Sabrina off of her. Then before she could react, he grabbed Lara and faded into the wind.

Sabrina cursed the minute Lara and the Renegade disappeared into the wind. Damion was the Renegade's name. She knew the sorry bastard. He'd been a part of the Renegade group who'd led Adam Rain to find out she'd been plotting against him with one of his own men. He was one of the Renegades who would surely lock her up for crimes against her country, just as surely as Adam would turn her into a sex slave in his breeding camps. She'd show them all though. Sooner than later, Serenity would be the last GTECH force standing, and she, its leader.

She found her gun on the ground, scooped it up, and turned to the fence. What she found as she peered through the gate set her blood to boiling. Several men— Renegades she assumed, based on Damion's presence— were herding the Russian and his family inside the hotel and out of firing range.

She yanked her pant leg up and shoved her weapon into the holster, then reached up to hit the mike by her ear, ready to call in backup. But she paused, realizing the implications of such an action.

The government officials contracting Serenity expected it to remain a ghost operation at all costs, until there was a track record of success that made their support publicly acceptable. Sabrina had been so sure she and Lara could take Damion on and kill him that she'd exposed herself as a GTECH to launch her attack. Then that little wench Lara had turned on her and her team, jeopardizing the entire program. Which made no sense. Lara, like the other members of Serenity, had been brainwashed under the top secret Bar-1 program. That program had been highly successful at targeting a female-specific section of the brain. It bypassed the GTECH's aggressive immune system that had destroyed any tracking device they'd attempted to insert and turned the female into a compliant soldier. Or so they thought. Something was horribly wrong for Lara to have the ability to be disloyal. Whatever that something was could jeopardize Serenity and Sabrina's security within the program, where she was hidden from Adam Rain. Even if the program went on, if confidence and funding were not compromised, Powell would blame Sabrina as the leader for this misstep. He'd throw her into the Bar-1 brainwashing program and strip her memories and her rank. Sabrina curled her fingers into her palms, anger and adrenaline merging inside her, making her heart pound. She could fix this, she *would* fix this. Her survival depended on it. Serenity wasn't compromised yet, but Damion would question if she were really working for Adam. He wouldn't know for sure, but a question was a risk. He'd have to die along with Lara. That meant capturing them, interrogating them, and killing them. Then she'd kill anyone they'd talked to. Serenity would be secure and so would she. Thankfully, Powell was away on a recruiting mission for Serenity, and she had until his return in five days to make this right, to make sure he never knew this had happened.

Blood glinted, and Sabrina bent down to look at the crimson-stained stone where Lara must have hit her head. She knew then how to find Lara before Powell returned, a realization that brought both relief and dread because it came with a price. Lucian, who'd betrayed Adam and was now working for Powell, was a Tracker. He could find a GTECH female through the essence of the blood residue that would follow her, wherever she went above ground. Lucian was loyal to Powell, but he was more so to himself, and she had something Lucian wanted. He wanted *her*, to turn her into a whore all over again, like she had been so many times. She'd been used and abused her entire life, and Powell had given her a chance to change that.

She'd thought that was behind her, thought that finally she was important, someone who made a difference, who mattered. That's what being the leader of Serenity meant to her. "You *are* making a difference," she whispered to the wind, a friend that allowed her the bliss of freedom. She wasn't willing to lose her new life, not to Bar-1, and not to death. Her lips thinned, and resolve formed. She would not be the tramp that was walked on ever again, the woman who was used and abused.

If that meant she had to pretend to be Lucian's whore for now, she'd do it. She'd tolerate Lucian if that's what it took to ensure her security and freedom. She'd use Lucian, as she'd been used by so many, as Lucian wanted to use her. If he became a problem, she'd get rid of him, as so many others had tried to get rid of her. Except Powell. For that reason, Powell had her loyalty, and she'd do anything to keep his. *Anything*.

Chapter 3

DAMION'S PETITE BUNDLE OF CAPTIVE WOMAN HAD A surprising amount of fight left, considering she was bruised, scraped, and had blood matted in her hair from a head wound. Just how much fight she had left was a little detail he'd found out the hard way when he'd ended their wind walk in front of a secluded cabin three hundred miles outside of Washington, and she'd tried to attack him.

Defending himself, he tried not to hurt her, his gut telling him there was more to this woman than met the eye. It wasn't easy to be gentle, when she twisted, kicked, elbowed, and then kicked some more. But he took it all, defensively, not offensively. Then she bit the heck out of his hand, which might not be what he'd expected from a GTECH, but it was pretty darn effective because it hurt like hell.

He recoiled from the painful bite, and she threw a punch aimed at his nose. That's where he drew the line. This had to end. He'd had his nose broken enough times to know he didn't want it broken again.

Damion, once again, found himself catching her fist not a second too soon. "Enough with the violence already," he ordered. "In case you didn't notice, I just saved your life."

"You didn't save my life," she ground out between her teeth.

"I suppose that woman you attacked back there was just trying to say thank you by beating you in the face?" he challenged. Determined to avoid her attacks, he shackled her wrists so she couldn't throw another punch.

"I can hold my own with Sabrina," she said. "And we both know you didn't do me any favors. You kidnapped me to drag information out of me."

When the truth might hurt, he'd learned, dodge or duck. He dodged and countered. "The last time I saw that rabid redhead, Sabrina was dealing ICE for Adam, helping him in his plot to get the entire city of Vegas addicted to a drug only he could produce." A good reason to think Sabrina had taken a supply of ICE before the Renegades destroyed the stockpile, and that both she and this woman were ICE users. Except ICE users couldn't wind-walk. No. They were full-blooded GTECHs, as impossible as that seemed. Back on point, he added, "Bottom line, Sabrina was kicking your ass."

An instant of surprise flickered across her face, her gaze clouded, then she opened her mouth to speak. He had the distinct, certain impression, that she didn't know Sabrina's history, but she quickly pursed her lips.

Damion arched an inquiring brow, letting her know he hadn't missed her reaction, which only served to tick her off all over again.

Her eyes sparked angrily. "She wasn't kicking my ass, and you will not bait me into telling you anything. We both know you're trying to manipulate me into giving you information, and that's the only reason you interfered in that confrontation back there. Well, you might as well move on to torture, because your manipulation isn't working. I'm not telling you anything." She tried to twist away from him.

That was it. Even a soldier with respect for women had limits. Damion was done with all this struggling. He pulled her against him and wrapped his arms around hers, so she couldn't move.

Fury and indignation burned in her stare. "Remember this moment when the tables turn, and I hold you captive," she said. "Because mark my words, the tables *will* turn."

Heat slid through his limbs—the idea of being held captive by this woman was not so unappealing. Somehow though, he doubted sharing his fantasy of them wrapped together in naked, sweaty bliss—with silk ties and bedroom sheets—would work in his favor. Damn the woman was infuriating and soft, and sonofabitch, she felt good in his arms when she shouldn't. She was a distraction, and perhaps that was what Adam had intended, a distraction that could turn deadly if he didn't get his shit together.

His lips thinned and his expression hardened. "If anyone here is doing any manipulating, it's you," he said tightly. "In fact, for all I know, that whole fight back there was staged to get me to do just what I did. Take you someplace off the grid, where I'm vulnerable to attack. You could be wearing a tracking mechanism, and trying to keep me outside where a gaggle of wind-walkers can trap me. Or maybe you don't need a tracking device. Maybe you're on a Tracker's radar."

"What's that supposed to mean?" she demanded.

He didn't answer, his instincts setting him on alert. A human woman who'd had sex with a GTECH put off an energy or essence. From that point on, unless that woman was below ground level, a gifted Tracker could find her. He was one of those Trackers, and he sensed nothing in this woman, but then she was the first female GTECH he'd encountered. Just because he didn't know how to track her didn't mean it couldn't be done. "That's it. We're going underground."

"I'm not going—"

"Oh yeah, you are," he said and bent over to pick her up. She yelped as he threw her over his shoulder and headed toward the cabin. He had a passage nearby that led to the underground emergency facility the Renegades had installed some time back, when more and more, they'd found themselves chasing Zodius threats to Washington. "And don't even think about wind-walking, because I promise you, I'll follow."

He walked toward the cabin, tuning out the female's curses, some of which would make a sailor blush. Hell, they might even make Chale blush, and that wasn't an easy task. Her nice, round backside, just above where his hand rested on her bare thighs, wasn't as easily tuned out. In fact, his hand itched to reach up and pop her right on one of those cute little cheeks just for making him notice it. Good thing she didn't notice his distraction, or he had a feeling her verbal bashing would get worse.

Right about then she vehemently vowed, "I'm going to kill you when I get down from here, and…"

Then again, maybe she had noticed. Damion sighed and started up the steps to the porch. This relationship was off to a beautiful start if he ever saw one.

—⁓—

Lara had a plan to escape the GTECH, and that plan didn't include being plagued by the dizziness that had started by the pool, which was made worse by blood rushing to her head that made her stomach churn. Nor the humiliation of having her dress fall to her waist, and her bikini-bottomed backside staring her captor in the face. It did, however, include cursing and yelling, both of which were meant to make him believe that was the only defense she believed she had left—that she'd accepted the inevitability of accompanying him into the cabin and just didn't plan to go quietly. She wanted him to believe that she'd accepted he was physically stronger, that she knew he could tag along if she wind-walked because he was touching her, so she wasn't going to try.

Then, at the right moment, she'd catch him off guard and wind-walk, before he could do whatever magic he was doing to stop her. He'd follow. She knew that. Gaining a precious few seconds lead on him was her goal, enough to allow her to reappear in a public place with lots and lots of people where he didn't dare grab her again. From there, well, she'd improvise. The most important thing, right now, was not getting locked in some underground cavern with a GTECH, who might not ever let her see the light of day again. Especially not when she knew he had to be the reason for her blackout, the reason she'd been incapable of wind-walking by the pool. She didn't know if she could wind-walk now, if surprising him would release his control over her, but she had to try, had to fight to survive.

The GTECH took the last step to the porch, and Lara blasted out one last rush of rants, surprised at how easily four-letter words came to mind since she'd never actually used them. Adrenaline rushed through her, with the urge to flee now, but she forced herself to be patient, to wait until the last possible second, to wait rather than act, for that second when he reached for the doorknob. His hand closed around it, and Lara called to the wind.

Instant, piercing pain ripped through her head and left her panting, head spinning, fingers digging into the hard muscle of the GTECH's back. He was doing it to her again. He was controlling her, and she couldn't do anything to stop him.

"Bastard," she hissed through her teeth the instant the pain began to ease, but physically she could feel her body weaken from the energy she'd expelled in her failed escape, her limbs growing heavy.

"So I've been told by you several times now," he said dryly, walking inside the cabin and kicking the door shut. He flipped a lock into place, and then walked a few steps, though she didn't know where, because she couldn't see anything except the floor. But he kept talking, kept acting like nothing was wrong—like she wasn't hanging over his damn shoulder in pain. "For the record," he continued, "I prefer my name, Damion, to *bastard*. What should I call you besides, 'the one with the wicked tongue and mean bite'?"

She wasn't about to touch that wicked tongue comment, which sounded a little too suggestive, making her wonder if he'd evoked some deep, dark, captive-princess fantasy buried somewhere in the recesses of her mind. Then again, considering everything, it might just be the blood rushing to her head. "My name won't matter if the blood keeps running to my head like this, and it explodes. Please. Put me down, and stop whatever else you are doing to me."

"It's 'please' now, is it?" he asked, but he didn't expect a reply, immediately adding, "You're a contradiction if I ever met one. Just a few more minutes."

She opened her mouth to argue, but the energy seemed poorly spent, the time for her yelling and ranting gone, a failed distraction she now couldn't afford.

It was time to be silent, to catalogue her surroundings for escape options, as Skywalker had taught her. She frowned, a funny flutter rushing across her chest. Skywalker? Who was Skywalker? Powell. She meant Powell.

The GTECH—Damion—stopped at a wall of some sort, and Lara managed a brief glimpse behind her of a worn, brown leather couch, two chairs, and shag throw rug on hardwood, before he started walking down a set of dark stairs. Automatic lights flickered to life as he began the descent, and Lara saw a sophisticated electronic panel close behind them. That wasn't going to be easy to get past again without a security code.

He entered an elevator and headed deeper into an underground facility. Once inside, with the doors shut, he put her down, to her surprise. In the process, his powerful arm did a slow slide down her body, his palm running over her legs, her butt, her back. She felt every intimate inch of herself touch every hard inch of him—and not without reaction. By the time her feet hit the ground, she was hot, so hot. Unnaturally aroused by a man who was her enemy, and it made no sense. She couldn't control what she felt. Forget the rush of blood to her head, it had all pooled lower—much *lower*.

Neither moved, their bodies still close, and the scent of him, all musky and male, enveloped her, entranced her. She told herself it was his unique GTECH abilities and refused to make eye contact, *afraid* to make eye contact. She stared at his chest, at her hands resting against the hard T-shirt-clad wall of muscle, and told herself to push him away. But, for reasons she couldn't explain, she resisted breaking the physical bond. *Push away!* she silently yelled in her mind.

His hands caressed a path down her sides, sending warm tingling through her limbs, and she was lost in the sensation. That was, until she realized he was pulling her dress over her backside, because it had been shoved up over her hips, and she hadn't even noticed. What was it about this man? She couldn't keep her dress down around him.

Lara shoved out of his arms and in just one backward step, hit the wall behind her. Instinctively, her eyes lifted, and before she knew what had happened, they locked with his. Lord help her, she felt the connection to her toes, the silent snake of awareness wrapping around them, curling low in her stomach.

"Stop doing this to me," she hissed, angry at his seductive abilities.

He arched a brow, amusement dancing in his dark eyes. "Stop doing what?"

The elevator opened, and before she knew what he intended, he hit a button on the panel, locking the doors open, and then spinning her to face the wall.

Once again, she was trapped, with the same big, strong, powerful GTECH body pressed hotly to hers, with no ability to use the wind to aid her escape.

Chapter 4

BEING TRAPPED WITH HER BACK TO A BIG, DANGEROUS GTECH, not once, but twice in an hour, growing more physically ill with each passing second, didn't exactly invite more of her bravado, but nevertheless, Lara gave it a whirl. "Are we really doing this little game again?" she demanded, trying to keep her voice as cool as the elevator wall that her hands pressed against, only to sound breathless, as though she were affected by her captive position, by the heat radiating off his big body into hers.

"You mean the one where I search you to make sure you don't get to keep your promise to kill me?" he said, his body framing hers, his hands sliding to her waist. "Yeah. We are."

"I guess Renegades don't believe in facing their enemies head on?" she taunted, trying to get him to turn her back around, before he found her weapon. Fighting him would be wasted energy she'd need when a real opportunity to escape materialized. Saving her weapon had to be her goal. "You just prefer to stab them in the back." That last part wasn't a question. She knew it was true. She'd witnessed it firsthand.

"I'm not the one threatening to kill *you*," he reminded her.

"It's not a threat," she managed, and to her dismay, he slid his leg intimately between hers and spread them wide. A sudden, unforgiving ache spread between her legs, an ache that belied who and what this man was. An ache he had to be creating, just as he was weakening her physically. He was messing with her mind, her skills, her body. "Then you know why you're facing the wall, and I'm not," he said, his tone low and sandpaper rough. "In fact, keep your hands on said wall until I tell you to move them."

"In other words, don't reach for the gun my bikini is hiding so effectively?" She tried to look over her shoulder at him, but froze when he framed her body, his hands covering hers and pressing them to the wall. His palms slid back down her arms, leaving a sizzling burn in their wake.

"Exactly," he agreed, his fingers framing her waist, and she could hear the smile in his voice as he added, "I fully admit to a macho need to be the only one of the two of us armed and dangerous in this relationship." His palms skimmed over her hips and down her thighs, until he was squatting down beneath her skirt, patting down her shoes.

"We don't have a relationship," she said, hating the unsteady, telling note in her voice that having this man sitting beneath the hem of her dress had created. "We are experiencing an unfortunate encounter that is outlasting its welcome."

"Sounds like the beginning of something wonderful to me," he commented, a moment before his warm, callused fingers traced her calves and moved to her knees.

"Hey!" she objected, reaching down and catching his hand, as she met his gaze. "Not under the dress."

"Oh yes," he assured her, an evil glint of mischief in both his voice and his expression, "under the dress. I promise to make it fast and painless. Now be a good girl, and put your hands back on the wall."

Why did this man telling her to be a "good girl" and ordering her to put her hands back on the wall sound sexy, rather than insulting?

"Painless for you," she ground out, clenching her teeth. "And I swear to you if I get even a hint of an idea you're enjoying this, you'll be sorry." She cut her gaze to the wall and steeled herself for his exploration—the outcome. He was going to find her knife. "Do it, and get it over with."

"Now there's a line to break a man's heart," he said with a chuckle, wasting no time skimming her skirt upward, over her thighs, until he caressed her hips and then her backside. She squeezed her eyes shut as his fingers slid to the V of her legs.

Instinctively, she squeezed her legs shut, and what a mistake that was. "You're pushing your luck," she panted, his hand now firmly planted between her thighs.

"I never had any luck to start with," he said, the fingers of his free hand splaying across her stomach. "Which is why I can't leave any bit of tiny bikini cloth unexplored." Before she could stop him, his hand slid between her breasts and pulled the blade free. A second later, her dress fell back into place, and he waved the leather-pouched knife between them. "Good thing I don't believe in luck." The knife disappeared.

"One last little inspection," he said softly, and pressed her head forward, brushing the hair from her neck. She froze with the knowledge of what he was looking for, with the sudden spike in sexual energy between them, with the sensual feel of him stroking the delicate skin of her nape.

Seconds ticked by, silent seconds in which the air seemed to thicken, and her skin tingled. She was warm all over, aware of this GTECH on levels she shouldn't be, and guilt twisted inside her. He was a GTECH, a Renegade, a betrayer and killer.

But when he turned her to face him, his hands going to the wall above her head, and she was captured in his downright scorching gaze, she was lost all over again.

"Just confirming you don't wear a Lifebond mark," he said.

The mention of the tattoo-like double circle that appeared on a woman's neck the first time she had sex with her intended mate set her pulse racing, though she couldn't say why. Of course, he wanted to check for the mark. If she had a Lifebond, he'd be hunting for her. He'd kill for her.

"I knew what you were looking for," she said, her throat ridiculously dry. She was a GTECH. She should have better control than this. But when his gaze slid to her mouth and lingered, and she knew he was thinking of kissing her, Lara burned so badly for that kiss. Wanted it to the point where she could have justified it, could have told herself it was to manipulate him, to earn her freedom.

"It appears," he said in a whisky-rough voice, "you belong to no one."

When Lara normally would have snapped back some reply like, "I'll never Lifebond with a GTECH," instead, for some reason, she simply said, "I belong to myself."

"Correction," he said. A hint of a predatory gleam flickered in his eyes. "Right now, you belong to me." He pushed off the wall. "Let's get your wounds cleaned up." He motioned her out the door and added, "Then we can talk."

Reality, and her foolish hormonal reaction to this GTECH, slammed into her with that one word "talk," a reminder that he was her enemy, who wanted information and would do anything to get it.

She straightened and gave her dress a tug downward. "No matter how much you mess with my head or use your seductive voodoo on me, I'm not talking."

She didn't wait for an answer. She stepped around him, exited the elevator, and then started down a narrow hallway to her right. She hoped like heck that letting him know she was onto his manipulation would shut him down.

She'd lost everything to the GTECHs, lost her family, her life, so this one—no matter how hot and sexy he might be—wasn't taking her freedom, nor would he deny her the vengeance she intended to have. Before this was over, he'd know a piece of it himself. Right then, she vowed, before this was over, this GTECH would learn those lessons in a deeply intimate way.

Chapter 5

Voodoo? Did she really just accuse him of working seductive voodoo on her? Unable to help himself, he watched the sweet sway of her curvy hips, and grew hotter and harder with every move she made.

Jeezus, he was in some deep shit with this woman, and he didn't even know her name. What he did know was that the chances were pretty damn high that she was baiting him, seducing *him* and trying to infiltrate the Renegades' operation. It was working too, because she was already inside one of their facilities.

He scrubbed his now lightly stubbled jaw and followed her down the hall. Either she was playing him, luring him into thinking he was doing the seducing, not her, or she really hated how much she wanted him. He wasn't sure which he preferred. Yeah, he did. The one that didn't include this woman conniving against him. If she hated him, at least that was honest, not some form of manipulation. He had no idea what it was about this woman, why he wanted to believe she was Adam's victim rather than the man's ally. All evidence, from the gun she'd been holding when he found her, to her very existence as a GTECH, said she was Adam's creation. But there was something about her, something that didn't ring true to the obvious. Something that made him want her in a bad way.

"What voodoo is it I'm supposed to be working?" he

asked, catching up with her when she paused under the arch that led into a giant room divided into four sections.

She turned to confront him with a defiant lift of her chin. "I'm no fool," she said. "I've studied the GTECHs. I am a GTECH. I know a good number of the GTECHs have developed special abilities beyond the basics. Like Adam can communicate with wolves. So I get that you can make yourself sexually appealing and climb inside my head and play around. Well stop. Just stop. Nothing you do is going to make me like you or talk to you."

They were close, so close he could imagine pulling her against him, imagine her soft curves melting into his body.

He grinned at the intense look on her face. He couldn't help himself. She was serious about the voodoo, and so furious at her reaction to him, she was fishing for an excuse to justify her desire. She wasn't manipulating him as he'd feared, nor was she here because Adam had told her to seduce him. She hated the GTECHs too much to believe she could want one. It was probably nuts, but that made him really damn happy. His dick too, judging from the thick, uncomfortable bulge in his pants.

Her eyes blazed at his smile. "I'm glad I amuse you."

"Sorry," he said, trying to sound sincere, but it was hard because *he* was hard, and his male ego was buzzing with satisfaction.

"Right," she said. "That's why you're smiling."

"I am sorry," he argued. "That is, sorry to disappoint you. But you can't blame wanting me on some seductive power I possess, because it doesn't exist. This thing between us, this relationship, or whatever you don't want to call it—is pure chemistry, sweetheart. And yeah, I know it sucks to want someone you don't trust. Believe me. I'm in the same boat with you and sinking fast."

She glared a look at him that would have flattened a lesser man, but her feisty spirit only made him burn more for her, made him wonder, in fact, just how feisty she would be all hot and bothered and naked—in his bed. Oh yeah, she could seduce him all night long if she wanted to, and he wouldn't regret it the next morning either.

"Right," she said sarcastically. "It's just chemistry. Just like you aren't causing me to hallucinate any more than you stopped me from wind-walking outside the cabin, now are you?"

"Whoa," he said with his hands up, stop-sign fashion. "You tried to wind-walk and couldn't?"

She crossed her arms in front of her truly spectacular chest. "Like you don't know."

"I didn't," he said. "And I admit I was sure you would try. I was ready to yank you right back out of the wind, and yes, I could have. Time and practice breed skill."

"I know you're doing this to me," she insisted.

"Contrary to what you seem to believe, very few GTECHs have special abilities beyond the basic wind-walking, he-man super strength, and speed, and I'm not one of them. If you're having hallucinations, you probably have a concussion. I'm sure that's why you couldn't wind-walk too."

"Good try," she said. "This all started by the pool before my injury, and as I figure it, about the time I must have hit your radar."

He wasn't so sure the knock on her head didn't have her confused on the facts, but it was clear she believed what she said. "I know it means nothing to you, but my word is as good as gold. And I give you my word—I have nothing to do with what's happening to you." In the giant room divided by four partitions, he motioned toward the first that doubled as a bedroom and a treatment center. "Have a seat on the bed, and I'll get that wound on your head cleaned up."

She cast him a silent "you're crazy if you think I'm sitting on that bed" look, walked to the big black chair next to it, and sat down.

Yeah, good choice, he thought. He could still feel her soft skin beneath his hands, her long legs aligned with his. His cock thickened, his zipper stretched. Oh yeah. A bed and this woman were just too tempting to be safe.

Damion claimed a rolling chair and eased across the concrete floor to the medical cabinet at the foot of the bed, next to a vitals monitor.

With peroxide and gauze, he rolled back to her chair. "Why don't you put your head in your lap so I can see the wound?"

"I'll heal from the physical wound without you doing this," she said. "I'm GTECH. Remember?"

"I remember," he said. "Do *you* remember? Because you act like all of us are assholes and bastards, and simply tolerate being like us. Physiologically, GTECHs are different from humans, but we choose right from wrong. Good from bad. All of us, including you."

"That's like comparing humans to butterflies, GTECHs to lions, and saying both are as likely to attack and kill their prey."

"Humans are far from butterflies," he said. "And if I'm a lion, so are you."

"It takes a lion to kill a lion."

"Is that what you want?" he asked. "To kill me?"

"Like you don't intend to kill me when you're done with me," she accused.

"I want to save you from Adam," he assured her. "But you have to want to be saved. And you have to talk to me. Make me understand why you would work for a man who's a seed of destruction. If you truly hate all GTECHs, then I have to assume you were forced into becoming one and forced into fighting as one. *Do* you hate all GTECHs? Or do you just hate the Renegades?"

"I know what Adam is," she said, cutting her gaze. She pulled her feet into the chair, with her dress and arms over her knees, giving him a glimpse of the fast-healing bruise smudging the pale ivory of her cheek.

She hadn't given him a direct answer, but then, he didn't need one. Emotions rolled off of her and slammed into him. Pain. Resentment. No one faked this kind of raw hurt. The soldier in him—who did everything by the book, who had no room for emotions—urged him to use this moment of weakness in her to push her for more, but he found the man in him could not. She'd shut down anyway, he could see that, and done so in a way that screamed *insurmountable* wall. She was angry and with reason, if she'd been abused in Adam's sex camps, and then forced to fight for him when she didn't find a Lifebond.

"Let me look at your head," he urged softly.

Her gaze shifted to his, eyes flashing stubbornly, a bit of that fight of hers returning. "I'm fine."

He rolled his chair closer. "You're not fine."

"I am," she argued.

Before she could stop him, he pulled her legs to

the floor, not allowing himself to think about the short, tempting path up her tiny dress. She was hurt, physically and emotionally. He knew that now, and it changed everything, even if it should not. He could have her, he knew, and she'd willingly give herself without much encouragement. But he was pretty sure she'd feel raped in the aftermath, which meant that right now, he couldn't have her, no matter how tempting she might be. Still, holding her knees steady, he ached to touch her, to allow his fingers to caress the smooth skin of her leg beneath his palm. "Put your hard head in your lap, so I can see," he ordered. "I'm checking your wound one way or the other."

Rebellion flashed in her bright green eyes, and her gaze collided with his in a silent clash of wills, a battle she simply wasn't going to win.

Charged seconds ticked by until her lips thinned, her expression shifted. There was a tiny flash of vulnerability in her face—a hint of what was beneath her façade of toughness—before she bent her head to her lap and allowed him to see her wound. With gentle fingers, he brushed her hair away from her scalp and studied the six-inch cut that would be gushing blood if not for her GTECH healing abilities. "Now that's what I call a gouge," he said with a whistle. "And despite your claim of being 'fine,' you aren't. You're going to need several hours of sleep to heal this one."

He rolled his chair back. "You can lift your head."

She peered through the mass of dark brown hair covering her face. "What happened to your cleaning my wound," she lowered her voice to imitate him, "'one way or another'?"

Though being mocked wasn't something he enjoyed, her attempt to make her distinctively feminine, almost youthful voice, deep and masculine, was fairly entertaining.

"Your hair's matted inside the cut," he said, watching as she straightened fully and shoved that mass of gorgeous hair from her face. "We may need to throw a few stitches in it to speed the healing." He motioned to the right. "You can use the shower in the back of the facility, and then I'll have another look. I need to check on my team anyway.

"And just so we're clear. If you get any ideas about an escape, don't bother. You're in here until I say you're out."

"Until I steal your gun, and make you let me out," she said matter-of-factly.

"Good luck with that," he said. "Why don't you wait until that head wound heals, and you're feeling feisty again?" He wiggled his eyebrows and grinned. "We'll have more fun that way."

"Fine then," she agreed. "That gives me time to plan the moment of revenge, when I turn you upside down like you did to me." She pushed to her feet and wobbled, reaching for the chair.

He rolled his chair forward and caught her, wrapped his arms around her—holding her steady, holding her close. She was tiny and soft and yielded to his touch—as if her subconscious trusted him, even if she did not. "Easy, sweetheart," he said softly. "I wasn't joking about how bad that head wound is."

She grabbed his arms and steadied herself, her eyes fluttering as if she were light-headed. "Thank you."

He narrowed a probing look at her. "You really are a contradiction, aren't you? One minute you have the vocabulary of a sailor, cursing up a storm, and the next, automatically saying 'thank you' and 'please.'"

"I don't curse like a sailor," she argued, and when he arched a brow, she indignantly added, "If you had your bikini-clad backside hiked in the air, in a strange man's face, I bet you'd discover a few four-letter words too."

"If I was wearing bikini bottoms, I hope and pray someone would kill me long before my butt was hiked in the air and in some man's face."

She laughed, her expression shifting to quick surprise, as if she couldn't believe she was sharing such a moment with him. "I'm trying to imagine you, the big, macho Renegade—in bikini bottoms." Her eyes actually twinkled as she added, "Maybe a pink pair with flowers."

"I'm going to take the big, macho Renegade comment as a compliment, but then again, with you, I'm not sure it is. And for the record, I'm not the pink flower type. I'm the American Flag type." And then, because he had the undeniable urge to hear that soft, sweet laugh of hers again, because laughter bred trust, he added, "Or Spider-Man. Nothing like a good pair of Spidey boxers." She rewarded him with a soft musical laugh, and he wondered if she realized she was still holding onto him, because *he* did. Every damn inch of him was alive with that little piece of awareness.

"You wear Spider-Man underwear?" she asked.

"You got a problem with Spider-Man?"

"No," she said, a smile lingering behind her laughter. "There's nothing wrong with Spider-Man. You're pretty funny. *For a GTECH.*"

"You're pretty funny too," he said. "*For a GTECH.*"

The smile on her lips faded into the crackle of spiking sexual energy arcing between them. She drew a ragged breath, and he knew then, she was aware of their nearness, of his hands on her hips.

She pressed out of his arms and took several steps to her right, out of his reach. "Where can I find that shower?" she asked.

With the discomfort of his bulging zipper, and a mass of frustration over her withdrawal, Damion ran his hands down his knees and stood, motioning for her to follow him. "This way." He started walking, letting her follow, giving her his back and his trust in doing so, even though she wouldn't give him hers. It was trust she didn't deserve when she wouldn't tell him her name… and swore she wanted to kill him.

In his head he heard Kid Rock shouting the lyrics of "American Warrior" from his tribute song to the soldiers, but he was thinking "American Fool" might suit him better. A fool for a woman.

Lara followed Damion toward the back of the facility, passing a tech center that would rival anything Serenity had and then some, on the way to what she assumed was a bathroom. His name repeated in her mind, and she stopped walking, flustered that she'd thought of him as "Damion." *Don't give a GTECH a name. He doesn't deserve a name*—a warning that had her gaze lingering, not where it should be, on the rows of monitors on the wall that might hold clues to escape, but on the man— the way his T-shirt stretched across impressively broad shoulders, and how his jeans hugged a hard, firm back-side. She shook her head, a mistake she paid for when stars exploded in front of her eyes and set her to swaying.

A gentle hand settled on her arm. "You okay?"

She blinked to find Damion—dang it, *the GTECH*—standing in front of her again, towering over her and ooz-ing a dominant masculine presence, lethal and sensual. He was too close, too big and bad and hot. Unbidden, an image of the two of them naked, entwined in bed, overcame her. She blinked it away and found herself looking into Damion's light hazel eyes, softening at the genuine concern she read in them. She caught herself swaying again, but this time toward him.

Frustrated, she stilled the sway and balled her fists by her sides, telling herself this feeling, this connection she felt to this GTECH, was a spell, some of his GTECH voodoo. "Don't worry," she said. "I'm not going to pass out before you can grill me for information."

"Good to know," he said, his lips lifting slightly. "Maybe I'll even find out what your name is before the night is out." He motioned her forward with a wave of his hand. "Ladies first."

She shook her head. "I'm no lady, remember? I'm a GTECH. You go first."

"Together then," he said, reaching for her hand and sending heat darting up her arm. "This way I keep you from falling."

They were in motion before she could object, and he didn't let her go until he set her down on a footstool in the center of a large dressing area, complete with a shower, vanity, and walk-in closet.

"You'll find everything you could possibly need

here," he said. "Clothes that should fit, and whatever cosmetics you might want. Several of our high-ranking Renegades have Lifebonds who frequently travel with them, and they keep the place well stocked. Many of our medical and research team are female as well, so we want them to be comfortable if they should be here."

"You have females involved in your operation?" she asked in surprised. "As in—not in sex camps?"

He leaned against the vanity. "I keep trying to tell you the Renegades are nothing like the Zodius. We've saved a large population of people and their families who were targeted by Adam for their skills or simply their bodies, and offered them safety and shelter." He crossed his arms in front of a truly stellar chest, and she tried not to notice his powerful forearms, or the light brown hair dusting them. "Everyone in Sunrise City, humans and GTECHs alike, share a goal—to stop Adam before he's unstoppable. And I know you find this hard to believe, but we try to make everyone's lives in Sunrise City as normal as possible. We have a school for the kids. There's no crime, no bills to pay, no need or want not provided for these individuals and families."

Families they had kept together, rather than killed, as hers had been—it sounded too good to be true. Images of her past twisted her into knots, images of her own family being killed at the hands of GTECHs. She remembered her father's new friend, who'd come to the house, and remembered arriving for a dinner just in time to watch him and a group of men slaughter her family. She'd gone into shock, but a moment before she would have been found, she'd hidden under the porch stairs, with bugs and mud, and who knew what else. That was where Powell had found her.

Powell's warnings came back to her as well. *The Renegades are worse than the Zodius. They pretend they are good, but they'll smile and then shoot you in the back.* These men had done just that to her father, to her family. Now this one was trying to do the same to her.

"I'll leave the door cracked," Damion said, moving toward the exit. "In case you need me or feel sick. But I won't come in. You have my word."

She actually believed him, which was a reason to disbelieve him. He could stab her in the back the minute she let her guard down.

He started to turn, and suddenly, she wanted him to know he couldn't fool her, he couldn't suck her in. "I'm Lara," she said, giving him the name he sought. "And I was created to kill your kind. And I *will* kill you before this is over."

He didn't react, his expression unchanged, his big body still loose-muscled and comfortable. "Since you plan to kill me, seems only fair I get to know my assassin's full name."

She realized that she wanted him to know too, and she wanted him to know what the Renegades had taken from her, why she sought revenge. Why she *would* kill him. "Lara…" she said, intending to give him her last name, but her mind went blank.

He arched a brow at her hesitation. "Lara what?"

She didn't know. She reached into her memories, but there was no name. Desperate, she tried to picture her past, her family, but there was simply more of that blankness.

"It doesn't matter," she lied, because it mattered more than he would ever know. "Lara is dead. My duty is all I have left." And she feared that was truer than ever, because no matter how hard she tried, she couldn't picture her family, couldn't see their faces.

He studied her a moment, his gaze hot and steady, probing and thoughtful. "Lara isn't dead," he said. "She's lost. And I'm going to help you find her again." He said nothing else, simply turned and left the room. He pulled the door shut, but for a small crack, leaving Lara to stare after him, *lost* in every way.

How long she stared after him she did not know, because at some point, she became aware of warm water running over her naked skin, of suds washing down the drain by her feet, of her own name on her tongue, as she whispered it over and over. She tried to answer the question the GTECH had asked her—*Lara what? Mallery*. Lara Mallery. But the instant the name came into her mind, it felt wrong. It felt empty and brought no recollection of the past.

Squeezing her eyes shut, she willed her mind to picture her family, to open herself to her memories. The GTECHs had taken her family. She would not let this new GTECH, Damion, take her memories. But the harder she strained to remember her past, the darker her mind became, until the name "Lara Martin" came to her. A sudden onslaught of conflicting, violent images flooded her mind. Of GTECHs killing her family, then of Sabrina dragging her up a set of stairs and ordering a man she didn't know, someone named Skywalker, to be killed. But Skywalker was dead, and it hurt. God, it hurt so badly.

Lara hit the wall of the shower, the deaths of family, of Skywalker, replaying in her mind's eye, over and over, and with them, the pain, the loss, sparking the hot flames of anger that the water had no chance of dousing. The need for vengeance, the familiar need for justice, roared to life—her only hope of sanity, her only reason to go on.

Chapter 6

IF ANYONE WAS WORKING SEXUAL VOODOO ON ANYONE, Damion would have sworn it was the woman in that bathroom, and on him. She'd just told him she was an assassin trained to kill GTECHs like himself, that she, in fact, intended to kill him, and all he'd wanted to do was strip her naked and take her right there on the bathroom floor. And the *man* in him could all too easily justify why he might act on his attraction to her. Some part of him rejected her as his enemy, and there was this uncomfortable ball of possessiveness growing inside him like nothing he'd ever felt for a woman, let alone one who wanted to kill him. Because, he told himself, assassin or not, when she'd declared that "Lara" was dead, he'd seen the vulnerability beneath the hard shell, seen the woman who was Lara, who he'd sensed existed even before he'd known she did. The woman who'd been hurt, who'd had something taken from her that she didn't think she could ever get back. Something she blamed herself for. He recognized that feeling in her, because he had the unique perspective of having felt the same way when his brother had died. Lara existed because Adam had stolen something from Lara's life.

For the time being though, he shoved aside such concerns and focused on the urgency of contacting his team, after too long without communication.

Damion sat down at the computer panel of the tech center and flipped a red switch on the wall. A satellite phone slid from beneath the tabletop, and he grabbed the receiver and dialed. At the same time, his mind hung on something Lara had said. *I was created to kill your kind.* He frowned. Why hadn't she said *to kill Renegades*? Maybe because she hated all GTECHs, no matter who was pulling her puppet strings, or maybe because the puppet strings existed.

Chale answered his cell phone in one ring, and Damion moved on to the urgent matters at hand.

"Talk to me," Damion ordered, bypassing "hello" himself this time. He and Chale were like brothers. They didn't need small talk. "Tell me Lev is secure."

"Where the fuck are you?" Chale shouted into the phone, proving the small talk assumption one hundred percent true. "I thought you were lying somewhere gutted, for God's sake."

"Yeah well, I love you too, man," Damion replied dryly. "I'm fine. Now answer the question. Is Lev secure?"

"As secure as sitting ducks, waiting for nightfall to get the hell out of Dodge."

"And the agents guarding him?" Damion asked. "Were they 'in bed' with Adam?"

Chale snorted. "Try in bed with the fantasy of early retirement—at least that goes for the agent-in-charge. He's planning to resign the agency in a month and went ahead and mentally checked out early." His tone turned muffled and scornful as it became clear he was talking to the agent. "Apparently agent-not-so-smart-and-thank-God-for-all-those-who-might-depend-on-him-that-he's-resigning wasn't thinking about actually living to see his resignation happen. His men should thank us for taking over, so they get to live as well."

He didn't ask if Chale was certain about the agent's story. Chale had his fact-checking in order, or he wouldn't speak. The man never assumed anything, which Damion liked about him.

"So what's the bikini babe got to do with us taking Lev and clan into custody?"

"Adam's put together a team of female assassins to do his dirty work now. *GTECH* female assassins."

"No f-ing way," Chale said. "Adam considers women baby-making machines, not to mention, inferiors. Are you sure?"

"One hundred percent," Damion said, without explaining. "I got some up-close-and-personal demonstration of what they're capable of."

"I take it you have the bikini chick in custody and talking?"

"In custody, yes," he confirmed. "But she's injured and not doing a lot of talking beyond promising to kill me."

Chale chuckled. "Now that sounds fun. Wish I was there. I do believe I'd enjoy interrogating a hot female assassin."

"Just make sure, later tonight, you're not the one getting interrogated by a hot female assassin," he said. "Watch your ass when you leave. They will be."

"You do the same," Chale said. "Because I saw that bikini babe's backside, and it's a distraction if I ever saw one."

He could say that again. And he did, one last time, after a discussion about their extraction plans.

Damion ended the call and dialed Caleb Rain, the

Renegade's leader, who was Adam Rain's twin brother. "Adam sent a team after the Russian. We were forced to take him into custody. Chale's moving him in your direction at nightfall."

"Why Chale? And why are you in the shelter?" Caleb said, able to see his location from the Sunrise tech panels.

"I captured a Zodius soldier and went underground for interrogation. A *female* Zodius soldier. And yes, you heard me right. Adam's converted a team of women to GTECHs. The one here with me claims she was created specifically to be a GTECH assassin."

"Let's take this on monitor," was Caleb's immediate response. "Michael's here, and I need him involved in this conversation."

Damion punched a button by the phone and set the receiver back on the base. One of the dozen monitors above the desk came to life, and the image of Caleb and Michael sitting side by side at the conference table of the Sunrise City war room filled the screen. The two were complete opposites, well beyond the obvious—Caleb's short brown hair and Michael's long black hair. Caleb was the honor-bound Superman of a graphic novel, while Michael was the dark persona of Batman, willing to do what Caleb would not in the name of justice. That was where Damion and Michael often found themselves at odds. Damion believed the Superman-style of justice was the foundation this country needed, now more than ever. Michael believed that foundation was a myth that had never existed.

Once Caleb briefed Michael on the situation, Michael's head snapped to the monitor, his hard gaze finding Damion's.

"Where's the woman now?"

"In the shower washing a head wound," Damion said. "And here's the interesting part. I didn't give her that injury. She attacked her commanding officer and kept her from killing Lev, but took a beating in the process."

"Why would Adam kill the Russian when he needs him?" Caleb asked. "And why did this woman stop it from happening if that was her intention to start with?"

"I asked the same," Damion confirmed. "She refused to answer, but I get the feeling Lara is all about killing GTECHs, but humans are another story.

"And one more important little detail that's going to blow your minds—the commanding officer she attacked was Sabrina, the ICE dealer who'd double-crossed Adam and stolen from him. And before you ask—no, these women aren't ICE junkies doped up on drugs that Sabrina stole before she disappeared. These women wind-walk, and Icers using the synthetic GTECH serum can't wind-walk. We're talking the real deal here. These women are GTECHs."

"Wait," Michael said, shaking his head. "You're telling me that Sabrina is alive and in a command position for Adam?"

"It's Sabrina, all right," Damion said. "The one I have here is Lara, but no last name so far. It would help if Sterling could run a check on missing persons with that first name. I have my hands a little full right now." Sterling was the Renegade's top tech guy next to Damion, and his brother ran the family-owned Megatech Technology, one of the top tech companies in the world.

"I'll get him right on it," Caleb agreed. "And I'll have him chase down Sabrina's trail. Her involvement in this makes no sense to me. Adam would have killed a traitor. Hell, my brother'll kill you for looking at him wrong."

"Not a woman who could potentially Lifebond with one of his men, no matter what she'd done to him," Michael disagreed. "Adam would have let the entire male population of Zodius have her. If she didn't find a match, which we can safely assume, then she would have been handed over to Ava for experimental fertility procedures. Ava must have convinced Adam that injecting a female with the serum would make her fertile."

"And when it didn't work," Caleb said, "Adam decided to put them to work killing Renegades."

"It's a good hypothesis," Michael said. "Now we just need to prove it."

"Doesn't seem a good strategy for Adam," Damion said dryly. "Not when the women are going to hate him for what he's done to them."

"Adam knows how to get loyalty," Michael said. "He wouldn't think twice about torturing these women's families and friends, maybe even kill a few to prove he would kill the others."

"Considering Lara has a boatload of raw hatred toward GTECHs," Damion said, "I'd say there is a good chance that's exactly what he did to her. She hates GTECHs, every last one of us. I get the idea she's just happy she gets to kill some of us."

"As far as I'm concerned, that's good news," Michael said. "If that's how Adam is operating, that's the best case scenario in my mind. It means we're dealing with a few females they've experimented on because that's all the serum Adam would dare risk, when he has so little." His jaw clenched. "Now on to the worst case, which in my experience is usually the one that applies to Adam. What if one of Ava's fertility experiments wielded a method of converting females to GTECHs without the original serum? Women become his army and the ticket to power that Adam is looking for. If that's the case, then we'll be outnumbered, and Adam will be a whole lot closer to creating a Zodius Nation that takes over this country."

Caleb and Damion both took that in with a long silence, before Michael added, "I say bring the woman here to Sunrise City, and let Becca extract her memories."

Damion ground his teeth at the callous suggestion. Becca was Sterling's Lifebond. Through a combination of experimental cancer treatment and her conversion to GTECH, she had developed unique abilities, like reading minds when she touched someone. Damion wasn't about to let that happen to Lara. Not now, not before she had a chance to talk on her own.

"Performing what amounts to a mental rape on Lara, when there's a good chance she's already been physically raped, makes us no better than Adam, and it isn't going to get her to help us. We have to assume she has access to Zodius City, and if there is some kind of new serum, we need to get inside to destroy it. That means gaining her trust. Show her we aren't like the Zodius."

"Assuming she's not already corrupted by Adam, and this is all a ploy to infiltrate our operation," Michael said, cynical as usual. "Becca's mental probe would let us know if she can be trusted."

"Both valid points," Caleb agreed. "Michael's right, though. We can't risk this being some sort of trap to get this woman inside Sunrise City. If we need Becca, we'll have her go to Lara." He homed in on Damion. "If you really feel Lara deserves a chance to come around on her own, we'll give it to her. But make this journey to trust a quick one. If Adam has the serum to build an army of female GTECHs, innocent lives could depend on it."

A female scream ripped through the conversation and was still clinging to the air as Damion ended the call on the move to the bathroom.

Chapter 7

DAMION FORGOT HIS PROMISE TO STAY OUT OF THE bathroom unless invited, blasting through the doors and then freezing at what he found. The curtain to the shower stall hung open, and a shivering Lara sat naked in the corner, her legs pulled to her chest, just out of the reach of a stream of water.

Quickly he scanned the room, relieved to confirm that the impossible hadn't somehow happened, and an intruder had gotten inside the facility. While there was no unexpected guest, and Lara was safe, it was also clear she was definitely *not* okay. He knew the signs of shock, having seen a few guys go off the deep end after missions turned bloody.

"Lara?" he softly called out, fighting the instinct to go to her, cautious so he didn't scare her and worsen her condition.

She didn't respond. There was no acknowledgment that he was present, not even a flicked gaze in his direction. Staring forward, she seemed to be seeing, but not seeing.

"Lara, sweetheart," he said. "I'm going to get you a towel and get you out of there."

She whispered softly, incoherently, and began to rock, but still she didn't look at him.

Damn it. Damn it. Damn it. This had to be the healing sickness the GTECHs suffered as a product of chronic low vitamin C that got worse with time. He might have prevented it from occurring with an injection. At a minimum, he would have lessened her suffering. But there had been no known case of a GTECH who'd been converted less than a year and who'd experienced the healing illness, so he'd assumed... well, he shouldn't have assumed anything.

Damion balled his fists by his sides and dared to step forward. He knew he had to ensure Lara was stable, that she wasn't going to surprise him, yet again, and do something none of the other GTECHs had done, like dying from the healing illness.

He closed the distance between them and stopped just outside the tiled rim of the shower stall, willing her to look at him. "Lara?"

She sucked in a breath at his voice, in what seemed to be the first definitive indication that she knew he was there, and then, as if in reaction to his presence, her petite frame erupted in violent quakes to the point he thought she might have a seizure.

Damion snapped into action, knowing he needed to get her warm. Quickly he shut off the shower, but not before splatters of icy cold droplets hit his arms and face, telling him just how chilled to the bone she must be.

He snatched an oversized towel off the silver shelf against the wall, his gaze sweeping over Lara, her beautiful pale ivory skin glistening with water, her teeth chattering. But the violent quaking he'd feared might be a seizure was, thankfully, already lessening.

"Lara, honey," Damion said, stepping back into the shower stall and squatting down in front of her, hesitating before he touched her. "I'm going to wrap this towel around you to get you warmed up." Easing her from the wall far enough to get the oversized towel behind her, he was able to wrap it around her shoulders and knees.

"Cold," she murmured. "So cold."

He rubbed where the towel covered her arms, trying to create extra heat. "I know," he said. "I'll get you dried off and warm. Can you stand up?"

She blankly blinked up at him with eyes no longer green but GTECH black. "Everyone is dead," she whispered.

A rare chill raced down his spine at the way she said those words. "Who is everyone? Who's dead?"

"Skywalker… is dead." She squeezed her eyes shut and stuck her hand through the towel to cover her face. "No. That's not right."

If she weren't GTECH, immune to drugs, he'd swear she was detoxing. "Does your head hurt, Lara?"

She grabbed his shirt, desperateness in her tone, on her face. "I can't remember who Skywalker is. I need to… remember Skywalker. I know he's important. I need—"

"You don't have to remember right now," he assured her, cupping her cheek with his hand and wondering why the idea of Skywalker being the man in her life bothered him so much. "All you need to do right now is get out of this shower." He started to pick her up.

Her tight grip shackled his wrist, compelling him to look at her, only to find her eyes so black he could barely see any white, her expression simmering with barely contained anger. "My family is dead."

Damion stilled with the icy clarity of her words. He'd been right. Adam had her family. "I'm sorry," he said,

but he'd barely issued the two simple words before he
knew they were a mistake.

Instantly, the black glaze in Lara's eyes crystallized
into hate. "The Renegades killed my family. *You* killed
my family."

"Whoa," Damion said, his hands going to her arms. "I
promise you, Lara. I… We didn't kill your family. We—"

The word was lost in the blast of her fast movement.
With all her GTECH strength, she shoved him away, and
he hit the floor with a hard thud. On some distant level, he
registered that such strength was impossible during a bout
of the healing illness. No, this was not the healing illness
at all. Whatever was going on with Lara was not that.

She came down on top of him, naked, wet, and ready
to kill. She was wild, angry, driven by the pain of loss,
her emotion swelling inside the small room.

She shoved to a sitting position, straddling him, naked
and fiercely beautiful, her high, full breasts thrusting
forward—a scene that might have been erotic, would
have been erotic, if she wasn't, once again, trying to
bust his chops.

Damion shackled her wrists and pulled her back
down, her perky little nipples pressed to his chest.
"Jeezus, woman, what is it with you and violence?"

She jerked against him, trying to sit up, but he held
her firmly, the tug-of-war ending with them so close, he
could almost feel her lips touch his. Instant electricity
crackled in the air, their breath mingling. "Let me up,"
she hissed softly.

"Not until you promise you won't attack me again."

"I will not be captive to a Renegade one second longer. You killed—"

"I didn't," he said, emotion welling inside him, memories of his mother and older brother screaming the same accusation at him in a hospital waiting room. "I didn't kill your family, and neither did any of the Renegades. But I know how losing someone you love feels. I know how much you need someone to blame."

God, he remembered his mother losing it, throwing fists at him until finally his brother had pulled her off of him, only to have his brother begin beating on Damion himself. He'd taken it all because he'd created their pain, because he deserved their anger, and because he wished he was the one with a sheet over his head.

"And you know what…" he said, sitting up with her, but leaving her on top, straddling him, the V of her body pressed to the thick pulse of his cock. He wanted her, wanted to slide his pants down and slip inside her, let her ride away her frustration. But she hated him, and she'd hate him even more if he let that happen.

So he offered her another kind of release, one he understood, one his family had needed, and he'd given them as well. "I'm good at taking the blame. If you really need to hit me, Lara, hit me." He released her hands and settled his on the floor behind him. "If that'll give you some sense of justice, then so be it. Hell—if killing me would give you some sort of peace, I'd give you my gun."

All the anger slid from her face, replaced by stunned disbelief that lasted—maybe fifteen seconds—before anger flared hotter than ever. "Damn you!" she said, flattening her hands on his chest and leaning into him. "Stop messing with my head. Stop manipulating me and playing with my emotions. I *should* hit you. I should take you up on that gun and kill you."

"Gun's in my right pant leg," he said, going out on a ledge, and he wasn't sure why. He needed to trust this woman—already did on some gut level that defied all reason. Or maybe she just opened an old wound attached to a death wish. "Either take it and shoot me, or stop threatening to do it, so we can move on to more productive things. Like putting clothes on you before you drive me out of my flipping mind."

She all but growled at him, her fingers curling in his shirt. "Damn you, GTECH—"

"*Damion*," he ground out, his hand sliding into her hair, tension rippling through his body. He was angry now too, angry and hard, and more sexually frustrated than he'd been in his entire life. "If you're going to curse me, hit me, threaten to kill me, while sitting naked on top of me and teasing me mercilessly, then I deserve to have you use my name."

"Fine," she whispered. "Damn you, *Damion*." And then, somehow, someway, without any coherent decision to do so, and with what felt like a physical demand, a life or death necessity, he was crazy-hot kissing her, his free hand melding to her back, pressing her close. Or maybe she was the one who'd kissed him. That possessive feeling he'd experienced with her a minute before expanded inside him again, a sensation like nothing he'd ever known, screaming *mine*. This woman was somehow a part of him. There was nothing but her, but them. All he knew was the rightness of this. They were wild, hot, and headed toward a firestorm of trouble he had to stop right now. But damn if she wasn't the sweetest thing he'd ever tasted, addictive and spicy sweet, and impossible to resist. *Impossible*.

THE DANGER THAT IS DAMION

—⁓—

Chale didn't dislike dogs. In fact, he liked dogs. But dogs, like kids and some adults, needed to be taught manners. The one presently growling and tugging at his pant leg, clearly hadn't been. For the entire hour since he'd talked to Damion, the wiener dog had barked, snapped, growled, and generally acted like a kid going through a bad case of the terrible twos, down to the "me-me-me or else I'll throw a tantrum" stage.

From where he leaned on the hotel nightstand, one leg crossed over the other, Chale stared down at the dog and waited for Lev to emerge from the bathroom in the doorman uniform he'd managed to scrounge. *No surprise Agent Wonderful had been desperate for some pool time.* Like the CIA agents who'd done a piss poor job of guarding Lev, the dog soon would be departing.

The Zodius would expect them to make a run at departure come nightfall. Chale wanted them to get what they expected, minus Lev and his family. Thankfully, Lev was more than agreeable to a plush, safe life under Renegade protection, as long as he knew his wife and kids were safe. Which Chale had agreed to—he'd expect nothing less from anyone who gave a damn about his family. Exactly why Lev's wife had already departed the room in a maid's uniform, the kids hidden in a laundry hamper. They were now being escorted by two Renegades, en route to Sunrise City.

"Houston!" Chale yelled toward the tiny kitchen area of the hotel suite—Houston being the nickname for Tommy Richards, their team's weapons expert, a name chosen not only because he was from Houston, Texas, but for reasons no one knew except Chale—that it was Damion's dead younger brother's name—Damion refused to call him "Tommy."

Fortunately, Houston loved dogs as much as he did gadgets. "The hotdog demands your attention."

Houston sauntered into the room, held up a bag of sliced hotdogs, of all things, and grinned. "Someone say *hotdog*?" He whistled. "Here, pup."

Chale would have rolled his eyes, but the dog, thankfully, was already darting toward Houston. Unfortunately, Houston teased the animal, and it started jumping, and Lord help Chale, barking. Chale grimaced and ran his hands down his jeans. "The idea is to make it *stop* barking."

Houston tossed a handful of hotdog pieces to the floor, and the dog instantly began to scarf them down in blessed silence. "Ask and you shall receive," Houston said, giving a big white smile that only made his long blond hair and pretty-boy face all the more… well, pretty. Houston was "pretty" in a cowboy, manly way that Chale had initially assumed meant wimp. Then in a confrontation with a Zodius, he'd seen Houston transform into something he could only liken to a pissed off alligator, and he'd forgotten that idea. Houston was a beast.

"He gets sick when he eats table food," Lev said from the bathroom door, now dressed in black slacks and a red button-down jacket about one size too big.

The dog started barking again, begging for more hotdogs. Chale motioned for Houston to give the dog what it wanted, and then tossed Lev a wig and bellman hat.

"We'll warn the kennel when they get here," he told Lev. "Put that on. When you exit the room, I'll have a man in the hallway to your right pretending to struggle with a key to his room. You go to the left and out the door. The minute you step outside, one of my men will join you and give you the code word..." He eyed the dog, and said, "*Hotdog*. That will let you know you are safe. He'll put you in a car and let you talk to your wife and kids. You'll connect with them a few miles up the road." He hit the mike on his ear and gave his team the code word, then pushed off the dresser. "Ready?"

"When will 'Molly' rejoin our family?" Lev asked in surprisingly perfect English, referring to the dog. "The kids are dealing with enough without losing her. We brought her with us."

"In a couple of days," Chale said. "We'll get her back to you. Right now, your safety comes first."

A knock sounded on the door—one, two, three knocks—a code. He and Houston exchanged a look, and Houston went to the door. He returned with Jesse Daniels, one of their own, dressed in the same uniform as Lev, down to the wig and hat.

"I came in," Jesse said, tossing the wig onto the bed, running his hand through his dark, rumpled hair and eyeing Lev. "Now you go out."

A few minutes later, Lev was on the move, headed toward several of Chale's team members, while Chale, Houston, Jesse, and the dog were left in the hotel room.

A knock sounded on the door, and there was no code. Just a knock. All three men exchanged a silent look and reached for their weapons. Even the dog went eerily quiet, as if it sensed what the men knew. Trouble wasn't waiting for sunset.

And while the Renegades enjoyed a good fight,

avoidance was the plan when innocent human lives were at risk, as was the case now with every human in the building. Chale pointed to the ceiling, and Houston quickly hopped up on the dresser and moved a panel to a crawl space they'd discovered that led to the kitchen—an exit strategy, but one that required a drop from the ceiling smack into a burning stove.

"Housekeeping!" came a female voice.

"No thanks!" Chale called, not believing this was housekeeping for a minute. Jesse lifted Houston into the ceiling, and Houston offered Jesse a hand to pull him up.

"Go!" Chale whispered to Jesse, and seeing his hesitation, added, "That's an order, soldier! I don't need a damn babysitter, but *you* will when I'm finished with you if you don't do as I say." Jesse hesitated again, but reluctantly disappeared.

The door of the room burst open, but caught on a chain. "I said, no!" Chale yelled toward the door and fitted the panel back into the ceiling. He jumped to the ground, rushing to the door to slam it shut. "I don't need service."

That was when not one, but three bullets silently slammed through the wood and entered his midsection. Chale grunted and bent at the waist, all too aware he'd been hit by the lethal Green Hornets, a top secret, Area 51 technology, and the only bullet that could penetrate the GTECH armor. The door opened again, and a pair of steel cutters appeared.

Somehow, Chale hobbled down the hall, into the bedroom and out of sight, behind a wall dividing the room from the entryway. Flattening against it, he fell to the floor and drew his weapon. Molly whimpered and hid under the bed.

"Smart dog," he murmured, glancing at his injuries, unable to stop the gushing from his stomach. As it was, he was so weak, his arms felt like wet noodles, and his gun, a fifty-pound barbell.

Too soon, before he was ready, a beauty of a woman, despite a bad blonde wig, sauntered around the corner, dressed in a maid's uniform. He hadn't even known when she'd entered the room, which told him he was in a bad way and fading.

He grimaced up at her. "What happened to knocking before you enter?"

"From the mess you're making on the floor, I thought you needed maid service." She straddled him, a gun in her hand, and even the conservative maid's dress she wore and a hole in his gut did nothing to stop his gaze from following the path up her skirt. If he was going to die, he was going to die happy.

He managed to lift his gun without using both hands. "I see we like the same toys." Spots splattered in front of his eyes. Shit. He was going to pass out.

She nudged his hip with her foot. "Don't you dare bleed to death until I'm done with you, Renegade."

"Hello, Chale," came a familiar male voice.

A man stepped forward then, removing a baseball cap he wore low over his face, to allow Chale to identify him.

"Thought Adam had killed you, greedy bastard," Chale said to Lucian, an Area-51 GTECH turned Zodius, who'd tried to overthrow Adam.

"You assumed what we wanted you to assume," Lucian said. "What we let you believe. Your plan to evacuate the Russian has failed. He's dead. I let your people keep the wife and kids. We have no time for babysitting."

Anger coiled inside Chale, and he tried again to lift his gun. The woman kicked it aside.

Chale raked his gaze over her in an intentionally hungry fashion. "Sweetheart," he drawled. "I can assure you, even bleeding to death, that I'm a better ride than this lowlife. Let me kill him, and we'll talk."

Lucian's boot connected with Chale's face in a blast that rattled his teeth. His ears rang from the jolt, and blood spilled from his mouth, but he laughed and looked at the woman.

"Jealous type, I guess," he said, a second before the next kick sent his head jerking to the left, and everything went black.

Self-preservation was all that kept Sabrina from shooting Lucian herself right then. "Are you trying to kill him before he tells us what we need to know?" she demanded. "You shouldn't even be here. Chale recognized you. Someone else might recognize you."

Lucian slid the cap back on his head, like it was really some sort of disguise. "Chale recognized me because I gave him the chance," Lucian said. "He won't live long enough to tell anyone. I told you to trust me. I covered your sweet little ass just like I said I would. I killed the Russian, and I'll kill Lara."

Never, in this lifetime or any other, would she trust Lucian. She never should have gone to him. He was setting her up. She could feel it in every inch of her body. "For all we know, she's already told the Renegades about Serenity."

"She believes they killed her family," he said. "I'm betting that hasn't changed."

"Excuse me if I'm not willing to gamble with my future," she argued.

"They won't trust her," he said. "Whatever she says is nothing without proof, and she won't live long enough to find any." He bent down next to Chale, snatched the Renegade's cell phone from his belt, and held it up. "We have everything we need to get to Lara right here." His free hand slid around her thigh. "*Trust me.*" His fingers brushed her crotch. "Do exactly what I tell you, and your place in Serenity will be secure."

Said the wolf to Little Red Riding Hood, and for the first time in a very long while, she felt like the girl with the red cape—helpless and at the wolf's mercy.

Chapter 8

WILD DIDN'T BEGIN TO DESCRIBE WHAT KISSING LARA unleashed inside Damion. He had never felt anything like he felt in this moment, never felt so out of control, so out of his own body. Somewhere, in the back of his mind, there was a warning, a voice telling him this wasn't normal.

One minute they were arguing, the next they were all over each other, touching, licking, tasting. Her naked little backside rubbing against his cock, driving him insane with need. He couldn't get enough of her. Couldn't make himself stop kissing her, stop touching her, couldn't resist molding her breasts to his hands and swallowing the moan that slid from her lips to his. He was a man who didn't lose control, but he was now. He was with this woman, this stranger. In some far part of his mind the word "voodoo" played again, warning him something wasn't right about his reaction to this woman, that she claimed something wasn't right about her reaction to him. He told himself to stop. Instead, they melted into one another, his tongue stroking hers. The wildness of passion exploded into an unfamiliar desperateness like nothing he had ever experienced with another woman, a need to escape into each other, a need not to speak, not to think.

Damion's hand slid up her back, into her hair, angling her mouth to deepen the kiss, to take more. Whatever happened beyond this moment, beyond the desire, it didn't matter right now. There was no right or wrong, no enemies or even friends. There was just feeling, needing, taking.

Reality slammed into him the instant her fingers touched the zipper to his body armor over his rib cage. Damion jerked back from her, suspicion over her motives a cold slap of reality. What the hell was he doing? Then, more importantly, what the hell was *she* doing? Accusation narrowed his stare. Had she ever been hallucinating, or was this all a ploy to take him out? Had she heated him right into a big pile of stupid?

She blinked up at him, her lips swollen from his kisses, her eyes clouded with desire that was quickly dawning with unhappy realization. *Aware.* She was now all too aware of what he was thinking, the distant confusion she'd shown minutes before, long gone. Long gone, like it had never existed. Damn it to hell, he didn't like being made a fool and didn't make a habit of it.

The phone on the wall by the door started to ring, a scream of sound in the midst of the silent tension that had Damion ready to roar with both irritation and relief at the timing. He needed space from this woman, but he didn't want it. Caleb and Michael had heard Lara scream, though, and if he didn't answer the call, they'd think something was wrong. Clearly there was, since she was naked and in his arms, and no matter how much he believed she was a victim, she didn't hide her desire to kill all Renegades, him included.

The phone was on the second ring. "I have to get that, or we'll have company I don't think either of us would welcome right about now."

She nodded tensely, her gaze, hot only moments

before, now downright icy. She slid off of him, grabbing the towel on the floor.

Damion sat there a moment, both with an ache in his groin at the sight of the ivory curves, but more so, with an odd sense of loss he'd never experienced before.

She glanced over her shoulder at him, her expression clouded, confused, wounded, rather than angry at his distrust. *Wounded*. This word sang in his mind, and with it, guilt in his gut about daring to touch her when she was vulnerable. *Unless she wasn't vulnerable, unless it was all an act.*

The phone stopped ringing. Damn it. Damion scrubbed his jaw and jerked into action, biting back a groan at the uncomfortable stretch of his zipper across his raging erection. He grabbed the phone attached to the wall and said, "2020," a code that changed with every use and indicated that the facility was secure and he wasn't under hostile takeover.

"That's one bit of good news," Caleb said in a heavy sigh. "Unfortunately, I don't have the same to give you."

Caleb didn't take the long way to a point, unless he didn't really want to get to it in the first place, and he was now. Damion glanced at Lara, not sure what he was willing to let her hear. She gave him a look scrubbed of any emotion and headed toward the walk-in closet, her hips swaying beneath the towel. His cock pulsed with the memory of what was—or rather was not—beneath that towel.

With a barely contained moan, Damion turned away from her and lowered his voice to speak to Caleb. "Did something go wrong with the extraction?"

"Lev is dead," he said. "Thankfully, his family is

safely in Renegade custody and headed to Sunrise City, but I'm not looking forward to telling them the news."

"How?" Damion asked, pretty damn sure he wasn't going to like the answer.

"Lev left the room in disguise and made it to the car we had waiting. That's when a wind-walker appeared behind Lev, shot and killed him, and shoved him into the car."

"A woman?" Damion asked, expecting one of Lara's people.

"A man wearing a hooded jacket with a baseball cap beneath," Caleb said. "He was there and gone too fast to make his identity. At about the same time, a woman showed up at Lev's room claiming to be maid service, we assume as a distraction, while the assassin did his job."

"Sabrina?" Damion asked.

"No one but Chale saw the woman. Chale sent Houston and Jesse through a passage in the ceiling, while he stalled the maid to give Lev time to escape. He was supposed to follow, but ten minutes later, Chale hadn't shown up, and he wasn't answering calls. Houston and Jesse went back to the room, and Chale was gone. That's how fast this went down. Ten minutes and Chale was nowhere to be found. His captors must have opened the sliding door and wind-walked with him out of there." He hesitated. "You should know, Damion... Jesse and Houston found blood on the floor and bullet holes in the door."

Damion's gut clenched. Blood could only mean one thing. "Adam Rain still has Green Hornets." The lethal bullets could not only penetrate their armor, but shred

bone and muscle, often beyond even a GTECH's ability
to repair the damage. Chale was in deep shit.

"We knew that when we stole Adam's stock, he'd
create more," Caleb said. "But I thought we had at
least a year, after we managed to destroy his blueprints.
Instead, we got a real fast six months."

And if Chale was really shot up with Green Hornets,
he had hours at most. "Chale's alive, or they wouldn't
have bothered taking him."

"We had Trackers on him within fifteen minutes of
his disappearance, and no one picked up a trail," Caleb
said. "And since I know Chale is smart enough to let
down his mental shields so we can find him, they either
took him somewhere close and underground, instead of
to Zodius City or—"

"He's underground," Damion said, refusing to hear
the end of Caleb's sentence that finished with "dead."

Someone spoke in the background, and Caleb offered
a muffled reply. "I need to go," he said. "Concerns about
Lev's death are being relayed from the White House. But
two things before I do. First off, something about this
Lev situation doesn't add up. The man was assassinated,
plain and simple. There was no attempt at capture. That
doesn't fit with my brother's behavior. If Adam knew
about Lev, he'd want him for his nuclear technology."

"Looks like Adam didn't want him to fall into our
hands," he said.

"That doesn't add up to me," Caleb said. "Adam
knows I'd never risk the fallout of human life associated
with nuclear weapons. There was no attempt to capture
Lev. This was cold-blooded murder. Another red flag is
Sabrina's involvement. Women as GTECHs is another.

The one person who might be able to give us answers, maybe even a location where Chale might have been taken, is right there with you. If you're going to gain her cooperation, now would be the time, before we find out there's a bomb somewhere—before it blows up in our faces."

Right. They needed Lara's cooperation. The same woman who believed the Renegades had killed her family. The woman he'd been foolish enough to almost have sex with, which might or might not have been her attempt to kill him.

"Right," he said, resting his head on the wall. "I'm on it."

"Just remember, Damion," Caleb said. "Trust and loyalty are earned." He hung up.

With those words vibrating through him, Damion stood there, facing the wall, a ball of anger in his chest. Trust and loyalty—Chale had earned both from him many times over, been there for him when no one else had. His younger brother was dead, and his mother didn't speak to him, let alone claim him, any more than his older brother did. But where had Damion been when his closest friend among the Renegades was getting shot to hell? Trying to get naked with a woman who hated his guts, who was somehow involved in the plot that had led to Chale's shooting. Could the knife twist any deeper?

Rage ripped through Damion, and he unleashed it with a hard punch against the concrete wall. "Damn it to hell." Pain vibrated up his arm, stickiness clung to his knuckle, but he didn't care. Not when it had been his plan, his orders that had backfired on Chale. He wanted to roar with the injustice of it. He reeled back, ready to blast the wall again, and suddenly he found his arms captured.

"Don't," Lara ordered roughly. "Are you trying to break your hand?"

He whirled around to face her, barely contained anger vibrating through his nerve endings. She was dressed now, in all black—jeans, shirt, boots—with loose tendrils of soft, half-dry, brown hair around her face. Her pale skin was bruised around the left eye and cheek, a reminder that Sabrina had attacked her. She softened him ever so slightly.

He wanted to trust this woman, wanted to trust her despite logic, and it made him angry at himself and at her. He wasn't a fool. He looked at facts, the right and wrong of actions. He wasn't logical about her. She was unraveling him.

So easily, she could be working him; so easily, she could be a part of the plan that had led to Chale's capture, maybe to his death. He wouldn't let anyone else die. He couldn't risk being wrong about her. He couldn't give her time to come around. He had to know what she was made of, and he had to know now.

"Isn't that what you want?" he demanded. "A chance to weaken me? To kill me? Isn't that why you tried to get me naked and out of my armor?"

"That's ridiculous," she said. "I was the one naked and unarmed. And you offered me your gun. I didn't take it."

"Then take it now," he said, bending down and yanking his pant leg up. He removed his gun, then grabbed her hand and pressed it into her palm, trusting his instincts that he wasn't writing his own death sentence.

Maybe, on some level, that is what he wanted. He was raw, an open wound, dripping blood. "Now you have no excuses. Kill me or trust me. Now. You choose."

"Are we really doing this again?" she challenged.

"You bet we are." He let go of her hand. "Do it."

She held the weapon, unmoving, aimed at his head, but there was a small quiver to her bottom lip, and the slightest shake to her hand. "And how do I get out of here once you're dead?"

He didn't flinch at the inference she was going to take him up on his challenge and kill him. If he died, he died, but he had to know where she stood, what she was made of. "The password for the security panel is 1850," he said. "Then enter my birthday, 8-8-1976." He held out his hands. "You're free. Do it."

Lara stared at Damion, telling herself to pull the trigger. He was a Renegade, a GTECH, a murderer. But there was a dull throbbing in her head, and she kept getting flashes of images, like a TV station being tuned in and out. Nothing about her past, her memories, made sense. She didn't know what was real and what was fiction. In the midst of it all, Damion was what felt real. Kissing him, touching him—she'd felt so much need for him. As if he were her past, her present, her... life. It made no sense, but there were those moments in the shower where there had been brief instances of clarity, of his tenderness. She wanted to scream in confusion. Everything was one cloudy mess inside her head, but when she'd kissed this man, the clouds had faded, as the dull throb in her head had disappeared. Reality had been present, and she desperately needed reality, to know she wasn't hallucinating. She had no way of knowing if he was causing the hallucinations, and then offering the cure—himself.

The idea that Renegades were masters of deceit scared her, and the fact that she wanted to trust him, scared her even more. But so did the idea of killing a man over a perception that she couldn't be sure was real. Not when the here and now was the only thing she was certain was real. He wasn't trying to kill her. He wasn't doing anything to make her feel in jeopardy. But Sabrina had tried to kill her, and Sabrina was in these flashes of memories in a very dark way, as someone involved in the murder of a man named Skywalker, who had meant something to Lara. Decision made, Lara flipped the gun around and pressed it to Damion's palm—God, he was Damion to her now, not the "GTECH."

"I'm not in the mood to kill you right now," she said flippantly, as if she weren't aware that her world seemed to be shattering around her. It resonated straight to her soul. He resonated straight to her soul. She couldn't let him see that, couldn't let on how he was getting to her. "Keep pushing me, and I might change my mind. And demanding trust... does that work for you often? Because it darn sure doesn't work with me."

Black eyes flickered to hazel, a hint of satisfaction in their depths, before he pulled her close, his hard body absorbing hers, his free hand sliding down her back. "I just trusted you with my life," he said, low and rough. "I think that deserves a little trust in return."

Her palm flattened on his chest, heat radiating up her arm, realization washing over her. The hum in her head was suddenly gone. When she touched him it was as if he healed her. She needed his touch, his connection, to stay sane and work through whatever was happening to her. *Which could be his plan,* she reminded herself.

She tilted her chin upward, met his stare, and thought about his lips against hers. It was better than replaying an image of Skywalker with a gun to his head, Skywalker going limp from a bullet wound. "I handed the gun back to you," she reminded him. "That's as much trust as you're getting."

"And if it's not enough?"

"It's all I have to give," she said softly, but it wasn't the truth. She wanted to give him her trust. She wanted to believe he was a friend. Her heart, even her instincts, said he was that person. Her training, her conditioning, told her he was the one causing her confusion, her physical illness, her dependency on him, and only him, to make it go away. He whirled her around, pressed her against the wall, and tucked the gun back inside his boot before he released her, his hands framing her face.

"*Again* with the trapping me against the wall?" she challenged him, knowing she didn't want to escape, and she should. The hum in her head had returned, and she barely contained the urge to reach out and test the theory that touching him would make it go away. Or maybe, she just wanted a reason to touch him again.

"You'll climb on top of me naked and kiss me, but you won't trust me," he said, as if he'd read her mind.

She shrugged and crossed her arms in front of her, trying to seem unaffected by his words, when she was anything but. "That pretty much sums up the last hour."

He studied her, his stare probing her with far too

much intensity for comfort. "You do know that's completely illogical."

Her chin lifted, and she tried not to notice the warm whiskey color of his eyes. "You don't have to trust someone to get naked with them." But she remembered all too well the trust she'd felt being naked *in his arms*, remembered the raw hurt in his eyes when he'd told her he knew what it was like to lose someone. How much she'd believed him, how much that didn't fit the perception she had of Renegades. How much she'd burned to lose herself in him, to hide from something in her subconscious that was trying to surface. It was why she'd kissed him then, and why she wanted to again—right now.

A muscle in his jaw flexed. "So that leaves us with an agreement not to kill each other." He paused. "For now, at least."

"I guess so."

"You talk big for someone who's in so much trouble. Adam will have you killed for defying him. What has he done to earn that kind of loyalty?"

He was talking about Adam, but she was dealing with Powell. "He saved my life and gave me a way to fight back."

Something dark glinted in his eyes. "And lied to you about what you were fighting for and why. We can protect you, offer you sanctuary. Offer your family sanctuary."

Emotion ripped through her, and she tried to push him away, but he was as solid as the wall behind her. "They're dead," she ground out, every nerve scraped raw by the irony of a Renegade offering such a thing. "They don't need sanctuary."

"So this is all about vengeance to you," he said. "Not about saving anyone's life."

"Of course, I want vengeance," she agreed. "And don't expect me to be ashamed of that. Not when vengeance means stopping your kind from killing innocent people, like my family." Those damn images flickered in her head again—a flash of Skywalker tied to a chair, a flash of her under the steps when her family was slaughtered.

"My kind," he said. "You keep saying 'my kind,' not the Renegades. Why?"

"You're all monsters to me," she said quickly, not about to let him corner her.

"And yet you didn't kill me when you had the chance," he said, his expression calculating.

"I might need you," she said honestly, not allowing herself to think of any reason that might be true, beside the need to control the hum in her head that was growing louder. His touch could make it go away.

His gaze darkened. "I thought you didn't want my protection."

"Who said anything about protection?"

He leaned in, his lips close to hers, his breath warm on her cheek, his body aligned with hers, but not touching, the air thick with sexual tension. "Then what, little Lara, would you need me for?"

Despite the hard bite of this man being a Renegade, every inch of her body screamed with awareness, with the need to touch him, and not just because of the hum in her head. She reached out and pressed her hand to his chest, testing her body's reaction, relieved by the instant silence in her head, the relief when all that was left was hot fire and *need*. "I think we both know what I need you for," she said, her voice raspy, affected, despite her efforts to be calculating, to try and get him to admit some sort of mental and physical manipulation.

The air spiked with electricity, heat, and mutual desire, before he turned his gaze upward and made a sound of frustration. His jaw set, his mood shifted, and his hand slid to hers, holding it over his chest.

"Do you watch the arena fights, Lara?" He surprised her by asking, his tone soft and lethal. "Do you sit and cheer when men and GTECHs alike, who have proven to be Adam's enemies, are ripped to shreds by his pet wolves until their bodies are beyond repair?"

"What?" she gasped. "No. Of course not." She'd heard of the coliseum, and it made her skin crawl.

"Sabrina took one of my men, Lara, someone who is like a brother to me," he said. "If you weren't here, if you were back in Zodius City, would you watch, would you cheer, when the wolves attacked him?"

"No." She repeated the one word with emphasis. "I am not a part of the arena games. I've never been to one, nor do I ever want to go to one." His hard eyes chilled her to the bone—eyes that were cold as ice, unforgiving, disbelieving, eyes that left her desperate to convince him of the truth. "My team isn't stationed in Zodius City. I've never even been there." It was an admission she shouldn't have made. She knew even before his next question.

"Where then?" he demanded instantly.

"You know I won't tell you that."

His hands went to her arms. "My man could be at your team's facility. I need to know where it is, and I need to know now."

"They wouldn't take him there," she said, and that was the truth. "No one outside the team is allowed inside that facility."

Disbelief shadowed his face.

"I'm telling the truth," she said.

He studied her a moment and pushed off the wall, hands on his hips. "So that's it then. I just sit back and wait for Adam to send us pictures of Chale shredded to pieces by those wolves."

Lara's heart twisted at the anguish in him; unnaturally, in an almost physical way, she felt this man's pain. He was a Renegade, her enemy, but... "No," she said quickly. "He won't be in Zodius City. I'm sure he's not in Zodius City."

He stiffened. "How would you know that if you don't know where he is?"

How? How would she know that without exposing Serenity? Lara repeated the question in her mind again. "My team is meant to operate off the radar," she said. "No one knows we exist. Anything we touch stays with us."

The phone on the wall rang again, shrill and loud, but for several seconds he didn't respond, then with a frustrated sound, he grabbed the receiver and listened. She saw his hand tighten on the phone, his knuckles white, and knew something was terribly wrong. She fought the urge to go to him, to comfort him, to touch him. *Renegade*, she repeated in her head.

Murdered. No. That felt wrong clear to her soul. Damion wasn't her enemy. Seconds ticked by like hours as she battled with herself, forcing herself not to touch him, until he slammed the receiver down again, and without a word, stormed out of the room.

"What just happened?" Lara called, racing after him. "Damion, please…? What's happening?"

She caught up with him at the computer where he punched a few buttons and brought the middle screen to life, showing a view of a man tied to a chair, his face swollen and bloody, his head slumped forward. Sabrina stepped into view and yanked his head back. The blood-ied man's eyes lifted as Sabrina said, "Tell Damion why you brought me here, Chale honey."

"Fuck you, bitch," Chale said. Someone shoved a woman in a maid's uniform to the floor at Chale's feet. She was young, twenty-something, tied up, with a gag in her mouth and crying. Sabrina smiled at the camera, but didn't let go of Chale.

"I'm going to kill her while you watch," Sabrina said. "And another one like her every fifteen minutes until you bring me Lara. Oh, and if you're thinking of calling for backup, don't. If I get even a whiff of a breeze that makes me think wind-walker, I'll put a Green Hornet in his head. In fact, he's a Renegade, and I hate Renegades. I'll kill him first. I'm going to give you exactly three minutes, not one extra second, and if you're not up here by then, I pull the trigger."

Chapter 9

THREE MINUTES TO DECIDE HER FUTURE, TO DECIDE IF Sabrina was here to save her or kill her, and act accordingly. To decide if she even wanted to be saved. She knew the answer. Sabrina was here to kill her and everyone else with her. She couldn't let that happen.

The computer screen went black, the reality of those short three minutes in full play now.

"I'll go," Lara said.

"Forget it," Damion said. "I'm not handing you over to Sabrina. I said we'd offer you protection, and I meant it. Chale only brought her here to save that woman and any other innocent lives involved. He expects me to work it out from here, and I will."

To save innocent lives. The Renegades wanted to save innocent lives, while the leader of Serenity was threatening to take them. None of what was happening computed with what she'd come to believe as reality.

"Then we'll work it out together," she said. "I'm going with you."

Damion unlocked a section of the desk and slid open a long drawer filled with an arsenal of guns, knives, and ammo. "Sorry, sweetheart," he said, quickly selecting an array of weapons. "But I'm a loner. Always have been, always will be."

She was going with him. He'd find that out when she

grabbed a weapon or two from the drawer. "Please tell me that doesn't mean you aren't calling for backup?"

"Every second I spend explaining the situation to someone else is one less bullet I load, and one less second I have to get top side." He reached for a Glock. She planned on claiming the one next to it as her own.

"Sabrina won't be alone," Lara warned. "And she has no intention of trading me for the others. She'll shoot us all the minute we reach the surface."

"As soon as *I* get to the surface," he corrected, shoving the Glock into the back of his pants. She ignored the assertion. "Is there a back exit, a way you can get behind the scene, so you don't get killed right out of the elevator?"

"One way in and one way out," he said, loading yet another Glock. The one she'd wanted. She'd settle for the Beretta a few inches up and to the right in the drawer.

"Can you call back to the surface?" she asked. "Tell Sabrina I have documents exposing secrets she doesn't want exposed, and those documents will be automatically delivered to a news station if anything happens to us."

His gaze snapped to hers, his eyes now black and hard. "Do you?"

She shook her head. "All that matters is that Sabrina thinks I do."

"I'm not wasting time on a bluff with a gun pointed at Chale's head," he said, reaching for the end of the drawer to shut it. Lara lunged forward, her hand snaking out for the Beretta, but Damion was too fast for her.

"You won't need that," he said, shackling her wrist. Before she knew his intention, he'd set her in the chair and cuffed her hand to the armrest. "You're not going anywhere."

"Are you crazy?" she demanded, aimlessly tugging at her arm, like it would help. "You can't do this alone."

"You're injured, you're hallucinating, and you're the one they want, which makes you the last person who belongs on that elevator going up."

"You can't go alone," she repeated. "Sabrina *won't be* alone."

"You'll be safe here until I return," he said, as if she'd said nothing worthy of reply. "We reprogram the entry codes to the elevator every time we use it, so right now, only you and I know the magic numbers. If something happens to me, the phones have a speed dial to Caleb. You can trust him."

He wasn't listening. She had to make him listen. "She'll kill one of the prisoners to force you into handing over the codes."

"I have a plan," he said, and headed for the door. Then with his back to her, he added, "I always have a plan."

"Damion! Damn it," she said, trying to roll the chair after him. "Macho stupidity will get you killed. You need me."

"Alive," he replied, stepping into the elevator and turning to face her. "I need you alive." She opened her mouth to scream his name again, to plead with him, but it was too late. The doors shut. He was gone.

Logically, Lara knew that the only reason Damion was keeping her safe, keeping her alive, was because she had information he needed. This wasn't personal. He didn't care about her, yet the idea of him dying because of her—dying, period—twisted her in knots, and it felt darn personal. Illogically, irrationally, the need to ensure Damion survived expanded inside her, screamed with the demand that she act.

Frantically, Lara turned back to the desk, her gaze catching on the phone. *If anything happens to me*, *the phones have a speed dial to Caleb*, he'd said. She didn't even hesitate, didn't think twice about the craziness of her need to save a sworn enemy, a Renegade, by asking for help from yet another Renegade.

She rolled to the desk and grabbed the receiver, punching one of the three numbers on the phone. Almost instantly, a man answered.

"Is this Caleb? Caleb Rain?"

"This is Caleb," he said. "Is Damion okay, Lara?"

"No!" she declared. "No, he is not okay. He needs backup, and he needs it now. He's headed top level to the cabin. Sabrina—he says you know her. She's here, and she's a GTECH now. She's holding one of your men and an innocent woman, threatening to kill them if I don't turn myself over in three minutes… about three minutes ago. Damion cuffed me to a chair and took off. I don't know how many others are with Sabrina, but she won't be alone. I can't help him. You have to help him."

He spoke in a muffled voice to someone else in the room and then returned. "Help is on the way, Lara."

"I have to go up there," she said. "I have to help. Where does he keep the key to the cuffs? Tell me, please. I know Sabrina. She'll kill your man and that woman, and more if necessary, to get Damion to bring her down here to get me. Then she'll kill us both."

There was a moment of silence. "Damion will set you free when he returns."

He hung up.

Lara clutched the phone and let out a frustrated growl. Then she dropped the phone to the table, not even bothering to hang it back up, and started digging through drawers. Nothing, nothing, nothing. That was, until her hand froze on a key chain under a cup. Bingo, five keys, and one was small. A cuff key. She freed herself, grabbed several weapons she'd found digging through the drawers, and headed to the elevator. With a punch of the codes he'd given her earlier, she expected the elevator to open, but it didn't. Damion still had it at ground level.

The Russian was dead, an innocent woman was being terrorized, and his friend was barely hanging on to life. Today was not a good day, and it ended now. Damion rode the elevator to ground level, on edge, ready for war, adrenaline like fire in his veins, ready to risk it all. *No risk, no reward*—that was the law of the battlefield, the name of the game. That was a soldier's life, his life, the only one he'd known since those early days out of college.

The elevator hit ground level, bringing him back to the battle ahead, and he shoved aside all thought—slid into soldier mode. Flattening against the wall, he waited. The doors opened, and Damion hit the button to lock it open, and then threw a smoke bomb into the room outside the car.

Shouts, both male and female, sounded. A rush of movement followed. One voice... two... both familiar.

He knew Sabrina, expected her, but who the hell did the male voice belong to?

"It's Damion," came Sabrina's sharp warning to whoever was with her, followed by a spurt of male and female coughs, the effect of the smoke's sinister burn. Damion felt it inflame his eyes and nose, felt the rawness of his throat, all the more motivation to get this done now rather than later.

Chale muttered something he couldn't make out, but it sounded like a taunt, and just hearing his voice, knowing he was still alive and fighting back despite the magnitude of his injuries, spurred Damion into action.

He hit the ground and began to crawl toward the area where he estimated he would find the captive female. The smoke was already thick, a wall of gray and black. He couldn't see his own hands, let alone his enemy's location, but then, they couldn't see him either. It would, however, be a real bitch to crawl right into his enemy's path, but whatever happened... happened. He'd deal.

"Move Lucian," a woman's voice rasped softly. "Move now."

Lucian. The only Lucian that Damion knew was a GTECH who'd betrayed everyone he'd ever come in contact with.

"There's two of them, Damion!" Chale shouted.

"Kill Chale!" the male voice yelled, from what sounded like the front door. Shit! That *was* Lucian all right. What the hell was he doing here? And what the hell was Lara involved with?

Damion hunched into a squatting position, ready to launch himself into action to save Chale, when he heard a female grunt and a moan of pain.

"I got the bitch!" Chale said. "Save the girl."

Relief washed over Damion, and he almost smiled as he realized Chale had just put his free assets, his booted feet and long legs, to good use. But it was relief blasted away with the sound of a gun firing.

"Chale!" Damion yelled, his heart jackknifing, certain Chale's attempts to fight back had gotten him killed.

"I said I got the bitch!" Chale shouted back, followed by the sound of something scraping the floor. A second later a gun hit Damion's hand.

This time Damion did smile as he snatched up the weapon and shoved it awkwardly into his rear waistband with the Glock that was already there. Still squatting, he followed the sounds of the whimpering female until he was at her side.

"Shhh," he whispered, leaning in close to her ear, placing a hand on her back and leaving it there a moment, to allow her to get used to his touch, before he scooped her up and charged through the smoke-filled room, toward what were thankfully still the open elevator doors.

Once he had her inside the compartment, he set her on the floor—leaving her gagged to prevent a telltale scream, while he keyed the security code. Holding the car open with his booted foot, he cut the ties on her arms and legs. "When you get to the next level, get out, and send it back to me." He moved out of the doorway, let the steel panels seal shut, and stepped right into a gust of wind so powerful he swayed.

The wind funneled out the front door as if sucked from a pipe, the room clearing almost instantly. Michael stood in the cabin's entrance, his long black hair rushing around his shoulders. His unique GTECH skill allowed him to control and communicate with the wind. Michael wouldn't know to be here if someone—Lara—hadn't told him there was trouble. Lucian and Sabrina were nowhere in sight. Too bad they'd been smart enough to get the hell out of Dodge. Damion had been looking forward to killing them both.

Even more so when he realized Chale wasn't moving, nor was his loud mouth spewing smart-ass attitude. Still tied to the chair, he lay on his back, blood spilling to the floor from his gut, darkening the bandages that had been used to help keep him alive until they didn't need him anymore—like now. Damion's and Michael's eyes met from across the room, all their differences cast aside in a rare moment of understanding, in what, at its core, was brotherhood. Neither wanted to know Chale was dead.

"How about… untying me?" Chale grumbled, with a squirm of discomfort that had him hissing in pain.

Michael and Damion both smiled, and in unison wind-walked to Chale's side. "I'll take him to Sunrise right away," Michael said, cutting the restraints around Chale's arms. "He needs immediate medical attention."

"How about not talking about me like I'm already dead," Chale complained. "I'm not, in case you didn't notice." He eyed Damion, sucking in a wheezy breath, before adding, "I kicked that witch's hot, little ass, even with my hands tied."

"How do you still have attitude?" Damion asked, as he and Michael each grabbed one of Chale's arms and helped him stand up.

"It's a gift," Chale whispered. "One that really pissed Lucian off." He wheezed. "Ate… that shit… up."

A tight ball formed in Damion's chest. "For once, no jokes." He didn't even try to keep the snap out of the order. War was serious, deadly, and joking got you killed. Damion had learned that the hard way, the day his baby brother had died. His brother had been just like Chale, a smart-ass, even as he'd been wheeled toward the ambulance after the car accident. *Next time I'm driving, Damion*, he'd said. *You need training wheels.* But there had been no next time. "Lucian would have killed you in the blink of an eye."

"Are we talking about the Lucian I think we're talking about?" Michael asked sharply, ignoring the rest of the exchange.

Chale's head dropped and lifted. "Yeah," he said in a barely there voice. "Not Zodius we are dealing with. Don't know who… they are… besides ass… holes."

Michael's eyes sought Damion's, steely with demand, though his voice was low, without emotion. "We *need to know* who we're dealing with here. And we need to know *now*. If you can't find out, if your morals keep you from pressing…" Translation, make Lara talk, or he would.

"I'm handling it," Damion said tightly. Michael wasn't getting anywhere near Lara. "And how you manage to have a Lifebond who is full of those so-called 'morals' and not find any yourself, I will never know."

"Cassandra is a constant reminder of what I have to protect, and why I'm not ready to die. If that means pressing one woman beyond your comfort zone, then so be it."

"And if that woman were Cassandra?" he demanded. "Would you press her then?" He had no idea where that had come from, the comparison of Lara to Michael's Lifebond, but it jolted him to the core, and apparently, it got Michael's and Chale's attention as well.

"What are you saying?" Michael asked. "That Lara is your—"

"I'm saying she's hands-off," Damion said. "*Mine* to deal with." He cut a look between the two men. "Chale needs a doctor. Get him out of here."

"Yeah," Chale agreed softly. "Good… idea."

Michael studied Damion a moment longer. "Jesse and Houston have the exterior of the cabin covered. I'll contact you as soon as Chale's in surgery." And then he was gone, fading into the wind, Chale with him.

For a moment Damion stood there, thinking about his reference to Cassandra. Correction. His comparison of Cassandra to Lara. He remembered Sterling doing something similar with his new Lifebond, Becca, before they were fully bonded. Damion's hand covered his face. Lara couldn't be…

The thought was lost to a sharp prick of warning, a premonition of trouble. His gaze jerked to the cabin door, which sat dangerously open, an invitation to a wind-walker. Everything seemed to go into slow motion as wind gushed through the entryway, and at the same moment, the elevator dinged.

Lara. And whoever was in that wind had come for her.

Backing up to the elevator door, Damion reached behind him, withdrew the two guns resting there, and stiff-armed them in front of him. The elevator doors creaked and opened slowly—too damn slowly to suit Damion, who fully intended to grab Lara and wind-walk her the hell out of here. A plan that shattered into a million pieces when three things happened at once. Sabrina appeared by the cabin door and slammed it shut, sealing out the wind he needed for escape. Lucian materialized in front of Damion, two of his own weapons aimed at him. The doors behind him fully opened.

"It's a good day to die, Lucian," Damion declared, praying Lara had the sense to stay behind him. "Take a step closer. Just lean closer, and give me a reason to show you just how good."

"I still have my GTECH armor," Lucian said, looking amused. "Your bullets can't hurt me, but mine can hurt you. I have Green Hornets. We want Lara."

"And the Russian wanted to see his kids tonight, but he won't have that pleasure, now will he?" Damion's hand lifted, his aim now at Lucian's forehead, a vulnerable spot, and they both knew it. "I'm a bulls-eye shot, so I say to you again—give me a reason to prove it."

He'd barely issued the warning when the sound of the windows shattering cracked through the air behind Lucian, to the left and the right, and blessed strands of wind mixed with the glass. *Thank you, Jesse and Houston*. Damion fired at Lucian, or rather, at empty air. Lucian had faded into the wind—and holy shit— Damion knew where Lucian was going to reappear. In the elevator with Lara… to kill her. And Lara couldn't wind-walk to safety.

Chapter 10

LARA LAUNCHED HERSELF TOWARD THE ELEVATOR exit, not about to risk the seconds a failed wind-walk would cost her with Lucian coming for her. Even if she got off the lethal head shot it would take to put him down, she wasn't likely to escape injury herself.

At the same moment she moved toward Damion, he rotated toward her, and in doing so, made the potentially lethal choice of giving Sabrina his back. Never slowing, acting on pure instinct honed from years of training, Lara recalculated her actions, taking the risk Sabrina represented into consideration. Rather than avoiding Damion's weapons and ducking, she ran straight at him, their eyes locking in a second of understanding before they both began firing to the sides and behind one another. The instant their bodies collided and a solid connection formed, Damion wind-walked them out of the cabin.

They materialized moments later, breaking apart, each using their guns to scan for danger, and finding all was clear. Lara found herself on top of a hill. The cabin was a mere speck in the dim glow of newly formed moonlight and stars.

"My men will keep Lucian and Sabrina occupied for a while," Damion said, shoving one of his weapons in his back waistband, the other in the holster under his pant leg. "But they won't give up, Lara. Lucian and

Sabrina are going to keep coming until you die, or they die trying to kill you."

Yes. *They* wanted her dead. Not just Sabrina now, but Lucian—Lucian was Powell's personal bodyguard, whom Powell presumably trusted. Lara let her weapons fall to her sides, squeezing her eyes shut as the adrenaline of battle faded, and her headache returned with nauseating intensity. Or maybe this time it was the hum of defeat.

"What is it they don't want you to tell me, Lara?" Damion asked.

With a twist in her gut, she turned away from him, offering him her profile, pretending to stare at the stars and moon, before she did something stupid like actually tell him about Serenity. She couldn't do that. Wanting to trust Damion and doing so were two different things. She'd trusted Powell, even Sabrina. Now... she didn't even know if she could trust herself.

"I know you aren't working for Adam," Damion said. "Not with Lucian involved."

She had no idea what Lucian's history with Adam was, but apparently, it wasn't good. "You guessed wrong," she said, training telling her to deny, divert, and repackage her cover.

Tense seconds ticked by, and though she didn't look at him, she could feel his gaze—heavy and probing. He didn't believe the picture she was painting. *She* wouldn't have believed her either. It was time to leave him now, time to escape, and go on her own.

"Talk to me, Lara," Damion urged, pulling her from her thoughts back to the moment. "Before more people die."

"More?" she asked, daring a look at him, and trying not to sound as affected as she felt. "Who died? Not your Renegade friend, right? Your people came and saved him." She shouldn't care about the Renegade named Chale, nor the fact that he was injured because of her. He was, after all, Renegade. But she did care, and she cared that he mattered to Damion.

"He's been taken to Sunrise City and into surgery."

"He's GTECH though," she said relieved. "He'll be okay."

"GTECHs aren't indestructible, especially where Green Hornets are concerned. Your friends pumped him full of them."

"No," she said. "That's not possible. We don't have Green Hornets."

"The bullets in Chale's gut say differently. I guess Adam, or whoever you work for, only gives his favorites the good bullets. Clearly you aren't one of his favorites, at least, not anymore. I guess you should have killed the Russian."

She drew her spine stiff. "I know what you're doing," she said. "And fishing isn't your sport. Maybe you should try hunting, and preferably, something other than me this time."

"Let's hunt the people trying to kill you, Lara," he said, reaching for her before she could stop him and pulling her close, lowering his voice. "*Together*. We'll do this together. Tell me what I need to know, and let's go get them before they get you."

Lara would have shoved him away, but the guns in her hands were a disadvantage, unless she wanted to shoot him and... she lost the thought as sudden realization overcame her. The pain in her head was easing with Damion's touch, as it had in the bathroom. If she stayed, she would give him her trust. It was almost out of her control, it was so certain. "I can take care of myself."

"You're in this thing too deep," he said, his hands reaching down to her gun, closing around her hands where they clutched the steel. "Let me help you."

"I don't even trust you," she said. "Why would I want your help?"

"Yet you called Caleb. You were worried about me."

"Self-preservation," she countered in what was only a half truth. She had been worried about him, and not in a small way. "I had a better chance of getting out of there alive with you, than without you."

"Then you'll understand me wanting you to put the guns down," he said. "Self-preservation and all."

"I thought you wanted me to shoot you?"

"Not so much right now."

"Fine," she said, bending her knees and disposing of the weapons on the ground. Then, straightening, her gaze lingered on his chest, avoiding eye contact for fear he'd read her sudden agreeability for what it was—a plan to attempt wind-walking to a public place where guns wouldn't be acceptable. "I don't have a macho complex like you do."

"Just a Renegade complex," he said, his hands settling on her waist. "I'd think the fact that we saved your life and that your people tried to kill you would have changed that."

Her gaze jerked to his, her hands covering his at her waist, intending to remove them. "You want something from me. They don't want me to give it to you. Let's not pretend that protecting me is anything but what it is."

He studied her a long moment, calculating, shifting to a topic he clearly believed would get to her. "They killed the Russian," he said. "He's dead."

Her fingers, still covering his, tightened uncontrollably before she could stop them. Damn it! His kids, his wife. Her heart bled at the idea that they'd seen it happen, or that they, too, were dead, but she didn't dare ask Damion. Already she'd showed her hand. Already he believed she was working for someone other than Adam. She still clung to hope that she worked for the good guys, yet she didn't want Damion to be the enemy either.

"The family's safe," he said, seeming to read her silent questions. "Under our protection and about to get the bad news, if they haven't already."

So they hadn't seen it happen. Lara squeezed her eyes shut, relieved, but rattled by the fact that Damion had read her hot points so well. There was only one way she was going to keep this man—this Renegade—at a distance, to sort through fact and fiction before she told him everything, regardless of consequence.

She inhaled, and ironically, his touch had made her stronger, her head clearer. At least right now, she wasn't hallucinating. She wasn't seeing flashes of images. She wasn't even dizzy as she had been during her previous failed attempts to wind-walk. Maybe... just maybe... she could pull off an escape.

Not giving herself time to think about what happened if she failed, or what would happen when he followed her, and she knew he would, Lara willed the wind to her. The familiar tingling sensation slid into her limbs, a moment before she faded into its depths.

—◆◆◆—

Lara materialized several minutes later in the alley behind the mall, out of sight. At least now she knew the wind-walking disability came with the dizziness. In its absence she was still mobile, but then, so was Damion. Her skills were back. Her head was clear. She had a window of opportunity to decipher fact from fiction, friends from enemies, Damion included. If he was intentionally using some GTECH skill to create her illness, she had no idea how close he had to be to do it. She didn't linger, didn't dare, knowing he'd be seconds behind her. Rushing onto the sidewalk speckled with shoppers, she charged toward the mall's main entrance, stumbling slightly as the hum in her head returned with full force, a rush of dizziness suffusing her.

She shoved it aside and entered the mall, urgently maneuvering to get out of the main corridor, and any chance of being within Damion's visual. Darting inside a large department store to her left, she headed past the makeup counters and straight to women's clothing.

Grabbing a few things off the racks—jeans and T-shirts—that she could change into, she headed toward the dressing rooms, which were unattended. As she hurried down the hall, she realized that the idea of changing clothes, and her appearance, though a good one, was hampered by a problem—she had no money, no purse, no resources—but she knew how to create an identity, even garner credit cards. She just had to get out of this mall and get to work.

Lara swayed, her steps uneven, but she didn't dare stop walking until she was at the room farthest from the entrance. She could feel the mental images, or hallucinations, or whatever these episodes were, coming on again. The fact that Damion wasn't here and couldn't be intentionally causing them was cold comfort. Or could he? How powerful was he? Enough to attack her mind from a distance?

Desperateness rose inside her to find a place that was secure where she could try to sleep off her weakness, a place where she wouldn't end up in a ball on the floor in public.

She opened the dressing room door and struggled with the slide lock, which didn't fit together properly, until she just gave up. At least it was a solid door, not a curtain.

Lara tried to hang the clothes on the wall hook, missing, but not caring. She couldn't settle onto the built-in bench fast enough. The hum in her head, in her ears, grew louder again, inescapable, and she had the impression of having a bad seat in a small plane.

Drawing her knees to her chest, she used them as a pillow, letting her head droop and her lashes lower. She just needed to rest a second, hide here until Damion gave up on the search for her. Out of sight, out of mind. Yes. Perfect. She'd rest, and he'd give up searching. If he was near, if he was causing this, maybe he'd just pass her by, and she'd be okay again.

<center>~~~</center>

No way was Damion allowing Lara to get away from him. There were too many unanswered questions about what she was involved in, and truth be told, this reached beyond duty and honor. Everything male inside him screamed "find her and protect her," and yes, "mine" in a ridiculous, primal way—feelings that were really going to bite him in the backside if she betrayed him.

Determined, driven to find her, he walked through the entrance to the mall and into the scurry of busy shoppers without really seeing them, stretching his mental feelers for Lara, seeking the familiar strand of energy a Tracker used to locate a target, usually an injured GTECH who couldn't maintain their shields, betting that Lara didn't have hers up. And if Damion could find her, so could Lucian.

Damion shut his eyes, ignoring whoever bumped into him, focused on Lara, on the moment he'd kissed her, on the taste of her, the feel of her, the energy that was her. Mentally reaching, touching, seeking, and then finding that wisp of her presence, different from the male GTECHs he'd tracked, and from the human females marked by sex with a GTECH—an energy that was both familiar and all Lara.

His eyes snapped open, and he started walking, cutting through the department store, heading straight to the ladies' clothing section and the dressing room in the corner. He entered the hallway to the changing areas without delay, following the energy, the essence that was Lara.

He didn't hesitate at the door, certain she was behind it. He turned the knob and entered the small room, shutting himself inside with her. The feminine scent of her— familiar like her energy, alluring and spicy—rushed over him, like flowers blooming on a hot, summer day.

But the sight of her, curled in the corner of the bench, much like she had been in the shower, legs pulled to her chest, sent a chill down his spine. It sparked fear that she was again lost between hallucination and reality.

"I'd make a scene and yell at you to get out if I thought you'd care," she whispered, clearly aware of who had joined her. She lifted her head slowly, as if it were a heavy weight, hard to endure, fixing him in a black-eyed glossy stare. Her soft dark hair. A beautiful mess framing her makeup-free, ivory face.

"And I'd ask why you ran," he said, "but I wouldn't like the answer, and it wouldn't change the outcome. I found you."

"How *did* you find me?" she asked.

"I'm a Tracker," he said. "That's what we do. We find people."

"Tracker," she repeated. "Is that some special boy's club I wasn't invited to or what?"

Interesting. No one inside Zodius City would be without this information. He leaned against the door. "It's a skill a select number of GTECHs possess. I'm one of those Trackers, and so is Lucian. That means if I found you, so can he."

"That explains so much," she said, the flip remark doing nothing to disguise the heaviness beneath it. "And how exactly do I hide from you and Lucian?"

A mental shield was as natural to a GTECH as breathing. Yet she didn't know what it was? Just another piece of a puzzle that didn't fit together, but he planned to try—just not now. Not when Lucian would be coming for her.

"You hide from Lucian by coming with me," he said,

sitting down beside her, his hand settling on her knees. "And by trusting me."

She sucked in a breath, as if his touch shocked her, but instead of shoving him away as he expected, she latched onto him and seemed to sigh a breath of relief, almost pleasure.

"Oh God, that feels so good," she said, dropping her head on her knees and scooting closer to him, until he wrapped his arms around her knees.

Heat rushed through him, hot and fast, a reaction to her soft sounds, her soft touch.

"Ah well, yeah, okay. If that feels good, you ain't seen nothing yet."

She lifted her head and stared at him, searching his face. "You really don't know what you're doing to me, do you?"

"If you're accusing me of sexual voodoo again," he said, breathing in the sweet, feminine scent of her, leaning closer to draw it in, his gaze sweeping her lush, kissable mouth, "I'm going to accuse you of the same."

"That isn't an answer," she murmured, the warmth of her breath teasing his cheek. "It's deflection."

He knew damn well things were getting too personal with Lara, that soldiers didn't do personal, they did duty. But still he found himself saying, "If I were going to deflect, I'd dodge and avoid. And I definitely wouldn't do this." His mouth brushed hers, a caress, barely there, yet it burned through him like a wildfire, lighting up every pore of his body.

It was a lingering kiss, a gentle kiss—at least it was until Lara moaned and pressed her hand to his face. In a slide of tongues, she was in his lap, his back against the

wall, her hips spreading his, and damn, he could get used
to her just like this. All over him, around him, on him.
The feel of her pressed close, the taste of her urgency,
her absolute need for him, was more than he could stand.
Damion slid his hand up her back, the other lacing into
her hair, deepening the kiss even further, drinking
her in—thirsting for her, like he'd never thirsted for a
woman. Knowing this wasn't a good choice, knowing it
was dangerous, for the first time since joining the army,
he didn't care.

His phone sounded, and damn if telephone calls
weren't his saving grace with this woman. The sound
jerked Damion back to his senses, and somehow, he
managed to tear his lips from hers. She tried to kiss him
again, and hell, he let her, wanted her to. Somehow he
yanked his cell from his belt, lavishing one last slide
of his tongue against hers, before he forced her mouth
from his, holding her back while he glanced at the ID
and answered.

"Talk to me, Houston," he said, his voice rough and
gravelly, even to his own ears.

"We tangled with Lucian and Sabrina, but they got
away," came the voice he recognized as Houston's.

Damion hesitated, debating about asking for backup,
and not because he didn't trust Houston, but because he
was quite certain that the woman melting like warm,
sweet honey in his arms could easily turn brittle and cold
if he made one wrong move. "Take care of the woman
trapped in the underground facility," he said, and gave
Houston the entry codes. "I'll be in touch soon."

He hung up, searching Lara's face. "Lucian and
Sabrina are on the move. We need to be too." Which

meant getting themselves underground and fast, before Lucian picked up Lara's energy path. His fingers slid around the back of her neck, and he gave her a quick kiss. "But later, we are going to talk about your need to jump my bones in unusual places and cuss me." He helped her to her feet and held her steady. "How do you feel? Are you okay to move?"

"Yes," she said, her gaze sliding to his chest. "I think I am now."

"What does that mean? You think you are *now*?" He'd seen how she'd been when he'd first found her. "You're still hallucinating, aren't you?"

"I'm okay," she said, and turned away, reaching for the doorknob, clearly doing her own share of deflecting. Damion pressed his hand to the wooden surface above her head. "If you run from me when we leave this room, I *will* find you. That is, if Lucian and Sabrina don't find you first and kill you."

She didn't turn. "I know," she said softly.

"So you aren't going to run?" he queried insistently.

Rotating to face him, she pressed her back to the door, tilted her chin upward to stare at him, her eyes now bright green and alert, a brilliant contrast to her dark hair and pale skin. "No, Damion, I'm not going to run. I told you I needed you, and that was the truth. I realize that now. I need you."

There were layers beneath that statement, layers he was going to explore and understand, some of which his gut told him he wasn't going to like. For now, though, he'd settle for getting them both out of here alive. "You'll be explaining that statement, and a whole lot more, in the very near future."

Chapter 11

WITH HER HAND TUCKED IN DAMION'S, LARA FOLLOWED him down the dressing room hallway, then watched him peer around the corner and into the store, watching the subtle flex of muscle along his shoulders, the lethal air of danger that seemed to radiate off him. He was tall, broad, and sexy—things that made kissing him oh-so-good and oh-so-dangerous. Because when she did, she not only forgot the hum in her head, but she forgot who and what he was. GTECH Renegade—one of the killers who'd stolen her family from her.

And so Lara had made a decision back in that dressing room, a decision that surviving meant not only taking things one moment at a time, but with her head in a muddled mess, she had to trust her instincts. The facts as she knew them were most certainly flawed. How flawed was the question she intended to have answered.

Going with the flow of that instinct, she believed Damion had no idea he could control her hallucinations with his touch, his kiss. He was right. She'd been desperate to save his life, willing to risk her own, known on some level that she was even supposed to. *Instincts.* Yes. They were all she had, and she was putting them to use. And Damion. She had Damion. Whatever that meant, good or bad, she was going with it and with him. Almost, but not quite, trusting him. There was something about Damion, something that spoke to her soul.

She didn't understand it and didn't want to try. She just needed him to be worthy. God, how she needed him to be one of the good guys.

He motioned her forward, and together they weaved a path toward the side exit, avoiding the main mall entrance, where Lucian and Sabrina would be likely to enter. They kept close to the walls, hidden by clothing racks. They eased into the main walkways only when moving from one department to the next.

The loudspeaker announced five minutes until store closing, and Damion cast Lara a displeased look. The crowds, which offered cover, were already thin, and they were about to get thinner.

They were close to the door though, only one department left to clear, and on the move again, in the home stretch and counting, when Damion suddenly yanked Lara into a corner. In an instant, her backside was pressed against his hips, his hand sliding intimately to her stomach, his mouth near her ear. "Shhh," he murmured, a second before Lucian and Sabrina walked by.

Heart racing, she shrank against him, her hands pressed behind her, flattening them on his powerful thighs, as she tried to melt farther into him, and into the shadows of several clothing racks.

His fingers spread on her stomach, his grip tightening, as if offering reassurance. She reveled in that silent communication, in the way he reached out to her, and the way that connection defied all she had ever been taught about GTECHs, Renegades included.

And so she waited, with this man, this stranger who didn't feel like a stranger anymore, this enemy who didn't feel like an enemy anymore, and prayed Lucian and Sabrina would pass them by. Watched as the two of them headed toward the mall exit where they would hopefully be locked out of the store as it closed. Just when Lara was ready to let out a breath of relief, and feeling certain they were going to get out of this all right, Lucian and Sabrina suddenly stopped in their tracks.

"Oh God," Lara whispered.

Damion turned her to face him, his hands on her arms. "We're running for it. *Now*."

"What if they shoot us?"

"Not likely in public," he said, dismissing her concern and moving on. "The minute we hit the door, we wind-walk, and I don't care who sees us. We don't have time for discretion. This is about staying alive." He didn't give her a chance to argue or contemplate the uncertain and very bad side of his "not likely in public" assessment. He grabbed her hand and took off running, her in tow.

It was a pure, adrenaline-driven, forty-yard dash that ended when a female in a suit opened the door and offered them access to imperceptible strands of wind.

Instantly, Damion grabbed one and took her with him, which she already knew from their poolside departure, wasn't so different from traveling on her own.

They reappeared in an alley, and she didn't have time to figure out where that alley was. Damion was already pulling her forward and down a stairway. *Subway,* she mentally computed. They were at the Washington subway.

Damion edged her in front of him, sheltering her against an attack from behind, she realized, urging her down the long, narrow passage of stairs. She didn't have to look back to know they were being followed, to know Lucian and Sabrina were there. She could feel them in the shiver down her spine, the hair standing up on her arms.

The ten o'clock hour meant only a few people would be dallying around, offering no crowd for camouflage, and she hoped Damion knew what he was doing.

"Jump," Damion yelled, as she approached the metal-armed ticket booths.

Lara didn't have to be told twice. In a well-executed leap, she scaled the rows of machines, ignoring shouts of some of the onlookers as she did, but weak, injured, and without the food and rest her body required to heal, she stumbled on landing. Damion was right there by her side, taking her arm and righting her footing, then pulling her with him toward the terminal. A hard thud of feet hit pavement behind them, and she didn't have to look back to know who followed.

A train stopped at the top of the ramp, the doors sliding open, and they made a run for it. They were close—so close, she was certain they were going to make it.

The rush of success already screaming through her, Lara was about a step from the car, when something latched onto her other arm.

Training and more of that instinct she'd relied on, mixed with a whole lot of adrenaline, Lara reeled around in fight mode, thrusting her flattened palm into what turned out to be Lucian's nose. A split second later, Damion's boot landed in the exact spot where her palm had been, and with such force that Lucian landed flat on his ass. Before Lucian ever made full ground impact, Damion thrust Lara into the car and kicked behind him, this time landing a blow smack in Sabrina's gut and thrusting her halfway across the platform.

On some distant level, Lara registered the observers, a few shouts and gasps, but she tuned them out. Lucian was on Damion again with a hard punch in the stomach resembling the one Damion had blessed Sabrina with, and Damion grunted and bent over at the middle.

Lara was behind Damion, holding the door, which was chiming angrily at her, trying to close, and she searched for anything she could use as a weapon. She found it in the form of an umbrella and launched the metal end over Damion's head and straight into Lucian's face, where it tore through muscle and flesh.

Damion yanked her fully into the car, and the doors shut. The excitement over, the few riders went back to their own business, like they were used to seeing weird stuff in subways—and they probably were.

"That was wicked," Damion said, straightening. "Remind me not to piss you off, will you? Oh right. I have bite marks to prove I already have." He grabbed her hand, angling toward the door that connected the cars. "Let's go."

"Hey!" an elderly lady shouted, standing in their path, all five feet and a hundred pounds of her, with her hands on her hips. "That was my umbrella. What am I supposed to do now?"

Damion and Lara exchanged an amused look. "Sorry about that, ma'am," Damion said, Mr. Perfect Gentleman in action. He fished a couple twenties from his pocket. "Hope that does you right?"

The elderly woman pursed her lips and gave a nod. "It'll do."

His lips curled in a smile. "Glad to hear it." He eyed Lara, the smile fading to a look of urgency. "Now we go." They traveled past the "do not enter" sign from one car to the next, until the train stopped, and they got off and then right back on yet another. And then did it all over again.

Finally, on the third train, the car was empty enough that she could risk conversation without someone overhearing. "How many times do we do this?" she asked, sharing a pole with him, all too aware of their legs touching, their bodies close, of the intimacy between them that seemed to grow with each passing moment.

"Until I'm sure we've got them chasing their tails well enough that we can go above ground without Lucian immediately tracking you."

Lara didn't like how that sounded. "So, anytime I'm above ground, a Tracker can find me? Please tell me there's a way around that."

"I'm teaching you one of those ways now," he said. "You dilute your presence and stay underground. A Tracker can't find you underground. We don't know why, but that's how it is. And it takes time and skill once you've lost the target's energy path to find it again, which is exactly why we're going to move around enough that Lucian won't have any idea where you go above ground again."

She studied him—his light brown hair, cut short, framing his handsome, strong face—looking for signs of worry and finding none. But then, he was a soldier, who'd likely been taught, just as she had, to *never let them see you sweat*. The thought brought an odd sense of discomfort to her chest—emotion and a hint of the memories that Damion's touch had been suppressing. She shoved it aside and asked the question that was bothering her.

"And when we go above ground," she said, "then what?"

"We get to another safe house, like the cabin should have been," he said, "so you can rest and get well."

"And this safe house. Will there be other Renegades there?"

"No," he said softly. "Just you and me, Lara. Someplace safe where you can rest and heal."

For a moment, she wanted to thank him, to simply trust him blindly. There was a cold, hard reality though that she couldn't escape, no matter what fantasy she might have over who, or what, this man was. No matter what she wanted him to be. "Then you bring in your people and start drilling me for answers. I'll be a prisoner."

"No," he said. "I meant what I said. It will be just you and me." He hesitated. "At least for now. I'll make that promise on one condition. I need to know that whatever you're involved in isn't an imminent threat to our country's security, and that it won't cost innocent people their lives. I need your word."

"You'd take my word on something this big?"

"Yes," he said. "I'll take your word."

Trust. He was giving her trust. Or playing her like a master musician. She studied him, reached inside herself, clinging to her instincts that told her he was real—the most real thing in her life right now. That he was the one person she could trust. She had to meet him in the middle. She had to go out on a limb with

Damion. "I thought I was protecting those very things, that the people I worked for were protecting those very things. So the answer is no. I'm not aware of any threat to our country or to innocent lives." She hesitated a moment, and then went on, charging into this full steam ahead. "The hallucinations don't seem to be hallucinations at all. I think they're more…" She choked on the next word. It unraveled all she knew to be real. "Memories. Like a past that was wiped away now resurfacing." She inhaled and let it out. "So even if I was ready to trust you, I don't know what's real and what's not." And then another hard admission. "I'm not even sure I know who I was before."

He reached up and cupped her cheek. "Then let me help you find out."

Her hand went to his. "Don't make me regret this," she said, knowing her statement, in and of itself, was admission of some level of trust.

"Nor you me," he said softly, a hint of tension in his voice, his hand falling from her face. "I don't throw caution to the wind, but I am, for you."

"Don't," she said, suddenly afraid of more than trusting him. "Please don't. I'm as afraid for you to trust me as I am for me to trust you. I don't know how I am or even what I am. So… don't trust me. Not yet."

"Too late," he said without hesitation. "I've already decided I'm going to do enough trusting for both of us. You can catch up later."

"And if I don't deserve it?"

"You will. And I will. Watch and see."

"You can't know that."

"Sometimes the facts aren't clear, and all a good

soldier has is his innate survival instincts. Mine are stronger than most. They've kept me alive too many times to count. I think yours are too, which is exactly why we're standing here now—united against Lucian and Sabrina. And it's also why we'd much rather kiss each other than kill each other."

They stared at one another, time standing still, a bond weaving between them, a silent connection that reached beyond the raw sexuality of their attraction, broken only by the announcement of their stop. The doors opened, and Damion grabbed her hand. Lara tugged him back, drawing his attention. "What if while we are trying to make Lucian and Sabrina chase their tails, we end up right back in their path?"

One corner of his mouth lifted, softening the hard lines of his expression. "We find another umbrella."

—∿∿—

Sabrina waited impatiently outside the subway while Lucian tended his wounds with supplies she'd bought at a drugstore a block away. Finally, he sauntered down the hallway leading out of the restroom, a large bandage taped on his face, looking tall and broad, his civilian attire of jeans and a T-shirt doing nothing to disguise the soldier beneath. The female in her warmed at the sight he made, but the *soldier* in her—the leader of Serenity— fumed at his slow, loose-legged swagger that said he was in no rush, making her want to strangle him.

Sliding her teeth together in a hard grind, she charged toward him. "They saw you," she said. "The Renegades saw you, and Lara was fighting against us. Serenity is as good as exposed, and yet you seem in no rush, as if you don't even care. *What* is wrong with you? We have to make a plan. We have to decide what to do now, not later."

He reached down and took the subway map from her hand, amusement in his dark midnight eyes. "What we aren't going to do is get desperate and behave foolishly," he said, his gaze and his tone hardening as he indicated the map. "And this is the kind of foolishness I expect from a follower, not a leader." He motioned toward the exit. "Come now." He started walking.

Dread curled inside Sabrina, a jab of searing warning. Calling Lucian had been a mistake, a desperate, horrible mistake, which had now trapped her.

Charging after him, she caught him at street level and grabbed his arm. "They know we aren't with Adam," she ground out. "Lara will tell them about General Powell. She was helping them. She was fighting with them."

He stared down at her, unmoving and hard, then suddenly grasped her arms and backed her into a dark corner behind a rank-smelling Dumpster. "Control yourself," he said, "before you convince me I should tell Powell you aren't capable of leading. Leaders lead. They solve problems. They don't panic like some schoolgirl princess who can't get a manicure on schedule."

He was so like every man who'd abused and used her throughout her entire life. She hated him. "What are we supposed to do?"

"One step at a time, doll," he said, brushing his fingers over her cheek. "Take out the targets, and then do damage control."

Doll. Oh yeah, she hated him all right. She despised him far more than the life that had ensured there would never *be* schoolgirl manicures, shopping malls, and family and hearth in her future. She'd always been alone until Serenity, until Powell. She'd foolishly created a situation that threatened to steal her security, her place where she finally belonged.

"She's underground," she said, resolved to deal with this problem before it got out of control. "You won't immediately locate Lara when she comes above ground again, and she's someplace secure."

He snatched Chale's cell phone from his pocket. "We have Damion's number. We call our tech team, and they signal us the minute his phone pings to life. Damion is a Renegade. Unless he feels imminent threat, he won't wind-walk in front of onlookers. We'll wind-walk to their coordinates, and I'll have Lara's energy link again. They won't escape. They die tonight."

What part of this didn't he get? "Even if that works, the other Renegades saw us, and we don't know what she's already told them. The damage reaches beyond their lives now."

"I'll smooth this over with Powell," he said, sliding his hands to her waist. "I'm to return to his side by morning, and by tomorrow night, he'll have made sure we're both linked to Adam as one big plot to undermine the Renegades. And neither Lara nor the Renegade with her will be alive to dispute that." His hands brushed up her rib cage and brushed the curves of her breasts. "Then we'll celebrate our new arrangement. You and I... leading Serenity."

You and I leading Serenity. The bastard was going to double-cross her with Powell, use this to jockey more control for himself, and less for her, just as she'd feared.

Even if she held onto her position as leader of Serenity, she'd be led around by his cock for the rest of her life. She was done with that life. She'd been a fool for calling Lucian into this. A damn fool.

He pushed off the wall and dialed their tech team, setting up Damion's phone trace. Sabrina listened, her heart thundering in her ears, her stomach so sick she wanted to throw up, on him preferably, but that would be short, cold comfort.

He flipped his phone shut. "Damion won't return to ground level anytime soon. He'll want to take his time diluting Lara's trail. So let's go eat. I don't like to kill things on an empty stomach."

He turned and started to walk away. Adrenaline rushed through Sabrina's body, and a sense of being out of her body, of acting without thinking, took hold. She'd fought too hard to get where she was to lose it now—she feared death, feared life. No. She couldn't lose it now, not over Lucian.

She pulled her gun with its silencer, pointed it at the back of Lucian's head, and fired the fatal shot, all too aware that even a GTECH couldn't survive a direct hit to the brain. Before he ever hit the ground she was behind him, wrapping her arms around him, and wind-walking to the top of a mountain near the cabin where they'd found Lara. It was too dark to see down the steep incline she knew to be to her left, but she could hear the river she'd seen earlier below.

She dropped Lucian's dead weight on the ground, removed both his cell phone and Chale's from his pockets, and then shoved the body over the incline, waiting until she heard the splash. Without hesitation, she wind-walked to the subway terminal, which she'd determined would be a good bet for Lara and Damion's exit, while studying her maps. A long shot, but one she had to take. At least she was a close wind-walk to any location the cell might ping to.

Sabrina waited for the tech team's call, thinking through what came next after she killed Lara and Damion. Smiling, she realized exactly what she'd tell Powell. Lucian and Lara had been plotting to take over Project Serenity, and she, Sabrina, his most loyal follower, had killed Lucian, Lara, and the Russian. But not before they'd potentially exposed Serenity to the Renegades.

Powell didn't want Serenity exposed any more than she did. He'd do damage control. He'd fix the leak of information, work his magic. Most importantly, she'd be given credit that he'd even had the chance to do that. It was perfect. She would look like a goddess and have more trust and power than ever before.

Chapter 12

THE TRAIN PULLED INTO A SCHEDULED SUBWAY STOP, and Damion motioned Lara forward. "We're getting off here."

"Right," Lara said, looking pale and tired. "We need to change directions again."

"No," he corrected. "This is it. We're going above ground."

Relief bled into her face, but to her credit, she wasn't willing to simply stop working their original plan. "I thought we were doing ten trains, not eight."

"This location was my intended endgame," he explained. "I miscounted the trains." Or rather, skipped a few after noting Lara's failing efforts to hide her weakening physical condition. She was pale and moving slower by the second. She needed rest, food, and probably a good dose of vitamin C—and she needed those things quickly. Truth be told, he needed food too. The GTECH metabolism had its plus sides, like rapid healing, but it also demanded to be fed, a large amount and often.

"Why don't I believe that's the whole story?" she asked suspiciously at the same moment the door's warning system went off, telling them they were going to miss the stop.

"I guess you were born suspicious," Damion said, latching onto her arm and pulling her out of the car.

"You know," she said, making an effort at feisty, but sounding exhausted. "If you keep manhandling me, I'm going to get mad."

"And here I thought I'd already made you mad a million times over." They were headed toward a concrete stairwell that would lead them to the landing of a main station. It was a weekend hot spot above ground that he knew well. It was the perfect Friday night, an eleven o'clock spot complete with a crowd for camouflage. "When we exit above ground," he said, taking the first step in unison with Lara, "if we turn right onto the sidewalk, we'll be headed into a popular area of nightclubs and restaurants. If we go left, we head toward a complex of retail stores that will be closed. We're going left and looking for a discreet corner to wind-walk."

She brushed wayward strands of rich brunette hair from her eyes to watch him closely. "And I assume I hang on for the ride because you aren't about to tell me where we're going."

"I haven't steered you wrong yet, now have I?" he asked in a light tone he didn't feel, knowing she wouldn't like hearing they were headed to an underground safe house in Nevada, near Sunrise City.

More and more, Damion suspected someone had messed around with Lara's head, and she needed medical attention. He intended to convince her of that much as well. Considering the Renegades had only human doctors who could not wind-walk, he wanted her as close to that medical attention as he could possibly get her, in case her condition suddenly took a turn for the worse.

A resigned sigh slid from those tempting, soft lips,

the lips he hadn't stopped thinking about kissing the entire eight train rides.

"Right now," she said as they stepped to the top of the ramp into the scurry of people that surrounded them, "all I care about is sleep and food."

"Ask and you shall receive," he promised, nonchalantly—when he felt anything but—and slid his hand down her arm to lace his fingers with hers. They crossed the platform and headed to yet another set of stairs, to what he hoped was an uneventful exit from the subway into the city, but truth be told, he had no idea how advanced Lucian's tracking skills were. Many of the GTECHs developed new abilities over time, much like Michael's ability to control the wind, and Caleb's ability to read emotions and to darn near read minds. For all he knew, Lucian might have the ability to track below ground and still have a grip on Lara's location, which meant they could be headed straight into the mouth of trouble.

But he would have charged right into that trouble if he wasn't stopped dead in his tracks by the sound of his cell phone ringing. Damion pulled Lara back down several steps, out of the range of a potential sniper shot, and snatched his phone from his belt.

She stumbled and fell against him, the soft curves of her body melting into his—a sign of trust, even if she didn't know it. But he did, and he also knew right now he didn't deserve it. Not when his nemesis of a cell phone that he shouldn't even have on his person was ringing.

Fuck! What had he been thinking? Hell, he was more of a tech guru than even his brother, the damn CEO of

Megatech, and he knew all too well that a cell phone could be traced. The chances that Lucian and Sabrina had his number after Chale's capture were pretty damn certain as well.

One look at the "unknown" on the phone's screen, and he knew he'd not only fucked up, he'd fucked up royally. Lucian and Sabrina didn't have to call him to track the phone, but he couldn't wind-walk and talk. Calling, getting him to answer, or even pause to check the number, slowed his progress, distracted him, and wasted precious seconds their pursuers would exploit.

"Damion?" Lara asked urgently. "What's happening? What's wrong?"

He closed his hand around the phone, his words low and tight, but without definitive explanation. "Stay between me and the wall." He didn't give her time to reply, not with this beacon in his hand announcing their location.

He tugged her forward, and the minute they were above ground, he chunked his cell phone as far as it would go, hoping it would be followed, knowing that wasn't likely.

"What the—?" Lara murmured beside him.

That was all the warning he got before she forcefully yanked him into the crowd. He held his footing, and her hand, and tried to redirect her. However, he quickly reconsidered his actions when he spotted the source of Lara's urgency—the rapidly approaching Sabrina. Parting the crowd, she wasn't even trying to conceal herself.

Lara whirled around to object to his delay. "We have to—"

"Go." Damion said, leading Lara back in the direction she'd wanted to go in the first place, distancing them from Sabrina, who could be packing Green Hornets. Though Damion was fairly certain that he and Lara were about to be sandwiched between Lucian and Sabrina, he didn't see he had much choice in direction.

He had to come up with a plan and do it quickly. Simply wind-walking to some random location wasn't the answer because Lucian and Sabrina would track Lara. But he couldn't stay in the crowd where innocents could be hurt either. Nor could he risk a confrontation with Lara in her current physical condition. The only safe destination Damion knew was the one where the playing field was so weighted in their favor, there would be no room for hostages and death bargains. A place Lara would refuse to go to if he gave her the option, and so he wouldn't.

"This way," Damion said, wrapping his arm around Lara and ushering her into the tiny pizzeria they were about to pass.

"Are you crazy?" Lara demanded, aimlessly tugging against the hand he'd wrapped around hers, already charging forward with a locomotive tug that did nothing to stop her objections. "We'll be like trapped rats in here."

He didn't reply, just led her past the empty red booths and the counter where pizza slices were displayed, heading to the concealed back hall and the rear exit that he knew from a past visit. The instant that Damion shoved the door open, he faded into the wind, taking Lara with him. They were headed to Sunrise City.

Minutes later, with Lara by his side, Damion materialized in front of the entrance to Sunrise City. High-
tech scanners instantly identified Damion as one of the
Renegades. The doors, hidden beneath stone and moun-
tainside, parted a hair's breadth—just enough to allow
a wind-walker entry. Taking Lara with him, Damion
faded back into the wind, and they reappeared inside
the facility, sealed in by the closure of the doors. At the
same moment, one of four elevators opened, and Caleb
and Michael strode forward.

"Damn it," Damion cursed under his breath, aware
that any chance he'd hoped for to explain himself to
Lara was now lost.

And sure enough, she shoved away from him, her
gaze ripping a path around the paved garage filled with
rows of motorcycles, where weapons and supplies lined
the walls, then back to the two approaching men, and
finally to Damion.

"You lied to me. You said you would keep this
between you and me, and you didn't." Her voice con-
demned, her eyes glinting with enough sharpness to
throw shrapnel.

"I can explain." Damion swore, stepping toward her
and stopping when her knees bent, her body readying for
attack, offering him a silent promise of retribution. "We
were being tracked, Lara. They would have followed
us. They would have taken human hostages to draw us
out again, like they did back at the cabin. I couldn't let
that happen. This was the only place I knew where he
wouldn't dare follow."

"But you didn't warn me," she rebutted.

"There wasn't time," he argued.

"I'm no fool, GTECH."

"My name is Damion," he ground out.

Her eyes flashed fury. "I know what our situation was, *Damion*, and I know we could have gone underground and talked. But you wanted a reason to bring me here." Her fingers curled into her fists by her sides. "We both know I'm your prisoner, and that's why I wasn't given options."

If he was honest with himself, she was right, at least partially. He'd wanted a reason to bring her here—he'd wanted her safe. He'd wanted her under medical care—and Sabrina and Lucian had given him that reason. But there wasn't time to deal with that now, as Caleb and Michael drew to a halt beside Damion.

"What's happening, Damion?" Caleb asked urgently.

Aware that he'd directly disregarded his leader's orders by bringing Lara to Sunrise City, Damion tore his gaze from hers and focused on explaining himself. "Apparently Lara is considered too valuable to be left free and alive. Lucian and Sabrina are not only working together, but doing so in an effort to kill her. As a converted female, she can be tracked as easily as a human female marked by sex with a GTECH. I had nowhere else to take her."

"I do not get any energy off the female," Michael argued.

"Stretch your senses beyond the familiar," Damion urged. "You'll find her. If she has the ability to shield her location, she doesn't know how to use it." His attention shifted between the two men. "They were on us like rats on cheese. I couldn't risk another hostage situation like the episode back at that cabin." His gut clenched at those words, at the reminder of just how bad things had gotten back there. "How's Chale?"

"Still alive," Caleb said, his attention remaining on Lara." "Damion did the right thing by bringing you here. No one can get to you inside our city. You're safe."

"Safe by your definition," she said. "I'm not—"

Her words cut off abruptly as she dropped like a rock, her eyes rolling back in her head, her body going limp as a noodle.

Damion cursed softly and caught her a second before she hit the ground, scooping her into his arms and immediately heading toward the elevator. "She needs a doctor," he said, giving the other two Renegades a quick rundown of her condition as they stepped into the car, and finishing with, "In short, I'm pretty sure someone's been playing around in her head. Now that they don't have a handle on her, she's having painful flashbacks, maybe hallucinations. She doesn't know who to trust, because she can't decipher fact from fiction, enemy from ally."

Michael keyed in a set of security codes, and a series of body and iris scans began on all three GTECHs. "Considering Ava has the ability to influence female minds, I'd say this was her doing, but that means she's overcome the need to keep the subject at close range."

The doors to the car began to close. "I'm still not buying the idea that Adam would allow Lucian or Sabrina to live, let alone, trust them," Caleb said.

"Maybe he's playing cat-and-mouse with them," Michael offered, "and fully intends to slaughter them when they've served their purpose."

The car started moving as various murmurs of

agreement filled the elevator. "These flashbacks Lara is experiencing explain the odd mix of emotions I'm reading in her," Caleb commented. "She's terrified that everything she's believed in is a lie. You were right, Damion. She definitely believes the Renegades and the Zodius are equally as evil. But yet... she feels the need to trust you, even protect you."

"That's because I don't want anyone to steal my thunder," Lara hissed softly, "and kill you before I get the chance." She lifted her head to stare at him. "Put me down."

"You fainted," he said. "I'm not putting you down until you see a doctor."

"I'm fine," she said. "But I swear to you, Damion, if you don't put me down right now, you won't be."

Michael chuckled. "I think I like this woman."

Damion ignored him, speaking to Lara. "Right after I find a doctor to check you out."

She glared at him, the vulnerability of a doe-caught-in-headlights just beneath the defiance, but still her chin lifted. "I might be here. I might be your prisoner, but I'm not done fighting."

"Good," he assured her, a smile teasing the corners of his mouth. "Because neither am I."

And he wasn't. He'd fight to protect her, to find out the truth about her life. He'd do both, despite a deep sense of uncertainty that told him there would be a price for doing so. His soldier logic told him that price might be too high in the big picture of war that quite possibly divided them. But to the man in him, holding her, feeling her warm in his arms, he was pretty certain logic had gone missing.

———

Deep beneath a Mexican mountain range in the Serenity headquarters, Logan Reynolds finished reading through the data on the latest Bar-1 conversion that one of his scientists, Jenna Jennings, had handed to him on a clipboard a few moments before.

"The subject's brain wave activity is peaking much earlier than we once thought possible," he commented, glancing up from the material and offering Jenna a satisfied smile. "Good news, considering Powell plans to bring us a new recruit next week. He'll be impressed. Now if only we had unlimited serum, we'd be able to create the manpower Serenity needs to truly shut down all other GTECH operations and secure our country from a takeover."

"You mean womanpower," Jenna teased. "And my team is working diligently on the serum, trying to re-create it, but it's not going well. And it needs to go well. I might not agree with all of Powell's methods of leadership, but Adam Rain's desire to create a 'perfect Zodius race' reads a little too close to Hitler's 'perfect Aryan race' for comfort."

"Agreed," he said, setting the clipboard on a lab table. "And Caleb Rain and his Renegades might say they're different, they might even be different, but they're too big a risk to leave alone. I am making some progress on Bar-2." That being the male version of Bar-1. "If I can perfect it, we can use it on the Renegades and the Zodius to control them, rather than kill them."

"You'll get it," she assured him and batted long lashes at him. "You're just that good, I guess."

She was a cute little blonde, and with her peachy perfect skin, she looked more like twenty-two than her real age of thirty-two. She had brains and a rocking body to boot. Not to mention how well she played the demure flirtation game, unintentional as it may be, to tie-him-in-knots perfection. "Not me," he corrected softly. "*We.* We're that good."

Their eyes locked and held, and while the look in hers was both shy and uncertain, his, he was quite sure, was far more hungry and primal than he should have allowed it to be.

The air virtually crackled with her unspoken question. *Am I crazy, or do you want me too?* A question he knew came from the ever-present call of passion between them that remained unanswered.

But there was what he defined as a "complication," a reason he didn't dare touch her. Still… Logan could almost convince himself nothing mattered but pulling her into his arms and tasting her.

Abruptly, that moment of fantasy came crashing to an end, quite literally when the lab door opened and slammed into the wall. "Get out!" came the harsh female command.

Both Logan and Jenna looked up to find Sabrina— the "complication" herself—in the entryway, and her attention wasn't on Logan. It was on Jenna.

"I said, get out," Sabrina repeated to the other woman through clenched teeth.

Jenna stood transfixed by the other woman's presence. Logan could see why. Sabrina was certainly a striking presence, posed in the doorway, her long flaming hair brushing her broad, but slender shoulders, her ripped jeans and snug Harley T-shirt molded to her lithe body like a second skin. Untouched by Bar-1, and uncontrolled by anything but her need for Powell's protection, she was as wildly arrogant and assuming as any of the GTECHs that Serenity was designed to destroy. One look at Jenna's pale face told Logan that Sabrina terrified her.

The urge to comfort her was strong, out of character. He didn't do the coddling, sensitive thing, but Jenna brought out urges in him he didn't understand. He actually cared that she was alone, without family, and that her work, her place here with him, was all she had. These were nonsense things that had nothing to do with duty and the job at hand, yet somehow they were important where Jenna was concerned.

The hatred burning from Sabrina's black eyes into Jenna told Logan that Sabrina knew Jenna mattered to him, and she didn't like it. "Give me a few minutes, Jenna," he urged, trying to get her off Sabrina's radar, out of danger. Sabrina *would* hurt Jenna—he had no doubt. Causing pain entertained Sabrina.

"And since they might be the last few minutes he knows in this lifetime," Sabrina said, "don't hurry back. I'd hate to taint your delicate sensibilities with the sight of blood."

Jenna gasped and turned to Logan in silent question.

"It's okay," he assured her, more than accustomed to Sabrina's threats, even physical demands, and then smiled. "If she kills me, you get to be in charge." Her eyes went wide, and he laughed. "I'm joking." He glanced at his watch, shocked at the time. "How did it get to be two o'clock in the morning? Go to bed, Jenna.

We'll start fresh in the morning. Or rather, later in the morning at this point."

"No." She shook her head. "I don't want to leave. I—"

"It's okay," he assured her, oddly warmed by the realization that she was worried about him. No one worried about him. He was a loner by design, by duty. Yet, even now, with his assurances, she looked as if she might dig in her heels and insist on staying. "I'm okay." He motioned to the door. "Go rest. Tomorrow is another day."

She didn't look convinced. "You're sure?"

"Positive."

She studied him a moment and then nodded before reluctantly heading to the exit opposite from where Sabrina stood, glancing over her shoulder as if she might change her mind.

The minute Jenna shut the door, Sabrina slammed hers. In a blink, Logan was shoved against the concrete wall. Pain bit a path down his spine, and air lodged in his lungs.

"You know I like it rough, baby," he said breathlessly, "but I thought we'd agreed to keep the violence in the bedroom, preferably with you naked, before we get started. Somehow that makes the pain endurable." Sadly, more than endurable. More like darkly erotic in ways he'd never thought possible. He hated this woman, yet he wanted her, and he had no idea why. Even now his cock was hard; even now, he was ready for her.

Not like Jenna. Jenna had changed everything, made him regret Sabrina, made him wish he didn't want her and wish he could turn back the clock. But it was too late. He was in too deep with Sabrina, and he couldn't turn back.

Sabrina's hand snaked out, a strong GTECH finger pressing to his throat, choking him. "Is that rough enough for you, Logan, honey?" she asked, her free hand sliding up his thigh and pressing to his crotch. "Because right now, I'm feeling like hurting you real bad. You converted Lara too quickly. She conspired with Lucian and sold us out to the Renegades."

For Logan, the implications of her words were lost to one need. "Air" Logan tried to gasp, but nothing came out. He couldn't breathe. Desperately, he grabbed at her fingers, trying to pry them free of his neck. "Please." The strangled word was barely audible. Her fingers dug deeper into his neck, and somehow he forced out the words, "Can fix... her... Lar... a..."

She glared at him, her eyes black ice, so cold he was sure he was a dead man. Instead, a disgusted sound slid from her lips, and she dropped him to the ground. "Pathetic human," she said. "Your begging disgusts me. It changes nothing." She whirled around, giving him her back, and sauntered to a lab table.

He sucked in the sweet bliss of air and rubbed his bruised neck. Contrary to her insults, he knew she loved when he begged, loved playing dominatrix—but he wasn't a fool. She would still kill him. She'd just drag it out and make him suffer first.

She leaned against a lab table, watching him with a mixture of amusement and lust. Hurting him turned her on. Damn it to hell, why did it turn him on too? Deep down, he knew. He wasn't going to pretend otherwise. Confinement to the Serenity lab had stolen that rush of danger, the high of living on the edge that being a CIA assassin had given him.

He felt it now through the rush, the adrenaline pulsing through him. He was standing on a ledge about to be pushed, and he freaking lived for this feeling. This was where he was best—on the edge, where his mind worked best. And why he'd been a damn good undercover agent.

"Bring Lara to me," he said. "The Renegades trust her. I'll reprogram her to use the Renegade trust to destroy them, and Lucian along with them."

"I killed Lucian, but Lara is already under Renegade protection," she said. "I can't get to her. The damage is done. Serenity is exposed."

"Powell is a master manipulator," Logan said. "He'll find a way to spin this with the White House. Serenity will survive this. It will go on."

"And so will I," she said. "Which means Powell has to know I dealt with those who failed him—definitively and decisively. You have to die, Logan." She shoved off the table and sauntered toward him, pressing against him. "I'll make it good for you, sugar. When you come, when you're feeling no pain, I'll end it then. For old time's sake."

"Why would you want to kill the one person who can give you Lara?" he asked. His mind raced, calculating how to turn the tables and make this work for him.

She laughed. "Right. You can give me Lara. I don't think so."

"Every GTECH subject I assimilated to Bar-1 has a built-in trigger," he said. "And that trigger, when activated, will bring them back to their old self. Use that trigger in the right way, the way I alone know to use it, and Lara will not only come running right back into your hands, she'll be a blank canvas ready for creation."

"You're lying," she accused. "The GTECH immune system destroys any foreign objects. A trigger wouldn't survive insertion."

"That's where my scientific expertise comes into play," he said.

She narrowed her gaze, angst in their depths that he read as fear that, she too, possessed such a trigger. "Powell knows of this trigger?"

"I never, ever, show my full hand until necessary," he said. "A way to ensure *I'm* necessary."

"Show me," she said. "Use this trigger now. Bring Lara to me."

"I'll use the trigger with Powell present or not at all."

Her gaze narrowed. "You failed with Lara once. Why would any of us trust you to brainwash her again?"

"Just because Lucian lured Lara to the dark side with the Renegades does not mean I failed," he said. "It simply means Lucian succeeded and should never have been trusted in the first place." Nor should Sabrina, he suspected, despite her desperateness to maintain the protection from Adam that Serenity offered her.

"If you're suggesting Lara turned on us, but didn't regain her memories, that we simply lost control over her, then that means we could lose control of every last member of Serenity. If you actually expect Powell to feel good about that—" She patted his cheek. "You need therapy. Sorry, sugar. You might as well face the facts. You're a walking dead man and not for long, because I can't allow you to live through this. Powell isn't going to trust you again."

"Oh, but he will," Logan said, his heart thundering in his ears at her threat. "He'll trust me again because he wants Serenity to be more powerful, and he wants the destruction of the GTECHs who are outside his control. I can give him those things."

"How?" she demanded.

"We send a newly brainwashed Lara back to the Renegades. Once she's inside Sunrise City, she places a few strategically located bombs inside, and it will be dust."

She studied him, her fingers doing a slow, calculating roll, back and forth on his shoulder, as if that were a part of her thinking process. "If I let you speak to Powell, there's a good chance he'll still have you killed."

Better odds than he had with Sabrina right here and now. "I'll convince him he needs me."

"And if you do convince him, and then you fail, I can promise you... you'll wish you were dead by the time he finishes making you pay."

"I won't fail," he assured her.

He'd barely finished the last word of the vow when a knife appeared in Sabrina's hand, drawn from somewhere on her person, and she pressed the blade to his face. "Sorry again, sugar, but I have to make sure Powell knows I made you suffer for your mistake. It'll ease his anger and make him focus on your plan."

The blade bit into his flesh, a small trickle of blood oozing down his cheek. In a quick shift of her wrist, she sliced it down his shirt, the steel grazing his skin, before her hand flattened on his chest, and she walked him to the wall. Her palm slid down his chest and settled on his crotch, a smile touching her lips when she felt the bulge there.

"Apparently," she said, "you know this is for your own good."

No. He was pretty sure, in fact, that this woman was as bad for him as a shot of arsenic straight into his veins, but he couldn't seem to care right now. Not when he was rock hard with anticipation and pure white-hot lust for her. A momentary mental image of Jenna's lovely face brought with it a sense of regret. Sabrina's teeth roughly bit at his nipple, pain and pleasure ripping through him, and he lost the image. There was nothing but the ache of wanting more—more pleasure, and yes, more pain.

Who was he fooling with Jenna? He loved the idea of her, but he could never be the man she needed—and deserved. No. He lived for the kind of high Sabrina gave him, the edgy, dark, perverse high of pain mixed with pleasure and the danger of going too far or not far enough—made easier by a shared desire to save the world before an uncontrollable GTECH population took it over.

Sabrina lifted him and then slammed him down onto a lab table before straddling him. Pain crashed through his skull as it hit steel, quickly forgotten by the demanding pressure of her tongue sliding into his mouth, the feel of her hips arched against his. *Oh yeah, baby*, he whispered in his mind. This woman, this GTECH, took him to the edge and kept him there—and the edge was exactly where he wanted, and needed, to be.

—∿∿—

From inside her private quarters, Jenna barely contained a scream as she watched the lab's video footage play on her computer—feeding to her from the camera meant to allow the monitoring of procedures when she wasn't present. Logan knew the camera was there, knew she had access to it as well.

It was almost as if he wanted her to see this, as if he were telling her what he hungered for. It wasn't little, sweet Jenna. She glared at the image of Sabrina roughly dominating Logan, of his grunts of pain and moans of pleasure, and then hit the end button. She couldn't watch another second.

All her life, the Sabrinas of the world—conniving sex vixens who took and bled you dry of happiness—had taken from her. Juliette Rogers had been the one before Sabrina, the one who'd stolen her husband and scientific mentor back at Yale. With him had gone her role in a cutting-edge research program. She'd lost her life, her happy, wonderful life. She didn't please him in bed, her husband had said, and then he'd gone on to call her boring and predictable, too naive and guarded to ever take the scientific world by storm.

Juliette had used her husband, screwed him senseless, and he'd not seen what she was up to until it was too late. Juliette had left him, and not only taken the funding for his research with her, but made it look like he'd stolen the cash. He'd lost everything, including his reputation. Just like Sabrina was going to destroy Logan, and Serenity, if something wasn't done to stop her.

Jenna flipped open one of the rectangular black boxes, one of seven she secretly possessed, which were now sitting on her glass desk. She stared at the row of filled syringes.

Each time she'd dosed Lara, she'd diluted her serum and taken some for herself. Jenna had calculated through her private research, with findings she had yet to reveal to Logan or Powell, that Lara would convert to GTECH just fine, and she had. Foolishly, Powell's previous scientific teams had been using more of the precious serum than needed. After skimming serum from Lara and the newest recruit presently undergoing conversion, Jenna had enough to fully change herself into a GTECH. Finally, she was ready to begin dosing herself.

With a shaky hand, she lifted one of the syringes and stared at the golden liquid inside—the unique DNA of an alien. The DNA that would soon pour through her body. The DNA that would give her the power Sabrina now possessed. She wanted that, yet the idea of injecting herself with it set her heart to racing, thundering loudly in her ears.

Desperate to regain her resolve, she reached forward and punched a computer key, bringing the lab back into view, letting the sounds and sights of Logan's desire for Sabrina fill the room, fill her mind, and expand in her chest. Logan's face contorted with so much lust and desire for Sabrina that it twisted Jenna in knots. She wanted a man to feel that kind of ultimate desire for her, but instead, the men in her life had wanted the Juliettes and Sabrinas of the world.

Why didn't Logan, and even Powell, see what kind of poison Sabrina was? She was no different than the GTECHs they were trying to stop—uncontrollable and power hungry. It was clear to Jenna, just as it had been with Juliette.

That needed resolve solidified, destroying what she recognized had been hesitation and fear, what had made her hands shake. They steadied, she prepared the syringe, and then, without another moment of doubt, she injected herself. This wasn't about Logan, or her ex, or even about the moans of pleasure filling the room that

Chapter 13

AWAKENING ABRUPTLY, LARA JERKED TO A SITTING position, finding herself on top of a bed with Damion looming over her. A bed she unnervingly realized he'd put her in while she'd been passed out.

"Easy, sweetheart," he said in a gentle tone, settling a hip on the mattress next to her. "You're okay. You're in the ER."

Her gaze swept the sterile hospital room, that could, she thought grimly, just as easily be a torture and inter-rogation room. She still couldn't believe she'd trusted him, only to have him bring her here to Sunrise City. "How long was I out?" she asked, afraid to think what might have happened that she didn't know about. "And has a doctor examined me?"

"Not yet," he said. "And you were only out long enough for me to carry you down the hall from the elevator."

Any relief she felt from that little piece of good news faded into another concern. "What about Caleb and the Renegade that was with him? Where are they?"

"They went to check on Chale," he said.

"So they're coming back?"

"Relax, Lara," he said. "If they do come by, it will be to check on your health and no other reason." His hand settled on her arm, oddly comforting considering he was the one responsible for her presence in a hornet's nest of

Renegades, and a Renegade himself. "No one is going to make you do anything you don't want to do."

"Until I refuse to tell you what you want to know," she said brusquely. "Who's going to torture me when that happens, Damion? You? Or maybe that big menacing one—Michael?"

He grimaced. "The Renegades don't torture people. I won't lie to you and tell you we don't want to talk to you. This is a war we're living, and you may well have information that could save lives. But we aren't doing anything until you get well. Besides, I've made it clear that the only person persuading you to talk—is me." There was a sensual heat to those words, an underlying meaning followed with a hint of a smile. "And so far, you've done a damn good job of letting me know when my methods of persuasion don't please you. I've got the bite marks to prove it." He patted her leg. "Why don't you try and rest until the doctor gets here?" He pushed to his feet, intending to let her do so, and she burned to do just that.

Every muscle in her body screamed for rest, but she moved as he did, twisted around to let her legs dangle off the side of the mattress, ready to launch herself into action if need be. Not that she had a chance in hell of escaping Sunrise City, but it made her feel better—more in control.

"Okay then," he said disapprovingly, noting her sitting position. "I guess you didn't like the idea of rest."

He'd placed himself between her and the door, and somehow it felt intentional, as if he didn't quite believe his claims about the other Renegades leaving her alone. She didn't miss the subtle tension etched in his handsome, chiseled face. He was the lean, mean soldier she'd seen by the pool, assuming a façade of casual that didn't fool her.

"Would you rest if you were in my shoes?" she asked.

"You're safe, Lara," he said, stepping toward her and settling his hands on her shoulders. "No one is going to hurt you here. I won't let them."

She felt herself melt into the touch, her body reacting to the intimacy without her consent. The smart move would be pushing him away, but like so many other times, she just didn't have it in her. "You didn't answer my question," she said instead. "If you were in my shoes, would you be able to rest?"

"I'd make myself rest," he said. "I'd want to be my best and my strongest as quickly as possible."

She made a sound of disapproval. "You wouldn't dare shut your eyes for fear you'd never open them again, and you know it."

He didn't bother denying she spoke the truth. "What can I do to prove to you that you're safe enough to rest?"

"I'll rest when you take me out of this place."

"That's not going to happen, not until I know you're well. So you might as well lie down and rest."

"You mean not until you have the information you want." She crossed her arms in front of her chest, silently declining. "Tell me about the doctor I'm going to see. What's her interrogation experience?"

He grimaced and ran a rough hand over the light brown stubble framing his jaw. "You have to be the most stubborn woman I've ever met."

She grimaced right back at him, comfortable with the combative exchanges they continued to share, even welcoming the familiarity. "I bet you say that to all the women you kidnap and tote around like luggage."

"I did not—" he started, but someone cleared her throat from the doorway, a delicate, feminine sound that had Damion turning and Lara assessing the petite, thirty-ish brunette in hot pink scrubs who'd appeared there.

"I didn't mean to interrupt," the woman said. "But I wanted you both to know Dr. Moore is on his way."

"Not Dr. Moore," Damion corrected. "I told you Dr. Petersen."

"Yes, but Dr. Moore is on duty, and he—"

"Treats humans. Lara is not," Damion said.

Surprise flushed the woman's heart-shaped face to a rosy red. Her attention jerked to Lara and honed in on her eyes. She knew what she saw—knew she was too drained to camouflage the black coal of her GTECH eyes.

The nurse's throat worked in a hard swallow. "Oh my," she said, the surprise she'd shown seconds before shifted to obvious discomfort—and fear?

"She's not a Lifebond," Damion said, as if answering some unspoken question. "And she's not bound to a Zodius. She was injected with the serum."

Again, Lara found the nurse's attention on her, this time with a mixture of stunned disbelief and horror in her face. "They injected you?"

A fizzle of unease went through Lara at the "they" reference. "Yes," Lara agreed, cautiously avoiding a lie and eye contact with Damion. "I was given injections." She could feel Damion's attention sharpen, almost hear his mind racing at her choice of words. There was no doubt, he suspected the truth—that Adam hadn't been the one to convert her.

"It was Ava, wasn't it?" the nurse asked, as if feeding off Damion's silent contemplation. "She convinced Adam the injections would bypass the Lifebonding process and make you fertile without it, didn't she?"

"Emma," Damion warned gently, saving Lara from pulling some brilliant reply from a hat, when there was no hat in sight. "Lara has a real need to see Dr. Petersen."

"Yes, of course," Emma replied, casting Lara an apologetic look. "I'm sorry. I didn't mean to pry or make you uncomfortable. I, of all people, know that's not what you need right now. I'll get Dr. Petersen for you right away." She wasted no time departing, pulling the door shut.

Lara stared at the door, a hollow, horrible feeling carving a home inside her as she replayed Emma's words. *I, of all people, know that's not what you need right now.* "She was in the sex camps in Zodius City, wasn't she?"

"Yes," Damion confirmed, stepping between her and the door, his arms crossed in front of his broad chest, and Lara couldn't fight a moment of pure female appreciation as she took in the sight of him—tall and hard all over—but his next words dashed her with enough ice water to end her distraction. "She's part of a group of fifty women we rescued last year. There were more than a hundred inside Zodius City at the time, but Ava's ability to brainwash many of them proved impossible to overcome during rescue."

"They force the women to have sex with the soldiers there," she said, the words heavy on her tongue. "Trying to find a Lifebond connection to make them fertile. She thought I was one of those women, and yet it scared her."

"Ava's able to brainwash most of the women into believing they want to be with the men," he said. "They believe becoming a Lifebond will make them royalty among the Zodius. It's a small comfort to know the women don't feel raped while they are there. But not all women are susceptible to Ava's skills."

"Emma wasn't," Lara said, reading between the lines.

He shook his head. "Emma wasn't. And now she's terrified of anyone who might be loyal to the Zodius, as are all the women we rescued from the camps."

"And if I had been a Lifebond to a Zodius soldier, she would have assumed I would be loyal to that Zodius."

"Exactly," he said. "Once a couple Lifebonds, they're bound in life and death—if one dies, the other will die. That's pretty intense loyalty by default. That loyalty is what Adam is counting on when he throws women like Emma to his men, like they're meat to the damn wolf packs he keeps."

Lara barely suppressed a shiver at the idea of being passed around a group of Zodius soldiers for sex. That was what Adam did to women, and what she'd thought the Renegades would do to women as well. They didn't though, and Emma was proof of that.

Suddenly, Lara just couldn't swallow the idea of connecting herself to Adam, allowing herself to be thought a monster in order to protect Serenity. "I was telling the truth when I said I was never inside Zodius City," she said. "And I would never be a part of something as horrific as what happened to Emma."

"I know," Damion said, sitting down beside her and gently pressing her back against the mattress. His hands settled beside her head. His eyes captured hers, reached inside her, and seemed to be searching clear to her soul. She could barely breathe with the certainty he could see too much, her heart and adrenaline kicking into overdrive.

"Emma made me remember one of my initial assumptions when I realized you were GTECH, Lara," he finally said. "The only way Adam would let go of his precious stock of serum for a female would be to breed you with his soldiers." Lara's heart slowed to a standstill, the room shrinking with the foreboding knowledge that she was cornered, with no escape.

"You would have been put through medical tests and subjected to aggressive attempts to Lifebond you, with hopes that you no longer needed that bond to get pregnant. You simply had to have enough sex. In other words, you would have spent lots of time in the sex camps long before you would ever be used for other purposes. You asked too many questions about those camps for someone who's been inside them. You aren't working for Adam. I've said that before, but always with doubt. This time, I know it's the truth. You're working for someone else." A knock sounded on the door, but he didn't move, his gaze locked with hers, as he added, "And you're going to tell me who."

Chapter 14

Sabrina had not only fucked Logan, she'd fucked him up. His eye was black, his lips swollen, his cheek ripped open from her nails. He sat in the chair at a desk, in front of a computer, with her standing behind him. A webcam chat displayed Powell—a distinguished, fifty-something man in full army greens, while Sabrina gritted her teeth through an explanation of why Lucian was missing. "Apparently he'd not only conspired against us with the Renegades, and planned to claim the Russian for their use, he'd involved Lara," she continued. "I killed Lucian and the Russian, but Lara escaped."

Powell didn't react, his jaw tense, his face an emotionless mask, the air thick with his silence. Sabrina had come to know it signaled an impending explosion she wished to avoid with Powell, and these were those signs.

Her fingers dug into Logan's shoulders. "But as you can see, Logan and I have been discussing options to present to you. He's assured me he can not only bring Lara back to us, but reprogram her and send her back to the Renegades as a weapon."

Powell's gaze narrowed sharply on Logan. "Explain yourself."

"Each of the Serenity GTECHs has a built-in mental trigger, a memory that will take the subject back to her real identity, but will also take her to an exact location I've programmed into her mind. Then she'll be yours—a clean slate, ready to recanvas. We then send her back to the Renegades, where she will be trusted. We can use her to destroy them from the inside out."

The muscle in Powell's jaw ticked. "Explain the trigger."

"It would be in our best interests to have this conversation *alone*."

Powell's eyes lifted to Sabrina. "Leave us."

"General—"

He cut her off. "Wait in your quarters."

Sabrina ground her teeth, barely containing the urge to scream with the injustice of the moment. Logan was going to pay for this, just as Lucian had paid for crossing her. She exited to the hallway and went to her room, a sterile white-tiled, white-walled duplicate of the lab, minus the tables, where she paced for twenty long minutes. Finally, the webcam program on her laptop beeped from where it sat on top of her white-and-glass kitchen table.

She rushed to the computer and hit the button to bring it to life, bringing Powell into view. "Who would you consider the best of Team Serenity, besides yourself, of course?" he asked, not bothering with a greeting.

Uneasiness fluttered in her stomach. "It depends on the mission."

"The best, Sabrina," he repeated sharply.

He studied her a long, hard moment. "Send Crystal to me here in Germany where I will remain for several weeks," he finally said. "She'll be replacing Lucian as my personal bodyguard. I won't be returning anytime soon, and I wouldn't want to take Opal—as I'm sure you'll be counting on her for your upcoming mission."

Damn it to hell. Crystal was power hungry and eager to win Powell's favor. "What mission?"

"First you will close the front of the facility. Move everyone to the west, bottom level, so that it appears we've evacuated. Lara will be spending a few weeks in the Renegade camp earning their trust, and no doubt, she will tell them our location. When they come looking for us, we will know our plan is working. Then, we will exploit that trust to its fullest potential. Understand me, Sabrina. If anything happens to Logan to prevent him from bringing Lara back to me, I will hold you accountable. Are we clear?"

"We're clear," she agreed tightly and without hesitation. She could cause a lot of pain without impairing his performance. And she would enjoy every last second of it.

―――∿―――

Lara heard the knock a second before Damion released her and pushed to his feet. The door opened and a pretty woman with light brown hair, about Emma's age, wearing a lab coat, came in the door and shut it behind her.

"Hi Doc," Damion said, his tone still tight from their confrontation. He motioned to the bed. "This is Lara. Lara, this is Dr. Petersen."

"Hi Lara," the doctor said, claiming a rolling chair and setting her clipboard on the counter that ran along the wall, before extending her hand. "Call me Kelly. It's nice to meet you."

Lara accepted her hand, surprised at the energy she sensed in her. "You're human."

"I am," she confirmed. "As are most women you

will meet here in Sunrise City, though we do have a handful of women converted to GTECH by Lifebond." She arched a curious brow. "But you were converted by injection, I understand?"

Lara nodded. "Yes."

"Are there more like you?"

"I'm part of a team of female soldiers," Lara confirmed.

"Soldiers," Kelly repeated, casting a surprised look at Damion. "I'm shocked Adam would choose women for such a task."

Damion's eyes met Lara's as he replied, "Women were meant to be surprise weapons," he said. "Created to kill GTECHs, but fortunately, Lara liked me too much to kill me."

Kelly's eyes went wide. "You're a Renegade assassin?"

Lara could feel Damion's attention, feel him watching her, feel the tension weave through the air, binding her breath for long seconds inside her chest. Only hours before, Lara would have proudly let Kelly believe she was a Renegade assassin, rather than a GTECH assassin, because that would point to Adam, not Powell. But now... it wasn't so simple, and she wasn't sure why. "This was my first mission," she found herself saying, making it clear she'd never killed a Renegade, avoiding a direct answer. Or she thought this was her first mission, and her gaze dropped, her lashes lowering, hiding her doubt. What horrible things might be buried in the recesses of her mind?

"They told her the Renegades killed her family," he said. "Promised her vengeance. Still Lara stood against them when they wanted an innocent human killed. Now they want her dead, and we're offering her protection."

Lara's gaze lifted to his, colliding with Damion's, and finding a silent reminder of his words. *And I'll keep protecting you.*

"I see," Kelly said. "How long ago were you converted, Lara?"

"As I remember," Lara said, meeting her gaze again, "six months ago."

"She has a head injury about twelve hours old," Damion offered, stepping closer. "And she's had no food, rest, or vitamin C since the injury. She's hallucinating, or she is having flashbacks that come on her almost like seizures. Twice now she's completely passed out. She's having trouble holding her camouflaged eye color as well."

Kelly arched a brow at Lara. "A dictionary of information, now isn't he? Anything you might want to add, since this is *you* we're talking about?"

"The first flashback was before the head injury," she said. "So the injury isn't the cause."

"And that rules out the healing illness," she said, making a note on her clipboard.

Lara didn't know much about the healing illness, but if it was ruled out, she'd leave it at that. She wasn't asking more questions that Damion might believe she should already know the answers to.

Kelly finished making her notes and set the clipboard aside again. "Before we continue, let me tell you a little about me. I can sense that trust is an issue for you, so I want to assure you that I'm your doctor, plain and simple. I make you well. The rest is between you and the others." She didn't wait for a reply. "I'm one of many humans who live and work with the Renegades, and I'm honored to do so. I'm as much of an expert on GTECH anatomy and health as one can be, considering the ever changing evolution of those converted. I was also one of the original doctors at Area 51." She frowned and eyed Damion over her shoulder. "You're hovering, Damion." She pointed at the chair. "Sit."

Lara drew back in shock, watching the scowl on Damion's face, shocked when it turned to defeat, and he stalked to a chair and claimed it. Kelly, a woman—no, a *human woman*—had just successfully ordered Damion, a male GTECH, to sit, and he'd done it. Blown away didn't begin to describe how the demonstration affected Lara. This display, and the trust she sensed in Emma for the Renegades, didn't compute. Damion didn't match the monsters she'd thought Renegades to be, the Renegades who would abuse and use women as the Zodius did.

Kelly eyed Damion. "Thank you," she said when he was settled, and then glanced at Lara. "Unless you'd rather Mr. Mother Hen here wait outside?"

Damion flew to his feet. "I'm not leaving her alone."

"You will if she says so," Kelly shot back, and then arched a brow in Lara's direction. "Lara?"

Her eyes went to Damion, who was staring at her, willing her to allow him to remain with her. Damion, Lara realized, was an anchor, the safety net her instincts were clinging to in all of this. He might be a devil in disguise, but at least, he was the one she knew.

"He'll make a scene if I don't let him stay," Lara said.

His scowl deepened, and Kelly eyed him and laughed. "That he will."

"Vitamin C has arrived," Emma said, rushing into

the room. "And I thought we should feed that GTECH metabolism." She held up two chocolate bars. "These should hold you over until we get you some real food."

Her stomach growling at the mention of food, Lara eagerly accepted. "Oh thank you. You're an angel."

Emma beamed. "I try." She glanced at Damion and pulled out two more candy bars from her pocket. "Brought you some too."

"She's right," Damion said. "You're an angel."

Three minutes later, Lara had inhaled the chocolate bars, and already she felt a little better. Five minutes later, she had vitamin C pumping through her. Thirty minutes later, she'd given blood, had her vitals and head injury checked, and there was an IV inserted in her arm. Forty minutes later, Damion was propped in the corner, looking as heavy-lidded as she felt, when Emma returned with her test results.

"Okay then," Kelly said, as she read the report Emma had brought to her. "Your vitamin C levels weren't overly low, which would have indicted the healing illness, but we pretty much knew that. Your blood levels are… a bit odd."

"Odd?" Damion and Lara said at the same time.

"It could simply be normal for a female converted by serum," Kelly said, dismissing concerns. "We have no one to compare to." She sighed. "I don't see any physical reason you should be having your symptoms. We need to do a CT scan and look at what's really going on inside your head."

"No," Lara said quickly, despite the heaviness of sleep overtaking her. "I don't want anyone poking around in my head."

"Lara—" Damion started.

"No," she repeated, holding a hand up to him, before he could even consider coming out of his chair. "Save your breath. I won't do it."

"We really need this test, Lara," Kelly said. "What about it is worrying you?"

"How am I to know the CT scan is just a CT scan?" She sat up and glared at Damion. "Was this your plan all along? To use some machine to read my thoughts?"

He was on his feet, towering over her in a flash of a moment. "The plan is to get you healthy."

"And you're trying to get information from me," she said. "You admitted that, so don't lie now and say you aren't, or I'll never believe another word you speak to me."

"I happen to believe that once you learn the truth about the Renegades and the Zodius, you'll freely share it."

"The truth or the truth you let me see, so I'll talk?"

He flung his hands in the air and then ran one of them through his hair. "Doc," he said. "Can you give us a minute?"

Lara started to get up, ready to rip out her IV to avoid whatever he had in mind.

Damion was on the bed holding her down quicker than she could move. "Oh no. You stay in the bed."

"Because you fully intend to force me to take the CT scan, or whatever it is, right?"

"You know what?" Damion said. "If that's what it takes to be sure you don't go and die on me, then yes."

"Because you can't have your biggest source of information die, right?"

"Chale's crashing!" Emma shouted from the door. And just like that, Lara was alone. Damion, Kelly, and Emma charged from the room, but not before Lara had seen the distress in Damion's face. Lara yanked out her IV, and quickly grabbed paper towels from a wall dispenser and folded them in the V of her arm. She rushed to the doorway and stood there, knowing she should use this moment for escape—a moment of indecision paralyzing her. Even if she could escape, which she doubted, she didn't know how to prevent Lucian from tracking her, or whether she was well enough to take flight without passing out again. Still… it was now or never.

Chapter 15

As Lara stood in the doorway of the hospital room, she envisioned the look on Damion's face when he'd heard Chale was crashing, and her stomach knotted. She shouldn't care about Chale—he was a GTECH. *Damion* was a GTECH. She was supposed to be their assassin, and they, as Renegades, were implicated in the murders of everyone she loved. Nothing she'd known to be the truth, up until the moment she'd met Damion, felt quite right. And she did care if Chale died.

She cared that it would be because of her, and she cared about how that would affect Damion, about how certain she was that it would hurt him deeply. It was time to face facts. She could reason away Damion's protection of her, by way of them needing her, needing information she possessed, even if that didn't feel quite right. Yet, a cold-hearted Renegade, a killer—as she thought all of them to be—wouldn't be hurting like Damion was about someone close to them. Lara glanced down the sterile hospital corridor where medical personnel congregated, and without taking time to second guess herself, she rushed toward them, rather than trying to escape.

Footsteps sounded almost instantly behind her. "What happened?" Caleb asked, rushing to her side, Michael with him. "Where is everyone?"

Lara stopped walking and turned to them, surprised

they didn't grab her and haul her back to the room she'd departed. "Emma ran into the room and told us Chale was crashing, and they all took off."

Caleb cursed softly and scrubbed a hand over his jaw. She saw the obvious angst in his face, before he and Michael exchanged a silent look. Caleb then rushed for the room where everyone had gathered, leaving her with Michael, who, she surmised, had been silently assigned the duty as her babysitter.

Michael glanced at her arm. "Aren't you supposed to be in bed? Or making a run for it?"

Yep. Definitely her babysitter. "I'm fairly good at doing exactly the opposite of what I'm supposed to do."

He studied her with calculating, crystal blue eyes. "Then we have more in common than I first expected. Damion, on the other hand, believes in doing exactly what he's supposed to do."

"You say that like it's a sin," Lara replied.

"I say that like the fact that it is," he said. "The rules are the rules with Damion. He doesn't break them. Not for anyone. Yet he brought you here against orders. You might not realize how significant that is, but we do. And so does Damion."

Her nerves prickled. "What are you accusing me of?"

"Nothing yet," he said. "I'm reserving judgment on what I think about you until I have more details. But it's fairly clear to me that either Damion has a strong reason for trusting you, or you have a real knack for manipulating him. You need to know right now that I plan to find out which it is before you hurt him or anyone else here."

Lara studied him, this fierce male who controlled the wind like no other GTECH. Digesting the power of his statement, and how it conflicted with everything she thought of this man, and once again, the Renegades. Despite the threat in his words, she didn't feel intimidated or afraid for one simple reason. He was telling her he would protect those he cared about, and that was something she understood, something she related to. "Then I guess it's my turn to say we have more in common than I first expected," she said softly. "Because I, too, will kill to protect those I care about, and those I've lost."

"And you think we killed your family."

"I guess I'm going to have to repeat your words once again. I'm reserving judgment. But if I find out you, or anyone else here, killed my family—I promise you, Michael—I don't care how wicked your reputation with the wind. I'll kill you."

Voices sounded near the room, and they both turned to find Emma, Caleb, and Kelly stepping into the hallway, along with numerous other personnel who quickly scattered. Caleb motioned to Michael to follow him and the others down a hallway, even as Damion appeared in the doorway behind them.

"Why aren't you in bed?" he demanded.

Lara took one look at the tightness of his jaw, the tension in his body, and she moved toward him, not waiting for an invitation. "How's Chale?"

"I'm just as fine as you are," Chale yelled from the room. "At least that's what Suzie told me last night."

Lara stopped in front of Damion, who was shaking his head at Chale's remark. "Try to ignore his misplaced, rarely funny, sense of humor." He then called over his shoulder. "And you're not fine, damn it. You almost died twice today." Then to Lara, "I have to wait for Emma to sit with him. But you need to get back in bed before you fall down."

After hours of touching him, depending on him, it was all she could do not to reach out and touch him now, to comfort him. She sidestepped him and entered the room, half expecting him to stop her, but he didn't. Instead, she heard Caleb and Michael speaking to him, murmuring something she didn't understand. She was by the bathroom, about to enter the main room, when black spots splattered in her vision. A sudden flash of images in her head had her swaying, and Lara grabbed the door frame, trying to force away a sudden piercing pain between her eyes. She blinked and shook her head, thankfully regaining her composure with ease, and then walked toward Chale.

The minute he saw her, he cursed. "Damn. I hate when people see me without my hair fixed." He was pale, his body shivering like he was cold.

"Stop joking around," Damion chided brusquely, joining them, his shoulder brushing Lara's as they stopped at the edge of the bed. "There is nothing funny about what's happening here." Damion glanced at Lara. "And I told you… you should be in bed."

"Surely you have a better pickup line than that one, man," Chale chided, and then moaned with pain before coughing.

Lara rushed toward the water pitcher and poured some in a paper cup. Damion came up beside her, their glances momentarily meeting, before he took the cup and handed it to Chale, who gulped it down and then tossed the cup toward a trash can.

"Did they teach you bedside manners in assassin school?" Chale asked, eying Lara.

"I wasn't aware I had one," she said, her lips lifting slightly.

"You aren't trying to kill me," Chale said. "That sounds like a pretty good bedside manner to me."

"Wait until she decides to kick you or bite you," Damion offered with a smile. "Then you'll change your mind."

Suddenly, Chale's eyes were shut, and Lara sucked in a breath. "Damion?"

"He's asleep," he said. "The Green Hornets shredded so much muscle and tissue that his body is working harder than usual to heal."

She wanted to ask more about the healing sickness, but didn't dare show her ignorance—at least not before she decided exactly how she felt about the Renegades.

"The sudden slumber is his body's way of demanding energy to heal," he continued, "*which* is exactly why you need to get some sleep."

Lara sat down in the bluish-green, hospital-style recliner. "I'll rest here, where I can keep an eye on you."

He arched a brow. "You're keeping an eye on me?"

"That's right." Her body relaxed into the cushions, reminding her how bone-weary she really was. "Got a deck of cards?"

"A deck of cards?"

She grimaced. "You know... cards. Kings, queens, jokers. That's what people do to pass time. They play cards." A sudden sense of confusion hit her. Why did she know that? Where had that statement come from when she didn't remember ever playing cards in her life? A flash of a man she knew to be "Skywalker" rushed through her mind, of him shuffling at their kitchen table, of her sitting across from him. She sucked in a breath at the vivid image, at the emotion that welled in her chest.

"What is it?" Damion said. He was kneeling beside her, with his hand on her leg—but she didn't remember him moving.

She blinked into his hazel eyes and wanted so desperately to tell him what she'd seen, what she felt, what she feared—that she wasn't who she thought she was, that Powell wasn't who she thought he was, that she wasn't really the good guy in all this. "I want to trust you, Damion," she admitted. "I do, but—"

"No buts," he said. "I trusted you by bringing you here when Caleb forbade it, for fear you were trying to infiltrate our operation. I listened to my instincts and took a risk. Now it's your turn. Take a risk, and trust me, Lara."

"It's not that easy."

"Who said anything about easy?"

Her gaze dropped to his hand on her leg, and she wondered at how right it felt there, how right his touch felt. Only a short while before, this man would have been her enemy. And maybe he still was, but no… he didn't feel like her enemy. She inhaled and lifted her gaze to his. "This really isn't even about trust, Damion. I just don't know what's real anymore. I have these memories surfacing, like pieces of my past that conflict with the past I know. I… can't even remember what my parents looked like, and… I keep remembering two different names." Was her last name Martin or Mallery?

"What names?" he prodded.

"My names."

He grabbed the stool and sat down, before rolling close to her again. "Lara isn't your name?"

"No," she said, shaking her head and feeling suddenly sick. What if she found out horrible things about herself that made Damion hate her? "Yes... no. I don't want to talk about this."

He rested his palms on his thighs and considered her a long moment. "You're afraid of what you're going to find out about yourself, aren't you?"

Her chest tightened, and for reasons she couldn't explain, her eyes prickled. "Wouldn't you be if you were me?"

"Of course," he said, surprising her with his honesty, and earning more of her trust. "I'd want to know the truth before anyone else did. There's no reason that can't happen. But you have to let Kelly run her tests and rule out any other cause for the mixed memories. Make sure it's not physical. Then, let her help us figure out how to separate truth from fiction."

"I already feel like someone has been in my head messing around, Damion," she admitted. "How am I ever going to know fact from fiction, if I allow someone else to do the same? I need to think about this." She reminded herself that his willingness to let her decide didn't mean he was honorable. She had every reason until today to believe the Renegades had killed her parents and had lured her father into a web of trust, and then murdered him. To dismiss those concerns would be as foolish as ignoring that they might not be reality.

Damion seemed to read her expression, her caution,

and he sighed heavily, then rolled to the edge of the bed and pushed an intercom button. "Anyone got a deck of cards?"

She softened inside at his actions, at his understanding—that he'd pushed her as far as he could and should back off. She didn't want his actions to be a form of manipulation that somehow replaced torture. She wanted it to be real—she wanted this growing bond she felt with Damion, the only thing that felt certain and real, to really be sincere. *Please, please, don't be the enemy, Damion.* But then, if *he* wasn't the enemy, what did that make Powell, or even herself?

Damion laid down his cards on the rolling table that he and Lara had stolen from near the bed almost an hour before. "Straight flush," he announced and wiggled an eyebrow. "I win again. That's four straight hands, but who's counting?"

"Apparently you," Lara said, tossing down her cards. "Shuffle, and let's go again."

Another two hands later, she threw down her losing cards and ran her hand through her hair. He loved her hair, so soft, like silk against his skin.

"You know," she continued with a glower. "It wouldn't hurt you to let me win a few hands."

"You get what you get honestly with me," he said softly, a hidden meaning in his words. He wanted Lara—wanted her in a bad way, in a way he'd never wanted a woman before. A way that defied the possibility that she was the enemy, that she'd unlock her memories and neither of them would like what was discovered.

She grimaced, when he'd expected something a little more intimate in reply. "Oh good grief," she chided. "That's exactly what Skywalker used to say and…" She paled and swallowed hard.

He stilled, his gaze searching her face, noting the instant distress in her eyes. "Who's Skywalker, Lara?" She squeezed her eyes shut, and Damion shoved the table out from between them and rolled closer, taking her hand in his. "Talk to me, Lara. Tell me about Skywalker."

"I don't know," she said, forcing heavy-lidded eyes open. "Someone who keeps finding his way into my thoughts, when… when…" She pressed her lips to his.

Heat rushed through him, and he wrapped his arms around her, pulling her close, and kissing her. Her arms snaked around his neck, her tongue reaching for his in hungry reply that threatened his restraint. "If this is your way of avoiding my questions," he said, his lips lingering over hers. "It's a pretty damn good strategy."

"It's not that," she whispered, brushing her lips over his as if she needed another taste of him. God, she was driving him wild. "When you kiss me," she panted. "I—"

He framed her face with his hands and leaned back to study her. "You what?"

"I—"

"How's Chale doing?" Kelly asked, rushing into the room for the second time since they'd started playing cards.

Lara pulled back from Damion, as if burned, and he silently cursed Kelly's timing. He wanted to know what Lara had been about to explain. Not only had he missed out on what was sure to be another kiss, he was pretty confident he had been about to make a breakthrough with her, that she would have opened up to him.

"He's sleeping soundly," Damion said, reluctantly turning to Kelly. "No signs of distress since you checked in earlier."

"Excellent," she said. "His vitals are strong and the worst is over." She rolled a blood pressure machine toward them before shooing Damion off her rolling stool. "Let me sit down and check the patient I'm really here to see."

He stood up and gave her the seat. "Her head hurts," he told Kelly, and when Lara opened her mouth to object, he said, "You furrow your brow when you're fighting the pain."

"Is that right?" Kelly asked. "Your head still hurts?"

Looking busted and surprised at his observations, Lara conceded. "Yes. It hurts."

"Lean down, and let me find the location of your injury," Kelly ordered.

Lara bent over and let Kelly check her scalp. "It's fine." Lara straightened, and Kelly gave her a puzzled look. "Describe the pain."

"A dull throb that worsens whenever I have flashes of images."

"Memories," Damion supplied.

Lara glanced at him and then back at Kelly. "I don't know." She sounded frustrated and a bit defeated, but no longer on guard. "I just really don't know much of anything right now."

Kelly pursed her lips. "You do know that the only time GTECHs get headaches is when they're vitamin C deficient, right? And let me have your arm so I can take your blood pressure."

"Honestly," Lara confessed, offering her arm to Kelly and obviously trying not to look at Damion. "I've never heard of this vitamin C thing that Damion told me about."

"Well, that doesn't surprise me," she said. "Adam isn't exactly one to tell a woman anything but to bend over and pant."

Damion and Lara shared a shocked look, and he almost choked on a bark of laughter. "I do believe you've been around too many soldiers for too long, Doc. You're starting to sound like one of the guys."

"Sorry, Lara," Kelly said with a shrug. "But I've got fifty women here who endured hell from that man in his sex camps, Emma included. It's hard not to get a little bitter about it." She released the cuff on Lara's arm. "Your blood pressure and your heart rate are fine. And no, you're not vitamin C deficient, and nothing is off in your blood work. So if you aren't willing to do the CT scan right now, which I know you aren't, then you need to rest—as in a good twelve to fifteen hours of healing sleep—and then we'll reevaluate. There are a few other tests we could try. A brain wave test might give us a clue as to any irregular activity. But right now, you need sleep to heal. And eat." She pushed to her feet and eyed Damion. "Feed her, and then get her to bed." She glanced at Lara. "I don't think you need to stay here in the hospital, but you shouldn't be alone either."

Damion's eyes met Lara's. "She won't be," he assured Kelly, fully intending to keep her close in his room. He wanted this woman, wanted her beyond reason, beyond the risk that she might still prove to be an enemy. "I plan to take care of her."

And he did. In his private quarters, where she could finish telling him exactly what his kiss did to her in vivid, intimate detail. Though he was prepared to be a gentleman and sleep on the couch while Lara claimed his bed, he'd much rather be in it with her. To hell with examining right from wrong and consequences.

───※───

A sudden rush of nerves and anxiety hit Lara as Kelly exited the room.

"The doctor has spoken," Damion said. "Let's get out of here and grab some food and shut-eye."

"And go where?" Lara asked, pushing to her feet, the not knowing killing her. Nothing was stable, nothing was controllable. It was driving her crazy.

"You can't be alone, so either you come back to my quarters with me, or you stay here in a hospital room."

And she knew what would happen in his quarters. She'd end up in bed with him. She knew it. He knew it. She'd never keep an objective mind if she slept with this man. "I don't want to leave the hospital."

"All right then," he said, after a long pause. "I'll get you some food, and then you can head back to your room."

"Where I'll have a guard at my door."

"You'll have *me* in your room."

"Because I'm a prisoner."

"You've vowed to kill all Renegades. We'd be foolish to leave you unattended."

He was right. He couldn't leave her unattended. *She*

wouldn't leave her unattended. But the idea of being here, where anyone could walk in on her while she slept... "And if I go back to your quarters with you?"

"I'm not going to tie you to my bed, if that's what you're asking. Not unless you want me to, that is."

"I don't," she said quickly, but the ache that tingled in her breasts at his words defied her statement.

"I guess that means I should take the deck of cards with us." He motioned to the clock. "It's nearly two in the morning. I'm starving, and I know you have to be. So why don't we go find some food, and then you can decide between the hospital or my room?"

"Yes, please," Chale murmured, pushing to a sitting position. "Go get some food, and send some my way while you're at it."

Lara glanced at Chale and then at Damion, and suddenly, all the tension inside her faded into unexpected, much-needed laughter. "I guess this means he's feeling better."

"*He's* feeling hungry," Chale provided. "I want three cheeseburgers from Joe's."

Lara's gaze caught on Damion's, warmth shimmering between them with undeniable distinction. Chale wanted dinner, and she and Damion wanted each other. The question was—was she willing to allow their desire to turn into reality?

Fifteen minutes later, Lara sat across from Damion at a table inside "Joe's Burgers," after they'd had Chale's food delivered via one of the hospital staff. "I can't believe you have an entire city underground," Lara said, marveling at the twenty-four-hour diner that sat in the middle of what appeared to be a sleepy town square, complete with every kind of shop and restaurant she could imagine. "How long has this been here?"

"You've really never been to Zodius City, have you?"

"Not that I remember," she said solemnly, honestly. "At this point, I can't say anything for certain."

"Including that the Renegades killed your family?"

"Including that," she agreed, somehow unable to even want to keep her guard up with Damion.

The awareness ever-present between them snaked a circle of silence around them, simmering in expansion, before Damion said, "Then tell me who you're working for."

"Not yet," she said. "I can't."

"So you admit it's not Adam?"

She wanted to say yes—damn it—she wanted to say yes to the point that she all but screamed it out, but she couldn't betray Powell. He'd saved her life, and so far, that memory remained true in her mind. "You didn't answer my question," she said, going into avoidance mode. "How long has Sunrise City been here?"

He sat there, his face expressionless for long seconds, before he snagged a fry and rolled it in ketchup. "We started building it right after Adam took over Area 51. Like I said back at the cabin, we have schools and about anything else that's needed to give the humans, and even the GTECHs here, a chance at a normal life. At least, the façade of one, which is a little piece of sanity we all need now and then."

"Even you?"

He finished off a fry, having already downed three burgers to her one. "The army is as normal as things have ever been for me."

"Where's your family?"

"My father and younger brother are dead. My older brother and mother—well, the less they know about me, generally the safer they are." He brushed his hands together, and the air prickled with his discomfort, with the sound of an invisible door being shut. "I'm about done. How about you?"

She hesitated, a bit taken aback by his brisk shift of subject and mood. She searched his face, remembering that moment when she'd been naked on top of him, when he'd told her he was good at taking the blame— when she'd felt his pain like her own. He wasn't some nameless Renegade to her anymore. He was a man, and she wanted to know what made him hurt like that, what *still* made him hurt like that. God, she didn't want to be his enemy, and she didn't want him to be hers. She didn't want to be the reason he hurt more than he already had. She saw it in his eyes, and she realized now, she'd tasted it in every kiss they'd shared.

"Yes," she said finally. "I'm done."

"So what will it be?" he asked softly. "Back to the hospital or to my quarters?"

She knew her answer, and she saw in his eyes that he knew too, that they'd both never questioned where they were headed.

Chapter 16

DAMION STOOD AT HIS DOOR, INSIDE THE LONG corridor of soldiers' quarters, his heart thundering in his ears, as he told himself that his to-hell-with-consequences attitude wasn't smart, nor was it safe. He knew his desire for Lara was dangerous, knew he should keep his hands off her. He would, he vowed, shoving open his door. He'd behave; he'd wait until he knew she wasn't the enemy, until he knew he wasn't treading dangerous waters.

He stepped back to let her pass, not trusting himself to look at her, all too aware of just how on edge he was, just how ready to pull her into his arms and feel those soft curves melt into his body. She moved forward, and his gaze brushed the soft sway of her hips, thickening his blood and his cock right along with it, the stretch of his zipper uncomfortable with demand. He'd held her, touched her, and had her naked in his arms. It didn't take much to envision doing so again.

He followed her inside and dimmed the lights. The narrow hallway was short and led to a room of white and gray tile, where the living room and the kitchen were one open space of black leather, silver, and glass—standard in all the quarters. Off to the left, the bedroom was, thankfully, through a door that both shut and locked. Lara paused, a few steps inside, turning to face him. He could feel her nearness tearing away at his willpower, threading through his blood, tempting him, calling him.

"Michael says you never break the rules, but you broke them for me," she said.

"Michael doesn't know when to keep his mouth shut."

"So it's true?"

"I told you I disobeyed an order by bringing you here."

"Is it true that you never break the rules, but you did for me?"

"Yes." And he didn't know why she made everything different, why she made him reconsider right from wrong—only that he'd do it all over again.

"Don't," she whispered. "Don't break the rules for me. Don't trust me because I can't risk trusting you. Damion, I don't know who I am or what I am or what I've done. I don't know if you're my friend or my enemy. I don't know anything except—"

He grabbed her and pulled her to him. "Except this," he said, his mouth slanting over hers in a deep claiming kiss he'd no more planned than he could now conceive of ending. She clung to him, melted just like he'd imagined a dozen times in the past few hours, her hands wrapping around his neck, her breasts pressed to his chest. "We want each other. What happens beyond that we'll deal with later."

"And if we regret it?" she asked.

He brushed his lips over hers. "I'm not going to regret this. No possible way." He kissed her, and somehow, he ended up against the door, her hand on his chest.

"We could be enemies," she reminded him. "We could be trying to kill each other tomorrow."

He molded her breast to his hand then pressed her shirt up, his hands touching the smooth, soft skin of her waist. He skimmed higher, to shove down her bra and caress her nipple. "You can try and kill me as many times as you want as long as you do it naked."

She bit her lip and tugged at his shirt. "As long as you're naked too."

"Oh yeah," he promised, pulling his shirt over his head and tossing it aside. "I'll be naked."

She ran her hands over the body armor he wore. "You mean you'd trust me without this on?"

"*Do* you trust me without my body armor? Because once it's off, there's nothing to hold me back."

"I'm counting on it," she promised, tugging down the zipper on his shoulder, and pressing her lips to the skin there. "Which is why I can't wait to get it off you."

He tugged her shirt up, and she moved to let him pull it over her head. Before she'd even managed to toss it aside, he'd unhooked her bra and shoved it down her arms, baring her beautiful high breasts for his viewing. Damion filled his hands with the weight of them, pressing them together, teasing her nipples.

She moaned, her hands covering his, her teeth scraping her bottom lip. "Kiss me," she commanded.

He tweaked her nipples, and pleasure rippled across her pale, beautiful face. "Where?"

"Everywhere," she said, leaning in to brush her mouth against his. "And why are you still wearing that armor?" A wild kiss followed, before her lips trailed his jaw, before she licked his ear and whispered, "Take it off before I get a knife and cut it off."

His hands slid into her hair, pulling her head back, baring her neck as he kissed a path down it and turned her to press her against the wall.

"What happened to getting naked, Damion?"

He let out a soft growl he barely recognized as his own—he was so aroused, so out of his own skin, yet never so inside himself as he was in this instant. The second she'd decided this was going to happen, the second she'd given herself, and him, permission to just be free, she had changed, and he with her. She was the woman from the shower now, demanding what she wanted, taking what she needed, and he was a man wild for that woman. There was something about her this way, about her ability to hold her own with him that turned him on in a way he had never imagined possible. She was no fragile flower, no delicate female who needed coddling. Just pure woman... sexy woman.

Stepping back from her, he made no effort to hide his lust, his desire. His gaze raked over her high, full breasts, and then lower—over her slender but curvy hips, her long legs that he intended to wrap around his shoulders, and then his hips. "Get naked," he ordered. "Take the rest of it off."

Her lips tilted seductively. "Already planned on it, soldier." She reached for her pants. He reached for his. They watched every zip, tug, and disappearing garment, until they stood there naked, staring at each other.

She smiled slyly, her gaze traveling over his body with open hunger, lingering on the pulsing thickness of his erection, before running her tongue over her lips. "You're even better than expected."

"And you are dangerously naughty," he said, reaching for her, only to have her dart past him and into the living room. He turned to catch the arousing image of her deliciously round and firm backside disappearing around the corner. "And you're killing me."

"I thought that was the idea," she purred in the midst of a sultry laugh.

Damion stalked after her. His blood pumped with a rush of adrenaline as hot as liquid silver. It was the primal high of hunting Lara, of the chase, unexpected—damn near uncontrollable—in its demand. He scanned the living room and entered the bedroom, only to have her wrap herself around him from behind. He turned to her, his prey, this tantalizing woman, who'd challenged him from the moment he'd met her, pulling her close and kissing her.

She clung to him, kissed him back, her tongue wild and hot, her hand wrapped around his cock.

"Something you want?" he asked.

She shoved him backward onto the bed and came down on top of him, reclaiming his cock with her hand. She cast him a naughty look. "I want this," she said and licked the head.

He moaned with the sensation only to have her straddle him, the wet heat of her settling across his hips, her backside pressed to his cock. "I want you," she panted and leaned over him, her hand sliding over his chest, her lips following, her teeth scraping his nipple. Her silky dark hair splayed across his chest just where he wanted it.

He rolled her to her back, pressed her legs apart to settle into the wet, slick heat between them, pressing her hands over her head and shackling them with one of his. "Clearly I have to take control."

"You can try," she challenged.

He ran his hand over her breasts, kneading and caressing before skimming a path down her slender rib cage, around her backside. She bit her bottom lip. Damn, he loved when she did that. Her dark lashes fluttered.

"I'd say I'm succeeding pretty well."

"Because I'm letting you," she whispered.

"Letting me?" he asked.

"Hmmm," she said, sucking in a soft breath, as he lowered his head and suckled her nipple, then took his time licking and teasing, while she arched her back, pressing the rose-red peaks toward him.

"Still letting me?" he asked, moving to the other breast to repeat his actions.

"Yes," she assured, as he slid his cock in the slick heat of the intimate V of her legs, even as she squeezed her thighs together, trying to draw him into her.

"So kind of you," he said, swirling his tongue over the stiff peak of her nipple.

"Isn't it just?" she agreed, a look of absolute lust in her eyes as she watched him lave her nipples, one after the other. She inhaled as his teeth nipped a stiff peak, his tongue soothing the tip, then whispered, "Especially since I intend to make you pay for every second of torture you're making me endure."

"If I ever set you free." He kissed her mouth, a soft, teasing kiss. "You never finished telling me what kissing me makes you feel." His lips trailed over her jaw, her neck. "Tell me now."

"Kissing you," she whispered, "makes the headaches go away."

He stilled with his mouth by her ear, lifting his head to stare at her. "What?"

She shook her head. "Touching you... stops the flashbacks. It—you—make them go away."

He released her wrists, dragging his hand down her arm, cradling her cheek. "I'm not—"

"I know. You're not doing it on purpose," she said. "I know you're not causing the headaches or taking them away." She tried to laugh, but it sounded strained. "I guess you could say I'm using you. I hope you don't mind?"

They stared at one another, the air around them, between them... shifting, hanging, intensifying. He knew her admission had come with a price, and that price had been trust. She'd just told him he had power over her beyond simple sex and attraction. Emotion welled in his chest at the realization, tightening his body, even as something unfamiliar expanded within him. Again, he had the sense of this woman belonging here with him, in his bed, under him, or on top him, or wherever she damn well wanted to be—but with him.

"Damion," she whispered, at the same moment he said, "Use me all you want."

He slanted his mouth over hers, his tongue stroking hers, caressing. He'd wanted women before, but never like this, never so completely—never with the sense of urgency that he did with Lara. Maybe it was knowing that he alone had eased her pain. Maybe that had created a bond. Or maybe it was the trust factor. Or maybe it was simply just the two of them together.

She sighed into his mouth, her fingers finding his neck, his hair. He trailed his lips over her jaw to her ear. "Do you have any idea how badly I want to be inside you?"

"Not as badly as I want you there, or you'd already be there."

He might have smiled at the witty remark that he was fast realizing was her way, but the words, the challenge, had his cock throbbing, pulsing. "I don't want to keep the lady waiting," he murmured, holding his weight on one elbow, his lips close to hers, his hand reaching between them to wrap around the thick width of his erection. He slid himself down the wet heat of her, back and forth.

"Then why are you?" she said, digging into his biceps.

He watched her face as he entered her, sliding inside her slowly, despite the near desperate need to thrust deep and bury himself in the farthest depths of her. Still, another part of him wanted to watch her face, to savor the moment, the pleasure. Slowly, inch by inch, he slid deeper inside the tight core of her, the wet wonder of her body drawing him in, until he was buried to the hilt.

"Is this what you wanted?" he asked, settling his elbows on the bed beside her head.

"Yes." She breathed out the word in a sigh and then taunted him. "But I thought you'd move or something."

He laughed, the sound tight with barely contained desire. He pulled back and thrust into her. "Like that?"

"A decent start," she said, her fingers curling into his backside, pulling him deeper. "But is that all you have?"

"You want more?"

"More," she agreed, wrapping her legs around his hips. "Much more."

It was a demand. She was panting, the feel of Damion inside her, filling her with heat and need, and she was holding nothing back. There were no inhibitions, not even a memory of past sexual experiences to guide her. There was an innate understanding of her own sexuality, of her comfort in it with this man, on the most intimate of levels. "More!" She arched against him, trying to pull him inside her, trying to take all of him when he refused to give it to her. He thrust deeply. Teasing mercilessly, he slid back slowly, until the tip of his erection was all that remained. Her hips lifted, chasing him. "You're killing me, and you damn well know it."

"Killing you softly," he promised, suckling her nipple and letting his next thrust tug deliciously against it.

"Killing me is better than torturing me," she assured him a moment before his hands slid under her backside, lifting her, as he pumped into her, harder and faster.

"How's that?" he questioned in a passion-etched voice that bordered on primal. Oh, and she liked primal, she liked over-the-edge—it's where she wanted to be, where she wanted him to be with her.

"Harder," she ordered. "Faster."

He lifted her legs to his shoulders, thrusting into her, watching her with a heavy-lidded stare. "More?"

"Yes. More."

His face tightened, his body flexing as he held her, as he moved in a fast, hard rhythm—deliciously male, deliciously hot.

"Yes." She wasn't sure how many more times she repeated "yes." The world faded into a cloud of sensation until she couldn't breathe, until every nerve ending she owned seemed to still and then exploded in an erotic rainbow of pleasure. Her body spasmed around the thick width of his cock, and he moaned—a sexy male sound that radiated through her—an intimate caress that intensified her release. Another stroke, another thrust, and his hands tightened on her legs as he shook and shattered. The wet warm heat of his release spilled inside her, before he settled her legs down and collapsed onto his elbows, over the top of her. For long seconds they lay there, their bodies intimately entwined.

Lara's chest tightened with a fist of emotion. Damion felt… right. He felt right—like someone she could care about, someone she already cared about. Yet he was someone who could be her enemy, someone who could be manipulating her.

She rejected the idea, the possibility, the reality of the truth—whatever it might be. She didn't want to think about it now. She wanted him, rejected the flashes of images, the pain in her head. "Just to be clear," she said, running her hands down his powerful back. "I'm not done yet. You better not be."

He leaned back to stare down at her, his hazel eyes shimmering with new desire, his strong jaw and high cheekbones sexy. He looked good enough to eat, and he felt good enough to drive her wild all over again. Yes. She wanted this man. She wanted to pretend that was all that mattered, all there was.

"You're supposed to be sleeping," he objected, but she could feel him thickening inside her, feel him growing aroused. "Doctor's orders."

"Because sleep was supposed to heal me," she countered. "I told you. You're a much better drug. The way I see it, the longer we keep at this, the less pain I feel, the more healing I do. I mean—you're GTECH. Doesn't that mean your endurance is superhuman?"

He smiled. "You're GTECH too, which you seem to keep forgetting."

"I'm not forgetting now," she said. "I have plenty of endurance." It was a challenge.

He rolled to his back, still inside her, and she sucked in a breath as a small tingling sensation started at the back of her neck, along her scalp. No. No. No. Damion was supposed to keep the pain, the images at bay. She grabbed his hands, pressed them to her breasts, and then bent down and kissed him. The sensation slipped away into passion, just as she'd willed it to.

***

Hours later, dressed in one of Damion's T-shirts, with him by her side in jockey boxers, Lara sat on top of the white down comforter of his king-sized bed and finished off a bowl of cereal. "I thought being GTECH meant I never had to diet again. Instead, it means refuel often or crash and burn."

Damion finished off a bite of cereal. "Exactly why I carry high-calorie supplements with me everywhere I go." Damion set his bowl aside and held up the box of cereal. "Still a little left if you want it?"

She shook her head. "I'm done." He took her bowl from her and disposed of it on the black and glass nightstand then leaned against the black wooden headboard, his long powerful legs stretched out before him, his back and shoulders rippling with the action.

Forget the cereal. She wanted to gobble him up. She sighed and dropped to her back, curling her toes in the soft blanket, her hand pressed to her overly full stomach. "It's been forever since I've had a bowl of Frosted Flakes. I forgot how much I love them."

"How long?" Damion asked. She stilled with the seemingly innocent question that wasn't innocent at all. It was the first bit of personal information he'd asked of her outside of what was directly related to her pleasure. He wanted to know who she was, and she didn't blame him. So did she. She wanted to answer him, but as she reached for the knowledge, she came up blank, an empty hollow in her mind, making a bigger one in her chest.

"How long have you been in the army?" she asked, changing the subject in what she'd intended as a smooth transition, which was more a train wreck of obvious avoidance.

"I went in when I was twenty," he said, showing no indication he'd noticed the dodgeball she'd thrown him. "I left when the army didn't differentiate between those GTECHs who tried to protect Area 51 and those who took it over. They wanted us all locked up until they could find a way to control us—thus the Renegades became the Renegades. We work with the army, but with due precautions. We as GTECHs—all of us, you included—are like commodities. We're weapons. Can you imagine what could happen if someone completely controlled an army of GTECHs, and that person wanted to use us for the wrong reasons?"

A chill ran down her spine. "Yes, and I don't want to." Even now, she thought of the order to kill the Russian, which had been wrong. What if they'd had some method of forcing her to do anything they wanted? Did they?

Was that why she was having the headaches? Because she'd disobeyed an order?

"How about you?" Damion asked. "Were you—are you—in the army?"

Powell was a general, but she'd never thought of Serenity as being part of the army. Maybe she should have? Maybe she should have thought of a lot of things. "*I don't know*. There is just the day my parents died and after. I don't remember my last bowl of Frosted Flakes, or Ben and Jerry's Chocolate Fudge Brownie ice cream, but I know I love it. I don't remember ever having sex before today, or ever being in love. But I know I've loved and lost." Her throat tightened, and her voice with it. "And I know I feel like I can trust you, Damion, or none of this would have happened tonight. So if you're manipulating me, if you're—"

"I'm not," he said, scooting down on the bed and pulling her to him, so they were side by side, facing one another. "I'm not manipulating you. If a Renegade killed your family, if a Renegade purposely took an innocent life, then they aren't welcome here. They're traitors. I swear it, Lara."

She buried her face in his chest, inhaling his scent, warm and masculine, and somehow familiar beyond their short attachment. Trusting Damion meant betraying Powell—it meant believing Powell was a liar, a manipulator—the man who she'd believed had saved her life, given her a reason to keep living.

Damion shifted to his back and snuggled her close to him, her head on his shoulder and her hand on his chest. "Rest and get well, and we'll figure it all out when you wake up."

Beneath her palm, his skin was warm, his heartbeat strong. Two days ago her life had been about justice and vengeance, two simple driving forces that had given her a reason to wake up. Now—now it was about truth. She told herself to search her mind, to find the answers, but her mind wrapped around the rhythmic thrum of his heartbeat, and she drifted off to sleep.

———

An uninjured GTECH didn't need more than a few hours of sleep every few days, and as much as Damion enjoyed sleeping with Lara, he was also concerned about her safety, and the many unknowns between them. He was awake in two hours, holding Lara, and staring at the ceiling, listening to her even breathing while his mind raced. By the time another hour had passed, it was already seven o'clock, and he was showered, dressed in black fatigue pants, boots, and a black T-shirt, sitting at his kitchen table, with his laptop in high gear, resisting the urge to call Kelly before eight. She was human and needed sleep. So he occupied himself doing a search for "Skywalker" and coming up dry. It was clear. He was going to have to get Sterling to put his magic fingers to work, as well as turn up the heat and hack the government's computers.

The instant the clock hit eight, he dialed Kelly. By eight-fifteen, Kelly was at his door with coffee in hand, her light brown hair neatly styled, wearing a navy blue pantsuit that would soon be covered with a lab coat. "How is she?"

"Fine for now." He stepped back into the hall to let her enter. "She's asleep." He followed Kelly to the kitchen table, where she sat down. Before joining her, Damion quickly and quietly pulled the bedroom door shut, so they wouldn't disturb Lara.

Kelly studied him a long moment when he didn't immediately speak. "Talk to me, Damion. What's wrong?"

"If she won't let us do a CT scan, then what?"

"She really doesn't trust us, does she?"

"I don't think she trusts herself at this point," he said. "How can she trust us?"

She nodded. "Well, who can blame her, really? I'd refuse the test too. Sleep is truly the best medicine for a GTECH. We might not have to do anything. The problem may solve itself. I don't think we have to push her about the CT scan. Not yet."

He considered that. "So when she wakes up, you think her memories might be restored?"

"I don't know, Damion," she said. "In theory, and in observed practice, every GTECH injury should heal with sleep. The question becomes—is this an injury? What if Adam, or even the government, found a way to put a control device in her brain that they thought her body couldn't destroy? The GTECH body adapts and learns to fight off any danger. So, what if her body is fighting to destroy a device?"

"Could sleep allow that to happen?"

"Maybe," she said. "If she's still having issues when she wakes up, you have to convince her to let me do the CT scan. If there is a foreign object, it might need to be removed. I need to stress that I'm speculating— making educated guesses based on my knowledge of the GTECH body and the limited symptoms described. Not only do I not have physical evidence, I am dealing with

the first female GTECH, and that's unknown territory."
She tilted her chin down, surveying him. "What aren't
you asking me that you want to ask?"

"I'm that obvious, am I?"

"You're fairly obvious."

"She said that when she touches me, the headaches
go away."

"Huh," Kelly said, spinning her coffee around and
around, as if it helped her think, before her gaze cut to
his. "When Adam used his son to attack Becca's mind,
Sterling was able to help protect her, even before they'd
completed their Lifebond. When Michael and Cassandra
refused to complete their bond, her body tried to do it
for her."

She was saying Lara was his Lifebond. He hadn't
checked for the Lifebond mark after they had sex. He'd
been afraid to—in denial, even. What if they were
bonded? And they really were enemies? What if she
woke up and hated him all over again? What if she was
manipulating him to destroy the Renegades?

Suddenly, he realized Kelly was standing up. "I'm
going to send Emma with some vitamin C for Lara.
Inject her immediately and then in another eight hours,
if she is awake. And call me when she does."

He nodded. "Right. Okay."

She finished her coffee and set the paper cup on the
table. "I need to say this. I wasn't going to say it, but
I have to. I saw the sparks between the two of you.
Before you hop in bed with her, Damion, think about
the consequences. Being a Lifebond is simply a physical bond that's the evolution of human love. People
who love each other hurt each other all the time. In

fact, sometimes when things go south, it's those who love us who lash out harder than anyone else. She thinks we killed her family. Being linked to a man she believes is tied to that loss—well, that would be hard for any of us, me included, Damion. If you have, or somehow end up, sleeping with her, you need to remember that once you complete the blood exchange, you're bound to each other in life and death. Before that, you can be separated from her. You won't like it. You won't want anyone else, but you won't die if she dies. Find out the truth before you let the bond get the best of you. *Please*."

Damion had gone icy from head to toe, frozen with the words she'd spoken, with the reality behind them, the "consequences" as she'd called them. That he hadn't thought of this before was a testament to how deeply involved he was with Lara, and how quickly it had happened. "I hear what you're saying."

She stared at him several seconds and then nodded. "I have to tell Caleb about my suspicions."

"Of course," he said. "It's your duty. I'd expect nothing less of you." He pushed to his feet, the gentleman in him kicking into gear automatically. He walked her to the door, his features carefully schooled when he was screaming inside.

"Call me when she wakes up," Kelly instructed.

"I will." And as she started down the hall, he shut the door and let his forehead fall to the wooden surface. He'd slept with Lara. If they were bonded, she'd now be wearing the Lifebond mark, his mark, on her neck. Lifebonds couldn't camouflage their eye color from one another, but then Lara wasn't able to keep her eye color camouflaged right now at all. She probably wouldn't comment if she saw his eyes as GTECH black instead of their human color. She'd likely assume he wasn't bothering to camouflage them from her. She wouldn't know enough about Lifebonding to think twice about eye color. No. He would only know whether they'd bonded if he checked her neck. It was as easy as walking into the bedroom and finding out.

He shoved off the door and walked to the end of the hall, stopping at the bedroom door. He pushed it open to find her curled in the center of his bed, looking innocent and delicate—a contrast to the fiery lover and fierce challenger that she was in her waking hours. The idea of her being his Lifebond shook him to the core—the idea that he had not only slept with the enemy, but bonded with her, almost impossible to conceive. Worse though, was the idea of her *not* being his Lifebond—that the absence of his mark on her neck meant they were not connected—that shook him equally so.

Fingers curling into his palms, Damion fought the whirlwind of emotions that had no place in a soldier's life. He turned, walked to the kitchen table, and sat down, keying his computer out of the dormant mode. If he knew she was his Lifebond, it might—no—it would dictate his actions, cloud his judgment. He had to find the truth about Lara first.

Sabrina collapsed on top of Logan, panting and sated, from what had been a damn good ride. She scraped his neck with her teeth. "I suppose as a human you will need time to restart your engine." She sat up and sighed. "You look good tied to my bed though, so you hang out here until I'm ready for you again."

"Damn it, Sabrina," Logan hissed. "Untie me."

"Not for a very long time yet," she promised, raking her gaze over his body. "Not until I know how you plan to bring Lara back to us."

"You know I can't tell you," he said. "Powell will kill me."

"An unacceptable answer. I wouldn't have been left in the dark if you hadn't insisted I be left in the dark." If Lara was allowed to live, Sabrina would risk having her lies to Powell exposed. That couldn't happen.

"Jenna is very beautiful," Sabrina continued, having contemplated an arsenal of ways to make Logan talk. "So sweet and delicate." She walked to the closet and pulled out a flogger, smacking it against her hand. "I'm really going to enjoy this." She whirled on her heels and headed for the door, while Logan roared in response. So she'd been right. Logan and the little lab assistant were into each other.

"I'll tell you, damn it!"

She smiled and walked back to the bed, before climbing on top of him, the flogger still in her hand. "Tell me."

Chapter 17

ON SOME LEVEL LARA KNEW SHE WAS DREAMING, AND she knew inside the darkness she'd find answers, answers she desperately wanted. She pushed through the black hole of slumber and reached for truth, for answers, until a vision appeared.

"Hello, hello!" Lara called out, pushing open the door to Skywalker's beach house, the warm, summer night air following her inside. Skywalker. She knew him, she knew his name, and she knew this place. Yes, she knew it well. She'd leased a place up the beach several years before, taking on a full-time job at the shelter. This was still "home." This was where she'd found safety and love.

Lara set the plate of cookies in her hand on the hall table and kicked the door shut, setting down her purse and key, and then pausing to glance at the pictures on the wall. One of her with Skywalker, and one of his beautiful brunette wife and teen daughter, Susan, who'd both been killed by a "spook," a rogue CIA agent who Skywalker had been hunting for the agency. That was only a year before Lara had met Skywalker. She knew now that she'd reminded him of Susan that night by the Dumpster, that he'd felt then, and still did, that they were destined to cross paths—her to fill the void left by his lost daughter, him to be the father she'd lost. And he had. A darn good one too.

She could hear the evening news coming from the living room, and Lara started walking. Feeling particularly nostalgic for no real reason, her gaze snagged on another photo—this one of her walking across the college graduation stage several years before, thanks to Skywalker's support.

A smile touched her lips as she called out, "Ms. Smith wanted to thank you for teaching last night's self-defense class." She cut around the corner. "She baked you cookies, though I have a sneaking suspicion this is her way of flirting."

A big, fluffy, brown sofa framed by overstuffed, comfy chairs came into view, and Lara sighed as she found Skywalker had deserted his regular news program. She was talking to herself. "Upstairs," Lara murmured. No doubt surrounded by surveillance equipment for the new "top secret" contract job Skywalker was working on. The one he wasn't talking about, despite her incessant prodding, and her frequent aid with research on past jobs.

Urgency as unexplained as the nostalgia overtook Lara, and she reached for the handrail. So much so that she would have double-timed the steps, if not for the shiver of warning that chased down her spine. Lara stilled, her senses reaching out, exploring potential threats.

After Skywalker had insisted she train, and train hard to protect herself, both physically and mentally, the shiver wasn't a feeling she was quick to ignore. He'd pushed her, tested her often. And she'd let him, well aware of the fear she saw in him that she would end up in a grave beside his daughter. To date, she hadn't needed that training, but it spoke to her now.

Cautiously, she inched back down the hallway toward

the cookies, or rather, the shelf beneath those cookies. One of many places Skywalker stashed weapons in the house. Not to mention she'd left her phone in her purse by the door. Suddenly, Skywalker's shout blasted through the air. "Run, Lara!"

Adrenaline shot through her veins, and she reacted instantly, doing exactly as he said. She ran. To the cabinet, to grab a gun. She was trained to fight. She wasn't leaving Skywalker. She wasn't losing Skywalker.

She fumbled with the cabinet and yanked it open, securing the Beretta PX4. The sounds of a struggle pounded out against walls and floors somewhere on the upper level, and she took comfort in the cold steel beneath her palm. She whirled around ready to fly up those stairs, when the weapon was ripped from her hand. A woman stood there, dressed all in black, long red hair braided down her back.

"Nice to meet you, sweetheart," she said. "Name's Sabrina, and we're going to be real good friends, you and I." A smile lifted her lips. "Once Skywalker is out of the way."

Anger exploded inside Lara, and she attacked, calling on the training Skywalker had drilled into her the last ten years. Kick, block, kick—all sidestepped and dodged as if Lara were an amateur, batting at a fly. The next thing Lara knew, the woman seemed to move at the speed of light, shackling Lara's arm, jerking a big glob of her hair and holding on. Then Lara was being painfully forced in front of the other woman and up the stairs—pushed with the force of a steamroller.

Fiercely, Lara fought, to no avail. The woman was taller than Lara's five-foot-five by several inches and outweighed her 118 by a good ten pounds. But she was also stronger than she was big. Abnormally strong. Insanely strong. Inhumanly strong. A crazy thought, but one hard to shake as Lara struggled against the attacker shoving her up those stairs.

No matter how she moved or twisted, nothing worked. She'd gladly lose her hair if it meant freedom, but she wasn't getting away from this woman without losing her arm—not an option.

Approaching the landing, Lara kicked her foot backward and tripped the woman. Unfortunately, they both tumbled forward, with Lara on the bottom. And since she didn't have control of one of her arms, she smashed hard onto the wood floor.

Her attacker leaned close, near her ear. "We don't want to mess up your pretty face just yet, so behave." Lara's head was jerked back, as her attacker yanked her up by the hair at her scalp, lifting Lara to her feet and shoving her toward the surveillance room.

It was then that her heart stopped beating, then that she saw Skywalker facedown on the floor, unmoving. And then that she saw another woman, a blonde dressed in black like the redhead, standing above him. The Beretta flew through the air, and everything went into slow motion.

"Kill him," the redhead ordered.

Lara screamed as the blonde caught the weapon, aimed at Skywalker, and fired. A second later, a sharp pain pierced her skull, and Lara went black.

Lara was jerked out of slumber with a gasp and the image of a gun held to Skywalker's head. Her gaze ripped around the room without truly seeing it, her fingers curling into a soft blanket. She was in bed. She squeezed her eyes shut, but the image of Skywalker's death was still vividly clear, and she tried to picture his killer—tried and failed. What had been clear moments before slithered back into her mind like a lethal snake waiting for its next attack.

Abruptly, the door to the room burst open, startling Lara's wide eyes, and Damion rushed toward her. "What's wrong? What happened? Are you in pain?"

Memories flooded her at the sight of him, the welcome thoughts of the two of them touching, kissing, pleasing each other, overriding those of Skywalker's last few seconds on earth—Skywalker, who had been someone special to her, a father figure. Yes. He'd been a father figure. She knew this deep in her soul, knew it in a way that defied the lack of memory, the lack of knowledge of the past.

"I'm fine," she assured him, not sure if that was true, not sure if she was ready to even talk about what she'd just seen. "I had a nightmare. That's all." Her gaze swept Damion, noting his faded jeans and a Super Bowl T-shirt. Clearly he'd been awake for a while, while she was still wearing just his shirt from the night before.

"That must have been one heck of a nightmare," he said, sitting down next to her, "because I don't think I've ever heard a scream like that."

"I screamed?"

"Like a banshee."

The screaming she now remembered from her nightmare must have been her own. "Sorry about that."

"Is she okay?" a male voice asked from the door. "I called Kelly."

Lara's gaze jerked to the doorway, where a man with blond spiky hair lurked.

"She had a nightmare," Damion called out over his shoulder. "Tell Kelly she's fine."

"Will do," he said, and gave Lara a quick, two-finger salute. "Scream again if you need anything." He shut the door.

"Is everyone around here a smart-ass?" Lara asked.

Damion chuckled, low and sexy, sending a tingle down her spine. She was way too attracted to this man for her own good. "Sterling and Chale excel, so the rest of us don't have to," he said. "Sterling's been helping me dig up information on Skywalker for you for the last couple of days."

"Couple of days?" she asked incredulously. "Please tell me I haven't been asleep for a couple of days?" No wonder he was clean-shaven and fully dressed.

"Okay, I won't tell you," he agreed.

"I was asleep two days?"

"Three."

"Three days! GTECHs don't sleep three days in three months!"

"Clearly you needed the rest to heal. How do you feel?"

Her stomach growled as if in reply.

He arched a brow. "Hungry, I assume?"

"Absolutely starving."

"Food I can handle," he said. "But what about your headache?"

"You know," she said, surprised. "I think it's gone.

Yes." She reached for her memories, for the faces of her parents, and there was nothing.

"You still don't have your memories back."

Her stomach clenched, and she shook her head. "No."

"Maybe once you're up and moving around, that will change."

She nodded. "I hope so."

He ran his hands down his legs. "I grabbed some clean fatigues for you, to get you by until we can get you some real clothes." He motioned to a door on her left. "They're in the bathroom, along with a bag of 'female necessities' that Sterling's Lifebond, Becca, put together for you. I didn't ask what that meant." He stood up. "I'll get you some orange juice and throw together some food."

She tilted her head to study him. There was a subtle tension that had replaced his concern of moments before. She yearned to make it go away, to cling to a little more of their fantasy of being friends and lovers. "Thanks, Damion. You're pretty okay—*for a GTECH*."

He didn't smile as she'd hoped. In fact, for several eternal seconds, he didn't move, let alone speak. Then finally, "You're pretty okay too. For a GTECH." He started for the door.

Lara stared after him, watching the lethal grace, the powerful lines of his body. She'd wondered what the morning after would be like with Damion. Now she knew. The morning after, he was more alluring and more dangerous than she'd ever imagined possible. Okay, so in this case, it was three mornings after—how had she slept that long?

Lara threw off the covers, a sudden urgency to get

dressed and gain some sense of her legs beneath her, to return to the safety of logic. Her attraction to him was a vulnerability she couldn't seem to fight. She needed to find out if she really could trust Damion, rather than hoping she could, gambling she could. That meant getting out from behind the bedroom door and investigating. She headed for the shower, and already her brain was starting to function more efficiently. The stream of hot water set her mind to racing, soothing her into a contemplative state.

Damion had claimed that the Renegades worked with the government. Powell had claimed *to be* the government, who he'd declared was an enemy of the Renegades. So either Powell was lying, or the government was feigning an allegiance with the Renegades. Or the other possibility, the one she should assume, but found herself struggling to accept, was that Damion was the one who was lying.

She was just about to turn off the water when a tingling sensation—not painful, but insistent—touched the nape of her neck. Frowning, she rubbed it, praying it wasn't a sign her headaches were coming back. The sensation intensified about the time a double-knock sounded on the door, a second before it creaked open.

"I brought you orange juice," Damion said. "Doctor's orders."

The sensation on her neck slid away, and with a smile on her lips, she peeked through a hole she opened in the shower curtain. "I never thought I'd see the day that I had a Renegade bringing me orange juice in the shower."

He handed her the orange juice. "Drink."

She did as he said, feeling weak from three days without food, and then handed him back the empty glass.

"Finally you took an order from me," he said approvingly.

She laughed. "Must be that voodoo of yours." A shiver slid over her skin. "My water is cold."

"You've been in there forever," he said, as she slipped behind the curtain and turned off the shower spray. "I was beginning to get worried."

"You should see how long I can stay in a bathtub." The statement froze in her throat. She liked hot bubble baths, so why couldn't she remember ever taking one? Another shiver slid down her spine, and she shoved aside the thought for a new concern. The idea of stepping out of the shower in all her chilled, naked glory was unnerving. Not because she was shy. The man had seen her body. This was about desire and willpower. She wanted Damion in a bad way, like she'd never wanted a man in her life. She didn't need memories to know that. She knew it with blind certainty, felt it to her core, which only made that vulnerable thing he did to her, all the more true, and him, all the more powerful.

"You coming out of there?" he asked.

She inhaled, steeled herself for the impact of his gaze, and pulled the curtain back. Damion held a large towel open and wrapped it, and his arms, around her. Their eyes locked and held. The attraction between them darn near sent the towel into flames.

"You're way too dangerous when you're naked," he said, his arms still around her, along with the towel. "You steal every bit of objectivity I own, and I swore I wouldn't let that happen again."

"Back at ya," she agreed softly, blinking away the water that clung to her lashes. "You naked... way... too... dangerous."

"So why do I want to drop this towel and get naked with you all over again?"

"The same reason I want you to." She sounded breathless. She felt breathless.

His lips lowered, lingered close to hers, teasing her with the promise of their touch. "And what reason would that be, Lara?"

"Yo, Damion!" came a male shout from the living room.

Damion's forehead settled against hers. "Sterling."

"Yo, Damion."

"And Chale," he added. "The two of them are the very definitions of perfect timing."

She inhaled on a sudden tightening in her chest, as their pretend world came crumbling down around them, or at least, around her. There was not one, not two, but three Renegades in this small apartment with her. Powell would say she was in enemy territory, and maybe she was. It was well past due that she proved him right or wrong, and before her attraction to Damion led her into trouble. "I should get dressed."

"Yeah," he said. "You should get dressed." And then he kissed her. A long, deep slide of his tongue against hers. "Just so you know. No matter how bad it might make my judgment, if Curly and Moe hadn't shown up, I would have licked off every drop of water on you and then done it all over again." He released her then, exiting the bathroom while she stood willing him back, thankful she didn't possess such a power. She so would have enjoyed him licking the water off her. Who was she fooling? There was no avoiding trouble where Damion was concerned. She was already there, in too deep, and ready to swim right back into his arms.

———∿∿∿———

Damion and Sterling were sitting at the kitchen table with laptops in front of them when Lara exited the bedroom. Damion's gut clenched at the sight she made, her long, dark hair sleek and silky around her face and shoulders, her lips lightly painted pale pink. The contrast to the rugged fatigue pants and T-shirt she wore, downright sexy. Then again, Damion was pretty much of the opinion that Lara could wear a paper bag and he'd think she was sexy.

"There she is," Chale said, exiting the kitchen with a spatula in hand. "Food's almost done."

Lara stood there, staring at Chale with a stunned look on her face, as if she couldn't believe Chale was cooking—that a Renegade was cooking for her. This was exactly why he had Sterling and Chale here now. To show Lara that the Renegades weren't the monsters she'd believed them to be.

Chale grimaced at Lara. "Don't look so petrified. I'm a damn good cook." He grinned. "I've never poisoned anyone." He cut a look at Damion. "And don't bring up the egg incident, or we're going to have trouble." He disappeared into the kitchen again.

Lara's eyes widened on Damion. "Egg incident?"

"He forgot to check the expiration date," Damion explained. "Tasted like, well, rotten eggs."

"Oh yum," she said sarcastically.

"Come sit," Damion said. "We won't bite." He

smiled. "Even if you do." Of course, he'd found other, interesting uses for his teeth during their little bedroom extravaganza.

Her eyes narrowed on his, lighting with the smallest hint of mischief. "We both know *that's* not true," she said, closing the distance between them to sit down at the table, across from Sterling and beside Damion.

Sterling snorted. "I know an innuendo when I hear one."

Damion motioned to Sterling. "I'm sure you've gathered by now, this is Sterling. King of smart asses."

"And expert hacker," Sterling added.

"Second best to me," Damion agreed.

"In your dreams," Sterling assured him, and then nodded to Lara. "Now you know our interrogation and torture methods. We seal you in a room with Damion and force you to endure his fantasies of grandeur."

"Breakfast for dinner, considering the 6:00 p.m. hour," Chale said, walking from the kitchen and setting a plate in front of Lara. "Cheese omelet and blueberry muffins." He cut Damion a hard look. "And yes, I checked the expiration date."

Lara looked down at the Texas-sized omelet and said, "Coercion by way of food?" She glanced at Chale. "And seriously? You made blueberry muffins?"

"What's wrong with blueberry muffins?" Chale asked.

"I like blueberry muffins," she assured him. "I just can't imagine you making them."

"He's a Harley-riding, blueberry-muffin-making contradiction," Damion concluded. "We don't try to understand him. We just eat the food." He glanced at Chale. "Where's my plate?"

"And mine?" Sterling agreed.

Chale's brows dipped to a grumpy line. "Get your asses up, and go get them."

Sterling reached over the table and took one of Lara's muffins. "Lara wants another muffin."

Damion stole one himself. "Make that two."

Chale grumbled and headed to the kitchen. Lara laughed, soft and sexy, the tension he'd sensed when she'd exited the bedroom quickly fading. The next thing he knew, they were all eating, arguing about who was the best quarterback of all time. Lara knew football—knew it well—and seemed to be a fan of the Dallas Cowboys.

"You know a lot about football for a chick," Sterling commented, after Chale headed for the door, claiming he had a "hot date."

"Yes, I…" Lara paled suddenly. "I know football, but I can't remember my last name, which has become a multiple choice equation."

A knock sounded at the door, and Sterling pushed to his feet. "I'll get it."

"Lara," Damion said softly, ready to talk her into the CT scan, when the two familiar female voices of Cassandra, Michael's Lifebond, and Becca, Sterling's Lifebond, touched his ears. "No, Becca."

The pretty brunette, who wore a pink, slim-fitted dress, threw her hands up in the air. "Full disclosure." Her attention went to Lara. "Lara. I'm Becca, Sterling's Lifebond, and if I touch you I will be able to see your past experiences. So I won't touch you unless you ask me to." Her gaze slid to Damion's. "And you should know me better than to think I would do anything sneaky."

Sterling wrapped his arm around her shoulders. "Yeah man. Chill already."

"Hey, Damion," Cassandra said, rushing into the room, her long blonde hair floating behind her. She looked casual and friendly in faded jeans and a T-shirt, until she turned, and he saw the "girls rule" logo—that told him he had absolutely no control over anything that was about to happen.

Cassandra offered her hand to Lara. "I'm Michael's Lifebond, and the only special ability I have is taming the beast otherwise known as Michael."

Lara stared at her a moment and then broke into a smile. "I've met him," she said, accepting Cassandra's hand. "That's definitely a talent."

Damion sank down into the chair again. "Welcome to Sunrise City," he said to her, in a sigh of defeat. "Where the women rule and the men just try and survive."

Cassandra grinned and sat down. "And don't forget it buddy." Then to Lara, "And welcome is the point, by the way. Me and Becca want to steal you away for a girls' night out—a little shopping and pampering. It's a way for you to get to know us here." Her eyes lit. "Oh. I didn't even tell you my name, did I? Cassandra. Cassandra Powell."

Damion felt the tension ripple through Lara at the name Powell, and his gaze locked with Cassandra's. She'd noticed Lara's reaction as well.

Everything became crystal clear. Adam hadn't converted Lara to GTECH. General Powell had, and if anyone could understand and explain, how easily that man manipulated and hurt other people, it was his own daughter. A little "girl time" was exactly what Lara needed right now.

Chapter 18

Several hours after leaving Damion behind in his quarters, Lara was still reeling with the knowledge that Cassandra was Powell's daughter, made more difficult to digest by the dull headache she was pretending not to have. Thankfully, the opportunity to sit had presented itself, and Lara found herself at a wooden table with Cassandra and Becca, in a quaint little coffee shop lined with shelves full of books and mugs. She even had a caramel latte in hand, and the bags by her feet held a variety of clothes and products that the two women had insisted she buy. Though Lara barely remembered what was in the bags, with her thoughts torn between her growing attachment to Damion, and the bombshell about Powell.

Lara glanced out the shop's window, feeling as if she'd entered an alternate universe where an underground military base had transformed into a town, with brick sidewalks framing stores and restaurants. This wasn't the world of vicious killers and monsters, as Powell had painted the Renegades.

"How long have you both been with the Renegades?" Lara asked, now that they had time to talk about something other than her wardrobe.

"A couple of months for me," Becca said, brushing dark hair from her eyes and resting her chin on her fist. "But it feels like a lifetime, so much has changed so fast.

One day, I was an astrobiologist with NASA and dying of terminal cancer. The next, Adam had kidnapped me, injected me with a synthetic form of the GTECH serum he'd created with his son's DNA, and told me my cancer was cured."

"Adam cured your cancer?" Lara asked, gaping.

"Right. Then told me the drug that cured my cancer was going to kill me if I didn't find an antidote. He'd wanted to create a worldwide addiction to a drug that only he could supply. He's a real charmer."

"Oh my God," Lara whispered. "Just—oh my God."

"It turned out okay," she said. "That's what counts. I found Sterling, and I got some pretty nifty abilities from it all." Becca looked down at the table and a container of sugar started to shake. Lara's eyes went wide, and her gaze jerked to Becca, who grinned. "Like I said—pretty nifty, yes? I have this little knack for putting a GTECH to sleep too—I think it, and they take a nap. It makes me a great tool for battle, but Sterling never wants to let me get involved. I'm working on that though."

"Unbelievable," Lara whispered. "They just fall asleep?"

"Drop like rocks," Becca said, smiling. "Too bad it won't work on Sterling. I could really make that work for me if it did."

Lara smiled. "I'll bet. Do you read minds too?"

"Memories and events," she said, matter-of-factly, like the gift wasn't amazing. "I liken it to replaying a DVD."

"That's just amazing," Lara said. "I can't imagine having such abilities."

"If you think Becca's amazing," Cassandra said. "You should see what Adam's son, Dorian, can do.

Thankfully, he's here at Sunrise City now, because that man is crazy powerful."

"Man?" Lara asked. "Isn't he a boy?"

"Ah no," Becca said. "He ages a year every few months. Which is why we have to bring down Adam's operation before he can have another child, or worse, before he figures out how to force Lifebonding so others in his operation can have children. Thankfully, right now, those who Lifebond are only those who fall in love. Judging from the number of online dating services these days, there's a lot of trying to fall in love, and not a lot of actually doing it. Considering Adam's version of Match.com is throwing people into a sex camp to see if they're destined for love by way of forced sex, success isn't likely. Who falls in love under such circumstances? And even if the Lifebond match occurs, thus far the ability to procreate is limited to one week per year. It's a really small window. For those of us not ready for kids, it at least makes for easy birth control."

"So the couple has to be in love to Lifebond?" Lara asked, hoping her interest didn't seem overly obvious.

"Well," Cassandra said, sipping her white mocha. "All of this GTECH stuff is really unknown territory." She snorted. "GTECH stuff. I sound so scholarly, don't I? You'd never know I was educated, now would you?"

Educated. School. College. Lara's stomach knotted. She didn't know if she'd been to college. She remembered Damion asking if she'd been in the army and not knowing the answer to that either. "Anyway," Cassandra continued, "from what we know—and this is fairly proven through the Lifebonds already in existence, and through laboratory testing—the Lifebond connection is basically the same as when two humans meet and fall in love. That couple has chemistry from the beginning, and love evolves. Lifebonds have that same chemistry, but our bodies seem to know, even if our hearts and our minds don't yet, thus why the Lifebond mark appears on the female's neck right after the first sexual encounter. We think the Lifebonding and human love connections are so related that it's spurred new studies relating to human attraction and fertility. In fact, it's opened the door to the question of just how interwoven the GTECH race might be in our human ancestry. Interesting stuff really, but it's all so far from answered. It's really just a bunch of question marks."

From the moment Cassandra mentioned the Lifebond mark appearing after the first sexual encounter, Lara had only been half listening. It was all Lara could do not to reach up to her neck and run her fingers across it. Lifebonding was a part of falling in love. *Love*. Was that what was happening to her with Damion? There was no denying that she felt things for him that defied circumstances and reason. Surely fate wouldn't bond two people destined to be enemies?

"So," Lara asked. "There is no real choice of who you Lifebond with then? Your body just decides for you?"

"If you're in love, you're in love," Becca said, sliding a lock of brown hair behind her ear. "It never felt to me like my body decided for me, even in the extreme medical condition I was in. I loved Sterling. I knew I loved him. If I didn't, I just wouldn't stay with him. You won't die because you're apart or anything like that."

"That's not completely true," Cassandra said. "Once

you do a blood bond, if one dies, the other will die. We know that for a fact now. We've proven it in the lab."

"But you and Michael were apart for years even after you Lifebonded, though you hadn't done the blood exchange," Becca reminded her. "You were fine without each other."

"I wasn't okay without Michael," Cassandra said. "I didn't want any other man. I didn't feel like myself. As cheesy as this might sound, I was incomplete without Michael in a way I can't begin to explain. The instant we were back together, my body tried to complete the process. Lab work showed that every time we had sex, I became more GTECH. So sex seems to fill in for the blood bond. Since sex seems impossible to resist when Lifebonds are near each other, distance seems to be the only way to prevent the life-and-death bond."

"So sex will complete the bond?"

"Not immediately," Cassandra said. "Time was a factor for me and Michael. We'd been Lifebonded for years without a blood exchange." She grinned. "And let me tell you—we had plenty of sex before our separation, and nothing happened. Eventually though, our bodies just said—this is it. You're bonding."

"The men have trouble with the life-and-death part," Becca said. "They don't want a bond that means every time they risk their lives, they risk our lives."

Lara glanced at Cassandra. "Is that why you and Michael separated?"

She shook her head. "No. When my father determined that the GTECHs with the X2 gene—like Michael—were volatile, he tried to lock them away. I was working at the Area 51 base as the psychologist, and my father knew I was in love with Michael, but still he not only included him on that list, he didn't tell me. Nor did he even try to find out if all X2s were dangerous. Michael has another gene that counteracts the X2. Anyway, Adam and the other X2s rose against my father. Caleb, good man that he is, led the X2 negatives against his brother and his followers, and tried to save the base. To make a long story short, Michael went undercover in the Zodius operation, trying to find the chemical weapons that Adam uses as a threat to stop potential attacks on Area 51. His Lifebond, Ava, was planning to use an experimental fertility drug on the women in the sex camps, a drug that had a high death rate. Michael helped them escape at the cost of his cover.

"Of course, nothing Michael or any of the Renegades do is ever enough to prove they are loyal to their country. My father wants them all destroyed, and he has done everything in his power to convince the government they should be."

Lara leaned back in her chair, the headache throbbing in her temples, while images of Skywalker being shot intruded on her consciousness, followed by another of herself in a jail cell, with Powell sitting across from her. When was she in a cell, and why was Powell there?

"Now the women he rescued call themselves the Wardens," Cassandra continued, pulling Lara back to the moment. "They monitor for high instances of female abductions, state by state, and then we send in a Renegade team when we feel we've found an area the Zodius are targeting."

"She fails to tell you," Becca said, "that she set up the program, and is now the 'Queen Warden,' as the girls jokingly call her."

Cassandra waved off the compliment. "Those women are the heroes, not me. Michael too, for saving them."

"You stood up to your father," Becca said, touching Cassandra's hand.

Lara liked these women, Cassandra in particular. There was something about her story that touched Lara on an almost personal level. "That was incredibly brave of you."

Lara's eyes met Cassandra's, and she saw the hurt there, the torment. Lara's stomach churned, and she had a horrible prickling feeling in her eyes, like she could cry—she didn't know exactly why. Only that she'd been prepared to kill as many Renegades as she could, thirsted for it like she did her next drink of water. Maybe she'd killed Renegades. Maybe she'd killed the friends and family of these women, of Sterling. How would she know? She didn't even know her own last name.

Cassandra cut her gaze to her cup and took a sip, and Lara had the sense that she was trying to regain her composure. When Cassandra set the cup down, she'd clearly checked her emotions, any signs of distress gone. "Would you like to see the Wardens Operations Center, Lara? Maybe meet a few of the Wardens themselves?"

Lara was stunned by the offer. "Aren't you afraid I'll tell Adam about the Wardens?"

"No," Cassandra said without hesitation. "I'm not afraid you're going to tell Adam anything."

There was a silent message to the words. Cassandra didn't believe Lara was working for Adam. Lara read it in the other woman's face and between the lines of the conversation here today. Deserved or not, Lara was being given the opportunity to see beyond Powell's version of the Renegades.

"Yes," Lara said. "I'd very much like to see the Wardens' operation." In fact, women fighting for women, standing against those who had wounded them, sounded like exactly the kind of cause that would call to Lara. She absolutely wanted to know more about the Wardens.

—⁓—

Once Lara had left for her shopping expedition with the women, Damion and Sterling went in search of Caleb. When they discovered he was spending quality time with his scary, freak-of-nature nephew, who, at one year old, was physically a man in his twenties, Sterling had taken off. Which was understandable, since Dorian had tried to kill Becca several months before.

Damion found Caleb, Dorian, and Michael watching *Star Wars* in Caleb's living room—a black and silver clone of his own room. The group sat around the now muted television, Damion and Caleb on the couch, Dorian, in a leather chair. Michael was standing, acting as a bodyguard to Caleb, watching the kid like he was a science project gone bad, which seemed more accurate than not: Dorian's hair, long and white blond, was tied at his nape—it had been midnight black only days before. No one but Caleb believed Dorian could become a trusted Renegade, but Caleb was determined to prove them all wrong.

Damion stared at the kid, hesitating to speak openly with Dorian present, despite the fact that the kid seemed uninterested and continued to stare at the screen as if he could still hear the muted soundtrack.

"You can speak in front of Dorian," Caleb said softly, drawing Damion's attention.

Damion tore his gaze away from the kid and gave a quick nod. "When Cassandra introduced herself as Cassandra Powell, Lara looked like she'd seen a ghost. She knew his name and knew it well."

"Damn," Michael cursed, scrubbing his jaw. "I'd hoped that man was long gone, never to be heard of again. If Powell is back, this is going to be pure torture for Cassandra."

"Knowing about Powell and *knowing* Powell are two different things," Caleb commented. "Let's not jump to conclusions." He glanced at Damion. "How close are you to earning her trust and getting her to talk?"

"Close," Damion said. "And right now, she's with Cassandra and Becca on the Strip. Cassandra noticed her reaction to Powell's name too."

"Well, you can bank on Cassandra making sure Lara knows what a monster her father is," Michael assured them. "On the other hand, you can also bank on Powell having painted us as absolute monsters. Whoever we're dealing with convinced her that we're the people who slaughtered her family. They even gave her memories of the brutal killings." He glanced at Damion. "She really needs to take that CT scan, even if you have to force her, man. I know you think I'm an asshole for suggesting that, but this time, I'm saying it for her own protection. If Powell or someone else has inserted some kind of device in her head, who knows what long-term effects it might have. God forbid that it might kill her."

Damion's gut clenched. "You're right. I hate that you're right, but you are."

"Not only is he right," Caleb said, "but time is critical. There is a massive difference between dealing with Adam and dealing with Powell. Adam wants me alive, so I can join him as a leader of a new world, and he wants me to bring my men with me. Powell, on the other hand, wants us all dead, because he can't control us."

"Bring the woman to me," Dorian said, fixing his swirling gray eyes on the room. "I will heal her and restore her memories."

"No," Michael and Damion said at the same moment.

Michael cut a sharp look at Caleb. "He is Adam's son. If we're wrong and this is Adam we're dealing with, not Powell, then Dorian could kill Lara to keep her from talking."

Dorian stared at Michael for several tense seconds before focusing on Damion. "If you do not wish me to save her, then you must save her yourself."

Damion went icy inside. "What does that mean?"

"Do the blood exchange, or she will die," Dorian said. He glanced at the television and back at Damion. "Did you know that Skywalker isn't his real name? It's Luke." And then he turned and focused on the movie.

Damion sat there, stunned into silence by this confirmation that Lara was his Lifebond, something he'd tried to avoid.

"How do you know that, Dorian?" Damion ground out between his teeth.

Dorian shrugged. "It's logical. You call someone Skywalker—it's a nickname for Luke."

"I'm not talking about Skywalker," Damion said. "I'm talking about Lara."

"Things come to me," Dorian said. "And no, before you ask, I don't have any more to tell you. I just know that without you doing the blood exchange with her, Lara will die." He turned back to the television, dismissing Damion and the problem, as if it were nothing but a mosquito he'd just swatted and killed.

Damion could feel both Caleb and Michael watching him, and he knew they both understood the silent message in Dorian's claim, the message that had Damion quaking from the inside out. Lara was Damion's Lifebond.

"I'll have Sterling look into any record of a 'Luke' in any of the government databases," Caleb said. "It sounds like you need to go deal with Lara."

Silence stretched heavily in the air, as Damion struggled with what he was feeling, what he was thinking, with the trust in Caleb's eyes, the confidence that Damion would do the right thing where Lara was concerned. For the first time since serving under Caleb as a Renegade, Damion wasn't sure he deserved that trust. He'd brought Lara here against orders. If she turned on them, he'd be responsible.

"I'll deal with Luke and Lara myself," Damion said finally.

Caleb gave him an assessing stare, but asked no questions. "Understood."

Damion inclined his head, and then walked toward the door and into the hallway. Michael followed him, and they stepped onto a moving sidewalk side by side.

"So she's your Lifebond," Michael said. "That explains a lot."

"Says Dorian," Damion amended. "And I don't trust Dorian and his motives any more than I trust Adam, no matter how much Caleb might."

"You're not wrong about her," Michael surprised him by saying.

"You can't know that."

"She's with Cassandra. If I didn't think you were right about her, do you really think I'd let that happen?"

Damion cut him a sideways look. "Don't trust me when it comes to Lara. *I* don't trust me when it comes to Lara. I'm not objective."

"You don't have to be," he said. "You know her. She's your Lifebond." He said the words as if they were not only proven fact, but some sort of profound answer to every question Damion might ask from that point onward.

As much as Damion wanted Michael to be right, he reminded himself he had to be objective about Lara. Anything that occurred as a result of her presence or involvement with the Renegades was his doing, his responsibility, which meant he needed to find out Lara's true identity, and he needed to find out now.

After traveling from the coffee shop to a separate operational wing of the city, Lara met several of the female Wardens, and now stood in a conference room where maps and sticky pins tracked abductions. "It's incredible what you're doing here," she told Cassandra and Becca. She discreetly pulled out a leather chair from around the long, rectangular table and sat down, trying to hide the growing pain in her head.

"It's not enough," Cassandra said, as she and Becca sat down as well. "Not when you think about what these women endure in those sex camps. We don't save them all, but it's better than doing nothing. For those women who are unable to leave here because the Trackers can find them, it gives them something to live for."

"Like me," Lara said softly. "The Trackers can find me as well." She was a prisoner here, no matter how she looked at it. If Lucian had always been able to track her, then she'd simply been on a leash that she hadn't known existed. Now, she was on another leash, because even if she could leave Sunrise and wanted to, she'd be hunted all too easily by too many potential enemies to count. Powell was no more what he'd seemed than the Renegades were the demons he'd painted them to be. He'd made her the Renegades' enemy, and she wasn't sure she could change that, no matter how much she might want to.

"You should have the ability to shield yourself," Becca said, drawing Lara back into the conversation. "It makes sense to me that you can't. But I'm not buy-ing the idea that because you're female you're incapable of such a skill. Both myself and Cassandra can shield ourselves from the Trackers."

Cassandra didn't look quite as convinced. "I couldn't until Michael and I completed our blood bond, and even then, it took me some time. You had unique abilities de-velop even before you Lifebonded, Becca." She looked thoughtfully at Lara. "Still, since you're GTECH, what-ever is causing your headaches could be interfering with your shielding ability."

Her voice softening, Cassandra continued, "Lara, listen. I know you don't know who to trust or what to believe. I even understand why. We're the good guys though. I really want to convince you of that." Becca held up a finger. "I have an idea."

The next thing Lara knew, she'd talked to an FBI agent in Nevada and an army sergeant named Ryker who knew Sterling well, both by way of Skype, and both well informed about the Renegades and the Wardens.

"So," Becca said. "Now do you believe us when we say we're the good guys?"

Lara nodded, emotion balled in her chest. "I do." Which made her one of the bad guys. What had Powell involved her in? What had Powell made her do that she might not even remember? And, oh God, what if the scenario was even worse? What if she was blaming Powell, when the truth was that she willingly, knowingly, without coercion, had done bad things—maybe even really bad things?

"So take the CT scan," Cassandra encouraged. "What if there's something planted in your brain that we need to surgically remove?"

Lara's gaze snapped to Cassandra. "Planted in my brain?" She shook her head. "The GTECH body destroys foreign objects."

"Typically, yes," Cassandra agreed, "but maybe my father came up with a way to prevent that from happening."

Her father. Cassandra had just said "her father," as if she was completely certain Lara was working for Powell. Lara wasn't sure how to respond. She wasn't ready to admit Powell was involved, because she wasn't sure what role she played in this nightmare. All she knew was that she had to know who she was, and what she'd done, before they did—*before Damion did.*

"I'll do the CT scan."

Chapter 19

AN HOUR AND A HALF AFTER HEADING TO THE SUNRISE Hospital, Lara had been poked, prodded, scanned, and thus far, given a perfect bill of health. As much as Lara would have liked to be happy about that news, it did nothing to give her back her memories, nor did it stop the flashes of images in her mind or the growing throb in her temples.

"A few more minutes," Cassandra said, sitting on the medical stool beside the leather hospital chair Lara currently occupied. A portable machine set between them, wires attached to the pads stuck to Lara's neck and forehead, to test her brain wave activity. So far, the test had been uneventful and painless, at least on her end. She couldn't see the monitor, and based on the tension she felt radiating off Cassandra, she was pretty sure she didn't want to.

Lara closed her eyes, willing the images into her mind, desperate for answers when that strange tingling sensation on the back of her neck started again. Lara opened her mouth to mention it to Cassandra, in case it affected the test readings, but before she could speak, Cassandra stood up. "One second. Michael is here. Let me tell him what's going on, and then we should be able to wrap this up."

Lara frowned. "How do you know he's here?"

"The Lifebond mark on my neck is like an early alert

system," she explained. "It tingles like crazy when he's nearby." She opened the door and stepped out into the hallway, leaving Lara gaping behind her with the implications of what she'd said.

Damion stepped inside the room and shut the door. Their eyes locked and held, and the room shrunk. There was something new in the air between them, or maybe she imagined it—maybe it was simply her knowledge of what the tingling on her neck might mean. Either way, big, broad, and lethal, he stole her breath and set her heart racing. The tingling faded to a warm caress across her entire body. Could this man be her Lifebond?

He sauntered toward her. "What happened to calling me if you needed to go to the hospital?"

"I was afraid you'd talk me out of it."

He grabbed the rolling stool Cassandra had just occupied and slid close. Lara remembered the cabin, remembered him doing the same then. She remembered every second with Damion, so why couldn't she remember the rest of her life?

"Seriously," he said, those hazel eyes of his probing hers, "what changed your mind about the testing?"

You. I don't want you to hate me. "It's that women's prerogative thing."

"Lara," he said softly.

"I'm tired of not knowing, but so far, this hasn't worked out how I'd hoped. There is no easy fix. My memories won't return with a snap of the fingers."

"I'm back," Cassandra said, entering the room. "Okay, Lara. We can unhook you now, and you can head out."

"What about the results?" Damion asked, rolling backward so Cassandra could get to the machine.

Cassandra didn't look up at his question, busying herself by pulling the pads from Lara's forehead. "Kelly and I are going to talk them over."

Lara knew avoidance when she witnessed it. Gently, she shackled Cassandra's wrist. "They aren't good, are they?"

Cassandra stopped what she was doing and turned so that she could speak to both of them. "Look. I don't want to jump to conclusions here. For a human, the results aren't good. In fact, they're downright unsustainable. But you aren't human, Lara. Sleep and time can do wonders for GTECHs, and since we didn't test you before the three-day snooze you took, we don't know if you are better or worse. So Kelly and I both agree that you should try to sleep another eight to twelve hours, and then let me re-run the test to see if there are any improvements."

"What exactly do you think was done to her?" Damion asked, taking the words right out of Lara's mouth. "What are we up against here?"

Cassandra pressed her hand to her forehead and then pressed her fists to her waist. "Okay. I wasn't going to talk about this until I did some more research, so let me preface this by saying it's pure speculation," Cassandra replied. "I did read a couple of studies on a sophisticated army brainwashing program when I was at Area 51. Which means my father had access to them as well. The end result of those tests wasn't good, which is why the techniques weren't used." She held up a hand. "But *those* studies were done on humans, not GTECHs."

"Brainwashing," Lara said, in stunned disbelief. "You think I was brainwashed?"

"Speculation," she said. "That's all this is. But yes. It seems logical and a way around the GTECH's ability to destroy any inserted object or device. However, the miracle of the GTECH body is that it evolves and adapts. My theory is that your mind is trying to heal itself and undo the artificial memories."

"Artificial memories," Lara murmured, staring at the ground. That was why she couldn't remember her family. They weren't real. But Skywalker was. Skywalker was real and he was dead. And Sabrina was responsible. Powell was too.

"You could easily heal from this, Lara, and even get your memory back," Cassandra continued. "We're gathering a scientific team to game-plan ways to stimulate the healing process under such unique circumstances."

Lara didn't look at Damion. She couldn't. She felt as if her heart had lodged in her throat. She pulled off two pads from her skin and sat up, somehow finding her voice. "Thank you for trying, Cassandra." She turned to face Damion, and she knew what she had to do. She knew that no matter what the consequences to her, she had to stop Powell from doing this to anyone else. She had to stop him from hurting the Renegades. "I need to talk to you."

Someone knocked on the door and it opened. "I'm supposed to get some blood from Lara," Emma said, appearing in the entryway.

"No blood," Lara said to Damion. "No more. I *need* to talk to you."

He glanced at Cassandra and Emma in a silent plea for privacy, and they quickly departed.

The instant the door shut, Lara started talking. "It's

Powell. I'm part of an all women's team of GTECHs called 'Serenity.' Counting me, there are—were—seven of us, but Powell was planning to grow our numbers. He said he was aligned with the government—that he *is* the government. That all GTECHs are the enemy. Lucian is Powell's personal bodyguard, and the only male GTECH I ever knew to exist in our operation. Sadly, considering I was taking orders from the man, I know little to nothing more about Powell and the operation. At least, not that I remember. We both know my memory isn't exactly golden at present. Bottom line here is that Sabrina and Lucian know I'm with the Renegades, and Powell will worry that I'm spilling his secrets, which is why I'm saying all of this now. Every second that passes gives him more time to escape before you can get to him."

"Where is it?"

"I'll take you to him."

"Not a chance in hell," he said, and before she could object, he added, "And no. It's not because I don't trust you. It's because I *care* about you. You heard Cassandra. You have to rest. You have to heal. When you're well, you can kick as much ass as you want, and I'll cheer you on. Powell isn't worth dying over. He's a smart man. The chances that he's still in the same location are next to zero. I'll send a team to scout. If they find anything, we'll decide what to do next."

Lara would have argued, but her head was spinning, images of Powell sitting across from her at a table in a jail cell flickering in and out of her mind's eye. "Mexico," she said, and then gave him exact longitude and latitude.

—⁓—

Thirty minutes after Lara had given Damion Powell's last location, Michael and a team of Renegades were planning to scout Powell's last known location under the cover of night. Easily reading Lara's unease after her confessions, Damion was now protectively ushering her back to his place where they could be alone.

Together they stepped onto the moving sidewalk leading to the soldiers' quarters, tension and unspoken words stretching between them, and it was all he could do not to reach for her. He could see the pain in her face, the tightness around her lips that told him she was suffering. He wanted to touch her, to use their bond to make it go away. He wanted to tell her he was in awe of her courage for doing what she'd just done, by giving them a shot at catching Powell. He could tell she was hanging on by a thread, either waiting to unload something she hadn't told him, or possibly, trying not to. Touching her before she felt more in control would be a mistake. He knew this. Maybe that was because they were Lifebonds, or maybe it was simply because they'd been through a lifetime of hell together already. They had that rare connection that friends and lovers felt, from the instant they'd connected, that allowed the Lifebond to exist in the first place.

When they finally stood in front of his room Damion keyed in the code. The instant the green light flashed on the panel, Lara pushed open the door and darted forward. Damion hesitated in the hallway, his body heating at the memory of her doing the exact same thing just a few nights before—remembering the naked, playful Lara who'd teased and pleased him for hours on end.

In pursuit, Damion entered the living room just in time to catch a glimpse of Lara cutting through the bedroom. He found her inside the bathroom, back to the mirror, holding a small compact and lifting her hair to see behind her. Damion stilled, catching a glimpse of what she was seeing in the reflection, of the etched circle with another circle inside it. The Lifebond mark. His mark, *their mark*. On some instinctive level, he'd known from the moment he'd first seen her by the pool—before they'd spoken, before they'd touched—that she was special, that this was where they were headed.

She let her hair fall to her shoulders, her hand dropping to her side, the compact crashing to the floor. "You already knew, didn't you?"

"I suspected." He forced himself to hold his ground, to give her a little more time, a little more space—no matter how much he wanted to touch her, to taste her, to hold the woman who he knew with certainty now to be his Lifebond.

"When? Why didn't you say something?" She held up a shaking hand to her face and dropped it. "It doesn't matter. We *can't* be Lifebonds. I can't stay here. I need a separate room. We have to stay away from each other. Cassandra said that when she and Michael—"

"You talked to Cassandra about this?"

"No." She cut a hand through the air. "She doesn't know about us. But she told me about her and Michael. They didn't have to do the blood exchange, Damion."

"They did a blood exchange." He took a step toward her.

"Stop!" she ordered. "Wait. Don't touch me. Listen to me, Damion. Please. The blood bond just speeds up the completion of the bonding. Cassandra started converting without it, just by being near Michael. I'm already GTECH. Surely it will be faster for us. You can't touch me. We can't even be near each other—"

Something dark and possessive stirred inside him. Anger, need, a burning. Damion pulled her close, turned her so that her back was against the wall, her body hugged by his. "Is it such a horrible thing to be bound to me, Lara? To a Renegade?"

"No," she rasped urgently. "Yes. No, damn it. It's not about you being a Renegade. It's about me—about me not knowing who I am, or what I've done, or to whom I've done it. We came together because we were enemies, destined to hate each other. We can't change that anymore than we can change whatever I've done in my past."

He kissed her, a passionate claiming that screamed of possession, of the first acknowledgement that she was his, and he was hers. "Do I taste like an enemy?" He kissed her again, his hand sliding over her waist, her hip. "Do I feel like an enemy?" He palmed her breast, wanting her naked, wanting to be inside her. "Do I *feel* like I hate you?"

"There's a fine line between hate and lust."

"That's love and hate," he corrected softly, before kissing her again. She shoved at his chest, trying to pull away, only to moan as his tongue found hers, stroking, caressing, demanding her response. He pressed his hand under her shirt, onto the warm, soft skin of her back, molding her closer, molding her breast with his palm.

"Stop," she panted, and then moaned again, arching into his touch, before tearing her mouth from his. "Damn it, Damion." Her fingers curled around his biceps. "What if I did something neither of us can live with? Something that will make me unwelcome here?" The desperation in her voice stilled him, and he pulled back to study her face.

"Is there something you aren't telling me?"

"No," she said quickly. "But that doesn't mean it didn't happen. What if I did things I can't remember? What if I killed one of your friends? People you care about?"

He ran his hand down her hair. "You didn't."

She grabbed his shirt and balled it in her hands. "Please listen to me. I beg you. You can't know what I did or didn't do. Powell told me the Renegades killed my family. No. It was more than mere words. He put memories in my head of the night they were killed. Until I met you, I *hated* the Renegades and lived for vengeance."

Tenderness filled him, and he ran his hand down her hair. "Lara, sweetheart. Whatever happened—happened. It's done and over with, and it can't be changed. You were brainwashed, and everyone here knows that. It only worked because you're brave, because there is an inherent part of your character that wanted to fight back for your family. It only worked because of who you are as a person. And that person happens to be amazing. I'm crazy about you." He picked her up.

"What are you doing?" she asked, holding onto his neck.

"Doctor's orders," he said. "I'm taking you to bed."

Logan entered his newly relocated lab office, tension rippling in his muscles. Opal was dead after suffering a sudden, unexplained seizure. She'd freaking *died*. She'd walked into his office and told him she wasn't feeling well and then just seized herself right to death. He and Jenna had tried everything to save her. Now she was lying in a lab room, waiting for him to explain why she was no more, when he finally got the courage to call Powell in Germany. This, after they'd lost their newest recruit during relocation, also to a seizure. He'd been certain that moving her during her Bar-1 assimilation had been responsible for the attack. Now though... now that Opal had experienced a similar fate, he was screwed.

He scrubbed his jaw, walked to the small fridge in the corner, grabbed a beer, and then put it back. This was a whiskey kind of night if he'd ever had one. Powell would kill him if Bar-1 failed. And then there was little Lara Martin. What if her trigger didn't work? What if she had a seizure and died before he was able to reprogram her and use her to destroy the Renegades?

He headed for his steel desk, sat down, pulled open the bottom left drawer, and removed the tequila inside. He was about to pour himself a shot, when a knock sounded on the door. Damn. He shoved the bottle back into the drawer. "Come in."

Jenna appeared in the doorway, looking delicate as a flower, too delicate and too beautiful to be mixed up in this hell of a war.

"Are you okay?" she asked.

Was he okay? He was thinking she was delicate, and she was asking him if he was okay. No, he was not okay. "I'm fine." He motioned her forward and lifted the bottle from his drawer. "Or I will be. Care to join me?" He set two shot glasses on the desk, next to the bottle.

She walked into the room, and her lab coat flashed open to give him a glimpse of a slender waist and a tapered black skirt. She had a body on her—a slender, curvy, hot body.

"Shut the door," he said. He wanted her. If he was going to die soon, he wanted a piece of this woman before he died.

She did as he asked and surprised him by walking around the desk to stand next to his chair. She leaned against the desk, and he filled the glasses, handing her one as well. He touched her glass with his. "To staying alive." They both downed the booze, and she coughed slightly.

He laughed and filled her glass again. "They go down easier the more you have." They both drank.

"Powell will kill us if Lara dies before we can reprogram her to destroy the Renegades."

"That's right," he said, and downed another shot. "Which is why I haven't told him Opal is dead."

"How do you plan to make Lara believe Skywalker is alive and set off her trigger? Because however you plan to do it, I say do it now."

"I assure you, we have a plan to do just that, but Powell is right about waiting. The Renegades need to trust her, and that takes time. If I rush this and fail to turn Lara into the Renegade executioner, I'll be dead. If I don't rush this, and she dies before that happens, I'll be dead." He moved her to sit in front of him and rolled her skirt up her legs, his gaze following the lines of her sleek thighs, to reveal thigh-highs. "If I'm going to die, I want to die a happy man." He pulled her skirt to her waist and glanced at her. "Why, sweet little Jenna—you don't have any panties on." He set her on top of the desk and spread her legs. "Here I thought you were a good girl."

"That's because you were fucking the wrong woman," she said. "Now I'm going to help you fuck the right one."

He arched a brow, aroused by this new, naughty Jenna. "And you would be the right one, I assume?"

"Literally, yes." She slid her high-heeled feet to the arm of his chair. "Fuck me, and fuck me well, because I've been waiting far too patiently for you, for far too long. Figuratively speaking, no. I was referring to Sabrina. If Opal just disappears, then she's Sabrina's problem, not yours. Sabrina will look incompetent, unable to motivate and manage her team. You will be the one person Powell can count on. The one who can make sure the Renegades are destroyed. When they are, he'll look like a hero to the government, and we'll get the funding we want to fix what's wrong with Bar-1 *and* replicate the GTECH serum." She leaned forward and grabbed his shirt, pulling him forcefully forward with more strength than she should possess. "And we won't tell him it only takes half the serum he thinks is necessary to convert a human to GTECH. That'll be our secret."

He stiffened. "What are you saying?" He tried to lean back, but she held him easily. "Jenna, did you—?"

She nipped his ear. "You bet I did. A few more weeks and I'll be as strong as Sabrina. I'll replace Sabrina in every possible way." She let him go and leaned back. "So you see… you don't get to die just yet. I'm not done with you." She slid one of her high-heels to his chest, pressing it against his flesh, the bite painfully arousing. "And don't even think about saying no. Sabrina isn't the only bitch in the house anymore. You have no idea the things I have in store for you—or her."

Logan smiled. "Right now, sweetheart, I've already died... and gone to heaven." And then he ripped her blouse open, but he was in some deep water, and he knew it.

This wasn't the Jenna he knew, the Jenna he'd wanted. This was someone else—another Sabrina—another GTECH on a power trip. If this could happen to Jenna, it could happen to anyone.

It was proof to him that Powell was right—the GTECH serum created monsters that had to be controlled. So he was along for the hot ride that Jenna offered, the short-term high, but he was officially Team Powell.

Chapter 20

THE INSTANT LARA WAS ON THE MATTRESS, SHE SCOOTED backward on her hands, trying to put distance between herself and Damion. Trying desperately to do what was right, to hold onto what little will she had to put space between them, while they still could. He captured her legs, stilling her retreat. "Damion, I—"

"Can't get enough of me? Want me?"

Her brows dipped, and she shifted her weight to her elbows to look at him. "I should say no, just because that was such an arrogant statement."

He smiled at her reply, satisfaction in his expression. He'd been baiting her into one of their familiar combative exchanges, and she'd fallen for it, hook, line, and sinker. "You're bad," she said. And sweet. He was trying to get her to relax.

"I could say the same of you," he said, maneuvering her under him as he slid on top of her, his big body framing hers. Their breath mingled, the air around them shifting, thickening with desire. The sexy male scent of him wrapped her in a warm blanket of desire. The lightness of his tone turned raspy, laden with desire. "I want you, Lara. I want you more than I have ever wanted another woman."

"Because of the mark," she said, speaking the fear she hadn't even admitted to herself. "It makes us want each other. What we feel isn't real."

"Ah sweetheart," he said, kissing her jaw, her neck, and then whispering near her ear. "That's where you're wrong. We created the mark. It didn't create us." His teeth grazed her neck, then her lobe. "And I wanted you the minute I set eyes on you, *before* the mark ever existed."

"That was the bikini."

"You, *in the bikini*," he assured her. He cupped her backside. "Have I mentioned how much I love your little heart-shaped backside, especially in that bikini?"

"You were on duty," she said, smiling despite herself, her fingers sliding together at the back of his neck. "You shouldn't have been looking at my backside."

"Exactly my point," he agreed. "I've never, ever been distracted on the job. But you... you stole my breath then, and you still do."

A mixture of heat, desire, and an emotion she was afraid to name, rushed through her. "Damion," she whispered, the hardness of his chest against her palms. He'd been there for her in so many ways, and she was falling hard. Too hard and too fast. "You are... you make me..."

"Yeah," he said softly, seeming to read her mind. "I'm afraid of caring about you too, but it's too late. I already do. I'm not running from it, and neither are you. Not because you're afraid. I won't let you. And I don't mean that like some dominating asshole either—we both know you can bust my chops if I get out of line." His voice softened again. "But if you try to run just because you're afraid of some past that doesn't matter, then I'll fight you on it. We're in this together now, Lara, and we'll deal with the past, one memory and one day at a time."

Yes. She wanted to scream, *yes*, but… "What if—"

"What if you stop saying 'what if' and just *be* with me? And 'what if' I do this?" He slanted his mouth over hers, his tongue parting her lips, pressing intimately into her mouth. She breathed him in, drank him in, until he gently nipped her bottom lip with his teeth. "And finally, 'what if' I give you an orgasm, and then do it again and again, until you forget all your reasons to worry." One of his hands slid over her breast, before he caressed a path down her sides, until he pressed her shirt upward and touched his lips to her stomach. Goose bumps prickled her skin, and instantly sent heat over her entire body.

He caressed her hips and then unsnapped her pants. "Unless you still want that separate room?"

She leaned on her elbows, and her head was clear, the pain gone. There was only pleasure and this man who'd taken her world by storm. "You don't play fair."

"Payback is hell," he said, reminding her of how mercilessly she had teased him several nights before.

"Remember that," she said. "Because payback *is* hell."

"I can only hope I'll be so lucky," he said, squatting and tugging her boots off. Then he pulled her to the end of the bed, her backside on the edge of the mattress. "It's time to get you out of these clothes." With deft hands he unzipped her pants, and she lifted her hips and let him slide them and the black panties she wore, away. He spread her legs, his palms skimming a path up her legs, even as he bent down and blew wickedly over her clit, teasing her with the promise of his mouth, his hands. He didn't give them to her though. Instead, he leaned back and tugged off his shirt. "Take yours off."

"You're bossy," she said, sitting up to do as he said.

"So are you," he reminded her. "And it's my turn. You had yours several nights ago if I recall. Believe me, I recall every last second."

So did she. Oh man, so did she. "I'll be a perfectly compliant little angel, as long as I get the same in return next time."

"Deal," he said, tossing his boots aside and reaching for his pants. "Take off the bra too,"

Lara unhooked the front clasp and tossed it aside. Damion kicked his pants and boxers aside, and stood there gloriously hard-bodied and naked, the bathroom light behind him illuminating his sleek masculine beauty. This man was her Lifebond, a man who would never want anyone but her again.

"I'm a lucky girl," she said, her gaze sliding over the ripples of his abs and then settling on the thick, jutting length of his erection. "You're spectacular."

He laughed, deep and sexy. "Exactly what I was thinking about you." He went down on his knees in front of her, his hands on her knees, which were primly pressed together. He kissed one, and then the other. "And you're beautiful, sexy, and *mine* tonight."

Mine. Heat sliced through her with the word, arousing her far more than it should. Memories intact or not, she wasn't the submissive type, nor was she the kind of woman who wanted to be possessed, except maybe by him—a desire made possible simply by knowing that he was willing to reverse roles, to allow her to take control.

Right now, not only was she not in control, he seemed to understand she didn't want to be. It was as if the world had landed on her shoulders, and she just couldn't hold it anymore. But he could. He could, and she wanted to let him, as he had said, at least for the night.

"Open for me, sweetheart," he urged, easing her legs apart, his fingers caressing the sensitive area inside of her knees.

Lara leaned back, her hands behind her on the mattress for support. She watched him, his eyes dark and greedy. Her body, just as greedy. She was wet, and he'd barely touched her, aching because she longed for him to do that and more. Anticipation rushed through her, building, as his fingers slid up her thighs, his lips trailing along her leg.

His eyes held hers as his thumbs stroked the delicate center of her body, and she inhaled with the sensation, biting her bottom lip as his fingers began to explore, tease. She leaned forward, wrapping her arms around his neck to kiss him. Before she could, one long finger slipped inside her, and she gasped, her forehead resting on his. A second finger entered her.

"That's it, sweetheart," he said, stroking her, in a slow steady rhythm that had her moving against him, had her hands clinging to his shoulders, her breasts arching into his chest. He palmed one of them, a rough, punishing, wonderful attack of pleasure on top of pleasure.

She buried her face in his neck, clinging to him, mov-ing against his hand—lost… lost in his touch, lost in the climb to bliss that came on her hard and fast. Lara sucked in a breath at the same moment that every muscle in her body coiled and then released into spasms of pure, white-hot pleasure. When she finally could breathe again, Damion brushed the hair from her face.

"What if I find another half dozen ways to do that to you again?"

She remembered him saying he'd found a little piece of heaven when they'd made love before, so she answered, "Then if I die tomorrow, I'll die a happy woman."

———

It was several hours, and several orgasms later, and nearly dawn. Though underground, Lara only knew this by way of the clock. She was wearing Damion's T-shirt, and they were both propped against the headboard of the bed, their shoulders and legs touching, while watching a Wesley Snipes *Blade* marathon. Thankfully, her headache was gone, and the flashes of images were held at bay.

"Maybe we should wear leather, like Wesley," Lara murmured. "That way we look really cool when we're fighting the bad guys."

"Too hot," Damion said. "And it's really not easy to move around in."

She glanced at him and lifted a brow. "You've worn leather?"

"I gave Chale's Harley jacket a whirl once," he commented. "Once was enough."

She laughed and scooted to lay on her side facing him, weight on her elbow, feeling oddly at home and safe, for the first time, well, *ever*. The rest of her memories were of Serenity—of loss and war. If there had been a time before that, she didn't remember it. She shook off that thought, clinging to this escape with Damion. "You are so not the Harley type."

"You won't get any argument out of me on that one."

"In fact, you and Chale are so different. It's amazing how close you seem."

"Sometimes I think he lives to agitate me, but yeah, we're pretty tight. He's my brother from another mother."

She wondered if she had any siblings, if the images of the family that were now indistinct shadows in her mind, would ever take shape again. "Did you say you have a brother, or did I make that up in my often confused thoughts these days?"

A subtle tension slid over him, a slight tensing of his jaw. The phone by the bed rang, and Damion hit the mute button on the television remote so fast, it was as if he welcomed the interruption. He answered the call, and the tension cranked up another notch. Suddenly on edge, Lara sat up, urgently seeking an update, suddenly terrified that someone had been hurt going after Powell, and she would be suspected of leading them into a trap. Why hadn't she insisted on going with them?

The call was quick, a few seconds in which he said nothing but "copy that" and "let me know if anything changes."

"Is everyone okay?" she asked, the minute he hung up.

He gave a slow nod. "Fine."

"Translation, not fine," she said. "The lab and Powell were gone, weren't they?"

He nodded. "The entryway into the facility was blown up, with rocks blocking the path. They're going to dig it out in daylight, and Chale and Houston are setting up surveillance."

Lara ground her teeth. "You won't find anything. He's too smart for that." She pulled her knees to her chest, his shirt to her ankles. "I should have told you about Powell sooner. I thought I was protecting someone who'd saved my life. Instead, I protected the man who has taken it, and for all I know, my family's lives too—if I could even remember who they are. I can't make out their faces. The only people I remember are those involved with Serenity, and Skywalker, whoever he is." She glanced at him. "My father. He feels like my father." She pressed the palm of her hand to her forehead. "I can't believe I let Powell get away. He's going to do whatever he did to me to others. He's going to keep trying to destroy the Renegades."

"Hey," he said gently and pulled her onto his lap. "Stop being so hard on yourself. It's not like you sat on the information for months or even weeks."

As Lara straddled him, a sudden rush of emotion overcame her, and she slid her hands into his hair. "Thank you." He gave her a wolfish smile, and she quickly added, "I'm not talking about all the wicked, wonderful things you did to me, so stop grinning like that."

He wiggled an eyebrow. "Wicked and wonderful. That bodes well for me being in control in the future, if I do say so myself."

"The future," she repeated hoarsely. "See, those words, that statement, is what I'm talking about, and why I said 'thank you.' Even when you thought I was with Adam, you tried to come up with reasons to believe in me. You asked me to give you a reason. And now, when even *I'm* afraid to believe in me, somehow you still do. All I can remember about the past is losing everything and being alone with nothing but fighting to live for. You make me feel…" Her voice hitched, and she swallowed. "You make me feel like I'm not alone."

He slid his hands over her hair and pulled her mouth near his. "You aren't alone, sweetheart. *You aren't alone.*"

For now, she thought grimly, until something happens, something surfaces to change that. "I swear to you, Damion—if we find out that I did anything to hurt you, or the Renegades, I truly believed it was to save innocent lives. I believed the Renegades were like Adam. I would never—"

"I know, and so does everyone else here."

"You don't know. You can't know. I need to know. I can't stand the not knowing. I'm almost desperate enough that I'd even let Becca read my memories in hopes of weeding through the lies to get answers. But as much as I want those answers, I'm terrified for her to see something horrible, something that no one, especially me, will forgive me for. I have to find out about me, and where I've been, and what I've done, before anyone else does."

"Stop doing this to yourself, Lara. Focus on now and the future."

She shook her head. "I can't start counting on you, and then wake up, and you're gone, like everything else in my life. Or worse, have you wake up and realize you're bound to me by this mark on my neck, and we despise each other. And don't tell me to stop saying that, or that it can't happen. We both know it could."

"It won't, but I'm not going to argue that point because I can tell it's a battle I won't win. So, most importantly, you need to know that the only thing the mark on your neck guarantees is that a blood bond makes us die together. We decide the rest." His thumbs stroked her cheeks. "I'm with you because I want to be, not because I have to be." He brought her lips a breath from his. "And I hope you feel the same way."

"I do," she whispered, her body tingling with sudden arousal. "You know I do."

"Then be with me, Lara. Forget everything else, and just be with me." He eased his hands under the shirt, calloused fingers skimming her naked skin, her bare breasts. "Just be with me."

His lips slanted over hers, his tongue pressing past her lips. The spicy maleness of him filled her mouth, drugged her, and claimed her very breath. Need built inside her, as a flame quickly ignited. "Lara," he whispered, her name on his lips somehow saying everything she was feeling, the wild frenzied need that was suddenly theirs.

He kissed her, or maybe she kissed him. She didn't know the difference. There was simply the burn to touch him, to taste him, to feel him closer. Until they were both panting as they shoved away his boxers, and he held her steady, so that she could slide down the hard length of him. He filled her, stretched her, completed her in a way that she didn't try to understand. It simply *was*... as they were.

"Are you with me now?" he asked, sliding his hand down her back and molding her against him.

"Oh yes," she assured him. "I am definitely with you now."

———

A good while later, Damion turned Lara on her stomach and kissed a path from one ankle to her gorgeous backside, and then all the way to her neck. He dusted the hair from her neck and traced the two circles etched on her nape with his finger, then pressed his body down over hers and kissed the delicate skin where the mark appeared.

"I know…" he said softly by her ear, "that I shouldn't say things like 'you're mine.' I know I sound like a caveman, but I can't seem to help myself. When I look at this mark, with you beneath me, it's what I feel."

She whispered his name, and he slid inside her, pressing deeply, melding his body with hers as the circles on her neck melded their souls as well. He was hot and hard, and something primitive and demanding ripped through his body. "Say you're mine, even if it's just for right here and right now."

"Yes," she whispered. "I'm yours."

He thrust into her, sensation sliding from his balls to his cock, twisting him in knots of pleasure.

"Yes," she panted. "I'm yours. Harder, Damion."

"You want harder, baby," he growled. "You get harder." He pumped into her, his hands traveling her body, curving under her to cup her breasts. More. He wanted more. She wanted more.

He wanted this to be about sex, about nothing but sex—sex didn't mean commitment. Sex didn't mean loss, or pain, or the opportunity to screw up and hurt the other person. Lara was the best sex of his life, but damn it, he knew this wasn't about sex. It was about a bond, a need, a connection that was so much more than sex. What they shared defied his vow. When he'd committed himself as a soldier for life, he'd promised never to let any woman mean anything to him but *sex*.

Lara cried out and stiffened beneath him, her hands pressing his hands to her breasts, her hips arching into his. She shattered around him, milking his cock with tight, hard spasms that ripped his orgasm from him. Damion arched his back with a roar of pleasure, his body shaking as he spilled himself inside her.

Long moments later, the two of them collapsed together, and Damion rolled to his side, Lara with him. He curled around her and brushed the hair from her eyes. "Next time you belong to me," she murmured groggily.

He smiled and nuzzled her hair, the soft strands tickling his chin. "Then you better sleep," he said, "because it's going to take a tough cavewoman to control this caveman."

"I'll be ready," she vowed softly, the words trailing off, her breathing slipping into a slow, rhythmic pattern.

Damion's chest expanded with a hard-earned breath. Lara had begun to matter to him. If he was honest with himself, it wasn't the bikini that had really worked him over. He'd started falling for her the moment she'd disobeyed orders and protected the Russian. She'd proven then what he now knew, and what she didn't seem to understand. That she was more than the sum of whoever controlled her, more than the façade of memories etched in her mind. He was falling in love with Lara, and it scared the hell out of him, and made him resist the blood bond, that final step in their Lifebonding—because at least physically, that meant every step he took, every action he put into play that might get him killed, would get her killed as well. No way. He'd lived that hell with his brother. It was one thing to play a sex game where she belonged to him, or he to her, but forever wasn't a game. He wasn't the man Lara needed in the long run, not once she found herself again. He knew it, and he was sure she knew it too, or she wouldn't be so freaked out about being bonded to him.

He had to tread cautiously with Lara, because Cassandra had told her the truth. Eventually their bodies would take over, and their final bond would be formed, whether they liked it or not.

Dorian's warning replayed in his head, the promise that without the blood bond, Lara would die from whatever Powell had done to her. If that were true, then there was no escape for Lara—Damion had become both her life… and her death. Conflicted didn't begin to describe what he felt, because after lying there, thinking about all the reasons he shouldn't want that to be the case, he found himself holding her closer, unwilling to let go.

Chapter 21

LARA WOKE ON HER STOMACH, THE MASCULINE, wonderful scent of Damion filling her nostrils—on her skin, on the pillow, in the air. God, she loved how he smelled, all spicy and deliciously male. Her lips lifted, satisfaction filling her. For just a moment, she simply lay there, drinking in a few moments of the naughty, wonderful, intimate things she and Damion had done together. Trying not to let herself think beyond this instant, beyond last night, not wanting to accept what, on some instinctive level, she already knew. She remembered nothing beyond a certain confined circle of information. That meant her headaches wouldn't be gone, not if things were as they were before her recent sleep. Cautiously, she resisted the urge to move, waiting a moment to see how her head felt, and then sighing with relief when there was no pain. In the background, she registered the sound of the television, and what she thought was the voice of a sports announcer.

"Morning."

Lara lifted her head at the brandy-rich male voice and turned to her right to find Damion sitting beside her, his long, muscular legs, stretched in front of him, and pressed to her side. He was touching her, and instantly her heart softened. He was trying to keep her headaches at bay so she could heal. Too bad, she thought, that her memories were still at bay as well.

She rolled to her side to face him, taking in his cleanly shaven square jaw and his handsome face. He wore faded jeans and an army-green T-shirt that told her she'd outslept him once again. She'd never thought army-green was sexy, but, oh man, had she been wrong. On Damion, army-green was downright sinful.

"How long have I been asleep?"

"Seven hours," he said, setting the computer that was in his lap on the nightstand.

"Seven hours?" she gaped and sat straight up, ignoring her nudity. It wasn't as if he hadn't seen everything about ten times over. She didn't feel shy with Damion, and she knew that meant something, but she couldn't focus on that right now. Urgency rose inside her. She had to find Powell. She had to find answers. "I can't believe I keep sleeping so long."

"Easy," he said, catching her wrist and pulling her to him, his hand sliding around her butt cheek as he molded her to his side. "You need the rest to heal. And don't panic. You didn't miss the NFL draft. I recorded it."

"NFL draft?" she asked, confused a moment, before she laughed despite herself, remembering the argument about football she'd shared with Damion and Chale. "You know that's not why I'm panicked." She shook her head. "And you recorded the NFL draft to prove you were right and I was wrong about the top picks, didn't you?"

"That'd be a yes."

"And was I right, and you were wrong?"

"I haven't watched it. I was waiting for you."

She had no idea why that announcement meant so much to her, but it did. Maybe because it felt like such a normal thing to do, and she felt so far from normal.

Or maybe it was simply that he'd waited for her, that he was sitting by her, caring for her.

She kissed his cheek. "I'll kiss you right—once I have a toothbrush."

"I'll hold you to it," he said, and released her. "And considering you're driving me crazy pressed up against me with nothing on, I highly suggest you go now, if you're going to go at all. Frankly, I don't give a damn about your toothbrush."

Lara bit back a smile and scooted off the bed to hurry toward the bathroom, all too aware of his eyes following her every step. She was about to shut the door when he called out, "I'll get you some food and call Cassandra, so we can get you tested again."

She stilled in front of the vanity. Another brain wave test. She didn't want another test. She *wasn't* taking another test. She felt fine, and even if she wasn't fine, there was nothing anyone could do for her. She didn't reply. She'd wait until she was dressed and ready to take on a real battle, be it with Damion, or her real enemy, Powell—the man who she was now certain had stolen her life, and all those she'd loved with it.

And no matter what Sabrina's role in all of this, no matter how much Lara wanted her blood, it was Powell she wanted the most, Powell she was going after. Determination formed inside her, and Lara quickly turned on the shower, praying Damion wouldn't join her, and then praying he would. No. She didn't want him to join her. He distracted her and made her want things she didn't dare want—a fairy tale of some happily-ever-after story that she clearly didn't have in her cards. She pulled back the curtain, and suddenly Damion was there, smacking her on the ass. Lara yelped and glanced over her shoulder. "Hey!"

"I owed you that from last night." He disappeared from the room.

She laughed and stepped behind the curtain, thinking of all the ways she'd teased him mercilessly. He was right. He owed her. God, how she wished she could turn back time and just live that night one more time. But she couldn't, and forty-five minutes later, Lara inspected herself in front of the vanity, ready to face the one real thing in her world outside of Damion. She was involved in a war, and not the one where she took orders from Powell, but the one against him.

Still, she found herself studying her reflection in the mirror. "Who are you?" she whispered, no answer coming to her beyond the superficial. Her skin was pale, her long dark hair straight and silky, compliments of her favorite shampoo and conditioner, which she'd been shocked to discover were available on the Sunrise Strip. Actually, she'd been as surprised by the development of this underground world as knowing that the coconut hair products were her favorite. It was just so darn odd that she knew so many things about herself, but had no idea where they originated.

Her gaze skimmed her slim dark jeans and black T-shirt with a light blue butterfly, still seeking some hidden secret to her identity. She liked butterflies. They meant something to her, something special. She sighed in frustration, about to dismiss the butterflies as another mystery yet to be unraveled, when she saw a flash of Skywalker's face—a strong jaw, a deep, familiar scar down his cheek that was as much a part of him as were the creases around his eyes and thick, graying hair. Lara saw herself, right there with him, a younger her, a teen maybe—yes, nineteen. She was nineteen.

Suddenly, Lara was in the past, in a karate studio, everything so vivid, down to her pink sweats and T-shirt, and Skywalker's gray sweats. Her feet were bare, a padded cushion beneath them.

She punched at Skywalker, then kicked. He avoided impact. She punched again, her brow damp, her determination strong. This time, she would take him down. This time wouldn't be like every other day this week, when she'd wound up on her backside. No sooner had she made that silent vow, than she had landed on the mat on her backside. Lara let out a frustrated sound, shoving herself to a sitting position.

Skywalker bent down in front of her, and she stared into a face of a fifty-something man, with intelligent gray eyes. He offered her his hand, and she glanced at his wrist, noting the familiar tattoo of a bald eagle with an American flag behind it. "Get up, my little caterpillar."

She ignored his hand and pushed to her feet on her own. He chuckled. "I'll make a butterfly out of you yet." She wanted to be that butterfly. She wanted to make Skywalker proud. Lara bent her knees and went into ready position. Skywalker grinned and did the same.

Then suddenly, the room shifted, and Lara stumbled. Shadows filled her vision, and then she was standing in a doorway, and Skywalker was tied to a chair, a gun to his head. "No!" she screamed. "No!"

Damion was standing in the kitchen when he heard Lara scream several times. Fear tore through him with the sound, fear for her carving a hole right in his gut. He took off running to find her, even as she went silent. The silence was worse than the scream. The silence that meant she could be—he wasn't going to consider where his mind was going—that anything could be wrong with Lara.

He charged into the bathroom to discover her sitting on the floor against the bathroom wall, her hands over her head and shaking. She was alive. Only then did he allow himself to fully realize what his fear had been— that he would lose her. That doing so would destroy him. That he had done what he'd sworn his entire adult life he wouldn't do—he'd allowed himself to care for someone, to feel responsible for someone, even if that person didn't see him that way. He *couldn't* lose her, no matter what that meant, whatever he had to do to keep it from happening.

"Lara, sweetheart," he said, squatting next to her, knowing he had the answer to the question that had been running through his mind. Sleep had not healed her. Sleep had not made this hell go away for her. "Lara." He gently eased her hands back from her face. "Lara."

"Damion?" she asked, looking confused, her eyes going wide. "What happened?"

"You started screaming." He brushed his thumbs over her cheeks. She was pale. Too pale. "Are you okay?"

"I screamed?"

He nodded.

"God." She pressed her hand to her forehead. "Will this ever end?" She started to get up, and he held her down.

"Maybe you shouldn't get up just yet," he warned, "Let me call Kelly and Cassandra before—"

"I'm fine," she insisted. "I don't need Kelly or Cassandra. I'm sick of being a wimp. I'm sick of being *sick*." She pushed to her feet, and he let her. "Really. Every second I spend sleeping and resting and complaining of headaches is time wasted. *I'm* the best shot we have of finding Powell. There has to be something in my head we can use to find him."

He leaned against the sink and pulled her close. Every instinct told him she was in trouble, and Dorian's words replayed in his head. *Do the blood exchange.* Damion had been scared shitless at the idea of doing the blood exchange. One mistake that could get him killed could get her killed. He'd spent his entire adult life making sure no one depended on him to survive, except a fellow soldier who lived to die, just as he did. He'd thought Chale was going to die, and he'd thought he'd caused it. When he'd heard Lara scream, he'd been afraid he'd already let too much time pass without doing the exchange, been afraid he'd already lost her. The bubble he'd been living in wasn't so secure after all, and he had a whole lot more to lose than he'd allowed himself to believe.

He ran his hands over her slender waist. "We have to run the brain wave test again."

"It won't be good. We both know that, Damion. Clearly, when you touch me, it eases the pain, but it doesn't solve whatever the problem is."

"There could be improvement," he said. "We need to know if what we're doing is working."

"I was just screaming and didn't know it. So the

answer is no. It's not working. So let's move on to more productive things than worthless tests that do nothing to help. Do you have a karate studio? Or a gym for training?"

"What?" he asked. "Why?"

"Because I need to stimulate a memory now, before I lose it."

"You have to eat to feed your metabolism after sleeping so long, or you'll fall on your face."

"I'll eat on the way to the gym." Her voice softened. "Please, Damion. This is important. I have to do this."

He ground his teeth, fighting the urge to throw her over his shoulder, as he had once before, and carry her to the hospital. "What memory are we talking about here?"

"Of Skywalker and me when I was younger. If I can remember him, really remember him, maybe everything else will fall into place as well. I just know it. I feel it, Damion. I just know he was my father, which is crazy, because I have this memory of a family, a mother and a father and siblings… only they don't feel real anymore. Skywalker does. He feels like the key to everything in my life. My trigger. The piece of history that will make everything fall into place." Her eyes softened, and she touched his face. "And you—you are my rock. The only person who's keeping me sane. Please don't pull back now. Don't stop helping me because of a medical condition you can't change."

But he could. If Dorian was right, Damion could change things. He could save her. "After the gym, we go to the hospital?"

She opened her mouth to argue. He saw it in her eyes, and he cut her off. "You can't win this one."

She clamped her lips together a moment. "Okay. After the gym, we'll go. I want to throw on some sweat-pants really quick."

"You really intend to work out in your condition?"

"I don't have a *condition*, but you will if you don't know karate, because I have every intention of sparring with you, and this time, you won't get the best of me just because you're bigger." She arched a brow. "You do know karate, right?"

"Something tells me I should be thankful the answer is yes."

A statement proven fifteen minutes later in the gym—empty but for the two of them—as Lara came at him with fierce determination. Kick, block, punch, block. She was fast and sharp.

"You're pretty good, for a girl."

"You're pretty good, for a GTECH," she said with a grimace, and threw another kick and punch, this time taking her game up a notch. Thirty minutes later, she was still coming at him, but he could see the pain radiating in her face, the tension in her lips, in her expression.

"Enough," Damion said, taking her to the mat beneath their feet, and laying her flat on her back before going down on top of her. She immediately tried to get up. He pressed her arms over her head. "Enough, Lara. You can't do this. You—"

"Damn you, Damion," she hissed. "Don't say 'can't.' I *need* to remember. *Can't* isn't an option."

He could see the desperation in her, and he didn't miss the slight twitch in her right eye that she couldn't seem to control. "Have you remembered anything else since we've been sparring?"

"No, but—"

"And you don't say 'but.' We *need* to get your exam done."

"I don't—"

"Another bad word," he said, before releasing her hands and resting his elbows on either side of her face. "The words 'don't,' 'can't,' and 'but,' are hereby outlawed for both of us. And I know you want to remember, which is why I've been doing some digging while you were sleeping." She started to speak, and he quickly added, "Don't get your hopes up. All I can really tell you at this point is what I've researched and ruled out as possibilities."

"I thought 'don't' wasn't allowed?"

"You got me on that one," he said. "Take the brain wave test, and then we'll sit down and go through what I've covered so far and where that leaves us."

"Tell me whatever you discovered now," she said urgently. "Please. I need to know now."

"Take the test first."

"That's blackmail."

"Yep," he agreed. "Sure is."

She grimaced. "Asshole."

He brushed the hair from her eyes and kissed her. "I can live with being your personal asshole, sweetheart."

"Apparently, everyday."

"If that's what it takes to keep you safe," he agreed, and pushed off her and to his feet. He offered her his hand. Lara sat up and stared at it for a long moment, and then glanced at him. "Skywalker had an eagle tattoo with an American flag on his wrist. I need to get to a computer and see if I can find the image."

"You don't need a computer," Damion said. "I've spent a good part of my army career finding people who didn't want to found, and helping people who didn't technically exist find those people. That's a Spook's tattoo. As in, a CIA operative that hunts down rogue operatives. That makes Skywalker one of the deadliest of his kind." He arched a brow. "No wonder Powell wanted you on his team. You were trained by a Spook."

She rested her weight on her hands, behind her long, silky hair that lay in a sexy, rumpled disarray around her slender shoulders. "Do you think that makes me a Spook? And Skywalker? Will this help us find information about him?"

He bent down in front of her. "Spooks are called 'Spooks' for a reason. They're ghosts even when they're alive, and they never existed once they're dead. And do I think you are—or were—a Spook? I don't know. My instincts say no, that Skywalker feels like family to you, so he probably was, but at this point, instincts are just that. They aren't facts. But I can tell you that I haven't found a 'Lara Mallery' or 'Lara Martin' or 'Lara' anything for that matter, who remotely matches your identity.

"And none of Caleb's government contacts confirm any involvement with General Powell. He's still MIA as far as they're concerned, and that includes our trusted contacts, who tell us what they aren't supposed to tell us. Both myself and Sterling are looking for your identity and that of Skywalker. We've checked out the name 'Luke,' hoping that Skywalker is a nickname, and have come up dry at every turn, in every facet of the government." He ran his hands down his jeans. "And now that I've pretty much told you everything I know when

I didn't intend to…" He reached for her hand and stood up, pulling her to her feet. "It's time for medical tests."

"I need a computer first," she said. "I have some ideas, and maybe I can—"

He kissed her. "A deal is a deal. Test first. Computer later."

She pursed her lips. "Fine. A deal is a deal. But I get a computer and Internet access when the test is completed, no matter what the test says."

"I promise."

—◈◈◈—

Sunlight would soon pierce the horizon, too soon for Jenna's comfort, considering the nastiness of the task ahead of her. She backed her car into the woods behind the rundown Mexican bar, her heart thundering in her chest, her fingers curled around the steering wheel. She inhaled the scent of Logan still lingering on her hair and in her clothes, a reminder of an amazing night, of why she was about to do what she was about to do and why.

For several seconds she just sat there, breathing in Logan, remembering the hours with him, and finding strength in those memories. She shoved open the car door and stopped at the trunk of the Ford Taurus before popping the trunk. Then she stared at the sheet-wrapped body of Opal, and suddenly wondered what she'd been thinking.

She wasn't Sabrina, not outside the bedroom diva fantasy she'd lived the past few hours. She could hardly believe she'd said and done some of the things she'd done with Logan. That character she'd played wasn't her, not really, and she wasn't a person who dumped bodies behind bars.

She squeezed her eyes shut, thinking of how good it had felt to control Logan, how amazing it had felt when he'd looked at her the way he'd looked at Sabrina. Her lashes popped open. Opal was dead. It wasn't like Jenna had killed her. Opal hadn't liked Sabrina any more than anyone else did, except Logan, of course. Jenna ground her teeth. She was doing everyone a favor by getting rid of Sabrina, and that meant she had to toughen up beyond the bedroom and the GTECH super strength.

She'd get rid of Opal's body, and then she'd get rid of Sabrina, so she and Logan could do their research, so they could stand together and make Serenity better. Powell would be happy. Logan would be happy. And finally, so would she.

Chapter 22

AN HOUR AFTER DAMION HAD CONVINCED LARA TO go to the hospital, he'd all but tied her to the recliner in the room, so Cassandra could run her test. Now, with the test complete, Damion stood behind Lara, while Cassandra and Kelly prepared to deliver the results.

"Small improvements," Cassandra said. "Not as large as I would have expected."

"Too small," Kelly said, hands on her hips, looking between Lara and Damion before settling on Lara. "We need to talk about options. Since you're Lifebonds—"

Damion stiffened, anticipating Lara's reaction. She whirled around to face him. "You told them?"

"I never got the chance," he said. "Dorian told them."

"Adam's son?" she asked in disbelief. "You told Adam's son about us?"

"I didn't tell Dorian," Damion said. "He told me. Dorian has unique abilities that include knowing things he shouldn't and feeling absolutely no need to explain how." He bent down in front of her, taking her hand in his. "And Dorian said that if we don't blood bond, you'll die. I won't let you die, Lara."

"Dorian isn't a doctor."

"Dorian knows things, Lara," he said. "And he's right too often for us to ignore him."

She searched his face, emotion pouring into her eyes,

before she jerked them to Kelly. "How can the blood exchange save me? I'm already GTECH."

"This is new territory," she said. "You're the first GTECH-to-GTECH bonding I've ever experienced, perhaps the only one that exists. Hypothetically, based on the research I've done on Lifebonding, the blood exchange makes you both whole, and thus stronger. All I can tell you, without question, is that you can't maintain this level of irregular brain activity without risking a stroke. With your GTECH metabolism, medications don't work. If I had your medical records, if I knew what had been done to you, I might have a shot at reversing it. That seems more of a long shot at this point than the blood bond."

Damion squeezed her hand, pulling her attention back to him. "We have to do the blood exchange."

"No," Lara said, her tone sharp. "I won't do it."

Damion felt immediate rejection like a punch in the gut, and it must have shown, because she squeezed his hand and lowered her voice. "You know why I won't do this, not like this, not with so many unknowns. Please, I beg of you. Don't read something into this that isn't there." Her voice caught. "It means so very much to me that you would be willing to do this, but it only makes me more certain I can't let you." She glanced at Kelly. "Instead of Damion healing me, how do we know that I won't cause him to stroke right along with me?"

Damion cut his gaze to Kelly, who reluctantly nodded. "She has a point. If she were human, you'd give her GTECH immunity. But she is GTECH, and we don't know what the blood bond means for the two of you, besides a connection in death. I know Caleb trusts what Dorian says, but I can't say that I do."

"I don't give a damn about the risks," Damion said, his attention fully on Lara. "Do you hear me? I don't care, Lara. We *have* to do this."

"No," she said softly. "We don't." And then, unexpectedly, she turned to appeal to Cassandra, who'd up to this point been silent, staying out of the argument. "Would you do this if you thought there was even a small chance it would hurt Michael?"

"Cassandra," Damion warned, willing her to look at him, but she didn't. She stared at Lara, responded to Lara.

"I would never do anything that would risk Michael's life to save my own," Cassandra said. "But he'd want me to, and he'd try everything shy of forcing me to accept the blood bond to save *my* life. If I'm honest, he probably would force the bond. But Lara, I love Michael. I'd know he did it because he loves me too. And being honest again—I'm not sure I could say I wouldn't do the same for him, if things were reversed."

Lara pushed to her feet almost instantly, a clear reaction to Cassandra's words, and Damion followed her to his feet.

"I won't put you at risk," she said. "End of story." He opened his mouth to object, and she pressed her hand to his chest. "*You aren't going to die trying to save me.* I won't let you." Her chin lifted. "And we had a deal. You promised me a computer and an Internet connection."

He pressed his hand over hers, over his heart, and considered arguing. Hell, he considered grabbing a knife and slicing their palms right here and now. That caveman feeling from the bedroom returned. She was his Lifebond, and he *would* protect her. She was also brave and beautiful, and she challenged him in every possible way. He wasn't a fool. He wasn't in denial. She was everything he could ever want in a woman, everything he'd never wanted to find, because finding it, finding her, meant he could lose her. He damn sure wasn't going to lose her when he'd just found her. "If you think I'm going to let you die, you can think again. This conversation is postponed, but it's far from over."

Lara studied him for several long seconds, and then turned to Kelly and Cassandra. "I want to have Becca try and read my memories."

"What?" Damion demanded. "You said—"

She turned back to him. "Everything changed when I found out I might die. I don't care about my past. I care about what happens in the future, and what I can do to impact it for the better."

Damion ground his teeth, his heart in his throat. "You're not going to die, damn it."

"You don't know that." She turned to the women. "I want to see Becca. Please. I want to get answers, and I want to get them now, before something happens to me."

"I can't approve this," Kelly said. "When Becca reads someone, it tends to be a major event, especially when she's trying to help them recover information. You're too unstable. We don't know how you'll react. It could send you into a stroke."

"I'm willing to take the risk," she insisted.

"I'm not," Damion, Kelly, and Cassandra all said at once.

"Let me speak to Caleb," Lara said, and then cut her attention to Cassandra. "No. Make that Michael. I've met him. He'll do what's best for the big picture, not what's right for me. And he'll convince Caleb of the same."

"You're wrong," Cassandra said softly. "He won't risk your life."

"Damn it, Lara," Damion said, his gut clenching, his hand claiming Lara's as he pulled her close. "You talk to me before you talk to anyone." He motioned to Kelly and Cassandra, who headed for the door. He wasn't going to lose Lara when he'd just found her, and she was about to find out just how stubborn he could be when something mattered to him. And she did.

The instant the hospital room door shut, leaving Lara alone with Damion, she was ready for a fight, something the two of them had excelled at since the moment they'd met. This wasn't a battle she was fighting with her fists though. It was one she was fighting with her heart. She pushed to her toes, and she kissed him, her fingers resting on his jaw. "Thank you for wanting to save me."

He wrapped his arms around her. "I'm not letting you die."

Her heart hurt. She cared so much about this man. She didn't know how it had happened, how in such a short while he'd become so much to her, but he had. "And I'm *not* letting you die."

His fingers twined in her hair. "Damn it, Lara—"

"Damn it, Damion," she hissed back at him. "You don't know me well enough to die for me. And I'm not selfish enough to let you either. I... I care too much about you to let you risk that." He kissed her. She didn't resist. She couldn't have if she'd wanted to, and she didn't. She kissed him back, wishing she could drag him back to bed and play that game of escape they'd been involved in for just a little longer. But they couldn't, and she was pretty sure he knew that too. This was real life and death they were dealing with, not a game, not an adventure.

He leaned back to stare at her, his fingers skimming over her hair, over her face. "I know you," he said softly. "I know you better than you seem to know yourself."

"Maybe that's true," she whispered, and then swallowed back emotion, willing her words through her dry throat. "But I'm not going to pretend my time may not be limited, and I'm not wasting what time I have by hiding from whatever is in my past. I want to help the Renegades find Powell. I want to go out with a bang and make a difference. I want..." Her damn voice hitched, her memory of that moment with Skywalker in the karate studio still in her mind. "I want to go out a butterfly, not a caterpillar."

"Sweetheart," he said after a long pause. "You are no caterpillar. If you're a butterfly, you're a butterfly with teeth. You want to fight then we'll fight. You and me—together. And for the record, you aren't dying. I enjoy fighting with you myself way too much to let that happen. We'll find Powell, and we'll get your medical records, right before we drag his ass back here and into a jail cell for the rest of his life."

Lara knew he was dreaming, fighting the wrong battle, the lost battle. It was the battle that allowed him to fight by her side, while she fought a different one—a battle to bring down Powell if it was the last thing she did, and it probably would be. The battle that convinced Damion there was an answer other than the blood bond, which she wouldn't allow. Not only did she love him for the vow he'd made to save her, to fight with her, but she was pretty sure she just plain loved him.

"Okay then," she agreed. "So we fight. How do you suggest we start?"

He took her hand. "We go to Caleb, and we talk through a plan."

Turned out, they didn't have to go far to find Caleb. He and Michael were waiting in the hallway, along with Kelly and Cassandra.

"You do know you should listen to your doctor?" Caleb asked, fixing Lara in a steely stare.

"I am," Lara said. "And the doctor said that she can't guarantee Damion's safety if we do the blood exchange. That means, I'm not doing the blood exchange. I won't let Damion be a fatality I create. Nor am I sitting back and waiting to die either. I want Powell, and I plan to get him. I'm hoping you Renegades want to come along for the ride."

Michael ran his hand over a strong, square jaw and arched a brow at Damion. "Got your hands full I see?"

"And then some," Damion agreed, wrapping his arm around Lara, his eyes touching hers.

"You're no walk in the park," she promised him.

"Not sure I ever aspired to be a walk in anyone's park."

"Maybe you should," she countered.

"She really does fit right in, doesn't she?" Michael asked, laughing at their exchange.

Cassandra hooked her arm with Michael's. "A chip off the old block, if I do say so myself."

"If that block is called 'stubborn,' then yeah," Michael concluded, staring down at his Lifebond. "I say so too."

Caleb crossed his arms in front of his chest, cool eyes touching Damion's, then sliding back to Lara. "I have an alternative to Becca. It's not a fast solution, or a miracle answer, but it's better than nothing."

Damion stiffened, tension crackling off him. "Not Dorian."

Lara studied Damion. "What would Dorian do to help? What do I still not know?"

"Not Dorian," Caleb agreed, as if Lara hadn't asked the question. "Me." He spoke the word directly to Damion, and then shifted his attention to Lara. "I can't read your mind, or even your memories for that matter, but I can read what emotion is real and what's not, even when you might not be able to. In other words, when you remember something, as we go through facts and dates, I can help you weed through the fiction. You'll have to tell me the details—good, bad, and ugly—for me to help. The best way to do that is for a group of us to sit down and weed through data, what we can find, what you can remember, and see where it leads."

"And I'm damn good at digging up information," Sterling said, as he and Chale walked up to join the group. "I'll work around the clock to help Damion find the information, so you and Caleb can do your thing."

Chale walked to Damion and clamped him on the shoulder. "I'll keep my boy, Damion, here in line. If he gives you trouble, Lara, I'm your man."

"Well then," Lara said. "I say, let's get started now."

Chapter 23

A WEEK AFTER DAMION HAD CONVINCED LARA TO TAKE the brain wave test, he was still trying to convince her to take another one, and she was refusing. It was late afternoon, and he sat next to her at the conference table of the Renegade's War Room. Cassandra and Houston, who'd once been an FBI sketch artist, were present, and Houston was working on composites of the various members of Serenity, to be searched in the various government databases.

"Amazing," Lara said, as Houston slid the picture of Opal across the wooden surface for her review, and then turned the University of Texas baseball cap he'd had on backward, forward again. Lara studied the drawing. "Yes. That's Opal for sure." There were five other drawings already on the table, and she added Opal's to the mix. "Amazing. I don't know her full name. Looking back I can't imagine never asking, but I didn't. We were like machines as members of Serenity, all driven by some façade of a personal agenda and purpose." She shoved a lock of hair behind her ear. "I guess I should be glad I remember what they look like at this point."

Damion squeezed her leg beneath the table, the pastel floral dress she wore a contrast to the soldier he'd first met—a delicate part of her that he hungered to discover, that she'd told him she wanted to discover with him. "If we can identify even one of these women, we're that much closer to any information about you and to finding Powell." For weeks now he'd watched her struggle to regain memories that simply weren't returning, and in the past few days, she'd stopped having flashbacks. Which would have been comforting, if the flashbacks hadn't become blackouts. "I'll feed these into the database," Cassandra said, collecting the sketches. "And wow, Houston, Lara is right. You're amazing. I can think of several ways the Wardens could put this skill to use, if you'll let us?"

"I aim to please, ma'am," he assured her. "Your wish is my command, but don't tell Michael I said that. I think he might hurt me."

She grimaced. "I hate when you make Michael sound so scary. He's not." She glanced at her watch and pushed to her feet. "Oh no. We're supposed to meet the gang at Moe's for Sterling's birthday in fifteen minutes, and I really want to get these composites in the database before I leave." The rest of the gang were Michael, Chale, Jesse, Sterling, Becca, and Caleb.

Houston pushed to his feet and patted his stomach. "Oh yeah. Time to feed the beast with some birthday cake. I'll head over and tell them you're on the way."

"Thank you, Houston," Cassandra said, as he headed for the door.

"You know, Cassandra," Lara said, as she and Damion stood up. "I've spent every day for a week looking through computer files for answers I never find. I was thinking maybe tomorrow I could join the Wardens and try to do something more productive." She glanced at Damion. "And you can get back to your regular duty and stop babysitting me. You can't stay by my side forever."

His gaze met hers, the silent message one he knew she'd read—forever, or until she agreed to the blood bond. "You could black out."

"Cassandra will be with me," she said. "And Kelly will be close."

"I'd love to have you help with the Wardens, Lara," Cassandra offered, glancing at Damion. "And we're not unfamiliar with hovering, overprotective Lifebonds." She held up the sketches. "Let's scan these into our government database, and see if we get a fast hit. Sometimes that happens when I enter a missing person's info." She headed for the door.

Lara glanced at Damion. "Stop acting like a papa bear. I'm fine." She started walking and swayed. Damion cursed, catching her against his body and the wall a moment before she fell, his heart frozen until she started to move.

She sucked in a breath and grabbed his arms. "How long this time?"

His ears were ringing. "A few seconds, and that was too long. I'm getting Cassandra to run a brain wave test now. Sit down while I get her." He didn't want to risk her falling and hurting herself.

"No," she said quickly, her feet planted, showing no willingness to sit. "We've discussed this. The test solves nothing, and besides, it's Sterling's birthday. A few seconds isn't a bad blackout. It was ten minutes this morning. It's probably because I'm hungry. I need to eat."

He slid his hand into her hair. "Damn it, Lara."

"Damn it, Damion."

"You're hiding from the test because you know you won't like the results."

"Because I know the results change nothing."

"Let's do the blood exchange."

Her eyes clouded. "Let's go eat hamburgers and birthday cake and drink beer. Isn't that what Sterling wished for?"

"Lara," he whispered.

She kissed him and then traced his lips with her finger. "I bet I can drink more beer than you without getting drunk."

GTECHs didn't get drunk. "I'm already drunk—on fear for you."

"I can think of much better things for you to be drunk on," she said, sliding her arms under his, her chest pressed to his. "I'll show you later."

"Maybe I should take you back to bed and tie you there," he said. "Then call Cassandra to do the damn test."

"You wouldn't do that."

"Yeah I would, on both counts, with varying degrees of pleasure."

She studied him, the humor fading from her beautiful, still too-pale features. "I would really like to go have a great evening and pretend to be a normal couple out with friends. I know, like so much else, it's a façade, but it would be a really, really wonderful way to spend the night."

Damn, this woman twisted him in all kinds of knots he'd never wanted to be twisted in. She thought she didn't belong here, that if she dared believe she did, it would be taken from her like everything else in her life had been. Worst of all was that she was right in some ways to feel such things. Time wasn't on her side, or his. He had to act, and he was going to. He knew what he had to do. He could only hope a night with friends, a night out together, would help her understand when he did what he had to do.

He drew her hand in his and kissed her knuckles. "I keep telling you, we're as real as it gets, and so are the friends we're about to spend the evening with."

———

Bittersweet. That's what a night out with Damion and his friends was to Lara. Moe's was hopping with Renegade standard black fatigues. It appeared Friday night in Sunrise City was like Friday night everywhere else—busy and fun-filled.

Sterling's party was, in fact, overflowing beyond the four square tables their group had turned into one long one, with regular toasts and shouts to Sterling from various locals. The immediate party, though, was Damion and Lara, along with Michael, Cassandra, Jesse, Chale, Houston, Emma, Caleb, Kelly, and of course, Sterling and Becca. There were pitchers of beer everywhere, and a Spider-Man cake in honor of Sterling in the center.

Apparently Sterling called Caleb "Superman" and Michael "Batman." Tonight the two had officially knighted Sterling "Spider-Man," which, Lara decided, seemed fitting, since apparently, pre-Becca, he'd done insanely ridiculous, highly dangerous things on a regular basis. She spent most of the next half hour after the food was cleared laughing at the outrageous Sterling stories, her back to Damion's chest, his hand resting on her stomach.

"My fondest memory," Michael said, from down the table, across from her, and next to Chale, "was when Sterling threw Damion across the conference table."

"Hate that I missed that," Chale said, directly across from Lara.

"Me too," Houston agreed from beside Chale.

Lara eyed Damion. "I guess you pissed him off?"

"He was delusional that day," Damion said, and held up his mug of beer toward Sterling. "Right Ster?"

Sterling lifted his mug in reply. "That's just how I say 'I love you,' man."

"Right," Damion said. "I say it right back with just as much feeling."

Caleb, who sat directly next to Lara, looked up from the deep conversation he was having with Kelly, a frown on his face that had Lara wondering if she was imagining a few sparks between the Renegade's leader and the doctor. "I seem to remember Michael and me having to hold you two back, you were feeling so much love."

Glancing at Damion, Lara reached up and touched his jaw, where a light, sexy stubble had started to protest its morning clean shave. "Sounds like an interesting story."

"He was feeling protective of Becca," Damion said, "and he wrongfully assumed I wasn't." He leaned in close to her ear. "GTECHs are protective of their Lifebonds."

Lara turned in his arms to face him, their eyes locking in the dim light, the awareness between them electric and instant. "I'm a GTECH too. Don't forget that."

"Houston, we have a problem!" Houston held up an empty pitcher. "We need beer, or we're never going to get drunk. It's your turn to buy, Damion." Like they could get drunk even if they tried, but they all seemed to enjoy pretending otherwise.

Damion leaned in and kissed Lara. "You think you

can handle another Sprite?" he asked, referring to her drink of the night.

"You'd be surprised what I can handle." There was a hidden meaning to the words, and she saw it register hotly in Damion's black eyes. Eyes that could no longer hide behind the human hazel color they had once been. Yet there were still so many secrets between them, so many things that could, and would, rip them apart.

"You can show me later," he finally said, his hand still on her leg, even as he shifted to push his chair back from the table.

Lara shoved aside the worries threatening to steal the happiness of her night out and eyed Houston. "Houston, we have a problem?" she asked. "Is Houston really your name?"

"Nah," Houston said. "Damion likes Houston, so I go by Houston, and heck, I'm from Houston. Nothing wrong with a tribute to the homeland."

"What's your real name?" she asked.

Damion's hand tightened on her leg ever so slightly, but the tension that rolled off him was a sudden white water crash that had Lara turning toward him.

"Pain in my ass is what I call him," Chale said, nudging Houston. "You think Damion might need that empty pitcher to get the beer or what?"

Damion cast Chale a tense look of what Lara would label appreciation, before he turned and headed toward the bar.

"I'm sorry, man," Houston was mumbling to Chale when Lara turned back to the table.

"Sorry for what?" she asked Houston, who eyed Chale with an appeal. Lara's attention rocketed to

Chale. "Talk to me. What did I just miss, and why is Damion upset?"

Chale, looking uncharacteristically uncomfortable, hesitated.

"Chale, damn it," she ground out. "Talk to me."

"I'm not talking," he said finally. "But you should. Talk to Damion."

She didn't need nudging, and these days, she didn't have a lot of time to waste. Lara stood up and went after Damion.

Chapter 24

TENSION CRAWLED DOWN DAMION'S SPINE AND BACK up again as he weaved a path through the crowd and set the pitcher on the bar. He didn't want Lara to know about his brother. Hell, these days he tried not to even think about Tommy because when he did, he could drive himself insane.

"Refill," he said to the bartender—Moe's brother, Mack—a tall, muscled dude who looked more Renegade than bartender, and who'd come to Sunrise as family to one of the Wardens, once a captive in the sex camps. They couldn't drag the guy anywhere near the war zone though, despite what his sister had been through, and no one knew why.

Mack saluted. "Coming up."

Damion gave a nod and pressed both palms on the bar, letting his head fall forward between his shoulders, and telling himself to calm down. Instead, a flash of Tommy's young face flickered in his mind, spiking his blood pressure to the moon. Holy hell, now he was the one having flashbacks. It was too damn long ago, well over a decade since Tommy's death, for him to still be this raw.

He shoved off the bar and toward the back of the joint, weaving through yet more people, and heading down a narrow hallway that ended with a turn to the left for men and one to the right for women. He walked left, and once out of sight, leaned against the wall, pressing his face in his hand.

"Damion."

The soft, familiar voice came seconds before the smell of sweet coconut and woman filled his senses, before Lara was there, wrapping her arms around him. "Talk to me." She urged gently. "What's Houston's real name, and why is it a problem?"

His heart exploded in his ears. "I don't want to talk about this."

"It has something to do with what you said to me back at the cabin, doesn't it?" she pressed. "When you said you were good at taking the blame for things?"

His heart was back in his chest, and with it a firestorm of emotion erupted. He grabbed Lara, pulled her into the restroom, shut the door, locked it, and then leaned against the wall with her pulled into his arms. "Yes. It has something to do with what I said back in the cabin. Houston's name is Tommy, and Tommy is the name of my dead brother."

She let out a breath, her fingers splaying over his chest. "Oh God, Damion. I'm sorry."

"He was sixteen, and my parents had grounded him for talking on the phone after bedtime. It was Saturday night, and our parents were at a movie. I stopped by to check on Tommy, who convinced me to take him to the fast food joint his girlfriend worked at." He pressed his forehead to hers, unable to look at her as he finished. Their breath mingled, and her fingers gently brushed his cheek then rested there. He forced himself to continue. "There was a box truck and a red light the driver didn't bother to stop for."

Lara gasped and pulled back. "No. Tell me no."

He nodded, because he couldn't speak, trying to swallow the emotion that had lodged where his heart had been a few minutes before. "He was a lot like Chale. Always joking around. My brother gave me hell for my bad driving all the way to the hospital. I thought that had to mean he'd make it, but…"

"Oh God, Damion." She pressed her lips to his, kissed his jaw, his cheek, her fingers sliding over his face. "It wasn't your fault. I can see—I can *feel*—you think it was, but it wasn't."

He dropped his arms from her and stared up at the concrete ceiling. "That's not what my mother and my brother thought."

She wrapped her arms around him. "They blamed you."

"Yeah," he said, tilting his head down to look at her, not even trying to wipe away the pain he knew had to be in his expression. "They blamed me."

"And your father?"

"Died of cancer five years ago," he said. "And I think my mother and my brother cursed him all the way to his grave for standing up for me. He'd wanted me to run Megatech, and that only made things worse. That's why I joined the army and got the hell out of Dodge. I thought he and my mother would be better when I was gone."

"But they weren't, were they?"

"No, they weren't."

"I've read about couples splitting after the loss of a child," she said. "There is an inherent need to place blame as a way to deal with pain. Now I know why you said you were good at taking the blame. You tried to make everyone happy. You left everything behind, trying to make everyone happy. That makes you a very, very special person that I feel honored to know."

He pulled her to him and slid his fingers into her hair. "I can't lose you," he said and kissed her, a passionate, desperate kiss. "I won't lose you." His hands started to travel, the need to touch her, to feel her, to know she was here, and she wasn't going anywhere, driving him wild.

"Damion," she whispered into his mouth, a moment before their tongues touched again, before the heat between them boiled to downright molten. Her hands slid under his T-shirt, over his chest, his back.

He palmed her breasts through the thin material of her dress. "I love you in this dress," he murmured, and turned her so that her back was against the wall, his fingers tugging up the hem of the dress, curving along the soft skin of her backside.

"I'll have to wear it more often," she panted, as he lifted her leg to his waist, stroking the tiny strip of her thong and then using his other hand to slide the silk at the V of her body away and stroke the wet heat. "I really need to be inside you right now."

Someone knocked on the door. "Go away!" they both said at once, and then laughed, their voices laced with passion.

"I really need you inside me too," she said tightly, reaching for the zipper of his fatigues.

Damion finished the task, pulling his cock from his pants and shoving her panties aside, urgency driving him. This wasn't about sex. It was about how much he needed this woman. It was about a bond they hadn't completed, that they were trying to replace with fire and desire.

She grabbed his shoulders as he penetrated her, her lashes fluttering, her fingers digging into his flesh, her breath coming in heavy pants. She looked so damn sexy, so incredibly sexy. He pressed into her, the wet heat of her surrounded him, blasting him a heavy dose of pleasure. She bit her lip, her gaze capturing his, passion burning from her stare, the connection between them expanding, consuming the room, consuming the very air filling their lungs.

Damion sunk deep inside her, sliding his hand to her face, the other around her backside. "You belong here with me," he told her, kissing her before she could object, before she said something that defied his claim. She tasted sweet, like honey, smelled like heaven, and felt like a hot, tight ride to ecstasy. He moved inside her. She arched into him, setting off a slow rhythm of movement that quickly turned to a frenzied rush of their bodies sliding together, of kisses, touches, and wild abandon where time disappeared.

"Damion," Lara gasped a moment before she buried her face in his neck, her body tensing before she spasmed around him, milked him, claiming his release as she had already claimed him the moment he'd laid eyes on her.

They melted into one another, panting into completion and then resting their foreheads together. "Tonight, Lara. Tonight, we do the blood exchange."

She leaned back. "No. We can't."

"We can."

She shook her head and pushed away from him. He let her leg fall and reluctantly eased their bodies apart. She quickly slid away from him, grabbing a towel and righting her dress, then standing there without turning. "I know you think you have to do this. I know you think you'll be to blame if anything happens to me, but…"

He turned her to face him. "No. It's not like that."

"It is like that."

"God, no." He pulled her close. "I'm pretty sure I'm falling in love with you, and before you say it's too soon, you should know that's the first time in my thirty-four years I've ever said the word 'love' to a woman, so it's not something I say lightly. Hell. I didn't want to ever feel this for a woman. I did my best to never let it happen. But it is happening—maybe it already has. All I know is you matter in a huge way to me, Lara, and I don't plan to lose you before I ever find out what that really means." His gaze swept the restroom. "And damn it, I would never have wanted the first time I said something like this to you to be in a restroom. This is definitely not my Prince Charming moment, but I'll make this part up to you. I'm not exactly used to these kinds of confessions."

"Damion," she whispered. "You don't even—"

"Know you?" he asked and didn't wait for an answer. "I know you. I don't give a flying flip about your past. I also know you're afraid you'll regain your memories with the bond, and then we'll hate each other, but that isn't going to happen." His voice softened. "We decide our future. We do, not the past, not Powell, or anyone else. Most importantly, we need to make sure we have a future. That means we have to complete the blood bond."

Her bottom lip trembled. "I stopped caring about the past when I learned what Powell did to me. You know that. You know that's why I confessed everything

I knew about him and Serenity. And I'm pretty sure I already love you too. I don't know if I've ever said that to anyone else, because I don't remember anyone else, but I know what I feel, and clear to my soul I know I've never felt for anyone what I feel for you."

Relief washed over him, relief and so much more. Damion scooped her into his arms. "You think you love me?" he asked, scared shitless of her saying yes and scared shitless he'd misunderstood and she'd say no.

"Well," she said, her fingers brushing his jaw in a way that was fast becoming familiar and endearing. "You enrage me, arouse me, and make me laugh. I frequently want to kiss you. I more frequently want to undress you, proven by our highly inappropriate rest-room encounter. Sometimes I even want to kill you. Not literally anymore, of course. So yeah, I'm pretty sure you've done the love number on me, Damion Browne, which is exactly why I won't put you at risk."

"I won't let you die, damn it," he said fiercely, the protectiveness in him expanding, threatening to take on a life of its own.

"I don't intend to die," she assured him. "I intend to find Powell and my medical records. You just reminded me of why I can't give up, which I almost did today. I have to find him, and I will." She pressed her lips to his, clearly trying to distract him, then said, "Take me to your bed and give me the good-caveman-you're-mine routine. I'm surprised how much I like it. While you're at it, *make love to me,* Damion."

"I'll take you to our bed," he said, drawing her toward the door. "However, this conversation isn't over."

"So you keep telling me and then proving."

He pulled the restroom door open to have a hand-written piece of paper fly to the floor that read, "Out of Order." He and Lara looked at it and then each other, before bursting into laughter. And as Damion led her through the restaurant, he sensed no embarrassment in her over their little encounter, clearly made public. There was simply an understanding of their connection, and their need to find privacy.

Damion had every intention of showing Lara just how well he could *make love* to her. Maybe—just maybe—in the heat of passion, he'd convince her to complete the blood bond despite how much the life-and-death bond had him shaking inside. One screw up, and she'd be dead right along with him. If they didn't complete the bond tonight, one way or another, they *were going to be*. Because if there was anything that revisiting Tommy's death had done for him tonight, it was to remind him how easily someone you loved could be lost.

———

Logan kissed Jenna and then set her back from him. He grabbed one of his kitchen chairs and moved it away from the table. He sat her down in it and then retrieved a pair of military-grade handcuffs made for the GTECHs from the slim black box on his bar. He dangled them in the air. "Hands behind the chair," he ordered.

She laughed nervously and motioned to her slim, prim and proper, black dress. "Shouldn't I get undressed first or something?" Her gaze swept his slacks and button-down. "And you too?"

"Hands behind your chair," he repeated in a soft, le-thal voice. Tonight wasn't about sex, though she thought it was. Tonight was about control and manipulation. His control, his manipulation of all the parties involved in Bar-1, to ensure he came out on top.

Her bottom lip quivered, telling him of her nervousness, but she did as he said. He had no doubt she would. Logan walked behind her and secured her hands. A moment later, he stood above her, staring down at her.

"Now what are you going to do with me, my mad scientist?" she purred seductively, but that hint of nervousness still teased the note, as if she sensed all was not right.

"It's not what he's going to do to you that you should worry about," Sabrina murmured to his left. Logan turned to find her in the doorway, holding a long knife, and hot as red fire in a tight leather pantsuit that would bring a man—this man, specifically—to his knees.

"Logan?" Jenna asked, panic sliding into her voice.

Sabrina licked the end of the blade. "Logan won't help you, honey. I do, however, have a mad idea he might enjoy watching." She strolled to Logan's side and wrapped herself around him. "You're going to enjoy this, now aren't you, baby?"

He didn't reply. Any enjoyment Sabrina gave him always came with baggage he wanted removed, and he had a bad feeling that wasn't going to happen. His gut said that Sabrina would be the last Serenity-bred GTECH standing—the only one who hadn't been brainwashed, and the only one who wasn't about to die from a stroke. The only one who hadn't been exposed to Bar-1.

"How long have you been shorting the GTECH serum?" Logan demanded, furiously certain that Jenna was the cause of Bar-1's failure.

"What?" Jenna asked, her voice cracking. "Logan,

please." And just like that she transformed, back to little Jenna, so innocent and in need of protection.

Logan didn't know what she was asking him to do, but he felt a punch in his gut, and he wanted to go to her. For an instant he forgot his discovery in the lab. This woman had quite possibly single-handedly destroyed Serenity.

"How long have you been shorting the serum?" he asked again, through gritted teeth.

"I told you," she said. "Just the new girl."

"No," he ground out. "You told me you'd shorted several of the subjects."

She shook her head. "I didn't."

Sabrina sauntered over to her and settled on the bed, then rested the blade on her stomach. "How many?"

"Just—"

Sabrina leaned up and put the knife to Jenna's throat. "How many, bitch, or I swear to you I'll gut you and let you bleed out and die."

"All of them, but the first." Jenna rushed the words out.

"Crystal," Sabrina said. "You're telling me you didn't short fucking Crystal?"

"Yes. No, I didn't short Crystal."

"Fuck!" Sabrina yelled, shoving Jenna's chair back so that it hit the ground. Jenna screamed, and Sabrina went down on top of her, straddling her. "Do you have any idea what you've done? I'm going to kill you. I'm going to—"

Logan grabbed Sabrina and pulled her backward, only to have Sabrina stiff-arm him and send him tumbling.

"Stop, damn it!" he shouted, pushing to his feet and grabbing Sabrina again. "We need her. We fucking need her, Sabrina! I need to run a brain wave test on her to verify my theory. I need to know exactly what I'm dealing with, if I have any chance of fixing this."

Sabrina whirled around to stare at him. "She destroyed Serenity. Opal is missing. Lara is with the Renegades. All the rest who are Bar-1 are going to die because she shorted their serum."

"No," Jenna said. "It's not because of the serum. It's because of Bar-1."

Logan glared at her. "Bar-1 kills humans. I started the process before the complete conversion, knowing the serum would heal any damage—not knowing that you'd shorted the serum."

Tears streamed down Jenna's face. "They fully converted. I did the blood work, I swear. I would never do anything to hurt you or Serenity. I believe in our cause. You know I do."

"You did the wrong test," he growled, pissed beyond belief. He'd thought he might care about this woman. She was turning out to be a bigger liability than Sabrina could ever have been. "I ran my own tests once I knew there was something to look for, including brain wave activity, on all subjects." Even Crystal, which had been hell to arrange without setting off Powell's alarms. He'd had to use the excuse of preventive action—reinforcing all subject triggers in light of Lara's betrayal. He grimaced. "Healing capacity for the women in Serenity, outside of Crystal and Sabrina, was diminished, and brain wave activity was erratic."

His gaze focused on Sabrina, who was still on top of Jenna, and again said, "I need to test her, Sabrina. I need to know if it's the low serum alone causing the strokes, or if it's the low serum combined with Bar-1. She's the only one who fits the criteria of low serum and no Bar-1 conversion. I need to compare her results to those with low serum dosage who've assimilated to Bar-1 to see if there's a difference."

Sabrina grimaced, looking as if she might refuse, then turned to Jenna and lowered her mouth to a breath from hers. "If I can't kill you, I *will* hurt you. Plan on it."

"I'll kill her myself if she destroyed Serenity for her own personal gain," he promised.

"Logan," Jenna hissed, a storm of tears bleeding from her eyes. "Don't do this. Don't turn me into the enemy."

He turned away from her, done with her tears, and walked to the closet to grab the supplies he'd stored there. He started to right Jenna's chair, and Sabrina grabbed him. "She stays on her back and as uncomfortable as we can make her."

Jenna sobbed, and Logan found it irritated him. He left her on her back. A few seconds later, he'd rolled a machine next to the chair and began connecting pads to Jenna's forehead, while Sabrina stood, arms crossed, above them.

"Logan," Jenna pleaded.

"Shut up," Sabrina spat. "Just shut the hell up."

Logan didn't bother to look at Jenna. He watched the monitor and the table, steady brain waves. Finally, when the truth was clear, his attention went to Sabrina. "Bar-1 didn't kill Opal."

Jenna gasped. "You told her about Opal!"

Sabrina laughed. "You didn't seriously think he'd hide anything from me, did you? I even know the exact Dumpster where you put the body. Powell would notice she was gone. I have to deal with that. Powell believes she's running a recon mission. Problem solved."

Jenna cast Logan a disbelieving stare that said, we had a plan to deal with Opal—us, not you and Sabrina. And they had, but after some evaluating and reevaluating, it had proven ineffective. He'd needed an ally to help him act before all the affected members of Serenity stroked and died—someone who wanted Serenity and Bar-1 to survive this disaster as much as he did. That someone was Sabrina. Once he was done with her, once he'd handed Powell the destruction of the Renegades, he didn't think he'd have trouble convincing Powell that Sabrina had to be controlled by Bar-1, that she was a monster, that all GTECHs were monsters—case in point, after all, being Jenna. Sweet Jenna, who was now a monster.

Logan stood up, giving Jenna his back. "Our one chance to save Serenity and Bar-1 is to use Lara to destroy the Renegades before she strokes. That alone will make the risk-reward ratio of any potential Serenity backlash worthwhile to Powell and the 'powers that be.' You already know I need Powell's involvement to properly pull off the scenario that will trigger Lara's memory recall."

"I couldn't agree more with the risk-reward assessment," Sabrina said, "but Powell wants to give Lara more time to bond with the Renegades."

"So I'll tell him my new testing shows the trigger weakens with time, thus we need to set it off now, not later."

A slow smile slid onto Sabrina's lips. "You do know he'll be pissed that you didn't know this in the first place."

"He'll get over it when we destroy the Renegades."

She inclined her head. "Well played, Logan." She motioned to Jenna. "And her? Can I kill her now?"

"Once we've proven ourselves to Powell, he'll hand over more serum. We'll complete her conversion and then use Bar-1 on her. She, Sabrina, will be your loyal subject when I'm through with her. You have my word." Silently he added—and you will be *mine*.

Chapter 25

WITH EACH PASSING HOUR, HE CARED MORE FOR LARA, and the ticking of the invisible bomb he imagined was attached to her head grew more deafening with every blackout she had. It was now Monday mid-morning, three days after their night at Moe's. At Caleb's summons, Damion and Lara entered the War Room, both dressed in black fatigues, which Lara had called "dressing for success." They were looking for a battle, and she not only intended to find it, she intended to be ready to fight.

And since they'd yet to have a hit off Houston's sketches they'd circulated through the government systems, they were both hoping to find out that had changed. Every other lead they'd worked had failed to produce any sign of Powell. It was all Damion could do not to live up to his words and tie Lara to the bed, and well—screw the brain wave testing she still refused—he'd jump right to the blood bond.

Caleb, Michael, and Sterling waited for them in the conference room. Damion quickly noted the sliding panel that hid a wall of six big-screen televisions had been opened. Damion and Lara settled down side by side at the table. "Tell us you have something we want to see."

Sterling rolled to a keyboard beneath the wall of televisions and keyed one of them to life. An image of what looked like a medical facility appeared.

"That's the Serenity laboratories," Lara said quickly.

"Right," Michael said, his long raven hair tied neatly at the nape of his neck. "There was something about the clean way the facility was left that bothered me. We searched for a connecting facility, but if it was there, we couldn't find it. Still, something bothered me."

"So we set up satellite surveillance," Sterling added. "A ten-mile radius in all directions, but the feed consisted of a few wild animals and some birds."

"So we decided to expand the radius five extra miles," Caleb said, leaning back in his chair.

"And lookie lookie what we got," Sterling said, and punched another few keys that brought a new monitor to life, showing what appeared to be cars and people at the foothills of a mountain range.

"You think it's Powell?" Lara asked, grabbing Damion's hand under the table.

Sterling brought what looked like an architectural blueprint of the inner caverns of several connected mountain ranges on yet another monitor that seemed to be linked by underground tunnels. "There's a straight path from the area of activity on the satellite images to the deserted lab. And you, Lara, would never have known that this path existed if Powell didn't want you to. It could easily be concealed just as the entrance to Sunrise City is."

"I'm taking a team in to run recon tonight," Michael said.

"I want to go," Lara said.

"Not until we know what we're dealing with," Damion said. "Not yet, Lara."

"We don't have time to waste," she said. "*I* don't have time to waste."

"Which is why we need to know what we are dealing with and have a plan when we attack."

"He's right," Caleb said. "Not yet, Lara. A few hours could be the difference between success and disaster."

Lara turned to him, the desperation in her black eyes burning into him. "I have to do this. I have to go."

"Turn on the television," Cassandra yelled, rushing into the room with her open lab coat flapping behind her. "Quickly. Turn on the news."

Sterling quickly did as she ordered, bringing a different station to life on every television. "Screen three," Cassandra said, stopping beside Michael, who was on his feet now.

Sterling brought the sound to the screen, and the mid-thirties, female newscaster's voice filled the room.

"The former top-ranking CIA official promises to expose the dirty little secrets of the agency that have kept him underground for a year now, and running for his life. The press conference scheduled at two o'clock tomorrow will be only a few miles from the CIA's Langley, Virginia, corporate office at the municipal building. That's what I call a statement, folks. This man is not only talking and talking big. He's doing it on the bear's doorstep."

The screen flashed with a series of images of a man in his late forties with gray hair and a scar down his cheek—walking to his car, shoving through a crowd on another occasion, and standing behind a desk.

Lara was on her feet the instant the first image was shown. "Oh God. That's Skywalker." Damion was behind her, pulling her close. She was shaking all over. "Skywalker." Her hands went to her head, and she let out a blood-curdling scream, a second before her legs went limp, and she went silent.

Voices sounded around him, worry for Lara. Damion caught her against him, fear ripping through him. He'd waited too long. He was going to lose her. "Lara! Lara!" He turned her in his arms, only to have her fall limp and unmoving against his chest. He went to the floor with her, his back against the wall, her body curled against his, as he checked for a pulse. In some far corner of his mind, he heard Cassandra screaming for Kelly, heard Caleb saying something.

Her pulse was faint, and suddenly she started to jerk. That was it. Damion didn't think—he wasn't losing Lara, he refused to lose her—and in a split second, he had his knife out of his boot. Another second and his palm, and then hers, were sliced open. He pressed the two wounds together and prayed. *Please, please, please, let her live. Let her be okay.*

The pain, God, the pain in her head, and the darkness. She was cold—so very cold. Somewhere in the distance Beatles music was playing. Where was the music coming from? She shook her head, tried to focus. Music. Right. Wait. She knew where she was. The music was coming from the nearby restaurant and bar. She could feel the cold breeze coming off the wintery Virginia Beach water.

Lara huddled behind a Dumpster—still cold—so cold and so scared. She wanted to be back at the girls' shelter. She wanted to be warm and safe. And the pain in her head. So much pain and blackness… nothing but black empty space. Until… wait. She was back—she was at the Dumpster, and the pimp had run away—the big man squatting down in front of her had scared him away. She blinked the stranger into focus, the streetlight brushing his high cheekbones, emphasizing the scar, and illuminating the lines around his eyes.

"You're lucky an old Beatles-loving Spook like me came along when I did," he said. "What are you doing out here alone?"

His face was hard, his voice steel. And he was at least her stepfather's age—late forties, maybe fifty. Yet he was nothing like her stepfather. This man felt… safe, like the great warrior she sometimes dreamed of protecting her. "I…I ran when he came after me. I've been hiding. I was… thank you."

"Running is good," he said. "But next time, you run into a public place and scream at the top of your lungs." He ran big hands over his jeans. "Why don't we go inside where it's warm and call your parents?"

She opened her mouth to explain and shut it, not sure what to say. He narrowed his gaze. "How long have you been on the streets?"

Lara hesitated, considering a lie, but discarding the idea. This man would know if she lied. "A while now," she settled for.

"You ran away because someone at home was hurting you."

She hugged herself and gave a quick nod. "Yes."

He studied her for a moment. "What's your name?"

"Misty," she said, and this time she lied. She wasn't giving him a way to trace her back to her parents.

"Funny," he said sternly. "You don't look like a Misty."

Feeling like a doe caught in headlights, her heart raced, and she blurted, "Lara. I'm Lara."

"I'm Luke," he said, offering her his hand. "Friends call me 'Skywalker' just to piss me off."

She shook his hand, and he added, "I'm retired law enforcement, Lara. Do private hire now, but I've got lots of friends who can take good care of you." He stood up, using her hand to pull her with him.

"I'm not going back there," she said, the defeat of moments before turned back into fight. Her voice lifted, panic balling in her stomach. "I can't go back there. I won't." She didn't know if he knew where she was talking about, and she didn't care. He just needed to understand. She wasn't going back. She wouldn't let him take her back.

Another long moment of contemplation, and then he surprised her by saying, "How long has it been since you had a good meal?"

Her stomach rumbled with the mention of food. "I've eaten," she said defensively, afraid he was making a case to send her home.

"Well, I haven't," he said. "Not for at least a couple hours, that is. How about we walk down to the diner on 21st Street and fill our stomachs? My treat. You can tell me your story, and I'll tell you mine."

She hesitated, knowing she should refuse, but a good meal tempted her resolve. Not that she thought this man would let her refuse anyway. Whatever her destiny, somehow he'd stepped in to play a part. "I... okay."

"Good," he said approvingly, and motioned her

onward. Side by side, they started walking, and he added, "Ever been to V's Diner?"

"No," she said. She'd eaten what the shelter gave her, nothing more. Every last bite of it and always wanted more.

"Mama V owns the place," he said. "She keeps the place hot like a sauna. You'll get warm and then some there. Good food though. 'Course, Mama has a mouth on her. Screams across the diner, like we all want to know whose order is up. I keep telling her, one day I'm going to pull my gun on her to shut her up."

Lara stopped in her footsteps. "You are?"

"Of course not," he chuckled, tugging her forward. "Mama V is ornery enough to shoot me with it."

Lara blinked and then laughed—laughter that would forever change her life.

A screech filled her head—pain, make it stop! Make it stop! Light flashed in her eyes, blasting her from the darkness. Suddenly, Skywalker's shout ripped through the air, and she was back in the hallway staring at photos on the wall, ready to deliver cookies.

"Run, Lara!"

Adrenaline shot through her veins, and she reacted instantly, doing exactly as he said. She ran. To the cabinet, to grab a gun. She was trained to fight. She wasn't leaving Skywalker. She wasn't losing Skywalker.

She fumbled with the cabinet and yanked it open, securing the Beretta PX4. The sounds of a struggle pounded out against walls and floors somewhere on the upper level, and she took comfort in the cold steel beneath her palm. She whirled around, ready to fly up those stairs, when the weapon was ripped from her hand. A woman stood there, dressed all in black, long red hair braided down her back.

"Nice to meet you, sweetheart," she said. "Name's Sabrina, and we're going to be real good friends, you and I." A smile lifted her lips. "Once Skywalker is out of the way."

Anger exploded inside Lara, and she attacked, calling on the training Skywalker had drilled into her the last ten years. Kick, block, kick—all sidestepped and dodged as if Lara were an amateur, batting at a fly. The next thing Lara knew, the woman seemed to move at the speed of light, shackling Lara's arm, jerking a big glob of her hair and holding on. Then Lara was being painfully forced in front of the other woman and up the stairs—pushed with the force of a steamroller.

Fiercely, Lara fought, to no avail. The woman was taller than Lara's five-foot-five by several inches and outweighed her 118 by a good ten pounds. But she was also stronger than she was big. Abnormally strong. Insanely strong. Inhumanly strong. A crazy thought, but one hard to shake as Lara struggled against the attacker shoving her up those stairs.

No matter how she moved or twisted, nothing worked. She'd gladly lose her hair if it meant freedom, but she wasn't getting away from this woman without losing her arm—not an option.

Approaching the landing, Lara kicked her foot backward and tripped the woman. Unfortunately, they both tumbled forward, with Lara on the bottom. And since she didn't have control of one of her arms, she smashed hard onto the wood floor.

Her attacker leaned close, near her ear. "We don't want to mess up your pretty face just yet, so behave." Lara's head was jerked back, as her attacker yanked her up by the hair at her scalp, lifting Lara to her feet and shoving her toward the surveillance room.

It was then that her heart stopped beating, then that she saw Skywalker face down on the floor, unmoving. And then that she saw another woman, a blonde dressed in black like the redhead, standing above him. The Beretta flew through the air, and everything went into slow motion.

"Kill him," the redhead ordered, and suddenly Lara knew who she was.

Lara screamed as the blonde caught the weapon, aimed at Skywalker, and fired.

The memory replayed with painful clarity, right down to the moment when Skywalker had been shot. Lara gasped and sat up. "Skywalker." Her eyes settled on Damion.

"Lara." His hand slid to her face. "Lara. Are you okay?"

Her hands went to his, and she struggled to grasp what was happening. "Damion?"

"Yeah, baby," he said. "You scared the hell out of me."

There were other voices in the room too, but she couldn't make them out, not in the whirlwind of past and present washing over her. All of a sudden, everything inside her crumbled into one big puddle of emotion. "I remember everything. I'm Lara Martin. I ran a girls' shelter where I'd once stayed myself, but Skywalker found me and took me in. He's dead, Damion. Powell had him killed to get to me. He died because of me." She burst into tears, a storm like she'd never known before, shaking from head to toe, and clinging to Damion, the strength of him all that kept her whole. It hurt. It hurt so badly to know she'd caused his death. Everything faded into that hurt, time fading away. All the while, Damion murmured near her ear, stroked her hair, her arms, her back. It was his voice, his comfort that finally calmed her, that finally eased the hurt.

She swiped at the wet mess that was her face and leaned back, remotely aware now that they were on the floor of the conference room. "Thank you. I'm okay. I..."

A biting pain in her hand had her gaze dropping to her palm, and for an instant, her heart stopped. There was a cut on her hand already healing from her GTECH metabolism, blood oozing from the seams.

Her gaze riveted to Damion's face. "*What* did you do?"

"I love you, Lara," he said. "I love you, and I couldn't let you die. And you were dying."

Anger, fear, and panic rushed over her. She had to go after Powell and Sabrina, even if it meant she died doing it, and now... now he would die if she died. Her fingers curled around his shirt. "I can't believe you did this. I can't believe you did this without my permission. Do you have any idea what you've done?"

Chapter 26

"DO YOU KNOW WHAT YOU'VE DONE?" LARA SAID again, shoving away from Damion and pushing to her feet. "Do you have any idea?"

Damion followed her to his feet, her rejection hitting him with what felt like the Mack truck of an emotional blast. "I saved your life," he said, all too aware of a growing audience watching this unfold. "I had to save your life, and I won't regret that. You don't have to live with me. You don't have to feel obligated to me."

She made a frustrated sound. "That's not what this is about. You don't even know if what you did worked."

"You're standing, you're fighting," he said. "It worked."

"So now what? You and I both die because of what Powell did to me? Damn you, Damion, you aren't supposed to die because of me. Skywalker died because of me."

Understanding hit him, and Damion reached for her, wrapping her in his arms. "Lara, sweetheart. I would rather die with you than live without you. I love you."

"You said you think you love me. That's a big difference."

"I know I love you. Believe me. I know I love you."

"You like me, and you didn't want to be responsible for my death. You didn't want the guilt. You felt obligation. You felt—"

"You're right on at least most of that. I do like you,

which is a good thing, since I also love you. You're damn straight I didn't want to be responsible for your death. But there was no obligation."

"Duty then. Call it what you want."

"You're right. It's my duty to protect my Lifebond, who happens to be the woman I love. So yes. It was my duty, and one I'm damn happy to live up to." He framed her face with his hands and bent his knees to force her gaze to his. "I love you, Lara Martin. I'll spend however long it takes to prove that to you. I won't rush you. I won't make any demands of you. I just want you alive and kicking my butt, while I try and win your heart."

"Damion," she breathed. "I can't believe you did this."

"I can't believe I didn't do it sooner."

"Ah, you guys," Cassandra interjected with obvious hesitation. "Why don't we do the brain wave testing and see where we stand?" She motioned to the machine on a roller cart.

"We don't want Lara to move until we test her," Kelly said, stepping forward, her hands in her lab coat. "You can both sit at the table. We'll make the setup work." She glanced at the room full of men—Caleb, Michael, and Sterling. "You guys are going to have to give up the room for a few minutes."

Damion arched a brow at Lara, and she nodded. "Yes. Let's do the testing."

He kissed her forehead. "It's all going to work out. I promise." Only his heart was heavy with what was still her rejection. For the first time in his life he'd not only fallen in love, he'd confessed it to a roomful of people. Sure, Lara was worried about his safety, but he didn't want her worry. He didn't want her guilt. He wanted her alive, safe, and happy—and he wanted her love.

Lara was in knots for so many reasons, she could barely process them all. After the initial brain wave test had been positive for both her and Damion, they'd moved to Damion's apartment, and the tension between them was thicker than the concrete floors.

Cassandra sat on the edge of the couch where Lara rested and removed the pads from a third brain scan, while Damion stood nearby, hovering. "The news just gets better," Cassandra said. "Damion's test results remain normal, and Lara, every time I run your scan, you are closer to normal. The magic of the blood bond is something that never ceases to amaze me."

Kelly spoke from the recliner next to the couch. "And now you are both alive and well."

She stood up. "We'll leave you two alone."

Lara pushed to a sitting position, and her gaze met Damion's, the connection spreading through her like warm sun on a cold day. She felt the pain in him. Pain he'd lived with all his life—pain she'd created. She felt it, knew it. This amazing, handsome, brave, and sensitive man didn't deserve to be hurt. Tall and broad—bigger than life—he was the only thing she had worth living for, except retribution for Skywalker, and he didn't know it. There was so much she wanted to say to him, so much she wanted him to know.

The door shut. The silence stretched until she started talking, making no discernible decision as to what to say or in what order. "My stepfather was a drunk who beat me. My mom didn't stop him. I ran away and ended up in a women's shelter where some pimp tried to recruit me. Skywalker rescued me and raised me. He was afraid to, though. He'd lost his wife and daughter to the job. They were murdered by a CIA agent gone rogue who he'd been trying to haul in. He trained me to protect myself—to be as lethal as anyone who might attack me, and…" Her voice hitched, and she had to inhale and exhale to gather her composure. "And still I wasn't good enough, or lethal enough, to keep him alive. So you see… that's why I didn't want this blood bond. I have to go to that press conference, Damion. I know it's a setup, and I know that no matter how much I want to believe Skywalker will be there and be alive, he's not. But I need to walk into that trap and turn it on Powell and Sabrina. I need to fight back. Skywalker would want me to fight back. But I'm scared to death. I want to be good enough, or lethal enough, to keep you alive. I love you, Damion. I love you, and I have to go after Powell. How am I supposed to do that now? How am I supposed to go after him and risk your life with mine?"

He was on his knees in front of her, before she'd completely finished the last word, kissing her senseless. Need overtook her. She needed senseless… intensely. She needed him.

"You aren't alone," he said, a full minute later. "Never again. I was willing to die *for* you. I'm damn sure willing to die *with* you. But I don't plan on either of us dying. We're going to go get our bad guys, and then, when it's all over, I'm going to do my best to convince you this is home for you, that *I'm* home for you." He stood and pulled her to her feet. "Let's go find Caleb and prepare our own trap." He led her to the door, and she knew she was already home. She just hoped they both lived long enough for it to matter.

<center>~~~</center>

Damion and Lara were back in the War Room, joining a meeting already in progress, but this time they had a larger crowd than before that included Houston, Jesse, Chale, Michael, Caleb, Sterling, and Becca, who had every intention of putting her gifts where they could help.

"I tracked all of the shots the newscaster showed of Skywalker, and all of them dated back ten to fifteen years ago," Sterling said, his gaze falling on Lara. "I'm sorry. I really don't think he's alive."

Damion watched Lara straighten, her chin lift. "Powell's the one who's going to be sorry. I can't wait to reintroduce Lara Martin to Sabrina. It's going to be special."

"I like you more every day," Michael said, his tone as serious as a funeral.

Chale grinned. "Me too."

"Add my name to that list," Damion said softly, lacing his fingers with hers under the table.

"This press conference is a trap, Lara," Caleb said. "You are clear on this, right?"

"Of course it's a trap," Lara said. "They'll know I know it's a trap, so they've got some spectacular plan, no doubt."

"Don't forget that we've got Becca," Sterling said, pride lacing his voice. "Powell has no idea what her abilities are. If she gets close to a GTECH, she can put them to sleep."

"A sniper can put a Green Hornet between Lara's eyes from a distance."

Damion ground his teeth. "Thank you for that ice-cold drink of reality."

"Hey, man," Michael said. "I'm trying to keep her alive. And your pain-in-the-ass self along with her, I might add."

"This is Powell we're talking about," Caleb said. "She's GTECH. They'll try to save her and brainwash her again."

"That's what I think too," Lara agreed, speaking to the group and then glancing at Damion. "I have to let them capture me if I'm going to get inside their facility and destroy it."

Damion wanted to object, to say no, but he'd vowed to do this with her. "Then I'm damn sure getting captured right along with you."

The room was silent a few long seconds, before Caleb said, "Then first and foremost, we need to teach Lara to use her mental shields. She can't use them until after she's captured, or they're liable to suspect her Lifebonding."

Damion's gaze lingered on Lara's a long moment, before he turned to the group. "I'll teach her."

"Becca and I are available to help, if you need additional training, Lara," Caleb offered.

From there, planning continued for a good hour, before Caleb ended the meeting, by fixing Damion and Lara in a somber stare. "Stay alive, you two."

The group adjourned, and Michael came up to Lara. "Don't get brainwashed again. I like you how you are."

She grimaced at him. "Don't worry. I won't forget how much I adore your cranky ass either."

Michael let out a rare chuckle and headed for the door. Damion smiled. "Ah, the magic of that tongue of yours. Glad to see the return of your memories didn't steal that away."

She turned to him and traced his jaw with her fingers. "I'm glad they didn't steal you away either."

"Nothing is going to do that," he assured her, running his hand over her back and molding her close. "I promise."

"Except death," she said grimly.

"I guess you didn't get the memo. We die together. That means when you go, I go. And wherever you go, I'm going too."

Her expression softened, the grimness slipping away. "How about I show you Virginia and my old hometown?"

"I'd like very much to see where you grew up." He wanted to protect and love this woman. He'd go to the moon with her, if it made her happy. But he knew this trip to Virginia wasn't about happiness. It was about the pain of loss, and that was the one thing he couldn't save her from.

―⁂―

After they'd changed into jeans and T-shirts so as not to bring attention to themselves, with Damion by her side, Lara appeared behind a house to conceal their wind walk. They moved to the sidewalk of 'Summer' street, standing across from the house where she'd lived with Skywalker. She stood there, frozen in place, unable to breathe for the knot in her chest.

Damion stepped behind her, his hands on her waist,

his strength and warmth radiating into her, comforting her. "That one?" he asked of the red brick beachfront, two-story house.

She nodded, unable to speak. Her mind went to the day Skywalker had died. She remembered pushing open the door of the house and walking inside, like it was just any other night. She remembered the warm summer air rushing in behind her, the salt from the nearby sea on her tongue as it was now.

"Hello, hello!" she called out and set the plate of cookies in her hand on the hall table. She kicked the door shut, setting down her purse and key.

She remembered pausing to look at photos on the wall, hearing the news coming from the living room television the moment she'd started walking toward it.

"Ms. Smith wanted to thank you for teaching last night's self-defense class." She cut around the corner. "She baked you cookies, though I have a sneaking suspicion this is her way of flirting."

She squeezed her eyes shut, knowing what came next, hearing Skywalker scream.

"Run Lara!"

Her eyes flashed open, and she took a step into the street, toward the house.

"Lara!" Damion grabbed her and yanked her back as a truck flew by, an inch from her body. "Easy sweetheart." He enclosed her in his hold.

"I need to see if he's there," she said, trying to dart forward, only to have him pull her back again.

"He's not there," he said. "He's not there, but I am. Right here with you, and I know what you're feeling. You know I know."

Her eyes prickled, and she held onto his arms where they wrapped her. "Yes." He knew because he'd felt loss, and he'd felt the guilt eating her alive right then. "Maybe if I would have—"

He turned her in his arms. "Don't do that to yourself."

"It's hard, Damion. It hurts."

"I know, baby."

At the sound of a car door behind her, she turned to find a van parked in front of her house, Skywalker's house, with a young couple and a child around ten years old climbing out. In animation they walked and talked and then disappeared through the front door. Gone. Like Skywalker.

She forced herself to turn away, rotating to face Damion. "There's someplace else I need to go."

"Take me there," he said.

Lara grabbed the wind, ignoring the chance of being seen, but Damion didn't complain. Seconds later, they appeared at the back of The Walker House.

———————

"Show me," Sabrina ordered, standing beside Logan inside a tech booth—one of many inside the Serenity compound. She was speaking to the human tech guy sitting beneath a wall where a huge screen displayed twenty-four windows, all with various real time shots of the Serenity perimeters, as well as surveillance sites. He'd called her and Logan there with the promise that Lara was on radar. Zach or Trey or something like that—she didn't know the human's name and didn't care what his name was.

The human punched a few buttons and one of the

windows moved to center screen, expanding to full-size with the image of a familiar house—the house where they'd made Luke Walker a thing of the past. The human rolled his mouse, and the screen enlarged further, the view expanding to show two people standing on a sidewalk.

"That's not real time," the human said, rolling his chair so that he gave them a look. "That's five minutes ago." He punched a button without looking away from Sabrina and Logan. "And that's where she is now."

Sabrina's eye narrowed on the equally familiar location before she turned to Logan. "Be ready. This won't take long."

Logan gave her a lazy look. "I think we've established I'm always ready."

Indeed, Sabrina thought. "Don't choose now to let that change." She was taking a big gamble on Logan against her best judgment. She was going to bring Lara back, reprogram her, and send her to the Renegades to destroy them. That was the best way to save Serenity. Make Powell and the program look like everything the government wanted and more—to seal her role as a leader of the most elite army of the world. That was the plan. Of course, it also included forcefully keeping Lara's mouth shut. If Sabrina failed to make that happen—well, she'd just kill the bitch.

Chapter 27

LARA STOOD IN THE FRONT YARD OF THE WALKER House for Girls, the shelter that had been renamed when Skywalker had donated money on her behalf, with not another house for several miles. Space that Lara had planned to use for recreational facilities one day. Wind gusted around her from the ocean that was practically a part of the backyard, once enjoyed by the many girls who'd found hope here. But the shelter was vacant now, run down to the point of broken windows and even some graffiti markings.

Protectively, Damion stepped close by her side, already having expressed his concerns about the wind masking an attack, especially since he'd only started teaching her to use her mental shield before they'd left Sunrise. But she didn't want to think about that now, not in this tiny window of time. There was a war she'd fight in only a few short hours—and fight it to win, she would.

"This was where I went to escape my stepfather's beatings," she told him, without turning to look at him. "It was my lifeline. So much so that when I graduated from college, I took over as the house mistress." She turned to him then. "Skywalker taught self-defense classes for me. I was going to renovate it with his help. It was going to be an amazing place."

"It sounds like it already was."

"It was, and they destroyed it."

"They were wiping away your history, making sure no one could track you down."

She looked back at the building. "When I heard about the Wardens, I was immediately in awe of what Cassandra and the other women are doing. I think on some level, my mind was remembering this place, even in the absence of my memories."

He motioned to the porch. "Take me on a tour. Tell me what it was like, and what you had planned. If you want to, that is."

She smiled sadly at him. "Yes. I want to."

They walked up the steps, hand in hand, and found the door unlocked. Lara led Damion from empty room to empty room, telling him stories of her time there—of Rebecca, who'd quite possibly saved her life by taking her in and getting her off the streets. It was somehow the salve to her wounds that she'd needed—this man, her past, the hope of a future that he gave her.

They ended up in the kitchen, leaning on the island counter. "If this place is where your heart is, we'll re-build it. We'll make it matter again. We'll remodel it and make Skywalker proud."

His words, spoken with such conviction and tenderness, touched her deeply. "I think... the past is the past. Not that I'm big on destiny and fate, but I think that maybe this place is gone because the Wardens are my future."

Damion's cell phone rang. "Caleb," he told her, looking at the ID.

She nodded and walked to the back door, stepping onto the porch and walking to the balcony, the wind whisking viciously around her as she stared at the

choppy surf the way she had so many times in the past.
She'd had to come back here to be able to leave it behind, but it would always be a part of her.

"Lara, sweetheart. You shouldn't be out there alone."

She smiled at his protectiveness—a real smile this
time—and turned to face him. At the same instant,
someone grabbed her from behind, and she felt a sharp
bite on both sides of her neck.

In what could have been only seconds, Lara found
herself face down on hard ground, that pinching feeling
in her neck. Oh God. It was a collar, a thick steel collar with something sharp digging into her skin, and she
could feel blood seeping down her neck.

A foot slammed into her back, and then Sabrina's
face was pressed near her cheek. "Every time you so
much as speak, the remote control in my hand will
pierce you with needles. If you really piss me off, the
collar comes equipped with blades. One press of a button and the collar will slice your throat, peel you open
like a nice, ripe peach, right to the core. So I might not
be able to sedate you, but I damn sure can hurt and even
kill you. And I'll keep you alive just because I enjoy
causing the pain." Sabrina jerked Lara back to her knees
with a chain attached to the collar. "Get up and walk."

Anger roared through Lara, and she shoved herself
to her feet, noting the exterior of a mountain that was
all too familiar. She was at the site the Renegades had
discovered. Suddenly, she realized she'd left her mental shield in place. She dropped it—or hoped she did,
considering how new this was to her, praying Damion
would find her through his tracking skills, but certain
he'd look for her here no matter what. Even if he did

not, she'd indulge in tears. Now, she was ready to fight. "You better hope I never get this collar off, because if I do—" Pins dug into her neck.

"Shut up," Sabrina said. "Just shut up and walk."

She'd shut up and walk, all right, walk right inside where she was going to destroy "Project Serenity" no matter what she had to do to make that happen. She straightened, and Sabrina shoved her forward. Lara ground her teeth. *Just wait, Sabrina, just wait.*

A few minutes later she was inside the high-tech underground world of Serenity once again, a world far more developed than she'd ever known. Then she was being shoved through a laboratory door.

"Well, hello there, Lara." The greeting came from "Doc Logan," as she'd called him since joining Serenity.

He patted a leather chair that resembled what you might see in the dentist's office. She'd never seen the chair before, or maybe she had and didn't remember. "Come pay me a visit, Lara."

Lara narrowed her gaze on him. She'd liked Logan, thought him brilliant and efficient. Apparently he was also a snake in the same grass as Sabrina. The brain wave machine sitting by the chair set her pulse racing, a bad feeling slithering through her. They were going to brainwash her again. They were going to steal the new life she was building, and as a pin jabbed into her throat, as surely as knives could as well, she knew she had to let them. She had to let them and then pray Damion could bring her back from wherever they took her, whatever they made her.

Lara had been gone for twelve hours, and Damion was climbing the walls of Sunrise City. Nightfall and the opportunity to rescue Lara came far too slowly. The moment when Sabrina had dragged Lara into the wind replayed in his head over and over, as he kicked himself for leaving her alone outside. It had been, and would forever be, one of the worst moments of Damion's life. So would watching the Renegades' satellite feed of Lara wearing a damn collar like an animal, while being forced inside the Serenity cavern.

Thankfully, without much ado, the Renegades had evaluated the situation and decided on an action, everyone rising to cover his back—and Lara's. He wanted her to know that. He wanted her to see how much she was now a part of this world.

It was straight up midnight when Damion and a team consisting of Michael, Chale, Houston, Jesse, Sterling, and Becca, all dressed in black fatigues, appeared just outside the mountain range where Lara had been taken, fully expecting cameras to capture them, and not caring. Without any interior beyond basic outlines or numbers of the enemy inside the Serenity facility, the plan was to make a fast, hard hit using their most lethal resources—Becca and Michael. Becca had insisted on helping, and Sterling hadn't argued. Like Damion and Lara, Sterling had said, *Becca and I live and die together.* She might as well be along for the "Welcome Home, Lara" party.

Several females charged them. Becca held up her hands—the way she'd learned to funnel her skills—and they crumpled to the ground in a heap of sleeping beauties, clearly GTECH since Becca's ability only worked with them. "Damn, it makes me hot when she does that," Sterling said, grabbing Becca and kissing her.

Michael lifted his hand and wind formed a ball on his palm. "Down," he ordered everyone.

Michael blew on it, and it busted through the cavern where they knew the door to be, creating a huge hole. Rock flew everywhere and back at them, hitting a wall of wind and falling to the ground. Michael charged forward, wind blasting in front of him into the building, as a protective shield. As long as there was a seam of air, a place he could reach the wind, Michael could use it underground.

Chale whistled. "I'm straight as a steel pipe, and Michael gets *me* hot when he does shit like that."

"That makes two of us right about now," Damion said, drawing two Glocks from his double-shoulder holster, and heading into the gaping hole Michael had created and entered.

He was going to get Lara—and he was bringing her home.

―――

Logan leaned over Lara, checking her vitals. "She seems to be doing just fine," he said, speaking to Jenna, who was on the opposite side of Lara, the steel bracelets on Jenna's arms his assurance that she would remain loyal. The bracelets operated like the collar they'd been forced to remove from Lara's neck to prevent interference with the Bar-1 machine. One click of the remote control hanging from his neck, and Jenna would lose her hands, and that would pretty much undo any glory she'd garnered from being a GTECH.

Jenna glanced at Lara's eyes, which flickered under her lids as she assimilated information. "Shouldn't we run blood work?"

"I have no concern about what her blood work says. She's dead soon anyway. We just need her to survive long enough to destroy the Renegades. Which means we need her Bar-1 procedure complete, so she can join the Renegades in the next few hours if she's to convince them she escaped. Their trust is the only thing that will allow her to act quickly."

Suddenly, the alarm screeched into a constant blast, and Sabrina busted in the door. "Hide Lara. They've come for her."

Shouting sounded outside the door, followed by a blast and the pelting of bullets.

"Fuck!" Sabrina shouted. "Get her somewhere, anywhere. Just hide her." She turned and headed out the door.

Logan whirled on Jenna, who was now standing. "Help me get her into the office, and get ready to fight."

Jenna held out her arms. "Not until you take these things off me."

He glowered at her. "One click of the button—"

"And you'll be on your own. Well, you'll have Sabrina. I'm sure she'll protect you. You must trust her to protect you."

If Logan had any doubt he was through with Jenna, it was gone. Another explosion sounded way too close. Jenna arched a brow. He growled low in his throat and reached for the remote at his neck. She didn't even flinch when he punched a button, as if she were absolutely certain that she had the control, that he needed her. And damn it, he did. The cuffs fell to the ground, and Jenna walked to Lara.

"We can't disconnect the machine or—"

"She'll gain consciousness," Jenna said, eyeing him with irritation. "I *know*." She picked her up, as if she weighed nothing. She glanced over her shoulder. "You think you can handle the machine?"

He ground his teeth at the inference that he was a weak human and lifted the Bar-1 machine. "Just go to the damn office."

A few seconds later, Jenna laid Lara on the ground, and Logan settled on his knees beside her to check the pads and connections.

Jenna headed for the door.

"Where do you think you're going?"

She didn't answer. She just disappeared into the lab. Logan cursed and quickly secured several loose leads to the pads on Lara's forehead.

A blast at the lab's door had him jumping to his feet and running for his desk drawer—his weapons. The sound of Sabrina's and Jenna's voices carried in the air, followed by a crash. Holy fuck! They were fighting. He yanked open a drawer, as footsteps pounded toward him, urgency charging through him.

The Renegade, Damion, the one who'd been with Lara on the video footage, appeared, and Logan wasted no time, survival his only motivation. He needed a head shot to kill a GTECH, but he just wanted any shot, any-thing to slow his enemy. He grabbed the military-issue handgun in his drawer and started firing the instant it was in his hand, too low for real damage, but it was a start.

Suddenly, pain pierced his chest, and he knew he'd

been shot. He tried to fire his weapon again, and another bullet hit his chest, and this time he had a few moments to think—*I'm dead*. There was no plank to walk, no mountain to climb, no exhilarating ride to the end. Everything just went black.

Chapter 28

"LARA! LARA!"

Lara heard Damion call her name in some far recess of her mind. He was far away, out of reach. No… no, he was here. They were at the shelter, but it didn't feel real.

"Lara!"

Lara's eyes lit with the sight of Damion as he exited the shelter's doorway, and she rushed toward him, and then… then he was gone. She was gone. Everything went black. There was so much darkness. "Damion! Damion!"

Suddenly, they were back in his apartment, and he was holding her, kissing her, telling her he loved her. And then he was gone again, as everything went black again. "Damion?" Panic rolled over her. "Damion!"

"Lara, sweetheart, please wake up."

He yanked something sticky off her forehead. Lara sucked in air and sat up, finding Damion holding her, the hard ground beneath her, unsure where she was. "Damion?"

"Oh, thank God." He kissed her forehead. "Please tell me you're okay. Tell me you're really you, not some brainwashed version of you."

"Where are we?"

"An office inside the Serenity facility," he told her. "Do you have any idea how scared I was for you?"

"Get up!" came a female voice. "Get up and turn around."

Damion's eyes met Lara's and everything came back to her. Sabrina and Logan. The damn collar.

"She's mine," Lara said. "Don't even think of taking that from me."

A slow smile slid to his lips. "Nice to have you back, sweetheart."

"I said, get up!" Sabrina shouted. "I have Green Hornets, and you can damn well bet I'll use them."

Damion moved so fast, Lara didn't even know he'd moved until he fired on Sabrina, shooting the gun from her hand. He pushed to his feet and tugged Lara up with him. "Now she's yours. The playing field is even."

Sabrina screamed in agony and outrage, holding her bleeding hand, and then dropping it to her side. "You want to fight? Bring it on, bitch."

"You bet I want to fight," Lara agreed, taking a step forward, ready for this like she'd never been ready in her life. Sure, they'd put their stupid machine on her, but it hadn't worked. She didn't know why, and she didn't care at the moment.

"Let's go, Sabrina," Lara said. Sabrina roared in anger and charged at Lara. Lara started toward her as well, when suddenly Sabrina dropped like a rock, flat on her face, blood pouring from her head.

Damion stepped up beside Lara. "If that's not anticlimactic, I don't know what is."

A petite blonde stepped into the doorway, a gun in her hand.

"Jenna?" Lara asked, shocked that the timid lab assistant had shot Sabrina.

"I didn't want things to be like this." She lifted the gun, like she intended to fire again, and then bam, she dropped like a rock too, only Chale was there to catch her. He lifted her and walked into the room with her in his arms.

THE DANGER THAT IS DAMION

"Someone order takeout?" Chale asked. "It's Becca's treat."

"Anticlimactic times two," Damion said dryly.

Becca rushed forward from behind Chale. "Lara!" She wrapped Lara in a hug. "Tell me you're okay."

Lara hugged her. "I'm good. I'm really good. I can't believe Sterling let you come."

"Anything to bring you back with us where you belong," Becca assured her, and Lara believed her. These people, who she'd once called her enemies, had become her family.

Becca grinned at Damion. "Told you it would work."

"What would work?" Lara asked, turning to face Damion.

"Thankfully you remembered to drop your shield before you went underground," Damion said. "Once you did, our blood bond created a link powerful enough for me to not only find you, but create a shield for you that you didn't have to maintain. I did it for you. But once you went underground I struggled to keep it in place. Becca managed to link to you through me, and she re-enforced your shield. In other words, aren't you glad we did the blood bond?"

Lara's heart swelled. She walked to Damion and wrapped her arms around him. "Yes. I'm glad. I love you."

"You can convince me later," he promised, his eyes twinkling.

"I'm taking our package back to Sunrise with the rest of the women," Chale said. "See you both back there." He disappeared.

"The rest of the women?" Lara asked.

"I gave the rest of Serenity a little nap," Becca said.

"Hopefully we can gather enough medical information to restore their memories."

"And Powell?" Lara asked.

Becca shook her head, and Lara glanced at Damion, who was still holding her. "What does that mean?"

"He's nowhere to be found, and Michael has pretty much gutted the place. He's still blasting walls, so there's hope, but…"

Her chest tightened. "We aren't going to get him."

"We'll get him," Damion promised. "Maybe not now, but we'll get him."

He kissed her. "Let's go home. *Our home*, Lara."

"Our home," she repeated, amazed that despite standing in the middle of the nightmare world of Serenity, this moment could be so perfect.

Epilogue

A MONTH AFTER THE FALL OF SERENITY, LARA AND
Damion ended a long evening stroll along Virginia
Beach at the back of the girls' shelter, the sand remark-
ably warm beneath their bare feet, the wind softly
blowing her long white sundress around her knees. It
was nearly summer, a perfect night as far as Lara was
concerned, the sky flawlessly clear with twinkling stars
dancing around a bright, full moon and illuminating the
beach like dim, romantic lanterns.

They sat down on the sand side by side, staring out
at the water, comfortable in their silence. She liked that
about Damion—the way they could sometimes just be
together and they didn't have to say anything.

Lara had done nothing but fall more in love with
Damion and become more excited about her role in
the Wardens. Not only was she helping to protect other
women from the Zodius soldiers that abducted them, she
understood what it was like to have your life change
overnight, to have it stolen from you. She brought
that to the women who used the Wardens to cope with
their past, like she was using it for herself. Thanks to
the medical records and some help from Jenna, who'd
confessed to having a lot to repent, the Wardens had
the former members of Serenity helping them as well.
Of course, Powell had done what he did best—as she'd
learned from the Renegades. He'd disappeared. She

shoved away the thought, not wanting to think about when Powell might reappear.

Lying down in the sand, Lara stared at the sky. "What made you want to come here tonight?"

"This," Damion said, setting something on her stomach.

Lara lifted her head and lost her breath. It was a ring box. She sat up and held the gift, and good gosh, her hand was shaking. "Damion?"

He moved so that he faced her, his legs in the opposite direction. "This is where you started a new life once before. I'm hoping you'll decide to start a new one with me here as well." He flipped the top of the box open, displaying a white-gold diamond band with the most spectacular stone she'd ever seen. She'd only just realized how much money he had from the family business, and how much he'd invested in the Renegades.

She blinked at him, stunned. "Damion, it's... big, too big. I can't wear something that cost this much."

"Oh, I bet you can," he said, smiling.

She glanced down at it. "It's spectacular, it's—" Why couldn't she seem to form a coherent sentence?

"Not nearly as spectacular as you," he said, his voice low, gravelly. "You didn't get to choose how we Lifebonded, and you didn't get to choose our blood bond." His fingers settled on her cheek. "I love you more than I thought it was possible to love someone. I would be honored to call you my wife. So I'm asking you now to choose me, to choose us. And I thought... we could renovate the shelter and hire someone to run it after we get married. I was thinking we could say our vows right here on this beach."

Her lips trembled, the emotion of this place, of what

she felt for this man, overwhelming her. Tears streamed down her cheeks.

He wiped them away. "Please tell me those are happy tears."

"Yes. I'm so very happy." She wrapped her arms around his neck. "And this is one name change I'll welcome." She smiled. "I really do like the sound of Lara Browne."

And so he made love to her, right there on the beach. Later, she took him home and tied him to *their* bed and made love *to him*.

Acknowledgments

To my Underground Angels—I love you guys. Special thanks to Wendy for being angel and super hero. Thanks to Aemelia, Kelly, and Fedora for reading *Damion* and helping me sprinkle some extra love on this manuscript. And this business is a little easier, the trials and tribulations a little less stressful because of author and valued friend, Donna Grant. Thank you, Donna! This book wouldn't exist if not for the wonderful efforts of the Sourcebooks staff who I appreciate so much.

The Legend of Michael

NEVADA'S AREA 51 WAS NOT ONLY THE SUBJECT OF government conspiracy theories; it was now, officially, her new home. A good hour before sunrise, Cassandra Powell pulled into the military parking lot outside the launch pad leading to the top-secret underground facilities where the launch of the Project Zodius GTECH Super Soldier Program was a year under way. The ride from her new on-base housing had been a whopping three minutes, which considering the inhuman hours the military favored, she could deal with. The simplicity of a standard green army skirt and jacket—required despite her contract status—seemed to be working for her as well. The cardboard bed, not so much. It had, however, made a great desk for her laptop and all-night reading.

And considering she was only three days on the job—taking over for the former head of clinical psychology who'd transferred to another department—she had plenty of work to do. The prior department head hadn't done one fourth of the studies that Cassandra deemed critical to properly evaluate these soldiers. And while the counseling aspect fell outside her clinical role, she wasn't pleased with what was being offered. She'd certainly be nudging her way into that territory.

Files in hand, she exited her red Volkswagen Beetle

and pushed the door shut with a flick of her hip. She walked all of two steps when the wind whipped into high gear, fluttering her suit jacket at her hips and tearing to pieces the blonde knot tied at her nape.

She shoved at the loose locks of hair and drew to a shocked halt, blinking in disbelief as four men dressed in black fatigues materialized in a rush of hot August wind at the other side of the long parking lot next to the elevator. She drew a breath and forced it out, trying to calm the thunder of her heart pounding her chest. Apparently she wasn't quite as prepared for the phenomenon of GTECH Super Soldiers as she'd thought she was. Or at least not this skill her piles of paperwork referred to as "wind-walking." It was one thing to be inhumanly strong and fast, even to be immune to human disease, but to be able to travel with the wind was downright spooky—and suddenly, so was the dark parking lot as the four men disappeared into the elevator.

Eager to get inside, Cassandra started walking, but made it all of two steps before another man appeared beside the elevator, this time with no wind as warning. Good grief, she hadn't read about that stealthy little trick yet. Special Forces soldiers were already called lethal weapons, but these men, this one in particular, were taking it to a whole new level.

Still a good distance away from the building, Cassandra slowed her pace, hoping to go unnoticed, but she wasn't so lucky. The soldier punched the elevator button and then turned and waved her forward. Oh no. No. No. Not ready to meet anyone yet. Not until she had a few of her ducks in a row. Cassandra quickly juggled her files and snagged her cell from her purse as an excuse to decline joining him, holding it up, and waving him off. He hesitated a few moments as the doors opened before he finally stepped inside and disappeared.

Cassandra started walking instantly, determined to get to the darned elevator before another soldier appeared. By the time she was inside, she had her file on wind-walking open—a good distraction from the entire underground, bomb-shelter-style workplace that made her more than a little uneasy.

Absorbed in her reading, head down, Cassandra darted out of the elevator the instant it opened, only to run smack into a rock-hard chest. She gasped, paperwork flew everywhere, and strong hands slid around her arms, steadying her from a fall. It was then that she looked up to find herself staring into the most gorgeous pair of crystal blue eyes she'd ever seen in her life.

She swallowed hard and noticed his long raven hair tied at the back of his neck, rather than the standard buzz cut—a sure indicator he was Special Ops. He could be one of the two hundred GTECH soldiers stationed at the base. *A Wind-walker*, she thought, still in awe of what she'd seen above ground.

"I'm sorry. I wasn't watching where I was…" She lost the final word, her mouth dry as she suddenly realized her legs were pressed intimately to his desert fatigues, and her conservative, military-issue skirt had managed to work its way halfway up her thigh. "Oh!"

She quickly took a step backward, righting her skirt in a flurry of panicked movement. Three days on the job, and already she was putting on a show. She pressed her hand to her forehead. "I know better than to read while walking. I hope I didn't hurt you." He arched a dark brow as her gaze swept all six-foot-plus of incredibly hot man, all lethal muscle and mayhem, and knew that was unlikely. She laughed at the ridiculous statement, feeling uncharacteristically nervous. She was five four in her bare feet—well, on her tip toes—and she bet this man towered over her by nearly a foot. "Okay. I didn't hurt you. But, well, I'm still sorry."

He stared down at her, his gaze steady, unblinking, the chiseled lines of high cheekbones and a square jaw, expressionless. Except deep in those strikingly blue eyes, she saw a tiny flicker of what she thought was amusement. "I'm not sorry," he said, squatting down to pick up her files.

She blinked at the odd response, tilting her head and then squatting down to face him. "What do you mean?" she asked, a lock of her blonde hair falling haphazardly across her brow, free from the clip that was supposed to be holding it in place. "You're not sorry?"

He gathered the last of her files, then said, "I'm not sorry you ran into me. Have coffee with me."

It wasn't a question. In fact, it almost bordered on an order. And damn, if she didn't like the way he gave that near order. Her heart fluttered at the unexpected invitation. "I don't know if that is appropriate," she said, thinking of her new position. She stalled. "I don't even know your name."

The elevator behind them dinged open, and Kelly Peterson, assistant director of science and medicine for Project Zodius, appeared. "You're early, Cassandra," she said, amusement lifting her tone. "Morning, Michael." She continued on her way, as if she found nothing significant, or abnormal, about Cassandra being sprawled across the hallway floor with a hot soldier by her side.

Cassandra popped to her feet, appalled she'd made such a spectacle of herself. Her sexy Special Ops soldier followed. "Now you know my name," he said, and this time, his firm, way-too-tempting mouth hinted at a lift. Not a smile, a lift. God... it was sexy. "Michael Taylor."

"Cassandra," she said, unable to say the last name, dreading it more with this man than with the many others she'd been introduced to in the past few days. What was she supposed to say? *Hi. I'm the daughter of the man who changed your life forever by injecting you with alien DNA without telling you first, and then claimed it was to save you from an enemy biological threat? Now you're a GTECH Super Soldier for what we think is the rest of your life, but who knows what that really means long-term for you. But hey, I promise I'm one of the good guys, here to ensure you aren't used and abused just because you're a macho, kick-ass, secret government weapon? And did I mention I'm nothing like my father?*

"Cassandra Powell," he said, handing her the files, leaning close, the warmth of his body blanketing her in sizzling awareness. "I know who you are. And no, that doesn't scare me away. I never run away from anything I want." He leaned back, fixing her in another one of those dreamy blue stares. "So how about that coffee?"

REBECCA BURNS WAS SITTING BEHIND A SCUFFED wooden table in the Killeen, Texas, library when he sauntered by, and every nerve ending in her body went on alert. "He" being Sterling Jeter, the hot blond hunk of a guy who'd graduated a year ahead of her. And try as she might to keep her attention on Bobby Johnson, the second-year high school quarterback who she was tutoring for his SAT test, she failed pitifully. As if drawn by a magnet, her gaze lifted and followed Sterling's sexy, loose-legged swagger as he crossed to the computer terminals he'd been frequenting the past three weeks.

Sterling yanked a chair out from behind a desk, and she quickly cut her gaze back to Bobby, who was still struggling through the worksheet she'd given him. Unable to resist, she slid her attention back to Sterling only to find him looking right at her. He grinned and winked, holding up a Snickers bar. She blushed at the realization that he'd brought it for her, after she'd confessed an undying love for their peanutty goodness just the afternoon before.

"I just don't get why I need to know algebra on the football field," Bobby grumbled. Reluctantly, Becca tore her gaze from Sterling's and refocused on Bobby who, at six foot two with brown hair and eyes and stud status at the school, was no grand dictionary of knowledge.

"Either you meet the required SAT score for the University of Texas," she reminded him, "or you'll be passing your ball to whoever is open somewhere else."

He shoved the paper away and scrubbed his hand through his hair. "This is bull. I don't want some fancy NASA-sponsored scholarship like you got, so I don't see why I have to be some geeky bookworm like you either."

She stiffened at the familiar jab, wondering why she let it bother her, why every once in a while she wished she was the cheerleader or prom queen. It wasn't like she wanted to be some brainless blonde beauty. Her mother was a teacher, both pretty and smart. Darn it, Becca liked having her mother's dark brown hair and brains, and she was proud of the NASA scholarship. Her parents were proud of her, and that's what counted.

Resolved to ignore his remark, she pushed the paper back toward him. "Let's try again."

"I'm done," he said. "I'm going to talk to Coach. He has to get me out of the SAT."

"Get you out of the SAT?" she asked. "You can't be serious."

He pushed to his feet. "As a touchdown." And with that smart remark, he headed toward the door.

Becca tossed down her pencil and sighed. Please let the summer end. She couldn't get to Houston and her new school soon enough.

The chair in front of her moved, and a Snickers bar slid in front of her. "You look like you need this urgently." Sterling sat down across from her, his teal green eyes a bright contrast to his spiky blond hair. She decided right then that her summer goal was to run her fingers through that hair just one time before she left for Houston. And kiss him. She really wanted to kiss him.

"It's a wiser and safer man who brings a Burns woman chocolate when she's upset. Or so says the Burns men. They swear it's a better survival technique than anything they learned in basic training." Both her father and brother were career military, same as her grandfather had been. She reached for the candy bar. "Thank you, Sterling."

He grabbed the worksheet Bobby had abandoned and started working an algebra problem with such ease that she assumed he was just doodling. They chatted while she waited for her next tutoring session, and she decided he was the best part of her summer wait for college. He took care of his grandmother by doing computer programming work. She thought that made him amazingly sweet.

When it was nearly time for her next student, he abandoned the worksheet and studied her. "I should go."

"Okay." Dang it, she really didn't want him to go.

He didn't go. He sat there, staring at her, the air thick with something—she didn't know what—but it made her stomach flutter.

"You want to catch a movie or something Friday night?"

She smiled instantly, knowing she should play coy— after all, Sterling was older and more experienced—but not sure she would know how if she tried. Dating wasn't exactly something she'd excelled at.

"Yeah," she said. "I'd like to go to a movie."

His lips lifted. "With me, right?"

She laughed. "Yeah, with you."

Once they'd arranged to meet at the library at seven the next evening, Sterling headed back to the computers. She glanced down at the math he'd done and smiled all over again. He'd gotten all the questions right. Good looking *and* smart. She might just fall in love with her hot cowboy.

———

With a smile on his lips, Sterling whipped his battered, black Ford F-150 into the driveway of the equally damaged trailer he called home and killed the engine.

He leaned back in the seat and pulled the wad of cash from his pocket. Ten thousand dollars and a date with Becca tomorrow night. He was going to kiss her, see what honey and sunshine tasted like, because that's what she reminded him of. Ah yeah. Life was good.

"Yeehaw," he whispered, staring at the cash again. How many nineteen-year-olds had that kind of dough? He was liking this new job. Hack a computer, get cash. He snorted. "And they say that government databases can't be hacked. This low-life trailer trash proved them wrong." That's what the kids at school had called him after his grandmom had gotten arrested for public intoxication. Trailer trash. Misfit. "Screw you," he mumbled to the voices of the past. "Screw you all."

Once Sterling had counted the money, down to the ten thousandth dollar, he grabbed a hundred for his date with Becca and stuffed the wad of cash back in his pocket. Then he snatched the bundle of flowers on the seat. He left the Snickers bar for himself and then decided better. Candy had worked with Becca, after all. And he'd need all the sweetness he could muster to convince Grandmom to head to that fancy alcohol-rehab center he'd arranged for her to enter up in Temple, Texas. It was even close by, only twenty miles away, which he hoped would help convince her to go. She'd curse and probably hit him. She was good at that, but it didn't hurt anymore. Hadn't for years.

He knew she couldn't help herself. He'd read enough about alcoholism to know she was sick. Yet she'd raised him despite that. Heck, he was to blame, he supposed. He was why his mother had died—the trigger that had set Grandmom off.

He climbed out of the truck and whistled down the path to the front door. The whistle faded the instant he entered the trailer. Grandmom sat on the couch, wrapped in the same crinkly blue dress that she'd gone to bed wearing, a big bottle of vodka in her hand. Two men dressed in suits sat next to her.

"Look what these men brought me," she said, grinning, holding up her prize.

"We know how you like to take care of your grandmother," one of the men said, his buzz cut flat against his skull.

"Kind of like your father took care of his family," the other man stated, a clone of the first one. They had to be army or government. *Fuck me!*

"The resemblance between the two of you is amazing," the first man said, picking up a picture of Sterling's father. He was standing in front of a helicopter, his blond hair longer than it should have been because he wasn't normal army. He'd been Special Forces, working undercover all over the map. And it had gotten him killed when Sterling was barely out of diapers. The man set the picture back down on the coffee table.